Deidre Knight

### Red Fire

"Scorching-hot with a pace that never lets up."
—Christina Dodd, *New York Times* bestselling author

"Deidre Knight has created a fascinating world of gods, demons, and immortal warriors. Her heroine, Shay Angel, is both strong and sympathetic, a woman discovering powers she never knew she had. Legendary Spartan Ajax is handsome, seductive, and haunted—a hero to inspire delicious dreams. I can't wait for more!"
—Angela Knight, *New York Times* bestselling author

"White-hot immortal warriors, heart-pounding romance, and thrilling action. It doesn't get any better than this!"
—Gena Showalter, *New York Times* bestselling author

"Hot Gates, hot men, myth, and magic in modern day . . . *Red Fire* flies above the rest. Sign me up for more Gods of Midnight!"
—Jessica Andersen, author of the Final Prophecy series

"Knight expertly blends scorching passion, gritty danger, and a wildly creative plot in *Red Fire*, the first in an edgy new paranormal series." —*Chicago Tribune*

"Knight provides an intriguing new twist to both Greek mythology and legendary Spartan warriors with this searing new series, as she sets up an alternate world that begs to be explored." —*Romantic Times* (4 stars)

"*Red Fire* is an interesting and sensual beginning to what looks like a fantastic series." —Romance Junkies

*continued . . .*

"*Red Fire* is a fabulously exciting and vividly portrayed page-turner of a novel with highly entertaining dialogue."
—The Romance Studio

### Parallel Desire

"[A] wonderful book . . . [an] outstanding series."
—*Affaire de Coeur*

"Riveting."
—*Romantic Times*

### Parallel Seduction

"You can always count on Knight to take an intriguing plot and bend it like a pretzel. This fascinating series is extremely intricate with its competing time lines and complex character growth. There's never a dull moment in this terrific series!"
—*Romantic Times*

"Deep emotion, fast-paced action, characters who come alive, and a plot full of surprises."
—Romance Reviews Today

### Parallel Heat

"Powerfully sensual and mind-blowing . . . a hot romance . . . a great paranormal."
—Romance: B(u)y the Book

"It totally dazzles . . . complex, compelling, [and] with a strong hero and heroine. . . . It's fast-paced, with enough twists and turns to keep the reader turning pages."
—The Best Reviews

"Deidre Knight once again hits all the right notes . . . a must-read."
—Romance Reviews Today

# Red Kiss

## A GODS OF MIDNIGHT NOVEL

# DEIDRE KNIGHT

A SIGNET ECLIPSE BOOK

SIGNET ECLIPSE
Published by New American Library, a division of
Penguin Group (USA) Inc., 375 Hudson Street,
New York, New York 10014, USA
Penguin Group (Canada), 90 Eglinton Avenue East, Suite 700, Toronto,
Ontario M4P 2Y3, Canada (a division of Pearson Penguin Canada Inc.)
Penguin Books Ltd., 80 Strand, London WC2R 0RL, England
Penguin Ireland, 25 St. Stephen's Green, Dublin 2,
Ireland (a division of Penguin Books Ltd.)
Penguin Group (Australia), 250 Camberwell Road, Camberwell, Victoria 3124,
Australia (a division of Pearson Australia Group Pty. Ltd.)
Penguin Books India Pvt. Ltd., 11 Community Centre, Panchsheel Park,
New Delhi - 110 017, India
Penguin Group (NZ), 67 Apollo Drive, Rosedale, North Shore 0632,
New Zealand (a division of Pearson New Zealand Ltd.)
Penguin Books (South Africa) (Pty.) Ltd., 24 Sturdee Avenue,
Rosebank, Johannesburg 2196, South Africa

Penguin Books Ltd., Registered Offices:
80 Strand, London WC2R 0RL, England

First published by Signet Eclipse, an imprint of New American Library,
a division of Penguin Group (USA) Inc.

First Printing, June 2009
10  9  8  7  6  5  4  3  2  1

*For Hope Edwards White,*
*a glorious star who will always shine powerfully bright.*
*I can't wait to meet you one day.*
*I know we will be fast friends.*

# Acknowledgments

So many to acknowledge! So little space! First of all, huge gratitude to Kerry Donovan, editor absolutely extraordinaire, for having shown River and Emma such tremendous love and care. Thank you, thank you! I am very grateful for all that you do, and I especially appreciate your giving River the love he deserves.

A huge shout-out to my family, as always, for keeping me glued together during the rough patches and late nights. The answer to "How do you do it all?" is my husband, Judson Knight. He's the real hero of every book I write. Tyler and Riley, keep reminding me that McDonald's is a curse word!! So are Wendy's and Burger King.

Major gratitude to my mother for those weekends when she gives me writing time. You're an incredible Mimi!

To my Madison posse, you know you rock my world. Still, love and hugs and major gratitude for all their support go out to Shawnee Mac, Scotty Mac, and Darreline. (No real names were used in the writing of the above acknowledgment!) Angel, you're the best fan ever! Jamie Miles, keep writing that novel. Mary Payne, your infinite knowledge of everything inspires my imagination.

Louisa Edwards White, you already know. But still, I'm putting it in print—thank you for everything during the writing of this book.

My TKA crew, you make every day an exciting, laugh-filled journey. Who knew that work could always be so much fun? Thanks to Pamela Harty, Elaine Spencer, Jamie Pritchett, Nephele Tempest, Lucienne Diver, Jia Gayles, and Melissa Jeglinski.

Jia, that party was one of the highlights of my life. Thank

you for such a great launch celebration, and for all the hard work you do every day. Your support is a huge gift.

Megathanks to my wonderful friend Angela Zoltners for her assistance and gracious reading.

Last, but certainly not least, big hugs and love to my sister, Pamela Harty, who also happens to be my amazing agent and dear friend. You rock *and* light my world.

# *Prologue*

More than twenty-five hundred years ago there was a land where the bravest, most valiant warriors were hammered like bronze, forged into human weapons by years of rigorous training and sacrifice. These men were noble, heroic, stalwart; they would willingly give their lives for their homeland and face down even the most terrifying enemy. Their home, called Sparta, lay nestled deep in the rocky heart of ancient Greece. Its people were private and plainspoken, their lives austere. The men made a life of war, always eager for the next battle.

Then there arose a threat of epic proportions, a Persian force numbering in the hundreds of thousands. The Spartans' Greek neighbors to the north reported that this Persian war machine had trampled entire villages, left forests devastated, the land ravaged and scorched, and that their ranks numbered more than the stars in heaven. Unbeknownst to these mortal soldiers, a much more sinister force stood behind the enemy's massacres. Djinn demons drove the bloodlust of the Persian forces and influenced the outcomes of the battles, on their own quest to carry darkness into the souls of mankind.

When this invading Persian army came, they seemed invincible. The Greek forces allied against them, but could not halt their advances. The Greeks were desperate for more time to plan and strategize since it was their only hope of stopping the Persian hordes. One man, King Leonidas of Sparta, announced that he would provide the necessary delay. That he would lead his three hundred most elite officers to make their stand against the invaders at the narrow spit of land known as the Hot Gates.

*Thermopylae.*

This pass, an opening wide enough to accommodate only a few men fighting side by side, would be the stage. There Leonidas and his Spartans would bottle up the Persian forces, using the Gates themselves as an advantage to limit the power of the Persians. They would fight to the last man in order to restrain the Persians for as long as they could—even until the very last Spartan lay dead. These three hundred would give up their lives for Sparta and Greece, for duty and loyalty, for homeland and family. And for a hero's passage to heavenly Elysium.

And so it was that for three sweltering August days this courageous, stubborn king fought alongside his crimson-cloaked warriors. There were no distinctions for Leonidas. All were soldiers, equal in battle, and all would drink from the cup of death as the gods decreed. Beside him, his senior captain, Ajax Petrakos, led charge after charge. Together they blocked the pass, warring with swords, shields, and eventually with only their bare hands.

The king and his captain never relented, never backed down, and on the third day when the burning sun began to slide behind the mountains that marked the pass, only a handful of Spartans remained standing. It was then that the final moments came, and one by one the last of these Spartan warriors, inseparable in life, fell together in death. With their passing the battle was lost, but their Spartan duty was fulfilled.

Captain Petrakos was the first to awake facing the River Styx, that boundary between mortal life and the mystery beyond. Next his servant Kassandros materialized beside him, the two linked together in death as they had been in life. One by one, other Spartans appeared out of the mist: Ajax's brothers, Kalias and Aristos, then Nikos and his fellow warrior Straton. And finally their beloved King Leonidas, battered, broken, and mutilated from battle, but standing tall among their ranks. But an unexpected being also emerged from the mist to stand beside their king. One beyond the warriors' imaginings. Before them stood a towering golden god, wearing a proud smile upon his face. It was none other than Ares, the lord of all Spartan soldiers, their god of war.

Ares had come to present an offer, one final choice, as the seven warriors stood at this place between life and death. They could lay down their swords and move on to Elysium and the afterlife that awaited them, or they could turn back to the world, take up their arms once more, and become immortal protectors of mankind for eternity.

They would fight every form of evil that threatened humanity, becoming battlers of demons and fighters of wars. They would serve under Ares, in the name of mankind. With the deity's offer, these warriors could ensure safety for their families, for Sparta, and for the sons and daughters of Sparta for centuries to come. In their immortal form, each man would possess abilities akin to the gods. They would be stronger than before, and in the heat of battle could assume the form of hawks, with the flight, lethality, and grace of these warrior birds. They would become dark angels, saviors of the night.

The will of warriors was in their blood and in their souls, and they knew in their hearts that it was a noble quest. But it was a noble quest for a capricious god. Still, they would have followed their king to the ends of the earth, to Hades itself if he asked it of them. And when they looked into his wise eyes, they knew his decision had already been made.

Leonidas did not beseech them; the choice lay with each man alone. But these were men born and bred to fight for the glory of war. Their duty, honor, and love for one another bound the warriors in unspoken agreement. One by one, each of the seven men drank from the River Styx, binding their immortality and their vow.

There was no time for second thoughts and no place for regrets. The seven Spartans, now the immortal protectors of all mankind, turned away from what might have been, and bowed down before the voice of war.

# Chapter 1

He refused to allow the water to swallow him whole. Immortals didn't die; they lived for eternity. Didn't they? That question had haunted River ever since he'd sunk deep beneath the water's surface. And it kept rising in his trapped thoughts, bobbing in his consciousness like a fisherman's buoy. He was immortal to the pinpoint blade of his soul, but *could* he still perish?

If he remained trapped as he was, in dagger form, eventually he would cease to exist. Although he'd never before found himself unable to return to human form after shape-shifting, he'd become convinced that his life force was now ebbing away. He knew it like he did the tides that moved him back and forth. Like the seaweed that sometimes tangled about him. As a weapon-shifter, he became whatever instrument each battle required for brief, intense periods of time. In his current fight—the one for his sanity and survival—he was turning hard and cold and violent. The very element of his soul was transforming into something he no longer recognized.

Soon, and he'd slip too far, lose that last tether to the man he'd been before. Perhaps one day years from now some mortal would find him and hold him in their grip. But it would be too late. His immortality would have faded away, his soul dying with it until nothing was left but the dagger shape he'd last assumed—the same one that held him captive now.

*I do not want to die*, he swore inside himself. *I want to be human again, to be free.*

Maybe he had always been no more than a simple ser-vant, but River had taken for granted that he, like his fellow Spartan warriors, could not be destroyed. He'd believed Ares' promise on that fateful day of their bargain, after each of them had died at the famous battle of Thermopylae. They'd assumed the arrangement would be eternally binding. After all, in the Spartan world fair was fair when you made a trade, whether for firewood, a better arrow, or a bowl of soup.

In the case of River and his six Spartan comrades, the exchange was more than adequate. For immortality and the salvation of their homeland, they agreed to protect mankind from every form of evil that stalked the earth. They questioned nothing. Spartans valued honor above all else, and that included their dealings with their war god. That had been the way of it from the very beginning.

Immortals lived forever; friends fought to save you; shape-shifters could return to human form. Certain assumptions lived inside of you, were true down to your very gut. Until they were shattered, that was.

*Assumptions.* He would have laughed bitterly if he could have. But instead there was only a dull, clanging ring that resonated in the depths of his hollowing soul.

He could no longer say how much time had passed since Sable, a Djinn and one of their greatest enemies, had forced him into this watery prison. They'd been fighting the centaur and his followers in Bonaventure Cemetery, a haven for demons near Savannah. In the midst of their skirmish Sable had seized possession of him.

"Go toss this vile blade in the river," he had commanded one of his minions with a flourish. "Make sure it hits the deepest part, the very center of the river, where the tides will wash it out to the Atlantic Ocean."

River had struggled to shape-shift while the demon held him, desperately reaching his internal energy toward the mental image of his true body. The one with a beating heart and flowing blood and tensing muscles. That was how he always returned to human form, but as he struggled that day, he realized the truth: It had become impossible for him to transform. He'd already remained a dagger for too long by that point, more than a full day of battle. Before then he'd generally spent no more than an intense thirty minutes in weapon form. Maybe once or twice he'd dared go for an hour, but never longer.

With one easy flick of the minion's wrist, River had gone sailing through the air and toward the flowing tide as if he were nothing more than a coin and the waters a wishing fountain. As if he were a piece of property to be disposed of when no longer useful, the slave he'd been back in ancient Sparta and remained throughout eternity.

The Greeks called their servants "speaking tools." Ares had underscored that point on the day of their bargain. He'd clasped River by his armpits, dropping him into the fiery waters of the River Styx, altering him forever. Afterward, River emerged from the depths as a gleaming, gorgeous sword. The most majestic weapon ever created by any god. Before, he'd been called Kassandros. From then on, Ares decreed, he would be known as River, named after the mighty waterway of his rebirth.

Then Ares commanded that although River was a fearsome weapon, he would serve his master Ajax throughout time as he had in life. The slightest need, the simplest call, and River would shape-shift from human form to potent weapon, joining the Spartan in battle. Gloriously powerful, with a special gift all his own, but River would never have the one thing he craved above all else: to be equal to the Spartans. To be free.

*I am a man!* he now thundered at the memory from within his shackled state. *I am still a man!*

A man who was discarded by a Djinn like rubbish, who met his true nature in these waves, in water, the source of his immortal name. What had followed was this slow decline into near-madness as he repeatedly tried, and failed, to become human again and swim to the water's surface. By now, he could be drifting anywhere in the Atlantic between America and Europe.

*No one is coming for you, fool*, River told himself, that seething, warring element of his curse taking hold. *You've always been a thing, now more than ever.*

He was becoming less human every day. More bloodthirsty and craven. Hammered by lusts that choked him. The longer his soul melded with the natural violence of the dagger, the darker he became. That violence threatened to become a permanent part of him. His soul and spirit were slowly seeping away, his immortality with them, overtaken by the violent urges of his inner beast.

Loins that were no longer a physical part of him wanted to thrust and grind within any female he could seize to appease the violent cravings. Focusing on the sex lust had always been his way of containing the brutal berserker that emerged whenever he returned to human form. It was his curse, the dark, hidden part of himself that was a by-product of weapon-shifting. He'd been unaware of that side effect at the time of the bargain. So by slaking his own needs, he'd successfully avoided killing any of his fellow warriors. Or any innocent humans. Except this new version of himself, the one that had been trapped as a dagger for gods only knew how long, was utterly unknown to him. Even if he could find a way to emerge as a human male again, he had no idea whether sexual release would prevent his berserker's violent rampages. But what he did know was that he had to find a way out of these waves, and back to the Spartan brotherhood, before he was permanently bound to the dagger's violent form.

*Someone*, he begged in silent prayer, *please, someone find a way to free me. But if you value your life, your innocent body . . .*

*. . . just don't stick around once the deed is done.*

It was all Evan's fault. Not the approaching storm, of course, but the fact that Emma was going to be stuck alone on Little Tybee, the uninhabited island where they'd been supposed to camp tonight.

Some best friend. He'd turned into the sort who was always pulling a Spider-Man vanishing act whenever you needed him most. What was the guy really up to lately, anyway? Emma had never kept secrets from him. So why all the mystery and running off? Sometimes she wondered if he had some secret lover on the side, and it wasn't as if she didn't know he was gay.

This weekend was supposed to have been about reconnecting, a last outing together before she returned to work in a few weeks. They'd been kayaking together for years and even as their lives changed, the two of them always made time for the last camping trip of the summer. Instead, shortly after they'd set up their tents he'd received a cryptic text message and announced that he had to leave. It had been low tide, exposing the sandbar, and he'd taken off across that natural bridge, tracking his way back to the main island of Tybee.

The contrast between Tybee Island itself, with its bars and surf shops and cafés, and Little Tybee's serene isolation never ceased to amaze Emma. That she could be so near civilization while feeling as if she were on an episode of *Lost* was downright surreal at times. She'd even joked with Evan about that comparison as he'd waded out to the sandbar.

"See you later, *Sawyer*!" she'd called, feeling agitated despite her attempt at humor. Something about his departure, about being left alone on the empty island, gave her a heavy sense of dread.

"Don't let any of the Others get you, Freckles!" He'd laughed, backpack over his shoulder and already on the move.

With the tide at its lowest ebb, there had been no time to discuss details. With a final promise that he'd use his own kayak to paddle back in just a few hours, he'd vanished from sight, leaving Emma all alone to wait for his return. Even the few people who'd been on the beach when they arrived had already left. The emptiness of the wide swath of sand gave her an eerie chill.

Here it was, hours later, and she was still waiting. No sign of Evan at all. She'd left her cell phone back in her car, and no way was she going to be stuck here on the empty beach when nightfall came. Cursing Evan's unreliability, she decided it was time to confront him, and trudged angrily toward their kayak. A plan was a plan, after all, and she was over all the mystery surrounding his recent activities.

She opened the kayak's storage bin, reaching inside for a rope to tie down Evan's paddle. As she stood upright again, a sudden gust of wind blew her shoulder-length hair across her face. Looking up she saw that fast-moving clouds had appeared suddenly in the distance. A rolling, dark thunder-storm was heading from the mainland, sending jagged bolts of lightning earthward toward the main island of Tybee. It was only a matter of minutes before it reached her current location, Little Tybee.

She'd never seen a storm appear so suddenly or violently. Sure, it had been overcast most of the afternoon, and storms did roll in quickly out on the barrier islands. But the surging dark clouds had seemingly appeared from nowhere. The temperature had dropped dramatically, too, an almost instantaneous change during the past few moments. The surf roared, rising waves crashing toward the beach, and the ocean suddenly seemed to be alive. Like a threatening, violent force that wanted to claim Emma somehow.

She shivered as she watched the tumultuous waves, unsettled by the image; it seemed far beyond a simple force of nature in its violence. It seemed . . . supernatural and dark. Then all at once it felt as if her stomach dropped inside of her and the hairs along her nape prickled, standing on end.

The massive waves seemed to transform before her eyes, time folding back, and she was nine years old once again. Watching a sudden, explosive set of waves rise from what had been calm water only a moment before. Out in those waters it was almost as if she could see small, flailing arms, tanned from a summer at the beach. Reaching up desperately through the surf, trying to grab at anything in a futile attempt to claw their way back to the surface. A head bobbed upward, rising briefly, and Emma caught a vision of long dark hair, wet and framing a young face. A face exactly like her own. But then the specter vanished completely beneath the waves, leaving nothing at all except those endless, devouring waves.

The violence of it all, past and present, hit Emma then. No wonder she'd distrusted the water for such a long time, after standing on the beach, watching her identical twin drown, helpless to stop it. After rushing into the water, screaming, and nearly drowning herself . . . she'd become terrified of every aspect of life. Anything unknown or that she couldn't control proved almost more than she could handle—whether a new teacher or friend, or traveling on vacation, all of it overwhelmed her.

Water, however, had become her greatest enemy, the truest source of threat and violence in her child's mind. It had stolen her twin from her, after all. Still, she'd gradually overcome those fears, not that she had much of a choice living in coastal Savannah, a city that was surrounded by a network of rivers and bounded by ocean.

At moments like this one, however, when the powerful waves rose higher and out of control, she felt as if she were facing down a monster from the deep. A true leviathan. And the long-ago fears came alive all over again, choking her, bringing back all the dark, tragic memories.

A massive breeze seemed to blow in from nowhere, growing with alarming intensity. Her hair whipped about her face, sand swept across the beach as if she were caught in a Saharan windstorm. Watching the turbulent waves, feeling the sting of sand against her skin, Emma became chilled to her very marrow. From the crown of her head to the tips of her toes, a sinister feeling overcame her in the space of a heartbeat.

*It's just the oncoming storm*, she tried telling herself, backing away from the ocean. *Of course it's windy.*

Glancing inland, she glimpsed their pitched tents, an illusion of safety between two swaying palm trees. Yet even those flimsy structures seemed ready to buckle beneath the wind's battling force.

A bolt of lightning split the sky, illuminating the cloud behind it like an eerie spiderweb. The atmosphere seemed to become electrified, threatening, the approaching force unlike any she'd ever encountered.

*God*, she prayed, *where do I go? I'm in danger here. Tell me what to do. I don't want to wind up as some cautionary tale on the Weather Channel.*

Spinning back toward the waves, she could have sworn that she heard a reply.

# Chapter 2

Ares reclined on a gold satin settee, an extremely large and ornate piece of furniture that accommodated his massive body with elegant ease. Unlike the god, however, Sable felt anything but relaxed, standing stiffly where he'd been ordered to remain. Ares occupied himself by nibbling grapes and allowing a maiden to brush his long blond hair.

Sable averted his eyes, but knew that the scene was intended as a blatant reminder. Not just of the deity's power here atop Olympus, but of the endless women who had once adored Sable's own beauty and now regarded his scarred form with distaste. The same distaste he observed on the face of the young nymph who currently attended Ares.

It wasn't as if he'd been born this hideous, with his curling horns and mottled, ravaged skin. Or with his heavy, awkward horse portion, either. As a Djinn demon lord he'd been created for dark pleasure, worthy of any nymph's adoration. All of that, of course, had been before his failures at Thermopylae. Because of his poor performance there, his own god Ahriman had sold him into bondage to Ares, who, in turn, proclaimed him a shame to his race. With one brush of the war god's glowing hand, Sable's beauty was obliterated, and he was transformed into a horrific centaur.

"Thank you, Elana," Ares purred, gazing up at the girl through velvet, golden lashes.

The female flushed, and bowed her way out of the deity's presence, casting a nervous glance toward Sable as she left.

"Ah, it's so lovely to be petted like that." The war god sighed lustily, sinking back on the settee in obvious pleasure. "Anyone pet *you* these days, my little pony?" Ares laughed. "No, I don't suppose anyone strokes you now, although that coat of yours isn't quite as mangy as I always expected it would become."

Sable's vision filled with a violent shade of crimson, the physical manifestation of his demon's fury, a reaction that he'd never learned to control. "I care for my coat diligently," he said through gritted teeth. "It gleams."

Ares pinned him with a calculating stare. "Of course that depends upon your satisfactory performance, old beast, or even that shall be taken from you. You were to bring two items today, my dagger and my looking glass."

A tight knot of dread took hold of Sable. "I have searched tirelessly for the blade—"

"For *River*," Ares corrected sharply, eyes narrowing to shrewd pinpoints. "That warrior is a mighty weapon forged by my own hand. Smelted in the flowing fires of Styx itself, bonded with the eternal power of the river. A display of my glorious nature. Remember that fact, centaur."

Sable blinked, inclining his head to appease the god. He'd never understood Ares' devotion to the seven Spartan immortals, and certainly a helot slave should be beneath his illustrious notice.

"So this is the news you bring today. That you have failed to locate River Kassandros."

"My lord, I have recruited a horde of crafty and seductive water demons for this task." Sable rushed to explain himself. "This crew understands that under no circumstances are they to kill Kassandros, should he return to human form. Nor will they destroy his dagger if he remains imprisoned. They *will* locate him, and I *will* deliver him to you."

"And you gave this task, one that I had charged you with personally, to slithering, mindless minions." Ares leveled him with a hard gaze. "Why?"

The throne room's warm atmosphere changed instantly, gloomy shadows replacing the golden hues that had filled the palace until that moment.

Sable took a jittery step backward, his hooves clomping too loudly on the polished floor. "Because I'm a centaur," he stammered. "Because I am a beast of your making, lord

Ares. These demons have access to areas I cannot penetrate in my hoofed form."

The god stood from the settee and roamed toward one of the open glass doors that led onto the stone patio. A silky white and gold cloak fell across his shoulders and draped about loins that were naked otherwise.

"Perhaps," he pronounced coolly, "it is time I bestowed a new form upon you, demon. One that includes fins and gills. You might make a fine water beast, and at least you'd be properly equipped for your assigned task. Perhaps I should contact Poseidon, for I hear he revels in such transformations."

Another shot of red fury swam before Sable's eyes. He would not grovel, would not beg Ares to spare him yet another curse. "The horde has already traced Kassandros's trail from the Wilmington out into the Atlantic, just off the Savannah coast." Sable kept his voice as steady as he could. "It's only a matter of locating him."

Ares growled in displeasure and filled a goblet with bloodred wine. Taking a sip, he said, "Tell me that you've at least located my mirror."

This, of course, was the worst of Sable's recent errors, losing the god's priceless Looking Glass of Eternity. He'd been using it in the recent battle against Ajax Petrakos when the Spartan's female intervened. *Interfered* was more like it. Shay Angel had stared into the mirror's captivating surface before he could use the object to destroy Ajax's soul. Not even Ares had realized that the mortal was a Daughter of Delphi, but Sable had glimpsed the genetic proof of that bloodline in her eerie, translucent blue eyes.

And no one, not Ares or demon or mortal, did harm to one of Apollo's oracles or their descendants, not without severe retribution.

"My looking glass," Ares said sharply. "What of its location?"

"I am searching constantly, war god." Sable lowered his gaze. "If Ajax's female hadn't interfered, then I wouldn't have—"

Ares cut him off in a thundering voice. "Forget that insolent and rebellious immortal and his mate! What of the

Spartan cadre as a whole? They've been silent for months, ever since that battle in Bonaventure."

For a moment Sable deliberated, not certain of what facts Ares knew, or at the very least, chose to ignore. Although powerful, he wasn't omniscient. That god's power was reserved for the One they never named among themselves.

Sable decided to plunge ahead boldly. "My lord, I assume you're aware that the Spartans moved their base camp from Cornwall to Savannah."

"Without my *approval*?" Ares roared in outrage, sloshing red wine onto the white stones of the patio. "Without seeking my advice or battle blessings?" Then he chuckled. "Of course I knew that, fool! You think I depend solely on you for my information?" Ares began pacing. "But if they no longer worship me, then it can be for one reason only. They must now regard me as a threat."

He gazed into the distance, an almost melancholy expression on his face, the golden blond eyebrows drawing tight. With a heavy sigh, he said, "My once-glorious plan for these immortal warriors has soured and failed. They have obviously turned their backs on me."

"My lord, you *did* have me attempt to kill Ajax Petrakos," Sable couldn't help reminding him. "Not that I wouldn't love to see that cursed warrior perish, but it's no wonder they've ceased following you."

Ares wheeled on him, eyes ablaze. "Those Spartans owe me their immortal lives! For which they must pay with eternal service." That gleaming stare silenced Sable from any further comment; he wasn't about to awaken more of the god's ire.

Once Ares appeared assured of Sable's silence, he continued more quietly. "I once thought that time would erode their human wills. That they could be made to serve my *own* purposes, to even battle the other gods if necessary, so my own power could increase and increase." He shook his head in disappointment. "Instead eternity has only made them *more* willful and their souls even stronger. This is why they must be stopped now; I must strip their immortality away if they refuse to serve me."

Sable snorted despite himself. "The original bargain was

for the warriors to protect mankind." *Not to serve you, vain god.*

"Why should I care about humanity?" Ares sneered, the red wine on his lips making the expression seem even crueler. "That was just a clever ruse to gain control over the Spartans. Mighty warriors such as they were, that selfless bravery they displayed at the Hot Gates . . . was simply too captivating a prize. I knew that last day at Thermopylae that even though mankind was yet young, there would never be warriors of their greatness and bravery again. I couldn't let them pass on to Elysium, not when they might have been turned toward my own purposes."

Ares swept his hand toward Olympus's peak. "My own quest for more power atop this mountain," he said ruefully. "All those fine plans have been crushed to crimson dust now."

"Because they've ceased worshipping you?"

"No, because they are beyond my control." Ares looked him hard in the eye. "It's become clear to me that they no longer serve me, their war god, but only the highest causes. Virtue, honor, goodness. Not to mention that they now listen to the one that they refer to as the Nameless or Highest God."

Sable trembled, hissing his basest reaction to such purity. "I don't like *that* God either."

"The Highest has more power than any god of Olympus." Ares didn't tremble or display fear. He did, however, seem aware that he was outmatched. "More power than all the ancient gods combined. That my Spartans now call him Master? This is the final proof that they must be stopped. They cannot be allowed access to the Nameless God's power. They must be eliminated before that happens. And before they become a true menace to me."

Sable wanted to rear up on his hind legs and thunder his enthusiasm about Ares' plan. Finally, the Spartans gone for good!

Ares placed a hand upon his shoulder. "Sable, you understand that I cannot have these warriors, ones whom *I* created and gifted with supernatural abilities, roaming the earth and exercising free will?"

He gave a vigorous nod of assent, swatting his tail several times.

"Good. Because from Leonidas on down, they are lost to me, and so they must be eliminated. To the last man, they must die."

"One question, lord Ares. How can these warriors be destroyed? Much as I hate to admit it, they're fair enough fighters, and they possess the unique powers you bestowed upon them. They've been honing those powers over the millennia and have been increasing in ability."

"This," Ares told him coolly, "is why I require the seventh warrior. River Kassandros, the one for whom you've been searching. Find him, and we have our key to destroying the other six."

# Chapter 3

Emma stared at the rolling waves, dismissing the idea that she'd heard a voice answer her initial prayer. As the wind whipped her hair across her eyes with a stinging slap, she lifted more silent prayers.

*I need help.* She pressed her eyes closed and made a conscious decision to open up to any divine guidance she might be able to hear. Her spiritual gift of supernatural listening, whether in prayer or with spirits from beyond, was something she'd avoided using for years.

*God, please. Tell me what to do.*

All at once she began to feel her ears literally burn deep inside the canals. Warm, tingling heat filled from within and spread outward until her earlobes grew fiery hot. God was going to answer her prayer! He would guide her on how to escape and what to do.

Lifting hands to both ears, she felt that opening sensation deep inside of her being; it moved far beyond her literal ears and speared the center of her soul and spirit. The warmth spread in tingling tendrils through her chest until she began to tremble from the intense impact of the awakening.

Then she heard something that made her shiver even harder. A husky, masculine voice that seemed to call out from the ocean's deepest heart.

*Help me,* the voice said. *I sense you; come to me.*

"Help me?" she repeated aloud in shock. Since when did God need help? No, it wasn't possible that the seductive, sensual voice belonged to *Him.*

*Please, help me. . . . I feel you near.*

*Definitely not God,* she thought, wiping blinding rivulets

of rain out of her eyes as she stared at the ocean. It must be someone who was lost out in that rough surf. Someone who was drowning.

She took a protective step back from the water, all her old fears of being pulled beneath the waves screaming louder than that man's desperate voice. She felt paralyzed, unable to breathe. Her mind screamed frantically, telling her to flee toward the tents, to race farther inland.

But then she heard it again, a truly spine-tingling cry. *Free me. I'm dying. . . .*

That rough appeal catapulted her beyond any fear and straight toward the ocean. She believed this man was dying out there, like he said. Her own terror had to be battled into submission so that she could save him.

He called out again, in a husky, hypnotic voice. *I sense what you are. Save me . . . please. I know that you can hear me.*

His words brought terrified tears to her eyes, made her feel hunted, from a realm beyond the one that she currently occupied. *I sense what you are.*

"How do you know what I am?" she demanded, staring at the consuming waves.

*Follow my voice. Will explain . . . later.*

This was no mere man, and his voice wasn't audible, at least not to regular human ears. She heard his words from the spirit realm, and that meant that he probably wasn't human. This realization only increased her horror, lent weight to the foreboding, chilling sense that the past few moments had given her.

When she'd opened herself to receive God's instruction and answer to her prayers, she'd obviously made a way for this entity to reach her. This was what she spent so much time avoiding: hearing voices from beyond the grave, the desperate pleas of wandering spirits who hoped to communicate with her. Even with her gift totally shut down they still tried to get through to her, but usually their cries weren't strong enough to catch her attention.

She stared at the waves, trying to keep her hair from blowing into her eyes. Maybe he wasn't a spirit at all, but a living, physical man who'd managed to reach her because of her special ability. Maybe he really was dying. No one deserved a fate like her twin sister had known. Nor would she stand paralyzed this time, not like she'd done while watching Leah drown, terrified and frozen to the point of inaction.

She rushed into the surf, her shorts soaking instantly, and focused her long-dormant gift. She'd done everything in her power to quash it permanently, but now a man's life depended on her awakening the supernatural power she'd inherited from her mother. Power that she had once promised herself she would never utilize or call upon again, a vow she upheld no matter how many spirits and entities had attempted to vault past her blocks during the past twenty years.

But this man was different, his heartfelt appeal unlike the others she'd forcibly tuned out for so long. Somehow, perhaps because of God guiding her or perhaps simply by instinct, she felt compelled to respond to him. His life could depend upon her heeding his pleas.

Someone who could hear him—it was more than River had dared hope for, even in his deepest prayers. He'd detected the woman's presence atop the waves the moment she'd glided near, gauging her to be only five or six feet above him. Perhaps in a vessel or out swimming, but didn't that place him closer to the shore than he'd believed? Her golden energy illuminated his dark world like a signal flare, that special brightness indicating her talent as a sentient.

He was certain that if he could reach out to her powerfully enough, project his spirit-voice loudly enough, she would hear him.

Summoning his remaining humanity, the part that he hoped would still be able to communicate with another living being, he called out as intensely as he possibly could. *I sense what you are. I know you can hear me. You can save me.*

Seconds later when he received a response, that fading part of his human soul sang with relief. He wanted to whoop and holler, to throw back his head and shout to the heavens, if only he weren't still a dagger. Then a name came to him.

Like a quick flash of her internal light, he'd perceived it psychically, by the same ability that allowed him to hear conversations when he was transformed into a weapon.

*Emma. Her name is Emma.*

But relief quickly turned to panic because Emma's wasn't the only response he received. A roaring cry of triumph sounded nearby, and he knew that he'd inadvertently summoned *far* more than Emma with his appeal for help. By finally crying out and with such strength, he'd aroused a deadly, sinister force, one that he'd managed to avoid during the long period of being lost in the water.

All around him he sensed darkness stir, felt it mass as one single being from the heart of the watery realm. He'd awakened the evil like a long-slumbering beast, a beast that was rising up now, emerging to come for him. No, damn it, for both of them, he realized, as he heard Emma call to him once again.

With his pleas for help, he'd dragged her into his own predicament. She was a mortal, one of his own, one of his protected. And at this dangerous moment, he had no way to defend her whatsoever. He determined that he would find a way to save her . . . if only she could release him from the dagger in time.


Emma's T-shirt was plastered to her chest, her shorts soaked through, and a strong undertow kept dragging her roughly by the legs. She was preparing to dive into the waves when the man's voice rang out again.

*Emma, be cautious*, he warned. *Find me, but be aware. Stay safe.*

Hip deep in storm-tossed waves that were crashing into her body, driving her backward, it was a fine time for her lost man to suddenly start warning her off. Besides, how did he know her name? Well, there wasn't time to think about that.

*Danger abounds, Emma. Find me . . .* now! *I will protect you if I'm able.*

"Who's gonna protect who here, bub?" she screamed into the spraying ocean. "You're the one who needs *my* help, remember?"

The voice seemed to howl above the wind, through it, underneath. It was everywhere and nowhere all at once, exactly as the voices had been throughout her childhood. The ones she'd silenced after Leah's death. Clamping hands over both ears, Emma prayed that whoever this man was, he'd shut up. That he would just shut his mouth, leave her alone, and go back to wherever he'd come from.

"I don't want this . . . not from you. Not from anyone," she shouted into the next set of approaching waves, three of them stacked right atop each other.

The softest moan, throaty and strangely seductive, answered her. *You are the only one. I am alone. Been lost . . . long . . . time. Free me. Must protect you, Emma.*

In reaction, an uncontrollable shaking settled into her frame, causing her teeth to chatter. These weren't cold chills caused by the wind or the pelting rain that fell from above. They were spiritual quivers, hitting her so hard that she could hardly keep her entire body from convulsing. She hadn't experienced anything like it since right before Leah died.

Feeling tears burn her eyes, she pressed them shut. "Where are you, then? *I* need help if I'm gonna find you. I can't follow your voice because the direction keeps changing. It's like you're moving all over the place."

*Follow me.*

Instinct took hold, and she dove beneath an oncoming breaker and skimmed her feet through the wave as it rolled overhead until she was sure she could surface safely again. Deeper and deeper the voice led her out from shore, until she could barely stand on the shifting sand.

She stamped her feet against the force of water, frustrated. "What kind of danger am I in if I don't find you? What's gonna happen then?"

*You are near. So . . . near. Gods, I feel you and your heat.*

A momentary lull in the waves allowed her to catch her breath. She stood on tiptoe, keeping her head above the rolling water, and slowly rotated in a circle. She listened for that deep voice above the wind and roaring surf. And then suddenly something stung the bottom of her right foot, making her cry out.

Had a shark bitten her? God forbid, had her stupid, bizarre-o talent reawakened only so she could talk to a flipping *shark*? One that had intentionally lured her out to where it could snap a sumptuous chunk right out of her foot before moving on to the rest of her body? Okay, that was just insane. She was clearly starting to lose it now.

"That hurts like a mother!" she yelled, taking hold of the injured foot. It had been sliced open from heel to toes as if someone had attempted to gut it like a fish.

*I am sorry. Hurting you was never my intention.* The voice was mournful, but oddly . . . hopeful, too. *But you've found me, and that wound will heal quickly.*

"You're a shark? A swordfish?" She put pressure on the gash to try to stop the blood flow, cursing at the pain. "What the heck are you?"

*A dagger. Dive to find me. You'll see the glint of my blade.*

She stared at the sky, sheets of rain blowing into her face, and decided she was acting drunker than a soldier on River Street.

"Evan Foster," she yelled at the sky, "if you're trying to play some really obnoxious joke on me . . ."

*My blade cut you. You felt it. Dive and search for me.*

Much as she wanted to dismiss the entire situation as being one of Evan's practical jokes gone wrong, she couldn't. In her heart, she knew the man calling for her was legitimate. Years ago, she'd used her gift often, and the way this guy's voice affected her was exactly as it had been all those years ago. Her eardrums tickled, her forehead hurt—two very familiar reactions to opening her spiritual hearing.

She set her injured foot on the sandy ocean bottom again, sighing. "Great. So, no, you're not a talking swordfish or shark. Not even a minnow." She raised her voice to a much higher volume. "Oh, no, you're something far more reasonable, totally normal. An absolute testimony to my mental health. You're a *talking dagger*."

*I am* not *a dagger.* He sounded miffed now, almost offended. *I am a man. A warrior who is trapped in this form. I've been lost for . . . I don't know how long.*

Her throat tightened and she thought of Leah. Of what it was like to be helpless and lost, in whatever way one might define that term. Still, she didn't want the poor guy getting his hopes too charged up.

"I probably won't be able to find you, you know." She stared down at the waves as if somehow he might be able to see her dubious expression. "Not in these dark waters. I'll be swimming blind."

His roar rang out across the water, a truly exultant cry. *Swim for me, before the danger arrives, Emma. I will protect you from the mounting evil. Don't you sense the demonic force that's surging closer?*

When she didn't answer, the mystical stranger spoke urgently and with renewed vigor.

*Feel with your hands.*

"So you can cut me again?" She laughed sarcastically, hoping he could actually hear. "Nope. Don't think so. I'm obviously not your kinda girl, bub."

*Any wound I bring you will heal quickly just as the first one I caused. I'll make sure of it.*

Slowly she released her injured foot, planting it on the soft, wet sand of the ocean floor. Amazingly, it didn't hurt anymore, just as he had promised. But she didn't have time to figure out how he'd healed her, not if she was going to find the man.

If he even *was* a man. Yeah, shark, dolphin, or some twisted merman was more like it.

She stopped and stood still, breathing heavily. Everything from her past seemed to be repeating in these few moments, memories she'd tried to bury along with Leah. She cursed herself for a stupid, crazy fool of a medium—correction, *former* medium—and was about to swim back to shore, when something in the atmosphere made her hesitate.

It was a marvel, but the stormy waves were suddenly growing unnaturally still. Supernaturally quiet. But then, farther out in the ocean, where the waves should have been lining up, Emma spotted something that sent her into tremors of terror all over again, yet paralyzed her with fear at the same time. Rolling as a mass, a single dark cloud covered the water. She might have mistaken it as another part of the storm except for the way the force gathered. The way it hovered, then funneled forward like a swarm of black locusts.

"Oh. My. God."

She didn't have the gift of seeing, never had. That ran in the other side of the family; her cousins Mason and Jamie Angel were demon hunters and could see the darkest entities of the spiritual realm. So could their sister Shay, if recent family rumors were true. In her own nuclear family, Leah had died too young to be sure exactly what talents she'd possessed, and her remaining younger sister Sophie seemed to have avoided the family gifts altogether. But not Emma; she was a *listener.* That's all she'd ever been able to do: act as a medium, hear the angels, sometimes heavenly instruction.

So she wasn't sure why she could see the demons that were swarming out over the ocean. Maybe it was simply a testimony to their own dark power; or maybe God, or some other force, was revealing them to her. Either way, she knew that her stranger told the truth.

"Uh, Dagger Man?" She wondered how fast she could find her promised protector. "You keep talking, okay? I'm coming for you *right now.*"

*Yes, Emma ... hurry. Do you sense the darkness? Hear it?*

She prepared to take a breath and whispered, "I hear and see it ... them." Then she filled her lungs with air and dove below the surface as fast and deep as she could.

# Chapter 4

Running onto the beach, Emma clutched the dagger in her hand and didn't dare glance over her shoulder at the approaching demons. No, she was going to move her feet as fast as she could and figure out how this speaking dagger was going to help her. Okay, even in her own head that sounded like something from a bad kung fu movie.

She reached the tents and leaned against one of the palm trees. The driving sheets of rain continued to sting her eyes, slapping her as the wind gusted. The storm had stilled only for that brief moment while she'd been out in the water, but it had been long enough for her to see the mounting darkness. Even now she could hear a buzzing noise, like many shrill voices speaking backward at once, and it was approaching both of them faster than she could formulate a plan.

She tightened her grip on the dagger, held it to eye level, and swallowed all pride. "Okay, pal, how am I supposed to free you? I found you; now what?" she demanded in alarm. "Because that evil is getting much closer, and you haven't said a word since I hauled you out of the ocean."

Nothing. Nada. She turned the weapon within her grasp, noticing how beautifully carved it was. She just hoped that such beauty was an indication of the entity's inherent goodness. With another glance out at the waves, she saw that the dark force seemed to be gaining strength. She squeezed the dagger tightly in her grasp. "Are you in there? Hello? I'm freaking out, out here."

*Em ... I'm weaker.* Long silence. *It took most of what was left of my ebbing strength to summon ... you.*

"Oh my God! You are so not leaving me out here with

no help. I think you're the one who woke those"—she pointed at the rolling cloud that was about twenty feet off shore—"creatures! They're demons and they're on me now, thanks to you."

She shook the dagger with both hands. "Wake *up*! Hop out! Do your thing!" She was nearly hysterical, tears mixing with the rivulets of rain that rolled down her cheeks.

*Your blood strengthened me. Briefly. But the effects are waning.*

"You want me to cut myself? Will that *strengthen* you again?" she suggested with a breathless glance out toward the advancing demon horde. "Will *that* get you out to help me?"

She didn't wait for his answer. Although she hated the idea of intentionally harming herself, if it meant that this mysterious warrior would be able to help battle the descending evil, so be it. She took the tip of the blade and sliced it across her thigh in a direction that wouldn't cause too much blood loss. For good measure, she ran the blade through the shallow wound a second time, wincing and biting back a raw cry.

"Did that work?" She kept her eyes closed, swallowing against the stinging pain.

*Yes. Not deep enough, though. It's too much blood that I need to bind us further.*

"Bind us? What does that mean?" She stood there, breathing heavily, willing her heart to stop its pounding.

And then, her hope rose just a little. The man suddenly sounded much stronger. *Ah, yes! Emma, I feel it now. I taste you and . . . I'm awakening more. Do it again.*

Without questioning the moment's reality, she took the dagger and ran it down her arm, spilling more of her blood. She swore she heard the man roar to life, a sound that hummed in her ears as something between a rush of power and a shout of exultation.

*Emma, you are bringing me back. Your blood . . . it makes me live.*

Before her eyes the wounds closed and vanished; not even a scratch remained.

*See? I promised that I would heal you, Emma.*

"I need your name." She pressed the dagger against her heart, feeling weak and dizzy. "You already have mine."

Rugged, muscular arms suddenly enclosed her; a warm mouth grazed her cheek, stunning her. "I am called River."

Emma jolted, about to scream in shock, but the very real and very *physical* man cupped a firm hand over her mouth. "Don't speak, Emma. Not a word." She shivered at the feel of his hot breath against her skin, at the growling sound of his voice. "The demons draw near, but I will protect you from them."

Thunder crashed nearby, but the storm was moving on, already more distant than it had been just moments ago. Or maybe it never had been a natural storm at all.

She tried turning in his grasp, but those lean arms of his were like a vise. She struggled, needing to see what he looked like, to verify that he wasn't a figment of her imagination. Yet the harder she fought his fearsome hold, the tighter it became, until with a growl he pinioned her against his hips. She would have sworn he was aroused; she felt something hard and solid press into the center of her back. She would have also sworn that, apart from some sort of rough covering around his groin, he was completely naked because she felt warm, human skin against her own body.

"I was trapped and you saved me, Emma." His warm breaths came faster, heating the back of her neck. Her body responded to that lead, her own chest rising and falling with tense, quick inhalations. He pressed his hips against hers, slowly rocking her against that smoldering spot where their two bodies joined.

His whisper fanned against her ear. "Your blood set me free, and I will do everything in my power to protect you." His fingers teased the edge of her bra, sliding beneath the cotton fabric. "And I do mean everything."

She shuddered against him, afraid that her feet might give way, but he held her steady and close. Good thing, too, since she'd obviously lost her literal foothold on reality. But somehow she knew that she'd always be safe so long as he stayed near.

*Maybe he's a beast, hideously ugly*, she thought. Not that

she'd even care; she was too lost to him, to all that he was
doing to her body with such focused, intense attention.

"Let me see you," she said.

She felt him shake his head. "You only need my touch."

It was as if he wanted to open her, unfold her body like
a flower, revealing one petal at a time. The feel of his hands
caressing her was staggering, unlike any sensation she'd
ever experienced in a man's arms. The crazed suddenness
only made the embrace more alluring, more thrilling. Yet
she had to take hold of her senses, especially considering
that demons still hunted them.

"Demons are coming," she reminded him, a new sense
of urgency sweeping through her.

"I might be, too." He laughed and moaned low as he
answered, sliding his other palm down along the center of
her belly. "*Coming*, that is. Especially with the way you're
pressing that hot, tight little body back up against mine."

Suddenly mortified, she tried wriggling out of his grasp,
but he'd have none of that. A firm hand anchored her by
the hips, pressing her against his groin, moving against her
in a slow, rolling motion.

"Oh, Emma, freedom tastes so sweet. I'm blood-tied to
you now," he whispered low against her neck, trailing hot
kisses lower and lower. "And you are blood-tied to me."
The words were threatening, seductive; God help her, but
they aroused her intensely.

"Blood-tied?" she asked. "What does that . . . mean?"

He spun her within his arms, turning her to face him,
and a blast of heat enveloped her. His tongue probed at
her mouth, urging her to open to him. He was all over her
with his body and hands and strength. Too close for her to
clearly see, he was a pouncing blur of golden brown, tawny
and lean like a big cat. Long wavy hair fell across his face,
brushing her cheek. With a blinking glance she saw that his
hair matched her entire impression of him; it was a mix of
light brown and gold, tangled as if he'd spent months in the
wild. She caught a glimpse of golden green eyes that were
as sensually feline as the rest of his body.

No room to breathe; no room to think. Or to question how River's sexual intensity had reached such a fe-

vered pitch, even with demons approaching. Strong hands
threaded through her hair, brushing it back as he deepened
the kiss, sweeping his tongue inside of her mouth, plunging and plumbing her depths. It was as if he didn't want
anything to stand in his way, not a single part of her. She
could feel the hard ridges of muscle that rippled across his
torso, could sense the power in his thick upper thighs, the
elegant strength in his long agile body. Leaving her helpless
to do anything—anything, that was, except respond to his
raw nature.

All at once a shrieking howl rang from behind them,
back down at the water's edge. River paused midkiss, his
entire body poised to listen. The only sound was that of
their heavy breathing.

After a moment, he pulled her closer, burying her face
against his naked chest in a shockingly tender gesture. "Now
that you've freed me, Emma," he told her intently, "now that
I'm here, holding you against me . . . you just may be in the
greatest danger of all, and not from those approaching demons. *From me.*"

He released her from his grasp with a forceful motion,
backing away with a low growl of warning. Or was it possession? Those golden green eyes of his were now bright
with an otherworldly glow; the gleaming look of a predator
filled them.

"So flee while I'm still capable of letting you do so.
Before I completely lose control, Emma," he warned in a
voice that was as strong as the distant thunder, "you must
get away from me. Before those approaching demons hunt
you down, you must go quickly. So, go, Emma, now! And . . .
*run!*"

Nikos settled into one of the two leather wingback
chairs that faced Leonidas's desk, and Ajax slid into the
other. Straton would be joining them soon, as would Ari
and Ajax's wife, Shay Angel. So they waited for the other
warriors, watching the king's silent meditation. He stood on
the other side of his desk, staring silently out the window
toward the darkening pasture.

Nikos fought a vague uneasiness at their commander's

continuing silence, letting his gaze drift around the intimate room. Leo's new study boasted floor-to-ceiling bookshelves, handcrafted from rich Carolina pine, and filled with beloved volumes from his library. Herodotus, Thucydides, Plato, and Plutarch were just a few of the ancient authors; then there were more recent works, too. Sun Tzu, Machiavelli, Clausewitz, Tolstoy, Malory, and Tennyson.

Nikos swung his gaze back toward the king, who continued to stare out the window. Suddenly their leader's preoccupied state became too much; Nikos just couldn't take the silence any longer. "My lord, what brings us here?" he asked. "Please tell me what concerns you this evening."

Leonidas turned to face them, blinking for a moment as if he'd been studying a long-lost memory or contemplating a battle plan. "I'm afraid you've caught me wandering in my thoughts." He smiled, the harsh scar that slashed through his lower lip making the expression seem more like a cruel leer. "Then again, what else might you expect from the Old Man?"

Nikos knew better. No heart was more noble or stalwart or kind than their king's.

Beside him Ajax growled. "Already told you, my lord. We call you Old Man as a sign of our allegiance. It's a private term of endearment among our ranks. Not a slight."

"Ah, but none of you are as old as I am," Leo said with a soft laugh, but it didn't hold much humor.

Ajax bolted out of his seat, beginning to pace. "Oh, bloody hell," he cursed, glancing toward Nikos for reinforcement. "Nik, you're what? Only six months younger than that half-decrepit fighter over there?" He jabbed a finger in Leo's direction.

Nikos growled. "I was thirty-four the day I perished at the Hot Gates."

"Ah, a young whelp." Leo gave him a flourishing bow. "Perhaps you should take my place."

Both Nikos and Ajax shook their heads. "Never," they murmured in hushed, reverent tones.

But Nikos wondered why their leader seemed downhearted. "My king, why are your thoughts so dark this evening?"

Leonidas's ruined smile faded, and he strode to his desk chair, settling in. After a moment, he released a quiet sigh. "I wonder why our Oracle does not counsel us. Ajax, you are the only one who has ever been able to hear and translate her words to our ranks. Although I gained the power to glimpse her in the past year, your role regarding her prophecies has not changed. You alone can tell us what guidance she offers about our battles."

"I have not seen her since the skirmish in Bonaventure, my lord," Ajax said, stating what they already knew to be the case. He'd never withheld news of their Oracle's comings and goings.

Leonidas nodded, continuing. "All these centuries, she's never stayed away for this long. She's always come to us when we needed her help. Yet River's been lost all these months, and I've not seen her since . . ." His voice trailed to nothing and he stared past them both. Almost as if he hoped his words might conjure the mystical female from the air in the room. Then Leo's expression changed, a vibrant, electric emotion filling his gaze, one that jolted Nikos because it didn't seem appropriate to the situation. Or to the king's need for his Oracle's guidance.

"You haven't seen the Oracle since when, my lord?" Ajax prompted, raking a hand through his shoulder-length black hair in agitation.

Leo's gaze refocused on them. "She gave me something to safeguard," their commander answered softly. "And I have watched this item as my soul's purpose. That was the last time she came to me, that day four months ago." Leonidas rubbed his fingers across the heavy, cracked leather of his desktop. "She should tell us what danger awaits. Why Ares sought to kill you, my warrior and friend." Leo stared pointedly at Ajax. "Instead . . . silence. Without her guidance it seems that every last standing rule of our original bargain has crumbled to dust."

Nikos swallowed hard. "It definitely looks like we're on our own now," he agreed. "First, Ares' betrayal in attempting to destroy Ajax. And now you're suggesting that he's taken our Oracle from us? Stripped us of her promised assistance?"

Leonidas rubbed the bridge of his nose, his eyes drifting shut. The Old Man truly did seem ancient in that moment, a fact that made Nikos's heart beat heavily in his chest. Their king was their ultimate guide. Yes, the Oracle was a great benefit to them, but seeing Leo in such a dark place made all the events of the past months seem even harsher and more ominous.

Leo sighed, his eyes suddenly lighting with renewed strength. "I know our Oracle. I know her character and her goodness. She wouldn't abandon us." He snarled roughly. "Not unless that treacherous god of ours commanded it. She'll return; it's only a matter of time. For now, new rules. New era. We must figure our own path."

"Are you going to launch a counteroffensive against Ares?" Nikos blurted, unable to hold back the thought. They couldn't sit still, languishing as nothing more than targets for the god they'd served for so long.

Ajax held out a staying hand, hitting Nikos lightly on the forearm. "I'm the one he tried to destroy, and even I'm not positive he's discarded us."

Nikos felt his blood boil. "You can't honestly think he still holds true to our bargain?"

Leonidas dropped a heavy fist on his desk, the sound a jarring, explosive noise between them. "He has gone after those I love, and that is enough evidence for me. But we remain immortal; we live on despite this breach. With the date of our vows approaching, we must be as one in this decision—that we will formally turn from the god. This is why I am eager for the Oracle's guidance. Because in just a few more days, we are expected in Ares' presence, required to reaffirm our pledges and loyalty."

Nikos shivered at the implication of Leonidas's words. Not once in all the past nearly twenty-five hundred years had they failed to mark the anniversary of their death and immortal rebirth by Ares' hand. He had them repeat the pledges in ancient Greek and numerous other languages from over the ages, unsatisfied of their full loyalty until he'd worn them down with their chanting words and prone bodies.

Leonidas lifted a hand, gesturing toward the door as

it opened. Aristos poked his head in, his massively broad shoulders filling the entire doorframe. "Straton and Kalias are on the way."

"Very good, Aristos. A monumental decision faces us now."

Aristos moved all the way into the library, leaning up against the shelves. "Is this about finding River?"

Leonidas nodded slowly in reply. "In a way, yes, it is about River."

"Has he been located, my lord?" Ari's face spread into a huge smile. "Is that the news?"

Ari was obsessed with his missing comrade, and Nikos understood the sentiment; he'd been haunted and driven to locate the missing weapon-shifter since he'd vanished four months earlier.

"I'm sorry, Ari, but there's been no word. However, we must decide, unanimously, if we believe the day has come to turn our backs against our war god."

# Chapter 5

Emma stumbled blindly as she tore through trees and brush that led to the tiny island's other beach. She charged forward, heeding River's warning, but despite how quickly she moved, she didn't reach safety. Not in time. Arriving on the distant beach, she heard a roar from farther down the shoreline. A horrible one like the time a tornado had passed over downtown Savannah when she was a teenager. Her family's entire brownstone had shaken, the windows rattling as if Satan himself were about to blow apart the old home. That was the sound that exploded behind her now.

River stood there on the beachhead, barely clothed except for some sort of leather loincloth, wielding a massive sword in each hand. She blinked because she swore those twin swords were—no way, they couldn't be—breathing fire. She blinked a second time, but the image had already transformed. Now the guy held a massive gleaming shield across his chest and a long spear in his hand. How had he located weapons so quickly? And why such antiquated ones?

Not that she'd complain. His unusual weaponry was making a fierce impact on the demons, the horde already seeming to retreat. The only evidence that remained of them was the sound of their high-pitched shrieking and squealing. Those hellions carried on like a load of pigs at the slaughterhouse. But the bloodcurdling sounds were much dimmer now, fading back into the ocean.

River was routing the demonic threat exactly as he'd promised after popping out of that dagger. She wondered what had happened to his dagger form. He obviously didn't operate like some genie in a bottle. No, the weapon had vanished as soon as River had emerged from that prison ... almost as if he *was* the dagger itself, on some elemental level.

None of it made sense. Well, actually one part did. River had made it clear that he posed a threat to her, claiming that a mysterious blood-tie existed between them. He'd warned her to run from him while she still could. Despite how bravely he now attacked the horrific demons, despite the kiss they'd shared, she believed him.

With one final glance behind her she started fleeing toward the sandbar. The tide was about halfway in. Maybe, just maybe, if she could make it to that submerged-yet-higher bit of sand, she could cross to the main island without having to swim too far in the Back River. Swimming *that* channel was the last thing she wanted to do. Just that morning she'd seen a school of nurse sharks in the river, and last time she'd kayaked near the sandbar, she'd accidentally hit a bull shark with her paddle.

She reminded herself of River's warnings about himself. That he wanted to harm her ... do something dangerous, based on the way he'd been nibbling at her ear and rubbing those hands up her belly. *All* the way up had been his obvious intention, and from his undisguised lust, even that wouldn't have been nearly enough of her to satisfy his raging appetite. Still, call her crazy, but that kind of attention didn't exactly feel life-threatening. More like extremely, dangerously satisfying.

Maybe the guy thought dizzying kisses could lead to murder; maybe for him they would. It didn't matter that she'd been willing at first. He'd been after far more than was appropriate for any stranger. With his warnings, he'd been blunt about how much more he would demand if she didn't escape.

Huffing breathlessly, she cleared her way to the far end of the beach. Neither River nor the demons should be able to see her here, she thought, sprinting toward the water. Then again, she doubted they would need vision to locate her, and that thought sped her movements even faster.

But her escape plan reached an immediate hitch. Right

as her feet touched the ocean something grabbed her by first one ankle, then the other. She screamed, feeling wet, slippery tentacles wrap tight about her legs, pulling her down hard. She landed on her side, slamming her left hip into the hard-packed sand with bruising force, and then the beast began surging back into the water, dragging her by her bound ankles. She could feel the demon that had hold of her even though she couldn't see a damned thing.

*"River!"* She screamed so loudly that it reverberated off the trees and echoed in the slowing rain. "River, help me!"

She dug hands and heels into the wet sand, and wished like crazy that she had one of the kayak oars to beat the thing with. Again she called out for River, and suddenly he was there. It was literally as if one moment he was far down the beach, then the next he was by her side, hacking with that powerful sword of his, freeing her.

He heaved heavy breaths as he labored, highly purposed and intense. With every motion of his sword, powerful muscles bunched and pulled, and she focused on that instead of the creature that held her. At last she felt the demon release her, but before she could move, another one seized her by both feet and began dragging her toward the water once more. Unlike her, River could obviously see the demons. He sliced at the invisible tentacles that tried to squeeze and pull her into the waves.

"A bigger one's rising up." River's gaze swung back and forth across the ocean, searching wildly, but he never stopped battling the fiend that had her in its grip. "As soon as you feel this one let go," he told her, "run back to the trees, to the highest ground you can find."

"What kind of demons live in the ocean?" She could barely get the words out, couldn't breathe. Her heart was beating a crazy, terrified tempo, hammering in her chest.

"Water demons," he said angrily. "Nasty, vicious, mindless creatures who only want one thing. To take you back into the deep with them forever. And trust me . . . you don't want that."

He kept wielding that gleaming sword, cursing and commanding the creatures to back down, but then he stopped speaking in English. He began booming away in what sounded like ancient Greek; she recognized the language because she was Greek American, and her cousins Mason and Jamie actually spoke the old language. It also explained the accent that she'd noticed earlier.

Suddenly, without a sound or word, he pitched forward, falling onto his knees. Had the demon pack injured him? Her own feet remained bound; he'd been stopped in the middle of freeing her. "What's wrong? God, River, are you all right?"

He turned to her, his stare wide and panicked. Those emerald golden eyes were truly otherworldly now, shining with a supernatural energy that made her shiver. But at that moment, the strength in his radiant gaze seemed to flicker, dim slightly.

When she saw his force ebb, she became truly terrified. Without River, she'd be sucked into the ocean, drowned like Leah. She began squirming and flailing against the demon that held her, but it reacted with a suctioning pressure, leeching onto her legs with new vigor.

"*River!*" she shouted, giving her legs another struggling kick. "Don't fade on me!" The creature reacted by dragging her several more feet into the water.

She jerked her head in River's direction, and was relieved to see that whatever momentary weakness had overtaken him, he was already getting back in the game. But he still looked pale, not as strong and vital as he had earlier.

"I'm . . . stronger," he said, shifting a sword in his palm.

She pried at the demonic grip on her body, but couldn't get a solid hold. Not that she could see the entity, but she could feel how slimy-slick and cold its tentacles were. They kept sliding out of her grasp with every attempt she made to fight back, cinching her tighter. As she battled the creature again, it began slithering one of its appendages along her inner thigh, seemingly intent on working toward a highly disturbing destination.

Feeling the motion, she panicked. "River? River! This is starting to get *way* too personal."

"I always protect my own," he proclaimed in a fierce tone, and began hacking at the unseen assailant. Finally, she felt the slippery creature release her and she scooted back on her bottom like a crab, scuttling as fast as she could toward freedom, not even stopping to draw breath or say a word. The demons' reach was obviously limited to the lapping edge of the waves, and although they could slither onto the sand, they were bound to the water itself.

Once she was out of the demon's grasping range, she scrambled to her feet and continued backing away from the horror she'd just experienced. No way would she let those demons grab her again. *No flipping way.* River moved with her, sword raised, and then when they reached the highest ground, he glanced at her.

"You're safe," he said in a rasping voice. "Good, Emma . . . stay here. Safe." Then he fell to his knees, almost as if he knew he could let go now. As if her safety released him to stop fighting whatever weakness kept hounding him.

She hesitated, looking between him and the shore, wanting to believe that she was out of danger, but worried about this brave man who'd saved her life. She reached a hand to his shoulder. "How can I help you? What do you need to be all right?"

He pitched forward onto his elbows, and for an eerie moment his entire form was covered by a silver cloud. It wrapped about him and he released an agonized groan.

Then, just as quickly, the haze disappeared. She rushed to his side, dropping to her knees.

"What's happening?" She brushed a tangled mass of waving golden brown hair away from his face, needing to see him more clearly. "Tell me what's happening to you, River."

"Protecting you." He obviously struggled to breathe, his strongly muscled chest heaving with every breath. On any other day, that gleaming and powerful physique would have had her ogling like crazy. Instead, she only noted his supreme physical beauty because it confirmed her earlier thought about his dagger—that his beauty reflected an inherent goodness.

Yes, that lean, rippling body had to be a physical manifestation of something much more powerful. More than that, deep in her marrow—that place of spiritual listening—she believed in the man's goodness. His soul and spirit hummed with a kind of noble purity, no matter how dangerous he claimed to be.

His head dropped forward, touching the sand; he moaned again and it was a deeper, rolling sound from the center of his body. She leaned closer, placing a palm on his bare back. "You're going to be fine," she whispered, hoping she wasn't offering a false promise.

He rocked slightly on his knees, keeping his head bent against the sand. It was as if he was trying to comfort himself—as if he'd been in this situation before, and had learned the hard way that only he could soothe his own suffering.

"Shh," she tried, stroking his shoulder, which was tanned a rich shade of sun-golden brown. A muscle rippled beneath her touch, one that was as finely sculpted and toned as the rest of his nearly nude body. *Beautiful. He is stunningly beautiful.*

Exactly like that dagger had been. In some way that she couldn't understand, they were one and the same, the weapon and the man.

River's eyes drifted shut and then a shimmer of silver flowed across his skin, a glowing pulse that seemed to run through his veins. Emma watched, refusing to fear the way his body morphed before her eyes.

"Listen to me." She clasped his shoulder, squeezing. "Why are you turning silver? Is it something to do with your dagger?"

Eyes still shut, he nodded his head with a slight moan. "It wants me. . . ."

Emma tried to restrain her panic at the thought of River vanishing on her. "You can't go back inside that dagger, River," she told him in a steady voice, trying to get him to focus on her words, to prevent him from disappearing. "I won't *let* you go back, you understand? Because those demons are all around us still."

His eyes drifted open again, and he focused their glazed depths back toward the attacking demons. The silver vanished completely, his entire demeanor becoming resolved and alert once more. She shivered, realizing that the glowing silver force had wanted to consume him, had tried to seize him. Or wanted to turn him back into a dagger against his will.

Struggling to his feet, River swayed a moment, then sank back down to his knees. "Emma, go. Leave me and get away from these demons. I'll hold them at bay while you escape. They're bound to the water, but the tide is rising fast because of the storm. You've got to get farther away."

She sprang to her feet, about to run for the trees as he'd advised, but she couldn't. She just couldn't leave this strange warrior man, not after he'd saved her and was now apparently in some sort of peril of his own. Having seen that strange silver cloud that tried to overwhelm him, and after hearing his frantic pleas for her help earlier, she knew one fact. He needed her as much as she needed him.

She reached him, taking hold beneath his arms. "Come on, bub. I'm getting you out of here." But he was so unbelievably heavy, his body slick with rain and ocean water. He was larger than she'd realized, solid, without an ounce of fat. Those hard muscles made him even more difficult to heft or move, especially since her grasp on him kept sliding and slipping.

He looked up into her eyes, his own green-golden depths growing unfocused, and his entire body shaking with unsteady tremors. "I can't hold my human form." He covered her left hand where it grasped at his arm. "Am going to be a dagger. Again. If I change, keep me. I promise . . . I won't hurt you. Will be careful with you, Emma."

Those gorgeous eyes slid shut, and he mumbled something else, something about Aristos, then Leonidas. Like the famous king from that *300* movie? Okay, he was obviously out of his mind with whatever he'd been through. And she wasn't much better; she felt weakness begin to overtake her, too, but she had to get River back to the main island, to safety. Maybe by the time she paddled them both there, he would be more coherent and could explain every living detail of this crazy nightmare he'd dragged her into. Or, then again, maybe she really was just dreaming, some horrible nighttime vision quest.

But unlike the nightmares where she sometimes had to seize control and wake herself, she remained on the wind-swept and rainy beach with the slumped warrior resting in her embrace. His ankles dug into the sand where she'd been dragging him, two small furrows marking where she'd already hauled him.

"Damn it, I'm getting you out of here, River. You saved me and I'm gonna help you now."

She gave his body a heaving tug, and there arose more howling, low guttural noises of the water demons. When she got out of this mess she was going straight to her cousins' house. Mason had always been a straight shooter, and they'd been really close at one time. He'd give her the skinny on what the living hell these water demons were all about. And how a man could turn human after being a dagger, or how he could even start out that way to begin with.

"Yep, Mason will get this all sorted out," she said aloud, working to calm her nerves.

"He's too far away," River mumbled, his eyes opening again.

"Mason Angel? How do you know Mason?" she asked in panic. Okay, the entire situation was getting weirder and scarier with every passing moment.

River began struggling against her, and rolled out of her grasp. He bent over double, his long hair falling across his face. She couldn't read his expression, not through the tangled mass of light brown hair.

"Em, please," he nearly begged. "The demons will keep coming for you, but if you get to the tree line, you'll be safe there."

She took hold of his nape, forced him to look up at her, and slapped him across the face. Not too hard, but enough to get him more alert. "No. Do you hear me, Dagger Man? No flipping way. You saved me, and now I'm gonna return that favor."

He grinned, laughed a little. "You saved me first, milady. Don't forget that."

And then, without any warning whatsoever, that silver cloud encircled him again. Or maybe it just swallowed him whole. She couldn't say for sure, but she no longer held a man's nape. That man had dissolved and vanished within her grasp.

Instead, she clutched a weapon that was so intricately carved and gleaming with silver brightness that she nearly had to squint just to gaze at it. There, instead of the man named River, she clasped a renewed and polished version of the dagger from earlier. *His* dagger, right in the palm of her hand.

"Oh, God, River," she murmured, holding his dagger form close to her. "What am I supposed to do with you now?"

# Chapter 6

Aristos would be damned if Nikos found River before he did. Who gave a rat's testicle if his Spartan brother possessed the gift of supernatural tracking, including the ability to generate multidimensional, organic maps mid-air? And who cared, while he was listing reasons why he shouldn't, that Nikos comprehended things from those living, reactive maps that the rest of them couldn't fathom? All because he could perceive entire ranges of the light spectrum that none of the rest of them could. Definitely beyond any mortal's range.

So, heck yeah, when Nikos swirled this latest map projection in the middle of the great room, it burned Ari up inside. Because of one simple fact: The tracker didn't even *like* River. For Ari, however, the slave meant the world and more. He was his best buddy, his closest confidant, his favorite wrestling opponent. River was the real deal. The friend who'd back your play no matter what kind of shit came down, no questions asked.

Ari's countless daytime trips out to the marshes, flying as a fully transformed hawk, had been a total waste of effort. He'd spent the past four months searching for any gleam of River's dagger in the shallow waters, able to fly in daylight because he was the only one of their corps who could transform completely into a hawk. Big fucking woo. That "gift" hadn't done jack to save River. And all the while Nikos had used his own unique, powerful, penetrating tracking talent . . . and turned up precisely squat.

Ari leaned back in the plush leather sofa that faced the center of the great room, folded both arms over his chest, and made sure every bit of his posture conveyed his total pissed-offedness about *who* was giving the talk. Nikos probed the visual display with his hands, even speaking to it in a whisper. He'd always treated his maps like living things, and treated River like a shithole.

Nikos droned on and on for what felt like forever, illustrating the probable trajectory that River's journey had taken him on. In response, Ari sank deeper and deeper into the cozy leather sofa, a new addition since their move to Savannah, as plush as the rest of the digs. Ari's eldest brother, Kalias, had located their new compound. An exclusive property, with a foreclosure price that was such a good deal, even their austere and simple-living king couldn't pass it up. A farm out in metro Savannah's Effingham County, it sat on more than one hundred secluded acres, a perfect location for training and drills.

But it was the house itself that had revved all their engines, with its ambient scent of fresh paint, and thick carpet that begged you to walk barefoot on it. The kitchen with its granite countertops and fine cabinetry defied their ancient imaginations. Leonidas, however, had remained nonplussed, declaring that he wasn't precisely sure what to do with a garden tub. "Grow flowers in it?" he'd asked dryly.

"Aristos? Any input?" Nikos's question brought him back to attention. He'd been attempting to appear as if he were actually asleep because he knew it would get in the freak's craw. "About the tidal patterns I was indicating?"

"You showed me the same thing two days ago. Seen it, done it, flown over it plenty of times."

"You think you can do a better job?" Nikos challenged, his naturally dusky face turning red with irritation.

"You know, yeah. I probably could."

Nikos gave a wave of his arm, indicating the hallway that led to the front door. "Have at it, my friend."

"Look, I'm not your friend, not right now, Nikos." Ari breezed past the Spartan with a cutting glance. "Until you find *my* friend . . . until I think your heart's really in it, you and I aren't pals at all. Got it?"

He stormed toward the hallway, so furious that his hands trembled. He balled them into fists, imagining getting some of the rage out. He knew he wasn't acting like himself, not being the good-natured friend that all his brotherhood normally counted on. He was supposed to be the one to lighten the dark days, to mend broken bonds between everyone else. But without River, he couldn't seem to get his usual good humor back. It seemed disloyal and wrong, somehow.

"Ari." Nikos followed close on his heels. Nikos never called him by that nickname, always kept his distance. "Ari, wait a moment."

Ari spun to face him, fury boiling up inside. "Yeah? What, *Nik*?" He practically spat the words, hunching his shoulders forward and assuming a fighting stance. *Just give me a reason, brother. Bring it on.*

Nikos's tough countenance seemed more open than usual, his black eyes searching and filled with something that Ari couldn't pinpoint. It was enough to make Ari relax his posture just a bit. Even though he'd gladly take the warrior out at the slightest provocation. "So what, Nik? What you want to say to me?"

Nikos drew in a breath, stared past Ari's shoulder. "I may not like the guy much," he admitted quietly, "but of course I care what happens to him. He's my Spartan brother, same as the rest of you."

"He's not a *true* Spartan, remember? You've always been first to point out that fact. The only one of us to point it out, I should add." Ari poked a finger against Nikos's chest. "River's just a lowly slave. Not worthy of your respect. *Kassandra*, isn't that what you nicknamed him, oh, more than two thousand fucking years ago? Don't bother trying to tell me you care about him. He's my friend and brother." Ari poked him in the chest again, harder. "Not yours."

"What's really eating you, Aristos?"

"You've been falling down on your job, dude, that's what. You're supposed to be able to find lost people . . . lost things, if that's how you prefer to think of River right now. But you know what? Trapped inside that silver dagger is still the guy I grew up with, the friend I miss who needs us to help him. So he's not a thing to me, and if you don't fucking find him soon, I'll feed your balls to you on the end of some *other* dagger. Get it now, dickwad?"

Nikos's shoulders slumped slightly, but he said nothing. Slowly, he turned away, walking back toward the great room. Ari rolled his eyes, heaved a sigh, and followed after Mr. Hangdog.

"Nikos, come on! You know it's true. You would've found anybody else by now."

The Spartan turned on him then, black eyes burning. "I can't find him, Ari. I have tried and tried." That desperate, intense look in Nik's eyes finally made a believer out of Ari.

Nikos continued, "He haunts my dreams, these images of him moving through the ocean. Sometimes I swear I can hear him calling for our help . . . for me."

The man's genuine remorse was more than apparent, and Ari clasped his shoulder with a brief squeeze of brotherly support. "I believe you, guy. I do. I get it now."

Only he didn't get it, not really. Nikos had always gone out of his way to give River all manner of shit, including calling him by the feminine designation of his last name whenever he could. *Kassandra.* Just because Nikos knew it got in River's craw. Now, remorse? Regret? *Peel an onion, find some unexpected layers*, Ari decided.

But it also reminded him of a hint Leonidas had dropped years before, that private remark to River—which he'd shared almost immediately with Ari since nothing was ever private between the two of them. That comment about there having been bad blood between River's servant father and Nikos's own Spartan warrior one.

"Nikos, what was the deal with your old men? Your father and River's?"

Nikos's black eyebrows cranked downward, his entire demeanor closing off in an instant. "Don't know about that."

"Leonidas once indicated—"

Nikos cut him off coldly. "Like I said. Don't know anything on that count." With that, Nikos turned away and focused on the glowing, swirling map that still hung midair where he'd left it. The conversation was over.

"Fine. I'm hitting the road, heading out toward Tybee again. Gonna search those marshes some more."

"Actually, I'd check the Back River area. As I've mapped the tides, I keep coming back to that and Little Tybee."

Ari opened the front door, and then turned back once more. "I'm never giving up this quest. Not if it lasts for eternity. I won't stop."

"Then we have something in common," Nikos said. "Because I won't either."

# Chapter 7

*Use the fool!* was the first cry that came to Emma as she sprinted toward the kayak. *Draw your own blood again; strengthen him! Give him to us.*

*Yes, us, us, us*, the water demons began chanting, the words rising up out of the waves themselves like some unholy catechism. *Save yourself . . . give the fool to us.*

She had to get out of here and take the dagger. *No, not a dagger, River*, she reminded herself. *He's a man, too, not just an object.* She had to get him to the main island. For crying out loud, he'd even seemed to know her demon-hunting cousin's name when he'd said Mason was too far from here. If they were talking one and same, then maybe her Dagger Man had dealt with her eccentric cousins before.

More ringing cries of instruction: *Use the dagger, draw your blood . . . he needs freeing. Free the man! Draw your blood, mortal!*

Keening cackles followed that statement as if it were the most uproarious idea in the world.

As she dragged her kayak out into the water, she kept River's blade inside her bra. If she put him in her pocket, there was a chance that the weapon might get washed out of her shorts and back into the ocean. So this was her safest option.

"You behave in there," she told him, trying to find some shred of humor in their dismal situation. She readjusted the dagger's sharp edge so that it faced the cotton fabric of her bra, secured it in place, and lowered herself into the backseat of the kayak. It would be hard to quickly steer the tandem rig by herself. *There's no other choice, though,* she thought and began working her way hard into the approaching waves.

*If I can just get past these demons, down into the river toward the main island, maybe we'll be safe.*

She guided the boat in that direction, trying to close off her supernatural hearing. It was bad enough to know that water demons were surrounding them, even worse to hear their taunts.

All at once, something made her grow still. She had the overwhelming urge to take hold of River's blade and use it on herself. To slice her wrists so she could bleed and bleed for him. Awaken him.

*Yes*, a deep and sinister voice cooed, *awaken your warrior. He will help you. Save you. Use the blade, Emma. Use it . . . use it. . . .*

"I'm not an idiot," she screamed into the howling wind. "You won't control my mind, or get me to do something insane and deadly."

*If you don't awaken your warrior, we will consume you. Drag you down to the depths and drown you.*

Emma pressed her eyes shut, but their threats stole the last remnant of hope that she'd been clinging to. Robbed her of that gut-level determination to escape their sinister clutches and the hope that she'd save River's own life in the process. Just as he'd already saved hers.

Maybe it was all some demonic mind game, she wasn't sure, but their strategy achieved its desired impact. Beginning to cry, she slumped forward in the kayak, feeling more helpless than she ever had before in her life. And she hated being powerless, despised that reaction in herself.

*Yes, you are weak now. Far too weak to battle us alone. We will swallow you in the depths of our realm. Take you under the waves.*

"You will never drown me," she argued, but her voice sounded halfhearted even to herself.

*Unless* he *comes to your aid.*

A momentary image of Leah being sucked beneath the ocean filled her mind, and with it came a flicker of defiant strength. That shot of determination grew, building off the rage that she felt at the memory of her twin's death, and her desire to fight off the demons was renewed. She dipped her oar into the waves, and paddled a few strokes, but again it felt as if the demons were tightening some invisible band around her mind.

*It doesn't have to be this way*, a falsely kind voice soothed. *The warrior can save you. Awaken River. You need help, Emma. You crave it, and you know you can't do this alone.*

River would battle them away if she brought him forth again. Oh, if only she could, Emma thought hopelessly. But that would require more of her blood, and she'd lost a fair amount already, even though River had healed her earlier wounds.

*But you can*, a lower voice promised. *You can call forth your protector. Use the blade and he will return. So easy, so painless.*

She shook her head, trying to fight the mesmerizing effect the watery voices were having upon her. "How do you know my thoughts?" she demanded.

*Listen to us.... Use the blade and your warrior will emerge. Use his blade against yourself.*

The voices sounded seductive and incredibly alluring. A strong sense of submissiveness overcame her like a warm, soothing blanket, promising safety. Protection. Peace. If only she would obey.

"Use his blade," she repeated, staring at her wrist. She would not die; River wouldn't allow it. He'd already healed her earlier wounds. But if she cut into an artery, there would be enough blood to truly revive him. She wouldn't be alone, unable to defend herself.

*You won't be alone*, that languid voice purred in agreement from against the kayak's side.

"I won't be alone," she repeated numbly and, reaching inside her bra, she withdrew River's dagger form.

*No, Emma!* He screamed the words from within his core, as loudly as he possibly could. Even if these were his final words, his last burst of strength, he had to stop her. Those water demons were hypnotizing her and directing her actions. It was one of the things they were renowned for, the basis for the old myth about the Sirens.

*Emma*, he tried again, *don't listen. Heed my voice, not theirs. They want to kill you. And they mean to awaken me in the process!*

If they could unleash River, then no doubt they would have their way with him, steal his immortal life one choking bit at a time. Or perhaps they only intended to kill Emma by using him, then seize his blade and carry him to the deepest part of the ocean and leave him there for eternity to agonize over what he had done.

Her blood penetrated his senses, arousing and waking him. He found it hard to fight with her, to beg her to stave off the demons. The taste of her was like nectar, and it stirred his lusts on the deepest level.

*Don't* . . . It was all he could manage. While nearly every part of his own mind, so ensorcelled by her blood, by his own berserker, wanted to cry, *Yes, Emma. Yes!*

Again she injured herself. He knew it because his formless, sightless world suddenly seemed to turn Technicolor, but he did not emerge. Instead he did something much more effective and helpful to Emma in her battle to survive the attacking demons.

He began to heal her, releasing power into her body with every swipe of his blade, and as he did so, something strong and binding knit between the two of them. A wondrous connection that was even deeper than the first touch of their blood-tie had been. Again he sensed her use his knife on herself, tasted her energizing, life-filled blood.

And again that beautiful tie between them gained power in the mingling of her blood with his immortal essence.

Emma stared down at her wrists, confused to see mild scratches. She wouldn't have turned River's blade on her wrists. That would have been suicide. But seeing the marks and her thick blood on his blade, it looked as if she'd done just that, and then he'd immediately healed the wounds.

She blinked, unsettled that she couldn't remember anything from the past few moments. A familiar hissing couplet of demonic voices brought all the details back. First the leader's more simpering timbre, urging her to use River's blade; then the second and weaker voice that kept repeat-

ing the same words in a loop. Clutching River's dagger
tight in her hand, she began swiping toward the sound of
their slithering tones, thrusting it in the air. He was filled
with supernatural power, so of course she could and should
use him to defend herself.

*You can get out of this, girl*, she told herself, sweeping
River again in a jagged, violent motion through the area
where she thought the demons were, but the voices kept
moving. Squinting for a moment, however, she would have
sworn that she saw a shimmering image travel through the
water. Like liquid within liquid, it moved, flashing gray-
green and then vanishing. Slimy scales emerging, then
submerging.

Oh, God in heaven. She could see these demons. She *was*
totally visualizing them just like her cousins Shay, Mason,
and Jamie did.

That had happened earlier after she'd turned River's
blade on herself to draw blood and give him strength. *I'm
a listener, I'm a listener*, she wanted to promise herself. *All
I'll ever be.*

It was bad enough to have her medium gift resurfac-
ing, literally, after so long, but now she was developing a
new unwanted ability? "Fine, I'll use it right now. Hey, you!
Freaks!" she called out, sitting tall and searching the water
for any sign of them, but there was only that iridescent,
sporadic motion. The demons were still submerged. "Ha,
clever trick. The ultimate Marco Polo game, bet you think.
Guess what," she taunted in a "neener, neener" voice. "I
can see you!"

The water began bubbling in a circular pattern and
Emma readied River's dagger, poised to strike the moment
the demons surfaced. Her advantage over them made the
gift not so unwelcome after all. She could figure out later
how to ditch it somehow. Maybe Shay could coach her on
closing down demon vision.

She tensed her hold on the blade, leaning out over the
bubbling area of water, but remaining careful not to over-
turn the kayak. And then, bingo. A blunt scaly head eased
itself out and a pair of beady, hideous eyes widened when
she struck out, hitting the thing right between those eyes.

It squealed vigorously, lengthening higher out of the water, which only gave her a longer portion of flesh to strike. She sliced into the demon and it went into a spasm, its evil eyes looking back at her.

And again, the foul eyes widened in surprise, only this time it shrieked, "Your eyes are . . . your eyes!"

"My eyes?" she shrieked right back at the minion as it kept babbling hysterically. "*My* eyes? Nothing's wrong with my eyes, pal!"

The creature said nothing more. It simply sluiced into the water with a squirming, inelegant dive and vanished into the deep.

Clutching River in her hand, Emma managed to drag the kayak onto shore. She checked her watch. It was almost six p.m. With one quick call, she could arrange for the guide company to pick up the kayak, and then she planned to drive over to her cousins' house as quickly as possible. In fact, she was going to call Mason first and make sure they were there waiting for her. And after that, Evan would be next, and boy, did she have an earful for that flake.

Walking up the wooden boardwalk steps, she began jogging toward her parked car, withdrawing the keys from her pocket. Her cell phone was in the glove compartment, and she was already planning what to say to Mason when an extremely large man stepped onto the sandy path, blocking her way.

Everything about him was dark. His eyes, his shoulder-length hair, his dusky skin. Although his sudden appearance should have made her feel threatened, especially after all she'd just been through, his face wasn't wicked or harsh at all. In fact, he seemed to be suppressing a huge, beaming grin.

"How's it going?" she mumbled politely, moving to step around him.

He matched her steps and gave her a gracious smile. She was about to try passing him again, but it became clear that he would not budge.

"Look, can I please get by?" She felt her face flush with anger and the first stirrings of fear.

"Totally." He nodded toward her hand, and she subtly shifted River's dagger within her grasp. "Once we've done a little business here, you'll be free to hit the beach, drink a few beers or, hell, go surfing if that's what you want. You can go on your merry way and live the rest of your life. So long as I get what I want."

Emma's breath caught. "It's daylight still; there are people all around. I'll scream and you won't get away with it."

"Oh, gods of Olympus, not that. No, no, that's not what I meant at all. I'm sorry, not trying to freak you out." He held his hands high, and then a little higher still, as if he were talking her off a dangerous ledge. "Really not that, I promise."

"Then *what*, for God's sake?" She nearly shrieked the words. Enough in one day was simply enough at some point.

"You have something that belongs to me." He stepped closer, pointing at River, whose silver form she'd been attempting to conceal within her hand. "I'm here to get it. To take it home where it belongs."

"*It?*" she challenged.

"Look, let's start over." He extended a large, bearlike hand toward her. "I'm Aristos Petrakos. Most people just call me Ari."

"I'm not most people."

He kept talking, ignoring her observation. "It's like this. That dagger you're holding is precious to me, beyond any bounty you might ask."

Emma thought as quickly as she could. The man's words sounded sincere enough, downright concerned and full of affection. Perhaps he really was a friend of River's. She held River's hilt in her grip, poised to strike out if physically assaulted.

"Okay, Ari," she answered carefully. "I have a question for you. If you had to name this particular dagger ... let's say if you wanted to, oh, try and find it like you would a missing ... friend." She paused, searching for just the right comparison. "Or, no, that's probably weird. More like a missing pet or something. Anyway, if you went calling for this dagger ..." She watched his black eyes flare in reaction to her words. "Tell me, Ari, what name would you use?"

"River," he said softly, holding out a beseeching hand. "I, and the rest of his brothers, call this dagger *River*."

"Good answer." She folded both arms over her chest, holding River even more tightly. "Now you just have to get me to trust you."

Whatever he said in reply, she didn't hear it. All at once her vision filled with bright floaters, sharp bursts of light that warred against growing darkness. She felt, more than realized, that her legs were giving way.

"Oh, God . . ." she said, right as the whole world went black.

# Chapter 8

"So, Petrakos ... that's Greek?" Emma sank down in the passenger seat of Ari's SUV, wishing she were more in control. More in the pink of things, as it were, instead of the bloodred state that had caused her collapse. She'd been given no choice but to accept his offer of a lift back into town.

"Yes, my ... friends and I are all Greek."

"Friends?" She wasn't sure what his vague remark meant.

"Those in my cadre, our circle." He made this statement as if it were the most normal, obvious answer in the universe.

"You're talking about that mysterious brotherhood you mentioned earlier, right? The ones who call my dagger River."

"*My* dagger," he corrected in a friendly tone. "He belongs with his brothers."

She let that comment slide for the moment. "So, okay ..." She pressed a hand to her eyes, a new wave of dizziness hitting her hard. All her earlier blood loss was taking its toll. "Brotherhood, cadre, whatever. You're using some kind of code language. Like in the Mafia. You're telling me that River is a"—she jabbed forceful quotation marks in the air—"*friend of yours*."

He cut a glance sideways at her, smiling slightly. It was hard to feel in danger around a guy who seemed perpetually on the verge of bursting into a huge, boyish grin. "*Our* dagger is Greek as well."

"River's my friend now, too," she said, although the seductive behavior he'd displayed definitely crossed the boundary of mere friendship. "So what does it mean that my friend is a 'friend of yours'?"

"We fight together. Seven of us." His tone was more closed off now.

"What, you're some sort of military unit or something? Who do you fight?"

"Who did River fight for *you*?" Ari countered, glancing at her bloody, torn T-shirt. "You obviously got into a major scrap together based on how rough you look."

She tightened her hold on River's cool silver form, pressing him harder against her right thigh. He'd saved her life, and until she could verify that Ari was on the up-and-up, she wasn't going to reveal too much.

"Not going to answer my question? No problem. I can already guess what the two of you battled. Demons of some particular variety."

Emma grew wide-eyed at the proof of just how well Ari obviously knew River. "Okay, but I still don't trust you." She leaned her head against the window, pressing her eyes shut.

"You got in the car with me." He gave her a stern glance, but mischief lurked behind his dark eyes. "I hope you don't make a habit of accepting rides from strangers."

"No, but then again I don't make a habit of fainting on boardwalks, either. Or befriending talking daggers." She laughed darkly. "Call it an unusual day, but I didn't figure accepting a ride from someone who was on a first-name basis with my dagger was exactly hitchhiking."

"How did you find him?"

"Just get me home . . . downtown, okay? I'll give you directions from there."

Ari cast a curious glance in her direction, but she felt exhausted suddenly, too tired to answer any more questions. Yes, sleeping would be wonderful. Even better was the thought of cuddling up with River right in her grasp or maybe beneath her pillow. The idea of him near her, even if he wasn't human right now, caused a wave of comfort to wash over her. She didn't have the strength to wonder why she felt incredibly tied to him now.

*We are blood-tied now.*

*Blood-tied.* River had used that phrase, had said they were bound together, linked because her blood had awakened him. That recollection caused her to sit upright with an arousing, powerful jolt. She blinked and found Ari's sideways gaze on her once again.

"You know, that weapon's been lost for a while." He spoke as if choosing his words carefully. "He's been missed. Especially by me."

"Why? What's he really mean to you, anyway?"

"Good question," Ari said. "What does he mean to *you,* Emma?"

Her skin prickled in reaction to the question, came alive with the same heat she'd felt emanating from River's muscular body every time she'd touched him or he'd held her close. At the memory, a sexual shock wave traveled from the crown of her head all the way to her deepest core. Dampness formed between her legs, an unstoppable reaction, almost as if River were stroking her body now.

*He is against my thigh,* she realized, snapping her gaze downward. But he remained a silver dagger, harmless enough. *Right, totally innocent, this one.* She wouldn't put it past him to have somehow been seducing her silently, creating the sudden wetness in her panties.

He'd nibbled and licked her as if she were a banquet laid out expressly for his benefit. That attraction, that heat, had been full-on real. Emma traced a fingertip across River's hilt, wishing that he were normal, like any other man she'd ever met before. Then again, if that were the case, would she have fallen for him so quickly? He was out of the realm of reality, literally, and that was part of his tantalizing, mesmerizing appeal.

They crossed over Lazaretto Creek where docks were lined with shrimp boats returning with their day's catch. Seagulls dove and hovered over the boats and their nets, creating a midair swarm. The birds were obviously hoping to filch a free meal. Emma shivered at the frenzied spectacle, the greedy gulls reminding her of the water demons that had tried to kill her earlier.

She shook off the creepy sensation and turned to Ari. "Tell me what River really is. Who he really is. I deserve to know that much."

He seemed to consider her question carefully, opening his mouth and shutting it several times before answering. "River Kassandros is my best friend," he said at last. "He's had my back for a . . . long time. I'm just returning the favor."

"He saved my life. So it's not just your back, it's mine, too, and I promised to keep him safe."

Ari laughed suddenly, such a warm sound that she couldn't help pegging him as a decent guy. "Good for River, placing himself in the hands of a gorgeous woman. Obviously very capable hands, I might add."

She frowned. "You make it sound like it was some sort of sex thing."

"Wasn't it?" Ari gave her a pointed look. "I do know how, uh, worked up the guy gets after he's been in weapon form for a little while. And this time out, it was way more than a little while."

A hot flush hit Emma's face, and she opened her eyes, sitting up tall. If River's supposed best friend knew exactly how he'd treated her back on the island, then that might mean that River's behavior hadn't been special. That *she* hadn't been special to him, just an available conquest the moment she helped spring him from dagger prison. She hated thinking that his touching and caressing of her had all been part of some sort of ritual, just his typical behavior whenever he popped out. Maybe he was like a genie, only a really horny one. The Don Juan of all genie daggers.

"He seemed pretty happy to . . . get out." She forced her words to sound far more neutral than she actually felt.

Ari really began laughing at that one. She tried to throw a glare his way, but the man was smiling too much for her to stay mad. "Yep, I'm betting that was a spine-tingling, toe-curling, dangerous kiss." His laughter faded. "But he didn't kill you, so I suppose that's a good thing."

She stifled a gasp of horror. "Has he killed women before?"

"God, no. I was joking. No way."

"But he's been into women . . . *done* them after?"

"Totally no! River's way too shy and . . ." Ari's words faded on his lips, and he glanced pointedly at her. "Uh, Emma? You do realize he's probably listening to all of this, right?" Then, in a much louder voice he boomed, "River man! So glad you're back. Missed you like hell, buddy."

"So, basically, River turns into a horn dog whenever he gets loose. That's what you're telling me."

"Horn dog?" Ari sputtered, his eyebrows shooting sky-high.

"Poon hound, whatever you want to call it." She hated herself for it, but the revelation left her feeling as if his caresses and nibbles had been something of a one-night stand. On a demon-infested beach. Yeah, maybe one-night stand was a little harsh, she decided, once again covering River's blade in a protective gesture.

"Hell no." Ari dropped his voice to a whisper. "Like I said, River's not much with the ladies. He's never had smooth moves, none of that. It's just that his special ability, the way he can become a weapon, like you obviously saw . . . well, when he comes out of it, it's rough. He's usually a little messed up in the head after."

"Messed up how?"

"Violent. Or sometimes heavily aroused."

Emma's body reacted powerfully to that simple statement. Her nipples grew taut, her whole body remembering how he'd stroked her. Her neck prickled as she thought of his warm, sensual mouth brushing against her nape.

"So he's really dangerous when he emerges?" She could hardly breathe, wavering between arousal and terror at the memory of having been so close to him after his change.

Ari waved off her question. "It's not a big deal. Not really. He's usually all out of sorts, trying to kill anyone in sight. Or needing a serious orgasm, whatever."

"A regular boy next door," she shot back.

Ari never even took a breath, just kept rattling along. "It's normal for him. That's the thing. The violence of what he has to do, how he bonds with the weapon, it takes a toll. But he's not violent by nature, and not dangerous so long as someone . . . usually me . . . is there to talk him down a bit."

Emma turned in the seat to face Ari. "I come from a family where everybody's got some kind of creepy talent, so I get unusual abilities. And I even get fighting demons. But what I *don't* get is this . . . how does a man pop in and out of a dagger like he does?"

Ari shook his head in obvious disagreement. "You really *don't* get it."

"Then explain it to me!" she shouted in mounting frustration. "Tell me about your Greek Mafia."

"I've said way too much already, actually." He seemed to finally realize how revealing his words were. "I'm just so stoked about getting River back or I'd have kept my trap shut."

"Why stop explaining now?" She hoped the question sounded innocent enough.

"I'll deal with it, no worries."

"Deal with it?" She jackknifed out of her seat, adrenaline energizing her fatigued body. "That sounds like more Mafia talk to me. You better not have bags of cement in the back." She tried craning her neck to make her point, but Ari held out a staying hand.

"Emma, you are perfectly safe with me just like you were with River. We don't harm people like you . . . we protect you. You're one of our own."

*One of my own, my protected.* Ari's assurance to her was an almost exact repetition of River's earlier words.

"You good now?" he asked, searching her face. "No need to be afraid."

"But how *will* you deal with the fact that I know too much?"

He shrugged. "You already knew too much just from encountering River," he said gently. "But that's my problem, not yours. You're looking pretty pale. Why don't you nap while I get you home?"

The thought of sleep was alluring, and Emma nodded her head appreciatively. Deep down, just as she'd heard River calling her, some element of her spirit knew that Ari would not hurt her. She slid her right hand over River's dagger, torn between feeling protective or aroused as she recalled his alternate, human form. But he was still a dag-

ger right now, so she'd just rest, hold him close, and hope
that when she woke, he would be human again. So he could
hold her close in return.

"So tell me where I'm headed, Emma."

"West Jones Street. I live at 109 West Jones," she said,
and would have sworn that he gasped slightly in reaction
to her address.

# Chapter 9

Of all the gin joints in the world, Ari's particular one, the brownstone looming straight ahead, really did want to fuck with him, didn't it? *West Jones Street—109 West Jones Street.* One helluva whopper as coincidences went.

He'd been speechless when Emma had given the address as her own. Then, finally recovering from the shock, he'd asked if she was sure it was correct.

"Duh, I know ... where I live," she'd mumbled groggily.

The sleepiness hadn't just been the result of her recent blood loss and demon fighting. During his conversation with Emma, he'd quickly realized that she'd learned too much about their immortal brotherhood, so he'd begun to erase her memories. Ares had given their corps that power to alter human recollection because there were some things that mere mortals were better off not knowing. Although most supernatural events were obscured from human sight, there were times when they glimpsed the forces of darkness.

And humans just couldn't deal with stuff like snap-jaw demons, or men sprouting epic black wings and flying away. That was too much for Starbucks-drinking, Panera Bread–eating mortals to deal with. Look at what had happened to all those folks who'd spotted Elvis in McDonald's. Now *that* had taken some serious memory mojo. Why hadn't The King just stayed dead like he was supposed to do?

Emma was an innocent. One who'd wandered into a demon battle totally by accident, or so it seemed based on the scant facts he'd learned about her interactions with River. She'd been in the wrong place at the wrong time, and it was his sworn duty to keep her blissfully unaware of the evil that surrounded her every day. So he'd tampered with her memories of River and the demon battle during the drive home. That's why she'd already been half asleep when he questioned her about the West Jones address.

Hell, talk about a crap-ass situation. That Emma, the one person who'd finally led him to River, would wind up living in this particular house. She could have given any address, lived anywhere downtown, even though the historic district wasn't very big. The coincidence gave him a thick, heavy feeling in the center of his belly. It felt as if events were starting to intersect—his own past with River's present, or maybe even all their pasts colliding together into one giant cesspool of significance.

Sitting up, he glared at the brownstone as he would at an opponent. "I'll get you for this," he threatened the dwelling in annoyance. As if *it* had been the cause of his heartbreak over the past hundred years. As if *it* were opening up his old wounds right now.

Gingerly he pried River from underneath Emma's hand; although she would no longer remember any of the afternoon's events at this point, seeing the dagger might release some piece of memory. Truthfully he hadn't wiped her memories clean. He'd simply locked them away within her mind, and, barring some unexpected trigger, they would remain hidden there. He tended to think of the action in modern terms: that human memories, once wiped, were much like a locked computer file. No password, no access.

Once he'd eased the dagger out of Emma's grasp, he held it in his hand for a brief moment and squeezed it. "We'll figure out how to free you, River man. Promise. Just gotta get you home first."

Then, reaching past Emma, he opened the glove compartment and gently slid the dagger into a leather case he'd been hauling around for whenever they found his friend. He locked the compartment, drew in a strengthening breath, and prepared to deal with getting Emma to her front door. Get the girl home, make sure she's safe and won't remember anything, drive on. Period. End of mission.

Yet somehow he had a bad feeling that none of what

awaited on the other side of that door would be quite so simple.

The demon horde's failure was utterly unacceptable. Sable stood on the remote island's beach, hooves slowly sinking in the wet sand, and contemplated some method of extracting his own vengeance for their failure. Just as Ares had promised to do to him if he didn't locate River. That hint he'd dropped about transforming Sable into an ocean beast made his current state, that of a smelly, ruined centaur, seem a downright appealing option.

Still, although he was far more powerful than the slithering water demons cowering before him, he might need them again in the future. Best not to burn all his bridges.

"Tell me how you had the warrior in your grasp," Sable sneered, "and yet allowed him to escape."

Malise, the leader, spoke up. "We thought he was a slave, but the power we sensed . . ."

His minions murmured their agreement in fearful wonder. "Too much for our horde, too much."

Sable sighed, actually trying to maintain some patience. If he blew his cool with Malise and his cohorts, he might miss out on important information.

"River Kassandros is no mere slave," he lectured smoothly. "He's a weapon-shifter and an immortal, capable of all sorts of treachery and cleverness. You knew this. You knew the depth of his power before you ever accepted the assignment."

Malise slithered closer, out front of his small band of demonic serpents.

Metallic scales rippled down the length of his back. "We remained in the fight for you, my lord, battling the warrior after he emerged. But that woman . . ." Malise's words trailed off, the scent of terror radiating off of his cool skin. "It was her fault. If it hadn't been for her, we might have succeeded."

Sable stamped impatiently, feeling his blood boil in frustration. The hair along his withers prickled and his vision swam red. "You let Kassandros get away and you're blaming your failure on a human woman? By the gods, what is demonkind coming to lately? She is nothing but a puny, pitiful mortal." Sable slashed his tail in violent disapproval. "A female with no power of her own."

"But, my lord, this is what I'm telling you. She does have power. Extraordinarily great power," Malise screeched in a burst of newfound boldness.

Well, well, curious indeed. Sable let his tail fall loose again, cocking his head. "Continue."

"It was her blood that freed him from the dagger. After being trapped so long, no mere mortal's blood could have empowered him."

"You don't know that. We have no idea how his blasted ability works. . . . Even he didn't expect to become trapped."

Malise cut him off. "Not only that, but when we compelled her to take her own life, to spill enough blood to draw him out for good, she didn't die."

"That means nothing! That warrior has the power of healing and life in his blade, not just death."

Malise hissed at him. "It wasn't just the warrior's power. She has power all her own, lord Sable. We saw it in her eyes, saw exactly what she is. We've encountered females of her bloodline in the past."

Several of the lesser minions chimed in, their voices a shrill screech. "Not to be touched! Not to be harmed."

A dark, troubling thought began to form in Sable's mind. He, too, knew firsthand that there was one group of women whom you never harmed. They were sacrosanct, not to be killed by any demon. And he'd already been burned recently by that hidden, holy line of powerful females. Ones descended from the original oracles of Delphi, who possessed the lightest of blue eyes and prophetic gifts that were handed from female to female throughout the generations. Shay Angel was one such seer, and he'd be damned if another female popped up and caused havoc in his life.

Sable studied the dirt beneath his fingernails. "And why couldn't this female be touched? Why would she, a mere mortal, be off-limits to your crew?" he asked as if it were only a casual question. Not one that had his heart pumping out a jittery beat, nor one that he had already answered himself.

Malise slithered backward, his long, scaly end retreating into the waves. "The female is a Daughter of Delphi, my lord. The proof was in her pale, unique blue eyes," he answered, far too much awe in his shrill, obsequious voice. "We can't touch one of Apollo's prophetesses or their descendants."

Sable reared in fury, unable to contain himself for even a second longer. "I'm well aware of the Daughters," he thundered, striking at the air with his hooves. "But this woman was not your charge, nor was destroying her." Sable dropped his forelegs to the sand, leering at the lot of them. Mindless, stupid demons. No wonder they'd bungled the operation. They lived among seaweed and crabs. "You failed me, and you'll pay. Maybe not now, but at some point, you will pay, Malise."

Malise slithered backward, hissing, saying nothing more. But the scent of his fear was strong, a wretched stench that burned Sable's nostrils. That was when Sable realized why his heart was hammering like the hoofbeats of a thousand wild horses.

Malise's failure was his own doom. Sable would now have to return to Ares and admit that he'd lost River's trail. And for that, Sable had no doubt, he would certainly be made to pay.

Emma slumped against him, but Ari kept her solidly on her feet and moving across the quiet cobblestone street toward her house. The brick and stucco structure loomed above him like a monstrous House of Seven Gables, one that sucked him closer and closer toward some predetermined fate. He shivered and then shook off that eerie thought like a dog would a sudsy, unwelcome bath.

*Not gonna do this shit. It's a house. It was once* her *house; it's not anymore. End of story.*

He focused on helping Emma to the other side of West Jones, checking traffic again since they were making slow progress. She wasn't in pain now, just woozy and confused. At least he'd managed to get her out of that tattered, bloody shirt by offering one of his own that had been in the backseat.

He glanced sideways and inspected Emma one last time. She certainly didn't look ready for a society ball, but she'd cleaned up pretty well. No one would guess that she'd been pounced on by the spawn of Hades.

As they reached the sidewalk below her home, she turned to him and squinted. "I'm sorry. Exactly who are you again?"

Okay, maybe he'd gotten a little overzealous with the memory erasing if she didn't even recall the story he'd planted in her mind a few moments ago.

"I drove you home from the beach." He left out the other suggestions he'd provided and kept things simple. She'd already been through enough in the past few hours, quite obviously.

"Oh, yeah." She leaned into him as they reached the marble steps that led to her home's entryway.

"Here we go. Home sweet home." He tugged her up the steps. "You got a key?"

"Just ring the bell." She shook her head. "Mom's car is out front; she's here."

"I thought this was your place."

She shook her head again, a little more weakly. "Live out back."

"In a trash bin?" he blurted, not quite able to stop himself from being sarcastic. That was how he dealt with uneasiness: making jokes, bad ones a lot of the time. It had served him well on the battlefield over the years, and this particular moment, with all its unsettling emotions, felt like warfare. It was as if the old place were crawling all over him, buzzing beneath his skin.

"No, in the carriage house." She laughed softly, and he caught a glimpse of what River must have already seen, keenly intelligent beauty and strength. He made a note to hound River for details once he was back for good and able to talk.

At last they stood at the entrance. He stared at the familiar Victorian-era door with its medallions and intricate, heavy knob. With a resolved nod, he rang the bell. And

Emma instantly sagged against him once more, listing limply like some strung-out party girl.

"Emma, get it together." He gave her a shove, trying to be gentle about it. "You don't want your mom getting the wrong idea here. Or, even worse, your father."

She shook her head. "Daddy died when I was little." She ran a smoothing hand over the front of her clothes, frowning at the oversized black T-shirt he'd loaned her.

She looked up into his face, blinking. "Now *who* are you again?"

# Chapter 10

"That Aristos looked extremely familiar, Emma." Cecilia had barely been given a moment to talk to the handsome, oddly behaving man. "Did he harm you in some way?"

Emma lay on the sofa, her head propped on a fluffy pillow. "Mama, I'm all right." She slid her gaze toward where Cecilia stood. "Ari just helped me home. Evan had left me out there, and a big storm came up. I had to paddle home alone and . . ."

"And?"

Emma shook her head. "I'm not sure. I fainted, so I guess that's why I can't remember." She closed her eyes tiredly. "We'll have to go back for my car tomorrow, though. And I'm making Evan go get the camping gear." Emma sat up and searched around. "Where's my cell phone? I'm calling that jerk."

"I'm not worried about Evan right now." Cecilia settled gently on the edge of the sofa. "I'm worried about you, darling."

"You're being overprotective and I don't need it."

Cecilia had to disagree with that particular statement. She'd already lost one of her three daughters, and had raised Emma and Sophie mostly on her own. Her husband, Ron, had died of a heart attack not long after Sophie's birth. But her vigilance didn't come from her years as a single mother. Emma was, and had always been, special. Her innate ability as a sensitive had atrophied at such a young age, leaving her in a spiritually vulnerable position. That hidden gift was a time bomb, always ticking away inside of her. It made her a potential magnet for all sorts of darkness, demonic forces looking to prey on her ability, manipulate it, and turn it against her.

Cecilia stroked a lock of Emma's dark hair away from her cheek. "How about a glass of wine? That might calm your nerves some, huh?" Cecilia rose and walked toward the kitchen.

"Where's Sophie?" Emma called after her.

"Out in the carriage house."

Emma huffed. "Why's she over in my stuff? I didn't tell her she could go in there."

"She's doing a photography assignment and wanted the light."

Cecilia's youngest daughter couldn't be more different from Emma. Always dreamy and unfocused, she was an extremely gifted artist, but unlike her sisters, she'd never exhibited any indication of paranormal abilities. Well, except for her downright ethereal nature, which did sometimes make her seem as if she were a visitor from another time.

That thought put Cecilia's mind back to Aristos and his odd behavior. She opened the refrigerator and, removing a bottle of Chardonnay, waited for her spirit guide to offer some opinion. The nameless entity had inhabited their home for as long as Cecilia could remember, never once identifying herself.

Cecilia had her guesses as to who the spirit might be, but whenever she tried to push or prod the woman for information, evasive answers were all she got in response. Cecilia only cared that the spirit's input never failed or misled her. The entity's aura was truly good, anyway, so she'd long ago shaken any concerns that the source was demonic in nature.

"Friend," Cecilia queried, opening the bottle of wine, "tell me if this Aristos is trustworthy or not. He brought my daughter home in an addled state, and it bothers me that he seems so familiar." Cecilia steadied her hands against the kitchen counter, battling a heavy sense of dread. "Emma is innocent. What should I be thinking right now?"

No answer came; only silence blanketed the kitchen. The lack of guidance when the spirit usually tended to be so garrulous annoyed her. With a frustrated sigh, she filled

Emma's glass of wine and was about to leave the kitchen when she heard the spirit's voice.

*Emma is safe*, that calm, feminine voice tinkled quietly. *The one who brought her to you is good. He will protect her. Not by sense, but by knowledge.*

Cecilia moved to the room's center, eyes searching in every direction, trying to find some physical proof of the woman who had directed her path unfailingly for so many years.

"Why is he familiar?" She needed to know that Emma wouldn't suffer Leah's long-ago fate.

No answer.

"Tell me why I recognize this man." She hoped she would stir some answer—from the angels, from God himself, and especially from the spirit who had just offered such vague instruction. She was met only with silence. She had no choice, then, but to trust the scant input. The spirit had already promised that Emma was safe, had vouched for the man who'd brought her home.

Whatever events might be unfolding, they would be for the best. Or at the very least, they would ultimately turn out that way.

It was the thought of the journey to that endpoint that caused Cecilia to tremble.

River would have clubbed Ari if he could have. Would have taken the big guy and boxed him right across the face. Why would his best friend have thought that shoving him into a leather box, of all things, would be a great idea? After such a long time lost in the water, being cramped up and locked away was hardly River's idea of big fun. He wanted to hear what was going on, to sense the people around him.

Apparently the warrior had wiped Emma's memories of him away, too. Or so River had gathered as he'd interpreted sensations and parts of their ongoing conversation during the car ride. River no longer felt Emma's strong, vibrant energy, that mortal spark that had drawn him toward her in the first place.

*Good job, Ari*, he thought sarcastically. *The one person*

*who has managed to free me, to communicate with me in my dagger form, and you lock her memories and leave her behind.* Once he broke free, he'd hug the huge Spartan, thank him for bringing him home ... then challenge him to a wrestling match and kick his ass.

For now, however, River was wrestling with something much more immediate: a returning sensation of hope-lessness. No, he wasn't in the water anymore, but without Emma's ability to hear him, he now wondered if his fellow warriors would understand how to free him from the dagger. Of course, Straton had the gift of hearing as well, and there was at least a small chance that River would be able to form a connection with his fellow warrior and communicate.

That thought should have quelled his anxiety, but it didn't, at least not completely. He hated the idea that she wasn't going to remember him, or those brief, extremely powerful kisses they'd shared. At the core of his soul, a quaking sensation began. If he'd been in human form, he undoubtedly would have begun shivering or trembling. And it wasn't remembering the warm, soft feel of her ath-letic body pressed against his that did it, or the sensation of their mouths opening to each other.

It was his sudden awareness of something even more powerful than his already intense feelings for Emma: the blood-tie that rippled between them. Back on the island he'd thought their bond was only temporary, but now, sur-rounded by silence, that connection began to sing to him. It came alive, like a living, vibrating cord that led from his soul's center, straight to Emma's. In fact, as he focused his energy on that pulsing link, he began to *see* it. Vividly.

It shone in his mind, glowing a vibrant shade of crimson, binding him with Emma as sure as if it were a solid, physi-cal rope. Not a chain, which implied bondage—more like a gorgeous trail of red stars, winding toward his sweet mortal. Guiding him toward Emma, who was now bound to him as surely as if they'd mated already. As surely as if Emma were his ...

Gods, his *what*? Soul mate? Wife? No, this blood-tie was more powerful than either of those concepts, far more mystical. He knew then that he would have to find her again, no matter how long it took, no matter what obstacles had to be overcome. Even if he had to be bound by chains to prevent his berserker from harming her, he would claim her physically as his lover. And then how much deeper would their strongly bonded connection become? They were already linked by that blood-tie that wove between them, and that gave him an idea. A thrilling one that might enable him to communicate with her despite their physical separation.

He could use that same link that connected them to reach out to her, to enter her subconscious mind. Perhaps while she slept or if she was quiet; he wasn't sure how to go about the plan because he was in uncharted territory. Never, not once in his immortal life, had he ever been blood-tied to anyone, just as he'd never been trapped in weapon form as he currently was. It seemed that only Emma's blood and mortal strength could free him from his shackles, and maybe, just maybe, that same supernatural strength would enable him to do what he never had before. Reach across the distance and link with a mortal. His mortal.

Moving with careful, methodical purpose, River reached out with his essence, feeling for Emma's strong pulse of human energy. He visualized her in the same way he'd always pictured his own human body while shape-shifting in the past, taking hold of it before it was a physical reality. He focused every ounce of his energy on that first shimmering link in the chain that connected their two souls, and began winding his way toward her.

# Chapter 11

With his spirit, River followed the glowing crimson thread that linked him to Emma. She'd seemed so groggy earlier, right before Ari had taken her away from him, and River prayed that if she was in a deep sleep it would allow him to use their connection and attempt to enter her dreamscape.

In what felt like a hand-over-hand motion, he moved his way along the chain. It was a little like traveling over a nighttime battlefront where only his intuition and heightened senses allowed him to maneuver. In this case, the dark land that he navigated wasn't part of the material world. He'd left that and his dagger form far behind. This shadowed place was the realm where his soul and Emma's joined as one. Their blood-tie overcame any possible barrier that might separate them.

So long as that bond remained, he had a prayer of stepping into her dreams. Not as a lifeless, violent weapon, but as a *man*. One whose body had come alive after only a few tastes of her blood, and then much more alive once he'd held and kissed her. Emma had transformed him back into vital flesh and bone.

Now if only he could reach into her subconscious, he had a hope of holding her again. He would reach into her heart and soul just as she had done his, hopefully releasing her hidden memories of him.

So long as he didn't lose control. *Highest God, please don't let that happen. Please keep my berserker from overtaking me as we meet in the soul realm.*

Drawing on every ounce of his warrior's discipline he made a vow. *I will stay rational when I reach her*, he prom-

ised God and himself. *I will restrain that monster that roams
my blood. Both for her safety . . . and for any hope of our
possible future together.*

With a new resolve, River focused on the fiery thread
that seemed to burn brighter with every forward surge that
he made. Emma was so near; he felt her spirit vibrating, its
heat and passion. If only he could see something, anything
at all. But the only source of light was their glowing link;
otherwise, inky blackness surrounded him. However, he
could sense Emma's personal energy pulsing strongly and
he made a desperate surge forward.

At that precise moment the shadows in her mind parted
like the curtains of a theater stage, giving way to a realistic
scene.

He blinked at first, shocked by the sudden brightness of
her dream, unsettled at how real the experience felt. He had
the strong sensation that he'd broken free from the dagger
again, and had to remind himself that this was only an illusion. A vivid one inside Emma's mind as she dreamed.
With another quick blink, he realized that she was dreaming about a living room of sorts.

But he barely noticed any physical details of the room
itself; his attention was riveted completely on Emma. She
lay curled on a long sofa, tucked beneath a blanket with her
cheek resting on her palm. She seemed relaxed and comfortable, and he decided that the room had to be part of her
home. He looked upward, taking in the high ceilings, the
intricate details and carvings overhead.

*Money.* Emma obviously came from loads of it. He
took a moment to study the expensive furnishings that surrounded him. He didn't know enough about décor to give
the proper names to the fancy china, the figurines, or the
furniture that he saw, but he definitely recognized wealth
when he encountered it. Gods of Olympus, he'd spent millennia on the lowest rungs of the social ladder. What could
a refined, cultured woman like Emma possibly have in
common with a lowly slave like him?

That thought caused his belly to clench with an emotion
he refused to identify. He had only just met the gorgeous
female; he had no right or claim to her, even though they

were tied together spiritually. As he glanced around once again, he became aware of one sure fact: He could never be enough. Could never move in her world or even know how to behave properly in it. The sinking realization gave him a sick sensation deep inside. It moved through his spirit like a wave.

No, there would be nothing between them except the one, leveling kiss that they'd shared back on the island. That, and whatever action it took on her part to free him from the dagger. Then he'd ensure that Ari got her as far away from his dangerous reach as possible. Somehow, too, he'd find a way to sever their bond.

But what if another taste of her blood was required for him to break free? Then would the blood-tie strengthen even more?

He gave his head a shake, determined to focus, to seize these few precious moments with Emma. Not just to convey how badly he needed her assistance, but to talk to her. To be with her. And without the specter of his berserker casting its violent shadow between them.

Here, in her quiet mind, he might even have a chance to show her that he could behave like something of a gentleman. Well, that was probably exaggerating things; no man of his common birth could ever be described *that* way. Especially not someone like him, a warrior who killed and maimed and battled the cruelest creatures that stalked the night. He released a dark curse of despair. Who was he kidding? He'd never have the smooth skills or fine words to impress Emma.

He'd never known what to say to females, not in any age. Whenever he found himself around the opposite sex, his tongue always twisted itself in rude, awkward knots. As for knowing how to *pleasure* a woman, well, he'd not lain with one in hundreds of years, and that last time had been disastrously awkward. He always handled his posttransformation release on his own; he couldn't trust himself in the presence of any female upon his return.

In near-panic he glanced down and discovered that he'd not remembered to create a clothed image of himself before entering Emma's subconscious. Gods, she might stir any moment and find him gaping at her in an extremely aroused state. His shaft protruded like the long, gleaming sword he so often became in battle.

His gaze shot to Emma who still slept on, unaware that he was gawking at her and palming himself, behaving like a craven, truly lowborn imbecile. And if she should suddenly wake, what would she think about him and his intentions? There would only be one conclusion for her to reach. Frantic and ashamed, he slapped one hand over his traitorous member and cupped his balls protectively with the other.

*Clothes, damn it. I need to be dressed when she wakes, not looming over her like a feral beast about to attack.*

His mind riffled through wardrobe possibilities, but he couldn't seem to conjure a single shirt or pair of pants. Damn it, he wanted to look handsome for Emma, yet he was utterly clueless as to what fashion she'd find attractive. His usual black T-shirt and cargo pants seemed dully functional; his armor would serve only to intimidate her. Holding both hands over his groin, his panic intensified.

That was the exact moment when Emma suddenly sat bolt upright on the sofa, blue eyes wide and filled with fear.

*She has no idea who I am. How could she?* Ari had erased her memory of him. Now he was the worst kind of threat: a stranger invading her home. A very naked, very aroused stranger standing only a few feet away from her, grasping his private parts like a wild creature.

"Emma, it's okay," he blurted. Without thinking, he extended both hands to reassure her, which immediately unveiled his rock-hard erection. Her wide gaze slid to the bull's-eye mark, locking on his protruding, pulsing length, then jerked back to his face in shock. A terrible strangling noise erupted from the back of her throat. He froze, standing there like some idiotic version of an ancient Greek sculpture, only he wasn't throwing a javelin or being crowned with laurel wreaths.

Oh, nothing so lucky for him. He might as well have been a marble depiction of a devil come to ravish a fair maiden. All he could do was stare at her with both hands raised, suspended between watching her horrified reaction to his nakedness and covering himself again.

At least she had the presence of mind to break the bizarre standoff. "Who the hell are you?" she demanded in a
high-pitched voice. "And why the hell are you in my living
room?" The words were almost a screech, not unlike his
hawk's voice. He hadn't heard her so frightened, even back
on the island when demons were bearing down on them.

With a jolt of awareness, he slapped both hands back
over his groin, trying to think of something to reassure her.
He only wound up sputtering like an imbecile.

She scooted back on the sofa in alarm, pulling the blanket over herself. "Get out of my house! Get out, right now!
I'm calling the police." She kept her gaze on him, but felt
around on the coffee table beside her, obviously searching
for her cell phone. "I'm calling them right now. And I'm not
the only one home, so you better leave while you can."

He tried to make his demeanor and tone as calming
as possible. "You're dreaming. It's just a dream, Emma,"
he said soothingly. It was the gentle voice he usually reserved for Ajax's horses when they got skittish. Too bad he
didn't have an apple or some sugar cubes. "Sweet Em, you
are soundly, deeply asleep just now. I promise that you're
safe."

She jerked her head around, then shouted, "Mama!
Mama? Can you come in here right now?"

River shook his head. "She's not going to come in here,
Emma, because you're not really in your house at the moment. Or *is* this your home?" He couldn't suppress a little curiosity even if it wasn't the right moment, all things
considered.

"None of your business, bub." She scowled at him, but he
smiled in return. She'd called him bub just like she had earlier today, which meant that he was getting through to her.

He couldn't help smiling even more widely. "Just trying
to gain your trust."

"By grilling me? By standing there naked and being
super scary? Don't think so."

She huffed, pulling the blanket up to just below her chin.
"You've got no right, showing up like this." She pressed her
eyes closed and started mumbling to herself. "Wake up. It's
time to wake up."                                      •

He could hear her thundering heartbeat, could smell the raw terror flowering all over her skin. That fear of hers was what finally brought him back to his senses, and he instantly summoned clothing. The soft cotton of his T-shirt covered his chest. Next, his favorite cargo pants formed about his legs, trapping his hard cock in a painful twist of fabric. Emma didn't even notice.

She pinched first one arm, then the other, still murmuring to herself. "Just wake on up, girl. You can do it." Then, as if calling out to someone nearby, she yelled, "Wake me up! *Wake me up now!*"

He leaped to her side because, damn it, he needed her asleep. Otherwise their communication would be dissolved. "No, Emma, don't wake up. Please," he begged. "I'm not here to hurt you, I swear it."

He dropped to his haunches in front of her, but she recoiled. "This dream feels wrong. You feel wrong. It's too real. Too . . ." She shut her eyes, shaking her head back and forth with a violent gesture. "Familiar."

He tried to reach for her hand, but she yanked it to her chest, growing agitated again. "Don't you dare touch me. Get out of my dream, freak. Now!"

He used the low, reassuring tone once more. "I feel familiar because you know me, Emma," he told her slowly. "And deep down, you know I would never hurt you. That I could never, ever hurt you, not intentionally. I saved you earlier. In your mind, you realize that, even if you don't remember."

She blinked back at him, her tense shoulders relaxing by a fraction. "You saved me in an earlier dream? Some nightmare? I don't understand any of this, or why my supposed dream feels like reality."

"If you'd just let me touch you, I'd be gentle," he promised. "I can help you remember everything." He extended his right hand, palm up, reaching tentatively toward her.

Her haunted blue eyes narrowed as she stared down, her expression growing much softer and open.

"Your hand is honest."

"How do you get that?" She was a sentient, a listener, but did she read palms, too?

She smiled for the first time since he'd pierced the walls of her dream. "You work for a living. Hard," she observed, still staring at his open palm. "But you don't try to hide that fact, or pretend to be something you're not."

Glancing down, he knew what she saw. Calluses covering the inside of his thumb and forefinger after millennia of handling weapons. Skin that was as sun-darkened as any Greek slave's had ever been. Gods, this one hand of his, the one he meant to calm her with, was hardly worthy of the beautiful, feminine woman before him. If he touched her, he might contaminate her somehow, stain her.

Shamed, he curled his fingertips toward his palm, not forming a fist, but wanting to hide the truth of himself from her. She jerked forward, seizing his palm firmly in her grasp.

"As close as you are, you could have put that hand around my neck. Could have choked me in the space of a second. But you didn't," she said. "You offered it to me openly. So don't pull away now."

"No. You saw enough." God, the dirt stains, the grime beneath his nails; he couldn't recall feeling so ashamed in years.

"You asked me to trust you," she reminded him. "Now you've got to give something in exchange."

# Chapter 12

Sable flinched as Ares' electrically charged palm slid down his back. His coat prickled and stood on end as if a lightning storm were approaching, his skin tingling beneath the deity's light touch.

"What are you doing to me?" Sable asked in a choked voice, knowing that this was the punishment he'd feared.

But then why wasn't he already in pain? Why did Ares seem to be adding more power to his demonic form rather than taking it away?

"You really are a magnificent beast." Ares' warm fingertips trailed along Sable's withers, lingering almost seductively. Stroking for one second too long. "But it's that thinking portion of yours that always gives me such trouble."

Sable lifted his head high, refusing to give in to the fear. Ares had often threatened to tether him to his chariot along with the fire-breathing horses that pulled the epic thing.

"Yes, this horse portion . . ." Ares paused, moving that potent hand all the way to Sable's rump, resting his palm there. The implied threat would have made the gentlest of beasts jittery, and Sable strained to keep from rearing away from the deity's touch.

Ares clucked lightly. "Working your beastly portions seems to be the only way I can control you, Sable. The only way to make you understand that you will not *keep failing me!*"

"It has never been my intention to disappoint you."

"Enough! You have had your time to please and appease me, centaur." Ares stepped away from Sable. "Now you must learn who controls your destiny—learn how you will help me defeat these Spartans. Suffering is the only way I've ever managed to teach you anything at all. So that will be the rod of discipline used upon your back now."

Ares raised a hand, unfastening his cloak, and with a flourish sent it sailing toward Sable. It billowed for a moment, hovering in midair, and then the warm fabric slid across the middle of his back. Did Ares intend to mount him to prove his mastery? Was this meant as a covering for that purpose? His mind raced over all the possibilities.

The war god's eyes narrowed, a smug look of satisfaction flaring in their cold depths. "My work is done now." He reached for the garment and at once an explosion of unbearable, piercing pain cascaded across Sable's entire back. Every place that the god's cloak had touched now began erupting with agonizing welts. Sable gasped, trying to remain steady on his four legs, and turned to see what was happening.

*Oh, gods, no. No! Not this.* Anything but what Sable saw forming across his withers and rump and sides. The pain of it was nearly unbearable, but that wasn't the worst part of this new curse.

The hideous spurs and horns that were piercing outward from the welts on his skin made his former scarred appearance look beautiful in comparison. He swiveled at the waist, trying to touch one of the spiking protrusions with a weak hand. Instantly he drew his own blood as it sliced into his palm.

"My handiwork is quite fine. Is it not?" Ares seemed to think this was a marvelous idea. "You'll be far more toxic and deadly than ever before. If you so much as charge an enemy, any portion of your anatomy will slice them. You're now a living cat-o'-nine-tails, Sable." Then the god laughed, tossing his head back in a great release of mirthful enjoyment at his own joke. "Tails. How appropriate for my equine servant."

"My lord . . ." Sable's chest heaved in anguish. He would not beg. He could not kneel before this god and ask him to take the pain. "It . . . the . . ."

Ares stepped close, a challenging gleam in his eye. "It what, demon?"

"You honor me," he said between gritted teeth. "This form . . . an honor to serve."

"Now those are fine words, Sable. Perhaps if you remain so grateful, I might find even better ways to honor you."

Sable nodded, took one step but faltered, his forelegs barely holding him. "I must leave," he said, trying not to collapse in the god's throne room.

"You have work to do, indeed," Ares agreed. "I will give you a deadline so as to, shall I say, reinforce the new discipline I'm providing you. Bring me River Kassandros in precisely ninety-six hours. Otherwise, I will double the number of spikes upon your body."

The Oracle watched Ares perform his torture on that cursed Djinn, and her heart swelled with compassion. She stood just behind the door, peering out cautiously, and her heart hurt for the demon in his suffering. It wasn't his fault that he'd been born half evil, half twisted. She'd seen the truth about his other, hidden half that day in Bonaventure. It wasn't a fact that anyone else would be able to discern, but as an ancient oracle, she saw the truth in his old eyes. There was a glimmer of good there; buried deep, yes, but it existed. Although her own brother had gone a long way toward destroying that tiny, golden spark that had come from the Djinn's maternal line.

Even now, as she watched the centaur's skin erupting in those horrid horns, she could practically feel his agony inside her own skin. She rubbed her nape and upper back in an effort to disconnect from the sensation of shared pain. Turning away from the door, she pressed it shut with a quiet motion so as not to arouse Ares' suspicion that she was spying on him.

And she wondered for the millionth time in her eternal life, why her half brother was always so cruel. How could he take such infinite pleasure from causing pain and destruction? It amazed her that they shared blood.

Then again, she was also her mother's daughter. She'd been raised in the human world until she'd come of age and been taken to Delphi. She'd never known her father's identity until that time. Even then the truth had been revealed only because of her immense prophetic gift. It defied human explanation, and when she'd tried to defend her visions to the others at the temple, her mother had finally explained the truth about her parentage.

Yes, she and Ares shared a father, but their familial connection ended there. She could never love or be loyal to a parent who had sold her into a form of bondage to this cruel brother of hers. She was little better than the Djinn she'd just seen brought to heel. Perhaps her brother wouldn't beat her within an inch of her life, or disfigure her. Zeus would never allow him that much control over her. But Ares had much more inventive, clever ways of extracting blood payment. Such as hiding her from King Leonidas for eternity, yet making sure she was repeatedly transported into his presence, a constant reminder that her beloved king would never glimpse her or know of her love for him.

And then, the recent change: Finally Leo had been able to see her—however, not because of any assistance from her own flesh and blood. No, it was because the Highest God had taken mercy on her. That One had allowed Leonidas to see her, to feel her . . . to appreciate her. It had been the sweetest, most perfect gift that she'd ever been granted. All the more meaningful because most of her life had been spent under the repressive thumb of her father or brother. And for one reason only. Her own mother had rebelled against Zeus. And for that defiance, she was made to suffer the consequences for eternity.

What sort of father tossed his daughter to the veritable wolves? She closed her eyes, sinking onto her bed. Flopping backward against the gilded linens, she thought about the words the Highest God had given her four months ago. He had made her a promise, given a prophecy especially for her. As a result, she no longer served Ares or offered his words to the Spartans, although Ares was unaware of the shift in her allegiance.

She rolled onto her side, remembering the Highest's words: "Little daughter, your faithful heart will be rewarded. But not without a hard test."

She was in the midst of a powerful test all right: one that she wasn't sure her heart could survive. Four months without Leo. How much longer would her brother keep her away from her beloved? Given the cruelty that she'd just seen him demonstrate, the answer was too depressing to contemplate.

Ares had laid down a new law after she'd last seen Leonidas. If she attempted to appear to him again—if she sent him even the vaguest letter or other form of communication—then Ares would strangle the immortal life from the king's body and spirit. Until the Spartans were brought back underneath Ares' full command, she would not be permitted to attend to any of them. It was a hard test indeed. One that left her lonely and lost as she imagined what Leo must be thinking about her long absence. Did he believe that she'd forgotten him? Turned away?

She pictured that moment in his chamber months ago, when they'd kissed and fallen onto his bed together. If she could scroll back the days since then, she would. She'd peel away all of her clothing and kneel before him, professing her love . . . her desire to let him have every bit of her virginity.

But it was too late. If she went to him now, then her brother would destroy him. That was too great a cost for any love, especially her own.

# Chapter 13

One by one, Emma unfolded River's closed fingers until his palm was spread open to her. "Your pulse is going crazy." She rubbed her thumb more forcefully against the underside of his wrist.

"You saw me naked, how aroused I was." He dropped his head slightly. "And it's only gotten . . ." He searched for the right words, not wanting to drive her away. "Stronger, now that I'm so much closer to you, Emma. You have me wound so tight, I can hardly hold back from you."

Staring into her eyes from beneath his lashes, he wasn't quite able to meet her gaze, but couldn't tear his eyes off of her either. "I need you to remember me, Em . . . to understand this moment. What's happening right here, right now. And to know what could exist between us in the future."

She pressed his palm closer against her leg, biting her lower lip. "But what if I can't?"

"I need you to, Emma. I need it more than my next breath, or . . . or my freedom."

"Your freedom?"

He didn't answer, and she pushed harder. "You're saying I already have memories, that they're inside of me."

"Yes."

Her voice grew louder. "I feel so close to you, care about you, but I don't even know what your name is. You know mine, and . . ." Her expression grew troubled.

*Yes, that's my strong fighter! You are so close!* He wanted to shout the words, but forced himself to be quiet and gentle. "You said almost the same thing earlier today, over on the island."

He lifted his thumb to her lower lip and was grateful

that she didn't pull away as he rubbed the pad of that finger gently over her mouth. "I am called River," he said. And wished with all that was inside of him that he could enfold her in his arms again just as he'd done earlier, that very first time that he'd pulled her close.

*Go slow, easy now. Don't make her jumpy.*

She nestled his hand closer against her thigh in an intimate, protective gesture. He'd have sworn he felt her do the same during the car ride with Ari.

"Yes," he encouraged, leaning closer. "You're remembering, aren't you?"

She searched his face, pale blue eyes moving back and forth. "I'm not . . . not sure. Why do I keep seeing you, then seeing . . . a knife?" She released her grip on him, demonstrating with her hands. "A silver knife."

"Dagger," he corrected, his chest tightening like a drum. The simplest mention of his alternate form had instantly called forth his berserker, sending a cascade of uncontrollable, feral sensations through him. He hadn't expected it to emerge right then, but he had no command over his cursed internal beast, not now.

Every other time that he'd weapon-shifted, he'd understood the ground rules, and had known how to dominate his berserker. But after four months trapped in his alternate form, he had no idea how to control the dark urges or any notion of when the violence might surface. He'd never traveled this landscape before; all was unknown to him. And, by Hades, he remained trapped in that cold, silver prison right now, even though he'd found a way to enter Emma's dreams.

It just wasn't supposed to be this way. Not here in her dreams, not when he wasn't set free yet. Still, the thrumming vibrato that began low in his belly instantly speared straight to his cock. He swelled within his pants, the bulge expanding, becoming even more shockingly large than the one he'd been sporting moments earlier. He bit back a groan as his balls drew tight, and a sharp, thick ache began pounding between his legs anew. The need for sexual release practically screamed in his ears. It hammered in his groin, demanding that he seize Emma. That he claim her in a raw act, branding her as his mate. His lover.

He began trembling as the familiar, crazed lust captured him in its predator's talons. The tense pressure between his legs intensified. He dug fingernails into his groin, hoping a sting of pain might rein in his beast before it lost control. And before it targeted Emma.

She'd obviously caught his sudden movement. Her gaze was locked low between his legs, a faint flush hitting her high cheekbones the longer that she stared. "Well, then," she finally said after a moment, laughing huskily. "Well, well."

And still she stared.

"Emma, look away." His thigh muscles tensed as he shifted position in a desperate bid to hide the thick proof of his lust. "Please, Em, just look anywhere else but down there."

He was about to leap to his feet, but she leaned forward, planting both hands on his shoulders. This time her gaze locked right on his face—right on his own eyes.

"I remember you, River." She gave him an almost shy, slightly hesitant smile. "I remember everything now. I hear your voice in my head. I feel you holding me from behind."

He kept his profile to her, feeling his face flush hot with raging lust. She was so unattainable that he might as well have lain in a meadow and stroked himself while hungering for the moon. With a wince, he recalled the first time he'd fallen for a woman. She'd been like Emma, too lovely for a helot servant who slept in his master's barn.

Emma stroked fingertips across his jaw. "I need to look into your eyes, River. It's important."

"If I face you again, I could hurt you." He hated how ragged his voice sounded. "I might not be able to stop myself from rushing you, from mounting you. Do you remember that much about me from the island? My lack of control, my inability to keep my hips from pushing up behind yours?"

He sucked in a tight breath. "Or perhaps you recall my tongue halfway down your throat, the only separation between us my leather waistcloth." He growled, whipping around to meet her gaze, knowing that his eyes were glowing silver-bright. "Or maybe you only remember the demons and have forgotten how dangerous I can truly be."

He lowered his head slightly, snarling, aware that his leash on the berserker had nearly snapped. As he stared at Emma through narrowed eyes, the silver filling his gaze had washed every part of his vision to an almost colorless state.

"Your eyes are beautiful like that." She planted a firm palm over his heart. "They were like that earlier today. Silver. Bright. And, yes, River, I remember every one of those moments you're hoping will frighten me." Her hand trembled against his chest, but she kept it there, right against his pounding heart. "The feel of your arms locking about me, of your hips pushing up against mine. Even those sounds you made."

"Then get away from me while you still can." He released a sharp cry, covering her hand against his chest. Somehow, perhaps because the two of them were only in this dream place, he managed to keep his berserker at arm's length. Then an arresting thought hit him: It was Emma herself who calmed his hot core. But he refused to count on the soothing way she tamed him.

"You have to stop touching me, Emma," he nearly begged. "Talking to me that way."

"What way?" Blast her, but the mortal actually gave him a wide-eyed, innocent look.

"Like you mean to fucking seduce me, Em," he shouted, rearing back from her. "Good gods of Olympus, don't you understand? You have to feel the beast that's barely manacled inside of me."

"You haven't hurt me yet."

"I am a mighty, fearsome force," he told her through clenched teeth. "So is the curse in my veins."

"Breathe, River. Breathe. Just one inhalation at a time."

Closing his eyes, he shuddered and did as she instructed. First one breath, then another, and yet another still. He found that his heart began to slow its jarring rhythm just a little, that his cock didn't ache quite so feverishly.

"There, that's good. See? You're calming. Remember what you told me earlier," she coaxed in an even voice.

"This is only a dream. You can't hurt me here. And you wouldn't hurt me, not ever. Not on purpose."

"You don't know how violent I can get after . . ."

"Ari told me. That it's a side effect of your weapon-shifting."

He tried to find words, keeping his eyes shut. So afraid that if he dared to look at her, this fragile hold on his control would shatter again. Then, a light brush of warmth touched his jaw, next his cheek. Her caress was so warm, so tender, that he began to tremble beneath it. Not from agitation, but . . . from something he couldn't begin to identify.

"What beautiful eyebrows you have," she said, tracing the length of his right one. "They're like wispy feathers, elegant. Graceful."

Unfortunately, the mention of feathers finally uncorked the raging devil in his blood, and his entire body jackknifed with compulsions. He had to kiss her, damn the consequences. Launching himself forward, he clasped her face in a rough hold, dragging her lips to his, forcing her mouth open as he tilted his face to the side.

And damn it all, she lunged for him at the exact same moment, driving fingers through his long hair and against his scalp. Lifting up slightly where she sat, she pressed into him as if she, too, were a devourer. Driven to consume him, body and soul, until she was drowning in him.

With a sharp gasp, she broke the kiss, keeping her lips against his as she dragged in urgent breaths. "Drowning in you," she murmured in agreement, once again reading his thoughts. Then he could feel her mouth turning upward in a smile. "Drowning in my River." But then that smile slipped and she withdrew from his arms.

Her cheeks were flushed, and her full lips had become swollen from that hard, probing kiss. Her eyes were shining, the pupils fully dilated with arousal. He knew that she'd loved that kiss. By Hades, she'd practically initiated it herself.

"Why did you stop?" He raked smoothing hands down his hair. He suddenly wished she would take a soft brush and gently work it through his tangled hair, one sensuous stroke at a time.

She reached toward his cheek again, a bittersweet smile on her lips. "I thought of you drowning in the waves," she admitted. "That's why I got upset. Drowning in someone you care about is one thing, but what you went through . . ." Her brown eyebrows furrowed sharply and she stared into her lap. "How long had you been a dagger?"

He shook his head. "I don't know. What month is it now?"

When she told him it was August, he felt that steely coldness seize him right through the chest. "Four months," he told her in a choked voice. "I'm still trapped. It's why I've come to you."

"You need my blood again." It wasn't a question.

"I need you, Em. But I need you to help free me first. You've got to go to Ari, but I don't know where he is."

She got an odd glimmer in her soft blue eyes and, leaning slightly forward, asked, "Do you know Mason Angel?"

His jaw went slack. How did she realize . . .

She seemed to read his expression. "You mentioned him on the beach today, but you were pretty out of it. It's not that common a name when it comes to demon hunters."

"I haven't met him, not formally. I was already a dagger when we . . . interacted. I know his sister Shay, though, but how do *you* know him?" River hated how jealous his question sounded.

She only laughed. "Uh, he's my second cousin?"

River couldn't help laughing himself. "So Shay's your cousin, too?"

"Yep, that's the math," she said, leaning forward and kissing him again. Her mouth covered his in a slow, searing seduction, her tongue stroking his lips until they parted. Just as quickly she jerked backward.

"Oh. My. God. Shay married a Greek man." Emma slapped a hand over her mouth, eyes wide. "A mysterious Greek guy named Ajax."

"That would be . . ." *My master*, he almost finished, but managed to stop himself. So Jax had made a formal bond with Shayanna? Good for his old friend.

Emma stared up into his eyes, waiting for him to finish the sentence. "Ari's younger brother," he said. "Ajax is my friend, just as Aristos is."

"Okay, so you know my cousins and I know your friend Ari. By extension, I'm sorta related to your pal Ajax, right? So I'm going to my cousins. I'm calling Shay and Mason . . . Jamie, too," Emma told him, head bobbing exuberantly. "We'll figure out how to break you free again. They've got to have your dagger. I mean, Ari's got it, but they're all together, and I'll tell them about my blood, and that tie between us. And how you came to me in this dream."

Her excited willingness, her desire to free him, was almost too much. He clasped her face between his palms and pulled her mouth to his, much gentler than before. He was crazy with desire for her, but his need was now tamed somewhat. Not lessened or diminished, just . . . calmer. With the tip of his tongue he urged her lips open, sweeping the warm, wet inside of her mouth. He used slow strokes, exploring her this time, savoring her taste by taste, inch by luscious inch.

His chest tightened with a spasm of need, and he growled low in the back of his throat at the sensation. But he kept his kiss under his own domination. Refusing to lose control to his dark side, he slid one hand beneath her chin, stroking light fingertips along the tender, sweet skin there, trailing his fingers down the column of her throat. Finally he reached the rapidly fluttering pulse at the base, and trailed his thumb over it exactly as she'd stroked the inside of his wrist earlier.

After a moment, she pulled away from him, staring into his eyes significantly. "See?" A slow, sexy smile spread across her face, and for the first time he realized that she had deep, twin dimples. He'd not yet been given much chance to see her smile so far. "River, you're under control. You're not treating me badly or going all horn dog on me. It's okay."

That quiet, low tone should have brought him down another few notches. So why in Hades' name did his desire crank upward by about ten additional ones? He balled both hands into fists, pressing them hard into his thighs, hoping that the sheer force of will would prevent him from finally unraveling in her presence. It didn't matter if it was a dream; he wanted to treat her like a lady, wanted to give her no reason to fear him whatsoever. Not ever.

"You're keeping it together, River. Besides, Ari says it won't last long once you emerge from the dagger for good."

"He didn't tell you what I really am, did he?"

"You're a weapon-shifter." She tilted her chin upward, and River was shocked and humbled to see a look of pride on her face. She just didn't understand the full implications.

"That's not all that I am," he told her in a flat tone. "I'm a berserker. Do you know what that is?"

"There's mythology, Norse stories—"

He shook his head, trying to find his voice, but his words came out in a rasping sound. "Not myth. Real. Goes back much farther than that. To my own people."

She shrugged; he might as well have told her that a fly was buzzing past her ear. "He said it's just part of what you are. What you do. But that it passes quickly."

She radiated goodness from the depths of her mortal heart. How could she understand the ugliness that had defined him for hundreds and hundreds of years?

"You're different, Em," he finally managed to squeeze out between light, panting breaths. "It's not just the berserker. It's you. You calm me inexplicably; you center me. But still, I feel so much more dangerous around you than I do the others."

"Other . . . who?"

"My fellow Spartans. We're guardians of mankind," he told her in a rush. "Even though I've tried to hurt them after shifting back to my human shape, it's not like . . ."

"Like what?"

"Like this raging hunger I feel for you. I'm calm now, but the risk to you is too great. I have to find another way to break free from the dagger. I was wrong to ask for your help. I refuse to put you in danger by using your blood again."

Even here in her dreamscape the threat remained that he could rape her, or spill too much blood. And the reality of that would manifest in her physical body the same as if he'd done it in the physical realm. For now, he had to return to the dagger. It was the only way to keep Emma safe.

Springing to his feet, he searched the room, needing to find that electric thread that linked them so that he could leave her subconscious mind and thoughts and return to his dagger prison. The only problem was that the recognizable deep crimson of their bond was washed out by the silver power flowing through him at the moment. It was like being a blind man as he stumbled through Emma's home, searching, knocking about. But if he so much as glanced her way, he feared that Emma's dangerous fate would be sealed.

"I'm going to Ari," she called out in a firm voice. "You're not going to shake me, or avoid me, River. I care about you. Already."

"I'm going to find another way; I can't put you in danger."

"We're tied together; you're the one who told me that. You're in too much danger if we can't break you free. I know it."

It was such a treacherous thing to do, but he couldn't stop himself from turning back one last time to stare into her gorgeous, expressive large eyes. She was the most beautiful woman he'd ever met, much less kissed or held, and the attraction he felt toward her was almost irresistible. But he knew that he needed to leave.

Backing farther away from her, he turned. "Emma, I've got to go. I . . . I want you to be safe."

"You can count on my help."

He ignored her pledge, feeling all about him for the connection that would lead him back to his dagger. But Emma wouldn't relent or back down.

She was so unbearably close, the heat of her body pulling him into the abyss, that swirling cauldron where his need for her could never be tamed.

"I will . . . find . . . another way," he said through gritted teeth. She was right up against him. He had to act now or he might never be capable of severing this intimate connection.

"You're dying if I can't free you, aren't you?"

He didn't answer, kept backing away.

"Aren't you? River, *aren't* you?" She became desperate,

rushing toward him with tears in her eyes. "You're dying if I can't free you."

He gave a single, firm nod of agreement, and then did something incredibly difficult and painful. He opened his mouth, threw back his head, and released the most deafening war cry he'd ever summoned. "Emma!" he thundered. "Wake *up*!"

And he was immediately hurled straight out of her dream, fully trapped in his dagger once again.

# Chapter 14

A ri paced the great room, unable to sit still as he watched his comrades pass River's dagger around their intimate circle. He should have been exultant, but something about the homecoming didn't sit right with him. Sure, his dearest friend had returned at last, but now that they had him back, Ari wasn't sure what to do. Hell, the guy had always handled his transitions easily and on his own until now. None of them even knew how he'd accomplished the shifting.

Pulling to a stop by the fireplace, Ari braced his hands on the mantel and tried to steady his breathing. He kept his back to the gathered group, all the Spartans and Shay seated around the room. Hushed, awed tones filled the circle as each greeted River in his or her own quiet way.

There was a shuffling sound behind him, and he could tell that another of the crew had accepted River into his grasp. At first there was a long silence, but then a heartrending sound had Ari spinning to face the room. His younger brother Ajax knelt in the middle of the floor, weeping as he held River against his cheek.

*You better be sorry*, a brutal part of Ari wanted to scream. His brother was River's master, after all, and held ultimate responsibility for his well-being.

"My dear friend," Ajax pledged, eyes shut, "I am the one who put you in such danger. Forgive me. I will find a way to free you now that you're home. You are with us again, where you belong, and you will be free, my faithful one. I swear it by the Highest God himself."

Ajax lifted River's blade to his own lips, kissing the hilt and blade. As he did so, the coppery tang of blood wafted through the room, spots of deep crimson beading on his brother's lower lip.

Ari reached for River's blade. "Give him to me." He knew his voice sounded pretty damned cold.

Jax blinked up at him, black eyes barely focused, and without a word, relinquished the dagger.

Ari sheathed River in his belt, moving back toward the fireplace, where he stopped to face the group. "It's going to take blood to free him. Like it did with the woman out on Tybee." He'd already given them a brief rundown about the human woman whose blood had brought River back to physical form. "One of us has to offer our own blood. We've got to use his blade against ourselves to bring him back."

Ajax rose from his kneeling position, stronger now, and strode toward Ari. This time his brother extended a hand. "I will do it."

"You already cut your lip a moment ago. That didn't do a damned bit of good." Ari shook his head. "Now it's my try, little brother."

"He is my servant, my ..."

Ari growled. "Don't you dare say *property*, Ajax, or we'll be heading outside together."

Ajax blinked back at him, his dark eyes widening in surprise. "Never. I was going to say ... my beloved friend. One of my dearest friends."

"You know, Ajax, although River is duty-bound to you, and although you may love him, for most of our natural and supernatural lives, he's been my best friend." Ari leveled Ajax with a hard, powerful stare.

Ajax met his glare, unblinking. "You blame me, don't you, Ari? That's why you're angry."

They should have been whooping and shouting and bringing out the wine. Instead, such sadness filled Ari's chest. "Look, Jax, I don't know how else the whole thing could have gone. River made his choice; he wanted to help protect you."

Shay cut in. "Ari, Jax tried to stop River from going. You know that."

Ari stared down at his younger brother. "Yeah, I know

you tried to keep him from going with you, and you even got in his face about it. But here's what I *don't* know. . . ." Ari couldn't help raising his voice now. "How you could have lost someone so dear to us all. You are his master, after all. You should have protected his ass like he's protected yours for more than two thousand years. It was your job to keep him safe, not lose him." Ari shook his head. "Gods above, that just makes me heartsick."

Ajax bowed his head, staring at his hands. "So you do blame me. Like you blamed Nikos for not locating him?" Ajax pressed. "Perhaps you want to add Leonidas to your list as well? He approved the plan."

"I would never dishonor my king that way," Ari snapped, watching as Ajax slowly rose to his feet and then stared him in the eye.

"Man to man, right now, brother." His younger brother got into Ari's space. "You need to own up to the facts, and deal with the person you blame most of all."

Ari gave him a challenging shove in the chest. "You're the only one on my list right now, Jax-ass."

"I mean you. Face up to it. You blame yourself for his situation."

"Blame myself for what?" Ari took several steps backward from Jax—he needed some space. "I didn't haul him over here to America! I didn't make him stay in weapon form much longer than he'd ever done. I didn't allow Sable to fling him away into a deep river, knowing, by the way, that he probably wouldn't be able to transform underwater. That he'd sink and be lost." Ari's face flushed angrily, and he shook with furious tremors. "No, I don't blame myself for a goddamned thing."

Ajax strode toward him, until they stood chest to chest, eye to eye. "You didn't do any of that, Ari," he said in an even tone. "You're right. But you *were* the only one he might have listened to back in Cornwall. And you said nothing. You let him choose to do it."

Ari flinched, feeling his eyes sting. Of course his brother was right. At the time, he'd been so worried about Ajax's safety in the upcoming battle with Sable that he'd thought the idea a brilliant one. "I never said I didn't fail him."

Next thing Ari knew, Ajax had swept him into an embrace, a bearlike hug that he rarely received from his more reserved brother. "Aristos, you brought him home. He will thank you for being such a faithful friend." Ajax slapped him on the back for a long moment, and then held him even closer. "What we do isn't easy, brother. And there are costs . . . debts."

Then Ajax pulled back, brushing a kiss against Ari's forehead. "Let's get our comrade free," he said.

Ari nodded, blinking quickly. Looking to Leonidas he asked, "My lord, may I please take River to my room? I need time to attempt communication with him. I truly believe I'm the one who can do it."

"Straton is the one with the gift of hearing," Leonidas told him quietly. "It would make most sense for him to attempt a connection with River."

Leonidas glanced briefly at Straton, who was sitting in the far corner in a simple wooden chair. He'd been sitting with his chin propped on both hands throughout the interchange, as silent and inscrutable as a fog over a battlefield. Ari didn't know him much better now than he had the day of their bargain.

*He's not the right guy to reach River*, Ari thought. *No matter what ability he possesses.*

"Straton," Leonidas asked, "I assume you understand why Aristos would want to attempt communication first? That you accept this plan?"

The fierce, monkish warrior inclined his head toward his king. The silent gesture was all they'd get in terms of commentary or discourse on the subject.

Ari gave a low bow and left the room. Behind him he heard Leonidas dismiss the meeting. "I need to inspect the wards again," the king announced. "I repaired them earlier, but they're still new and possibly vulnerable. Let's convene in another two hours. At twenty-three hundred hours, we will evaluate our situation."

Two hours. Ari would love to return to that meeting with River at his side. Talk about a true homecoming. That would be one worthy of the ages. Quickening his steps, he began to whistle.

But he could not shake the nagging sense that the dagger in his hand felt utterly lifeless. It seemed to lack every bit of animating spark that his friend's weapon normally held. The joyful tune died an abrupt death on Ari's lips, as for the first time he wondered if River might never emerge again.

As soon as River severed his dream contact with Emma, he began listening to his physical surroundings, trying to confirm his current location. Although he couldn't identify any warrior in particular, he detected the familiar presence of his fellow Spartans, and all but sighed with relief.

Excited and nearly humming with joy, he sharpened his hearing, expecting the raucous noises of homecoming. Loud cheers, flute songs, thundering war chants. To his shock, however, everything around him was muted and subdued, lacking the warriors' usual degree of hubbub. The Spartans might be famously spare with their words, but these days talk flowed more freely between them. They constantly ribbed and joked, giving heaping amounts of good-natured shit all the way around.

The absence of all that clanging noise confused him. Maybe he wasn't with his fellow warriors after all, but if not, where was he? He summoned powers of perception that had grown dull and flabby during his months in the ocean, pressing to hear a voice. Anything that would place his position, and hopefully indicate the presence of his comrades.

As he concentrated, a sudden scent wafted around him, an earthy and familiar one that mingled with the odor of burning candles. Next he caught the quiet rumblings of murmured words, spoken by a familiar voice, a deep and beloved one.

*Ari!* He wanted to shout in relief. *Thank the Highest God that I'm still safe in Ari's keeping.*

Ari was normally a whirlwind of noise, full of swaggering bravado and chatter, but he was totally silent now. River could think of one occasion when the boisterous Spartan grew so quiet: when he offered prayers to the gods.

Well, he certainly hoped Ari wasn't making the mistake

of appealing to Ares. Any Olympic deity would be better than that betraying, bloodthirsty fiend, but what other god would Ari be praying to? If he could have spoken to his friend, he'd have guided him toward the Highest God, the one who had saved River by sending Emma to rescue him.

Yes, Ares had turned on all of them completely, and if his fellow warriors didn't see that fact already, he'd convince them once he returned to physical form. Surely the god's attack on Ajax had already shown them the truth, even if his own recent fate had not. Then again, maybe they didn't consider losing him reason enough to turn against their war god; perhaps they'd not thought him worth such a bold stance.

With that sudden doubt, a splitting pain shot through his soul. One part of him remained hounded by the notion that none of his Spartan brothers had searched for him, and another remembered how happy Ari had seemed to see him again.

"River man! So glad you're back," he'd heard the Spartan boom. "Missed you like hell, buddy."

There was simply no way that Ari had left him languishing, and deep down he knew the others hadn't either. Those bitter doubts had only one source—his berserker nature. The evil curse that Ares had placed upon his immortal soul, bending him to twisted, wicked compulsions, filling his mind with whispered lies and doubt. All of it came from that moment long ago, when he'd submitted to Ares by the River Styx. The god had taken him in hand, meticulously forging him as a new creation, one birthed in fire and darkness. The god had declared River his finest creation, a potent weapon possessing the power of life and death.

Perhaps the god had seeded some of his bloodthirsty, violent nature inside of his soul that day. His core nature had changed, had kept on changing ever since. No wonder weapon-shifting left his soul stained and he always returned to human form in such a wicked, depraved condition.

River forced the infernal thoughts from his mind. He needed his wits about him, to be as sharp as his dagger's blade in order to secure his freedom. He trained his senses on Ari, trying to understand what was happening *outside* of his dagger in the material and true world. Ari was speak-ing, and although the words were impossible to understand, he definitely recognized a pained tone to the words. The warrior sounded heartbroken, deeply grieved. On the day when River had finally come home? That made no sense.

*Surely he doesn't grieve for me. Not because I remain in-side this weapon.*

Ari had to understand how near River was to freedom. By the gods, it was so close he could practically taste it. And Emma was so near that he could practically taste her, too, he thought, flushing with warmth. Oh, he had a long list of plans for that mortal once he was back in the physical world. Plans to nibble her, stroke her, and that was only the beginning.

*Ari! Friend! I am home. Don't fear for me, don't grieve. . . . I am home. Now that I'm here, I will be freed somehow.*

He heard no answer in return, but wasn't surprised; Ari didn't possess a gift for hearing or perception. At that precise moment, his blade began to hum. Not from blood as it had done after Emma cut herself, but from some un-known cause. What exactly was Ari doing, and what was causing the buzzing sensation? An unfamiliar taste speared through River's senses—one much saltier than the ocean he'd just been in.

Next, a low, rolling moan vibrated through River's sil-ver form. Gods above, Aristos was crying. The strong, wise-cracking, good-natured warrior never wept or grew sad. The man spent most of his days smiling and laughing, getting a kick out of just about everything. His best friend should have been exuberant, clapping all the others on the shoul-der, laying bets as to how long it would take River to sate himself after assuming human form once again.

*What, precisely, have I missed during these past four months?* River wondered in alarm.

*Aristos, friend*, he tried one more time. Silence met his appeal, and stretched on for an eternally long time until River heard another quiet sob. Then he caught one word. It was clear, so audible that River might have been standing right beside Ari, instead of frozen tight within his dagger. And it was a woman's name.

*Juliana.*

Ari spoke it again, a wounded murmur that rang painfully through River's center.

Who, by the gods, was this Juliana? And how had she hurt Aristos? He knew every woman who'd ever mattered to the man, so she had to be someone new, someone whom Ari had met during his recent absence.

*Juliana, I failed you.*

The words unsettled him. This Juliana clearly meant something very significant to Ari, but he'd lost her.

But the Spartan's next words chilled him even more. *He can't die, too*, Ari whispered. *River cannot die.*

Before Emma found him, he'd believed the same thing: that he was barely holding to his sanity, turning deathly silver in the center of his soul. But she'd changed all of that and brought him roaring back to life. She'd set him free physically, given him a burning hunger that he'd not known in years. His craving for Emma pulsed and heated him even now. Finding her had given his existence definition, made his warrior's life purposed once again. Surely all of that linked him to life, to his human form and to the ones that he loved so dearly. Didn't it?

But Ari's words haunted him. His friend knew him better than any of the others; he would probably be the first to recognize the signs that River had crossed over into the abyss.

*If I were turning into this dagger, becoming one with its form permanently . . . Ari would know.*

And in that moment, River understood why the atmosphere all about him was so deathly silent. Why Ari wasn't celebrating and the warriors weren't toasting and singing chants. Because they believed he was forever lost to them, so far gone and lacking any lively spark that they saw no hope for his redemption.

*But Emma! Ari, get Emma. She can still save me.*

He cried out, called, thundered and stormed, but nothing changed at all. Ari couldn't hear a word that he shouted. He was trapped, smothering—incapable of being heard by the one friend who cared for him most of all.

He slammed against the walls of his prison. *I am still*

*here. Still a man . . . and I do not want to die. Not when I've found Emma.*

*I am alive. Still.*

*I am better than this blade, more than just a tool created for other men to wield and use. I am more than this—than what I've been.*

All at once a bolstering strength shot through him, re-igniting his dimming hope. Emma had promised that she would move every obstacle to reach him, and quickly. Although he'd claimed he would find another way, he knew Emma already. She'd said she would help him, and she wouldn't back down from that. Her voice had been fierce and strong, and so had her promise. Holding that hope like the vibrant, electric blood-tie that linked them, he felt himself grow stronger.

Free me, Highest God, please. Let me serve you. Give me the chance, I beg. Just let Emma reach me before it's too late.

# Chapter 15

It had taken plenty of stealth by Emma just to creep out of the house. Her mother had been fussing over her all evening long. Emma had waited, albeit not very patiently, until she'd heard the upstairs television go silent. Slipping through a window on the back of the house, Emma had swung two feet across to her carriage house steps.

God, she hadn't snuck out of the house since high school, and it was downright ridiculous at twenty-seven years old. Now as she sprinted into the carriage house she found Sophie sprawled on her belly in the middle of the living room, digital camera in hand.

"Why are you still here?" Emma asked her little sister in annoyance. There wasn't time to explain where she was going.

"I'm working on a big project." Sophie rolled onto her back. Propping herself on her elbows she stared up at Emma, wide-eyed. "Wow, what happened to you? You're, like, bloody. Nasty. Disheveled. Choose your own descriptor."

Emma tossed her a glance, heading toward her bedroom. "And look who's talking." Sophie's short corkscrew curls were askew, shooting in every direction.

Sophie followed her and hopped onto Emma's queen-sized bed. "Where are you going?"

Emma tossed a small overnight bag into the mattress's center, flinging a few pairs of jeans and tops along with it. "I'm going to see Shay. Mason. Jamie."

Sophie scooted up to the headboard, fluffing the overstuffed pillows and leaning back against them. "Uh . . . why?"

"Look." Emma halted with a pair of khaki shorts mid-toss. "I need you to cover for me with Mama tonight. She's freaking right now, being totally overprotective."

"Uh, *yeah*. She's clearly off the grid." Sophie rolled her clear blue eyes in an "I'm so sure" expression. "Em, you do look awful. What happened? I thought you were doing your camping thing with Evan."

"He wound up taking off and leaving me." Emma hurled underwear and socks onto the bed. "Jerkwad."

"Gay guys are supposed to make loyal friends." Sophie made this pronouncement like it was a universal truth as she leaned forward, starting to fold Emma's clothes into the overnight bag, chattering in one long train of words that never had a caboose. "You need to align with someone more reliable. And fashionable. He wears Crocs, for God's sake. This is bad. Very, very bad. Not that you need fashion input, of course, but he's a *Project Runway* reject and . . ."

Emma tuned out the rest of her sister's soliloquy, moving into the bathroom. She gathered her grooming items onto the counter: shampoo, hairbrush, deodorant. No telling how long she'd be gone, so it was better to go prepared for the long haul. She dropped the supplies on the bed; Sophie began packing them neatly into the bag's side pocket without missing a beat.

She felt a familiar wave of guilt; Sophie was forever trying to nurture her, a true birth-order reversal since Emma was the older sibling, even if only by eighteen months. It was almost like her baby sister panted after her, craving approval or love that Emma could never bring herself to fully give. Not when she'd closed off that portion of her heart the day that Leah died. It had been heartbreaking enough to lose one sister. She couldn't risk facing those emotions a second time.

"You should tell me where you're going," Sophie pressed as Emma headed toward the door.

"Look, just cover for me," she answered vaguely. "And please take Mama to pick up my car. Tell her I'll call later . . . soon."

Sophie watched her go, not saying another word, but Emma glimpsed hurt in her expression. There just wasn't time to deal with that emotion at the moment, not with River's life depending on her speedy actions.

Emma turned right on Bee Road, picking up speed as she drove toward the Harry S. Truman Parkway. If she was lucky, she'd get to her cousins' old plantation house in less than fifteen minutes. Now she just needed to be sure that they were going to be there, ready and waiting to help her with River. Talk about an otherworldly debriefing; it would take some fancy, fast explanations to get Shay up to speed with her own version of current events. Then again, from what River said, Shay was in deep with the Greek Mafia, her new husband one of their chief members.

*Spartans,* she reminded herself. *All of them, River included, are Spartan warriors. Immortal protectors.*

The thought was so utterly surreal that it almost didn't faze her. It went beyond the freak-out zone and existed on an entirely different plane where you had no choice but to calmly accept the insanity. River's life depended upon her remaining calm and taking swift, appropriate action. So she refused to collapse into a puddle of emotion and fear.

Afterward, maybe she'd allow herself the luxury of falling apart, at least a little. Then again, if she was with River when he broke free, she might be otherwise occupied with something more thrilling. Being ravaged and kissed and pleasured until the only falling apart she'd want to do was beneath his touch. That one thought finally did make her flush and tremble, but definitely not out of fear. It also gave her an even stronger sense of urgent purpose.

Never taking her eyes off the road, Emma found her cell phone on the passenger side of her mom's Volvo. Holy crappola, her mama sure was going to be pissed.

"Sorry, Mama," Emma said aloud, cradling the phone in her palm. Traffic was heavy, and she changed lanes, weaving through the flow, opening Shay's listing in her cell phone directory. She clicked the number, and waited through at least four rings before her cousin finally answered, sounding confused and surprised that Emma was phoning at a fairly late hour.

"Are you okay? Is everyone all right?" Shay asked.

"Look, we have to talk. I need to see you tonight," Emma blurted, accelerating and switching lanes. "Are you home? I'm heading toward your place. You do still live there, right?" She'd assumed that Shay and her new husband were living in her family's old home, and felt guilty that they were so out of touch that she didn't even know for sure.

"Emma, slow down. Tell me what's going on," Shay told her calmly.

Emma drew in a breath, and this time tears filled her eyes. She'd wanted to cry from the moment she'd heard Shay's comforting voice. "I need to go to wherever you are . . . to wherever he is."

"Emma, you've got to slow down and start from the beginning."

"No! I don't need to do that," she shouted in annoyance. "I need to help him. He's going to die otherwise."

"*Who* is going to die?" Shay asked impatiently.

Emma knew that if she started trying to explain everything now, before she stopped driving, then she might really lose it. "River," she blurted, shaking all over. "I have to save River's life tonight. If I don't, he's probably going to die."

Stunned silence hit her hard from the other end of the line. What if River was a figment of her imagination? What if he wasn't even real and she was losing her mind? Maybe she was like Jimmy Stewart and River was her own personal Harvey the Dagger. Even worse . . . was he Wilson to her Tom Hanks?

She panicked. "You do *know* River, right?" When Shay didn't answer, she felt like she might be physically ill. "Shay? Shayanna?" she called more loudly.

Still no answer, but she realized that Shay had covered the mouthpiece and was talking to someone else. There was the deep murmur of several male voices in the background, and then Shay returned to the line.

"Em, we're taking off right now, okay? Are you sure you want to meet at the house?" Shay asked in a gentle tone; yeah, her cousin knew this was a serious step for her.

"Yes, the house. It feels right for some reason, and . . . I'm trying to do better about listening to that kind of thing."

Admission. Big admission. That she'd cracked open that door she'd padlocked shut on her gift.

"That's good, Em. If that's what you're hearing and feeling, we're there. It will take about fifteen minutes, but we're on our way."

Emma let out a tight breath. "Just make sure Ari comes along; he'll explain everything. And what about Mason and Jamie? Are they part of the whole Spartan thing, too?"

Shay sucked in an audible breath. "Shit, Em, how *did* you manage to wander into all this?"

"Geez, I don't know, Shay," she shot back. "I guess it was just lucky *fucking* dagger day for me! I mean, you know, I absolutely expected to be mauled by demons on the beach, see a man pop out of a weapon, and then practically bleed to death. Not to mention your pal Ari swiping my memories. Yeah, that was a great twist."

Shay laughed a little. "Welcome to my world."

"Already there and living large, let me tell you. Right now, I just want to help River get free. I promised and . . . well, I just have to do it." She wasn't about to tell Shay how much she already cared for River or about their blood-tie.

"Sweetie, we've all been trying tonight."

"And it wasn't working, was it? Because it's only my blood that can free him. Just mine. Why don't you tell Ari that while you're at it? If he hadn't done the Jedi mind wipe on me, River might already be free right now."

Shay dropped her voice low as if not wanting to be overheard. "Don't blame Ari, he's a good guy. The best. And he'd do anything to protect River."

A surprising thought hit Emma. "He hadn't told you anything about me, had he? That I had River with me when he found him? No, he couldn't have, because you were so surprised to get my call."

Shay hesitated. "Emotions were running pretty high tonight . . . after he brought River home. He mentioned that a human woman had helped River, but didn't give a name."

She heard the sound of several male voices, one more impatient than the others, and then Shay answering in a rush. After a moment her cousin returned to the call. "Okay, Emma," she said, "I'll see you in a few."

"Just tell me that Mason and Jamie are coming, too."

"We'll all be there, Em. I promise." Her cousin's words were gentle, steady, and for a moment Emma truly believed that River would be all right. She had no other choice but to hope and trust that he would live.

Her cousins lived on the Isle of Hope, their old home one of the last remaining privately held plantations in the Savannah area. It had been on the National Register of Historic Places for decades, and tourists sometimes tried to poke around wanting to take pictures of the house and grounds. But they quickly realized that trespassing wasn't welcomed, not on Angel land.

The locals were much more savvy and fearful. The legends and rumors that orbited about her cousins were enough to keep all those native gawkers away. Until they needed help, that was, whether with demons or spirits or any of the other supernatural areas of the Angel family's expertise. Mostly, however, her cousins hunted demons. They were the fifth generation of a secretive, supernatural fighting clan known as the Nightshades. Or Shades, for short. That name alone kept most everyone outside the brick gates.

Emma shared that unease, but it hadn't always been that way. As a child she and her sisters had spent endless summer days with Shay, the four of them crabbing and fishing. The group of cousins had been like a set of stairsteps, from her little sister Sophie, the youngest, all the way up to Jamie, the oldest. Of course he hadn't paid them much attention, whereas Mason had never grown impatient with them no matter how many times they begged him to play with them.

But all of that had ended abruptly with Leah's death. Emma'd been terrified of so many things after that. The water, the dark, her own gift. Facing her cousins' spooky house had been scariest of all. Its shadowed doorways were always filled with whispered hints about battling demons and dark spirits. Emma shut down her gift of supernatural hearing then, no longer willing to listen to the other side, terrified of what she might hear. Including the possibility of Leah's voice blaming Emma for not preventing her death. In her little girl's mind, she'd become convinced that because she'd received no hint of what was to happen to Leah, she'd actually been part of killing the person who mattered most to her. Who was her other half, her completion.

And with Leah gone, she'd never felt truly whole again, a piece of her soul forever missing. Because she'd failed. Because her gift had failed them both at the most crucial moment. She'd closed down her blossoming ability as a medium the night of Leah's death, closing off that part of herself.

Emma and her cousins drifted apart after that, although they'd seen each other at her mother's house for holidays, or bumped into each other around town often enough. Shay, too, had reached out over the years, calling Emma to make plans. There'd been the occasional lunch at Mrs. Wilkes' Boardinghouse or the rare night out on Congress Street. Sometimes Shay would drag Mason or Jamie along, and they'd have a good time. A nice, easy, superficial time. One that didn't touch on past secrets or involve any real closeness.

No wonder Shay had been surprised that Emma wanted to meet at the plantation, her unvoiced question practically hovering between them: *Why now, Emma? Why are you finally coming back now after all these years?*

The reasons were so complex and myriad, and it would take more time than they had to understand those feelings herself, much less explain them to Shay. But the one thing Emma did know was that River would be safe there, on land that had been protected for centuries.

*I'm coming there for him*, Emma answered silently now. *I think I'd willingly face down anything or anyone to save him. Even this.*

Even the scarred pain of her past. That she barely knew River was irrelevant. In a way that Emma didn't fully understand, she did know him, and in the deepest way that you could know another being. Literal time had no part in her feelings, maybe because *River* existed far outside of human time and space. She wasn't sure how to explain it, and didn't care. She knew only that some quiet, very strong part of her heart had already begun falling in love with him. Love wasn't a rational, scientific process; no more logical than River was himself. And it was that specialness, his strangeness and magic, that made her believe in love's illogic. More than she ever had before finding River.

She guided the Volvo onto the sandy, unpaved drive that led through arching live oak trees. Funny, but they seemed much smaller now, as if time had somehow shrunk them, turning them into miniature versions of the towering giants from her childhood.

Up in the distance, blazing lights illuminated the otherwise pitch-black night, casting a halo outward into the moss-draped treetops. She sped up, and then the house itself came into view, every exterior light thrown against the darkness, and almost every interior light shining outward from within the sagging, graceful old house. A lump formed in Emma's throat at the sight, the years peeling back in the space of a single heartbeat.

This place had once defined family for her, even more so than her parents' brownstone on West Jones Street. She could only hope that River, too, would find himself back where he truly belonged, where he was destined to be, encircled by his Spartan brotherhood, held close by all those he so clearly loved.

She stepped out of the Volvo and immediately spotted Shay, who moved briskly toward her, arms open. "Hey, you." Shay's words were muffled against Emma's cheek as they embraced. "Hard day, huh?" Then Shay started to move away slightly, but Emma latched on, holding her even closer. This precious moment was healing, and she wasn't going to let it slip away too fast.

"Two words for you, Shay." She laughed, wrapping her arms around Shay's upper back. "Water demons, baby."

"Oh-kay. I've never even heard of those."

"Exactly."

"It's going to be okay, Em. It really is." Shay laughed, a warm gust of air hitting Emma's cheek. "It's weird, all of this. Totally. But not nearly so weird as you probably think right now."

Then Shay pulled her nearer, saying nothing more. That sisterly embrace spoke more than thousands of words might have at that particular moment.

Emma gave her cousin one last squeeze, hoping she'd know how much she'd missed her, and was surprised to feel extremely developed muscles in Shay's upper back. The woman was so fit it was downright shocking; that strength rippled with a kind of power that Emma had never noticed before.

"Geez, you're really buff, girl." Emma stepped backward, breaking their physical connection. "I heard you'd started using your gift, hunting demons and all that." Emma studied her cousin from head to toe, shocked at how simultaneously feminine and strong she'd become. Yes, this was all very new; if she'd doubted that fact, the shy pride she saw gleaming in Shay's eyes would have told her otherwise. Besides, Emma had seen her at Aunt Joanna's funeral back in the spring, and she hadn't looked as strong and empowered and . . . alive as she did now.

Emma suddenly remembered her mother sharing details of Shay's recent marriage, how she'd met that "nice Greek man" shortly after her mother died. So, was this what happened to you once you cozied up with a Spartan warrior? You turned all Catwoman, got more gorgeous, and nearly purred with an energy that said you were extremely well tended to at the end of every day. Good to know, she thought. Good. To. Know. She'd never longed for River as much as she did at just that moment.

Extending a shaking hand, she murmured his name. "River," she said. "I need River."

Shay broke into a huge smile, one that said she knew exactly how Emma felt. And exactly how badly she needed her dagger man.

Shay laughed low in her throat, reaching for Emma's hand. "Come on," she said, leading her toward the house. "We've got lots to talk about."

Emma took her cousin's hand as her gaze moved to the brightly lit mansion that loomed just before them. Funny, but that fearful lurch she'd expected when she returned to this house wasn't there like she'd imagined it would be. Her heart and mind had moved on, and to someone much more important than stale, painful memories.

Her gaze wandered to the three extremely large, dark-haired men who stood talking on the veranda. They'd arrived with Shay, but quickly had moved away to give the two of them a quiet moment. Somehow Emma figured that it wouldn't be a great idea to go demand anything out of that towering crew.

"I need to help River," she told Shay softly, pointing toward the other men. "It's urgent, but I'm sure *they* already know that."

"You have no idea."

"I'm also thinking that getting possessive about him, right off the bat . . . well, that it might not be the best idea with the Greek Mafia over there. Am I right?"

Shay smiled a little, but worry kept it from reaching her eyes. "They'd defend River to the death."

"I don't want to hurt him," Emma rushed, but Shay lifted a hand.

"Of course not. I'm just saying that you can trust these men. Even if right now you're feeling connected." Shay stopped walking a moment, her gaze lifted upward. "Protective of him, maybe."

Emma shook her head in disbelief. "How do you know . . . how can you possibly get it like this?"

"Oh," Shay said with meaningful slowness, "I so, so know what you've got going right now." Her cousin's gaze moved toward the porch, toward the tallest of all the warriors. "I live it every day. You're bound to River somehow, that much is obvious."

Emma nodded, wanting to reveal everything about the blood-tie that she shared with River, yet also wanting to keep that bond a secret for some reason. To let it stay sacred for just a little longer. Finally she managed to whisper, "Yes, I feel very . . . bound to him. That's exactly how I feel."

Shay nodded, walking again, but said nothing. As they reached the steps that would lead Emma back into this home from her past, a monument to memories and pain, and also the opening door to her future, Shay turned to face her. She gave Emma's hand a squeeze, releasing it and looking into Emma's eyes. "You feel bound to him because you are," she said in a very low voice. "It's real, so trust it. But they're bound to him just as strongly, sweetie. They'll need a little time to trust you because they're not of this world. Not anymore. But I vouch for you and that helps a lot."

"I only want to help him." Emma felt fear surge again, that sense that River's time was running out.

"They know that." Shay began walking up the steps, and all three men turned toward them. All three taciturn, brooding, beautiful men.

"He's running out of time, Shay," Emma whispered, quavering beneath the collective gaze of those warriors.

"They know that, too. You just stick close to me, follow my lead, and it's going to be okay, I promise."

"I'm not worried about me."

"I'm talking about River," Shay said in one last rush. "You and River. It's all going to be okay. So is stepping back into this house."

Emma swallowed hard, too overcome with emotion to respond to the comment. Shay didn't give her time to, either. "Okay, gang, let's go inside."

When the intimidating circle split apart, she recognized Ari in the center. He wasn't looking particularly happy, not like when they'd met earlier. His dark features were now a threatening glower. The other two men threw her equally stormy looks, and for a moment, she would have sworn that she wasn't in Kansas anymore. That this childhood sanctuary of hers wasn't even real, and that any minute the Great and Powerful Oz would appear there right between them all. He'd materialize in a smoky, green explosion and explain that this was all an elaborate fantasy.

She actually held her breath, some part of her wishing that would happen because then she'd know it was all a dream. Instead, she got the wake-up call to end all wake-up calls. Ari stepped close, extending that same pawlike hand he'd offered before. "Hello again, Emma," he told her quietly, almost smiling. "I'm guessing my memory mojo wasn't so effective after all."

"Well, at least it's official now." She smiled, taking Ari's massive hand, which felt perfectly familiar and real. "I'm really not in Kansas anymore."

And she wasn't sure she wanted to go back, not without River.

# Chapter 16

They sat around the dining room table, and Shay slid a cup of coffee in front of Emma. It was eerie how little the house had changed. The furniture and family heirlooms were configured in nearly the same arrangement that Emma remembered from twenty years earlier. But that's how it often was with old family estates.

Talk about a circle of testosterone. Ari hunched across the table from her, dwarfing the fine Henredon chair that he sat in. Nikos, whom she'd met as they entered the house, sat next to him. He was closer to the doorway, pushed out from the table so that his back was flush against the wall as if he couldn't stand to be exposed, even here inside the protective shelter of the house.

Sitting next to Shay at the end of the table was her new husband, the extremely fierce-looking man named Ajax. She gave him a hesitant smile, wondering how Shay had possibly managed to relax around him long enough to fall in love.

She glanced at the warrior called Nikos. He was much less handsome than Ari and Ajax, his features too harshly defined and swarthy. At the same time, however, there was a kind of beauty in his brutal visage and long aquiline nose. His were ancient features, she realized after a moment of consideration, almost like something you'd see on a crumbling bust in the Louvre, except he was real. A true warrior, hulking across the table from her.

Aristos spoke first, which made sense. They'd forged a tentative friendship during the drive back from Tybee. "Emma, tell us of River."

She sat up as tall as possible in her chair, which didn't feel very tall considering how giant the men were circling her. "He's asked me to free him again, like I did on the island." She swept her gaze about the table. "So I need his dagger now. I need to take him somewhere private and ..."

Ajax cast his intense, piercing gaze toward her. "And do *what*, Emma?"

Oh, good grief, why was it so hard to just say it out loud? She cleared her throat after a moment. "I have to use River's blade on myself. Maybe several times until he emerges, but the point is that it's my blood that frees him. He said we have a blood-tie."

Nikos folded both arms over his chest, got a really smug look on his face, and said, "Never heard of that."

"Why would I make this stuff up?" Emma cried out in frustration, starting to worry that if she couldn't act soon, it might be too late for River to find freedom.

Shay tapped the table. "Boys, look, this is how it's gonna be. You're going to let Emma do her thing right now, and here's why." She slid an arm around Emma's shoulder, showing solidarity. "This is my cousin, right? I'm the one who brought her here to the so-called inner sanctum. The only reason I did that is because I've known Emma Lowery for my entire life, and I trust her. And y'all trust me, right? I'm on the inside here."

They made murmurs of acknowledgment and Shay continued, "So, yeah, you trust me, all of you do. Hell, you'd trust me with anything. You already have lots of times, agreed?" There were more rumblings of assent, and this time a few sheepish glances.

"I wouldn't dare cross my wife." Ajax drew her hand to his mouth, kissing it. Emma caught a low whisper from him about trusting Shay with his heart and soul.

Shay didn't wait for anyone else to say a word. She thrust her hand out, wiggling her fingers as if time were slipping away. Which it was. "So, you are going to give my cousin ..." Her voice suddenly grew loud as a deep trumpet. "River's *goddamned* dagger *right now*! Now, boys, now!"

The moment Emma saw River gleaming in Ari's palm, she sprang forward, reaching halfway across the table. Her hand shook with tremors, and Ari didn't miss that fact, reaching to steady her grasp as he gently slid River into her palm. "He's yours," the man said softly. "Be good to him; keep him safe."

"Thank you for trusting me with him. I won't let you down." She started to push her chair back from the table, trying to think of the best place to go with River.

"You're not doing that alone." Ajax's voice sounded a stern warning. "Not happening, Emma."

She slid back into her chair, tightening her grip around River's hilt. "Oh, really," she fired back just as coolly. "Well, why don't we ask River what he wants?" She immediately strained her ears, hoping to hear some quiet reply or whisper from the man.

"Nice idea," Nikos said, checking his watch. "Only it's never worked like that."

Shay gave her a sideways smile. "Go on and tell them, Emma," her cousin encouraged. "So they'll know what you mean. Tell 'em how you can hear River."

Emma froze; she wasn't sure why, but she felt frightened about admitting the details of her ability. Then again, until today she'd never even planned on reopening that vulnerable part of herself. Talking about it took that level of nakedness to a whole new dimension.

She gave her head a little shake. "Shay . . ."

"*Shayanna*," Ajax echoed. "What do you mean? There's no one capable of hearing River's voice when he's in weapon form. Not even Straton has that ability."

"He's not the only possibility," Shay replied, looking toward Emma to fill in the rest.

She took in a strengthening breath, knowing that what she said next would mark a point of no return. A willingness to open her heart to the pains of the past and the uncertainties of the future. Both of which were emotionally dangerous propositions. With one more deep inhalation, Emma chose to step beyond the veil.

"I'm a medium. I hear voices from the other side." She stared down at the table, not quite sure if she could put the rest into words, especially the part that involved explaining *why* she could hear River. But they needed to know how critical things had become for him.

"I've listened to spirits, angels, even God himself," she continued, her throat going dry. *Or that's how it used to be,* she wanted to say, but didn't figure admitting how long it had been since she'd used her gift would convince them of her legitimacy. "But mostly, it's those on the other side who like me. They're the ones always trying to get my attention. Like River."

All four of them stared at her; Shay actually paled visibly, and shivered, hugging herself. "But River's still alive. You saw him, talked to him," Shay reasoned. "So what do you mean about the other side?"

Emma bowed her head slightly, not wanting to reveal her suspicions or upset River's friends, but she'd been given no choice. They had to understand how dire his situation had become if they were going to let her be alone with him.

"It's one reason I want to be alone when I do this," Emma told them. "So I can hear him if I need to, without the psychic noise of all of you. His voice is thin, faint . . . or it was earlier. But time is running out."

"What do you mean?" Ari asked, his warm eyes filled with something akin to terror. "Are you saying his spirit has moved on to Elysium?"

"He's not dead yet," Emma admitted, "but he's getting dangerously close. When he was in the ocean, and reached to me, he told me he was dying. And although he emerged after that and my blood gave him strength . . ." Emma shook her head, feeling the stark truth in her heart. "He's hovering very close to the veil, and has been ever since I met him. He's growing nearer with every moment that we waste right now."

Ari's stare became resolved. "Then you do whatever you have to do, Emma," he told her. "And you do it right now so that our brother can come home, where he belongs."

She gave River a squeeze, shoving back from the table quickly. "I'll work as fast as I can," she assured all of them, but Ari's gaze was still on her, unblinking and deathly serious. His next words chilled her to the bone.

"Do it," he said. "But just make sure he doesn't kill you in the process, Emma."

\*       \*       \*

Emma stared down at River's blade. This was the moment. She could finally free him, and in the process they'd be free together. If he stayed with her this next time, if he remained the very real, solid man who'd held her before, then she could hold him in her arms and truly love him. She knew it was irrational, feeling such tenderness for a man she barely knew, but nothing about River was typical or boringly normal. No wonder she was falling in love with him shockingly, ridiculously fast.

He'd made her feel more alive than any man she'd ever been with, already. But what would happen once they came together without demons after them? He was an ancient warrior, something so beyond the realm of normal that surely he'd grow bored with her. And fast. Except every touch, every word he'd given her had made her feel more special. As out of control as he'd been, she'd felt safe in his arms—as if she would always be treasured and worshipped so long as they remained together.

Despite that fact, she felt unsteady as she clutched his dagger within her hands. Her heart slammed like a madman inside of her chest, and her palms were so slick with sweat that she could barely keep him steady. He'd turned her life upside down, sending every belief and concept of the known universe scattering like some skittish house cat. She trembled and shook as she sat on the bed.

*Right.* She could kid herself all she wanted, but she knew it was his fate that she worried most about. A heavy, sinking sensation clawed at her, suggesting that she might never break him free again, but he didn't need her fear right now.

What he needed was her blood.

"River, I'm going to use your blade." Her voice trembled audibly and she cleared her throat before continuing. "I'm going to use your dagger like we did on the beach, and that's going to make you stronger. Set you free."

She closed her eyes, and listened for his voice, waiting for whatever reply he might be able to make. *What if my gift is too underdeveloped? What if it isn't strong enough after so much time?*

On the beach she'd caught his voice, even over the

noise of the waves and storm and despite that deafening terror she'd felt about opening her gift. She hadn't heard him during the drive with Ari, but by that point she'd been weakened from blood loss. And there'd been so much noise between them. Not just her conversation with Ari, but the confusion of trying to figure out who River was, and as she later realized, because Ari had been working away at her memories at the same time.

Here in Shay's quiet bedroom, however, with only the low motorized hum of the air-conditioning droning in the background, it was more like it had been on the island. So maybe that would enable her to hear him again. She was ready to draw blood, but at the same time she didn't want to just go slicing away at herself if he wasn't on board with the plan.

"There *isn't* another way, River," she told him fiercely, squeezing his hilt. "I know you said you'd find one, but none of your friends know how to help you. I'm the one, and you've got to use me as your bridge back. It's a fair trade, okay? My blood for your life."

She waited, hearing nothing but the steady rumbling from the air-conditioning vent on the floor. That cool pulse hit her heated skin, and chill bumps rose along her arms in reaction. Drawing in a strengthening breath, she tried again. "River, I'm ready to try this. Can you hear me?"

She heard him at last, the weakened sound of his voice a cold shock. The thin thread of his words sent fear cascading through her, more terror than she'd felt since the crazy situation had begun.

"Tell me again," she encouraged, not even sure of what he'd just said to her. His voice had been so dim that she'd barely heard those dully murmured words. The ebb of his life force was obvious, the intensity of it much less vital than it had been back on Tybee, and that realization brought tears to her eyes.

Again, she heard something of a whisper, his deep voice moving across the surface of her thoughts. *Emma. You . . . are too good. . . .*

"I'm not doing this because I'm good." She clutched him tighter, hoping he could sense the warmth of her hand. "I care about you."

*Too good ... to ... me ... for ...*

He didn't finish, and she didn't like the direction he seemed to be going. "You're going to be fine and real again. Do you hear me? You will be all right," she babbled, ignoring the solid knot of fear that had lodged inside her chest. "I'm going to use your blade now, going to get my blood to you, and it's going to awaken you or whatever it is that it does. And then you're going to ... to ... pop out! Right? You're just going to come on out and it will be okay. You won't hurt me, nothing like that." Preemptive measures were best when dealing with dying dagger men, they had to be, and there wasn't time for him to resist her efforts. Not a moment for him to worry he'd harm her.

*Heal you ... you know that.*

"You think I'm worried about it hurting? No way. So, yeah, I'll just go on and do this." She placed the sharp-edged blade against her upper thigh.

She closed her eyes tight and slid the blade across her skin. There was the biting sting of pain and then the metallic scent of her blood. She didn't wait for him to ask for more, not this time. Again, she drew his edge across her skin, deeper this time, and then repeated the motion with another fast swipe.

The room filled with an otherworldly noise, a pure kind of energy that drowned out the purr of the air-conditioning. Bright light followed next, filling the room with that same surging silver that had consumed River out on Tybee. She held her breath, moving backward on the mattress until she was flattened up against the headboard. She'd needed to be alone with him; she'd known it by instinct, but now that this swirling energy surged ever stronger all around her, she couldn't help feeling afraid.

He'd warned her repeatedly about his frame of mind when he emerged. What would happen now that he was about to become human again?

River came free of his bondage with a roaring awareness. He blinked against the silver that blinded him, barely making out his surroundings. Slowly his vision improved, and he saw the only thing that he craved right in front of him. Emma lay there on the bed, ready, clearly waiting and hungering just as he was. His stiff cock twitched and bounced as he took purposeful, slow steps toward her.

He should have felt self-conscious or apologetic like he had in her dream. Instead he slid fingertips along his shaft and began stroking himself, stepping closer to her. Then closer still as his hunger to press it between her warm legs intensified.

*No, no, I have to calm down*, he thought, some dimly reasonable voice shouting into his thoughts. His feet moved forward again as if driving him toward her with a will of their own.

"It's all right," Emma told him softly, seeming to lean forward slightly as he approached. He couldn't quite be sure, though, not with the silver raging through his eyesight.

"Oh, it's more than all right," he purred back, pushing a knee onto the edge of the mattress. "Far, far more than all right, sweet Emma."

The grinding, thrumming need that shot through his body was the only thing he could feel, the only thought he could heed. And it wasn't his berserker this time, at least not completely. It was her. His Emma, sitting there waiting and reaching for him with more trust than he even remotely deserved. That gentle faith made him want to be the finest and most noble male she'd ever encountered.

He thought of an uncontrollable stallion, the untamed sort that could never be bridled no matter how long you trained or worked with it. Except with Emma, *he* was that stallion, miraculously soothed by her presence, broken in and ready to ride because of how she gentled him. There had never been anyone, not in the past thousands of years, who could take the edge off his berserker. Until Emma.

"If I just focus on you, on this . . . need . . . I won't hurt you," he reassured her, moving onto the bed completely. "You want me." He knew it, wasn't asking permission. But so long as she was willing for him to lie with her now, there wouldn't be pain, there wouldn't be rape.

She opened her thighs to him, taking him atop her and into the welcoming cradle of her legs. "Yes, I want you, River. You know that I do."

Her hands moved to his hair, brushing it back from his face, and as he stared into her eyes—truly looked at her—the silver gave way to human sight. Oh, Highest God, what a revelation! Emma was gorgeous, even more than he'd realized or seen out on that beach. His breath caught, a surge of desire spearing him hard in the groin, warm heat flooding his whole body. Rolling down like a wave from his flushing face, all the way to his already saber-hard cock.

"You've got clothes on," he told her, not caring that it was an asinine observation. She hadn't made him feel clumsy or stupid, not one time since he'd met her. This woman was safe; her arms gave him peace. And her body gave him a thrill and longing that soared far beyond any he'd ever known in his immortal life.

"I can fix that," she said, smiling up at him. Her hands twined in his hair, holding it back from his face. "Or you can."

With a needy growl, he reached for her shirt, and jerked it open. Then caught himself, realizing how aggressive his behavior must seem.

"Won't hurt you," he promised, swallowing hard, already considering a more gentle way to get rid of her tight little shorts. "Just . . . a little . . . urgent."

Still poised between her legs he rose up on his knees, staring down at the khaki shorts. "Hate those. Off."

He couldn't form full sentences; the rushing torrent of lust was too strong. Although his berserker was keeping itself politely out of sight in the wings, it was driving him, cornering him somewhat. He began trembling, watching as she wriggled out of her shorts and underwear. He moved over her right leg, freeing her to discard the clothing, and at last she settled down beside him. Naked and gorgeous, dark hair falling loose against the pillow, tanned body welcoming. She let her legs fall open to him, and for a moment he was transfixed. The craving hum of lust burned all through his body, his need for her spiraling to epic proportions.

"I've never taken a woman, not after . . ." He was embarrassed to tell her. Thank the Highest God that she seemed to understand.

"After you've come back?" she prompted gently.

He swallowed, nodding, and kept his gaze on the wall behind the bed. There was a movie poster hanging there, and he wondered dimly whose room they were in at the moment.

"So if you've never been with a woman after emerging, but the dagger makes you ... well ..."

"Not just a dagger," he told her, swinging his gaze to hers. "I'm able to become many different weapons, and for ... many different purposes."

He couldn't bring himself to tell her the rest. That he was created to serve, to fight in his master's grip and that unlike her, he'd never been free. Shame swamped him in a heartbeat. She deserved to know exactly what he was. For this intimacy to be real, to be honest, she deserved all of him. He opened his mouth, about to confess his full history, but she spoke first.

"Okay, so if you've never been with a woman after your change, then how have you always dealt with your needs?" She hesitated, brushing a hand through her rich mahogany hair. "I mean, you warned me on the island. And Ari talked about it."

River moved between her legs, making sure to be gentle. "Sexual release is the only way to control the bloodlust I bring back with me."

She gazed up at him, her brows furrowing slightly. "So if you've never taken a woman, then what have you done? I mean, how did you ..." All at once she blushed, and placed her hand over her face. "Sorry, totally dense moment."

"Servicing myself, that's how; it's never been very special." He laughed, hoping to turn it to a joke. "I've dreamed that one day I'd return from battle and have a woman like you waiting for me. A gorgeous, beautiful female who ... who ..."

*A woman who loves me; a good woman who is my wife and mate.* He ached to tell her all of his secret hopes, but was afraid of frightening her away.

"I care for you. Already," she said.

"Perhaps you should be more cautious, sweet Em."

She shook her head vigorously. "I might not understand how fast this is happening, but I'm more than sure about what I feel here. I care about you already, River. You need to know that I don't do this lightly." She gestured toward her supine body. "Or with just any ole guy. I usually go really, really slow."

"You don't have to rush into this now. I—I can handle myself, if need be." The tremors that already shook his body instantly grew far more intense. "I . . . I can do it . . . on my own."

"No way. "She gave him a cat-eyed look, pressing her knees together until they brushed against his outer thighs. "I know what I want, and that's to feel you, River. All of you deep, deep inside of me."

# Chapter 17

The front door opened and closed with a loud rever-
beration, and they all looked up at the noise. Shay's
brothers tramped into the long hallway, their deep voices
echoing into the dining room. They were midconversation,
voices becoming louder. Nikos felt his whole body grow
tense and edgy at the familiar sound. He braced himself for
the arrival of both men, clenching both hands involuntarily
where he held them in his lap.

It wasn't that he didn't like Shay's brothers—quite the
opposite. They were fellow warriors in this fight now, and
he felt a sense of camaraderie with both men, especially
Mason. As a former Marine the human thought in ways
that Nikos found familiarly comfortable. Far *too* comfortable, he'd discovered over the past few months.

They'd formed an easy friendship, the kind that never
had been easy for Nikos. They'd talked combat, compar-
ing the differences between modern military strategy and
ancient warfare; they'd watched *Aliens* together, Mason
griping about newly added scenes that seemed perfectly
fine in Nik's opinion. They'd discussed the movie's military
characters, too, including the tough-as-shit female marine
named Vasquez who Mason got him to agree was "sort of
hot." Only Mason's voice turned husky and strange at that
moment, a little guilty almost.

Nikos's belly grew tight in reaction to the sound. And
it wasn't the only part of him that did, either; definitely
not. The hard, muscular Vasquez, with her body armor
and weapons and ammo, was about as unfeminine as any
woman ever got. Nik watched her, shaking, wondering why
Mason Angel suddenly scared him so much.

The shaking that started inside him that night, well, it hadn't ever let up. There wasn't a place for friendship between them, not with the way Nikos was wired, not with the way Mason wound him edgy and tense. He'd kept his distance ever since, sad to see that thousand-yard stare return to the former Marine's eyes, the look he'd recognized the day they'd first met. It was the hollow regard of a soldier who'd glimpsed far too much, and Nikos knew it well.

That had been a month ago, maybe more, but now with Mason's voice echoing in the hallway, he'd walked back into Nikos's life. Nik tensed in anticipation, not knowing what to expect.

Jamie entered the dining room first, heading toward his sister. "Isn't that Cecilia's Volvo parked out there?" he asked. "Only one like it around Savannah, far as I know."

"Yeah, Emma's here," Shay explained as her brother bent and gave her a quick kiss. "I've been trying to call you for the past hour, ever since she called me."

"River Street, Sissy Cat," he said. "You know how crappy cell coverage can be down there." He took a breath, and then kept talking. "Evan had to meet us. . . . Oh, shit." Jamie stopped suddenly, seeming to remember something. "Emma's *here*? For real?"

When Shay nodded, Jamie cursed again, then glanced at Mason, who finally entered the room. "Dude, Em's here," he told his brother.

"That's not good," Mason offered with a slight nod of agreement, glancing toward his sister. He propped himself against the doorframe, never meeting Nikos's eyes. "She coming downstairs anytime soon?"

"Could y'all sound a little happier, huh?" Shay fired back. "You both know what a big deal it is that she's here at all."

"Sissy Cat," Jamie said again, "it's not Emma that's the problem at the moment. You know that. She's got no clue about Evan being involved with us."

Nikos watched Mason as he shoved off the doorframe and stepped toward the table; he kept wishing the man would just make eye contact. He wanted to give him a friendly look, and basically apologize in one glance for having been such a dick recently.

Jamie scooted his chair to the side, making room as Mason pulled up a seat of his own, dropping into it heavily. "Evan's hosing some demon blood off the grill of his SUV, but he's coming inside any second."

Nikos cleared his throat. If he spoke up and joined the conversation, then Mason would be forced to deal with him. "I'm not following here," he said quietly, and Mason finally gave him a quick glance. The expression in his eyes was unreadable, and he looked away just as fast. He turned to Shay while answering Nik's question.

"Well, it's just that our cousin . . . Emma, she's really close with Evan, but he's kept this from her. He knew she'd be upset that he was part of the Shades, Nik," he answered quietly. "He didn't want to hurt her or bring up old . . . pain."

Old pain. It was all Nikos could do not to physically wince at those words; old pain was what had spawned his recent coldness toward this man. "What . . . uh, kind of . . . old pain?" he managed to ask, and for a long second Mason stared at him, barely blinking, and Nikos felt powerfully arrested by that long gaze. Then shaking his head slightly, Mason stared down at his hands and said nothing.

Shay finally answered, "Emma lost someone, and she stopped her gift as a medium for a long time. Until . . . now. So Evan was afraid that if she knew he was a demon hunter, it would hurt her."

"Yeah." Mason sighed, still keeping his gaze down. "Yeah, I better go make sure he doesn't come in here right now. Emma's been through enough, and you're right, Shay, it's big that she's here and we have to support that."

Mason stood, walking toward the hallway with a weary, heavy posture, and as Nikos watched the man leave, he thought of how deadly old pain really could be. Not just the weight that Mason carried, but because Nikos's own past was the wall that kept him from getting up and following after him.

A dangerous, familiar buzz began under River's skin. Maybe beneath his muscles, he wasn't sure exactly where it started. His only awareness was of the fiery silver that, without any warning, erupted along his spine, the burning fire that chased through his torso.

"No!" He shook his head, blind with the primal force of his curse. All rationality fled him and he was atop of Emma before he could stop himself, seizing her hips in his hands. She was silky and damp for him, so welcoming and ready. He worked his erection against her opening, his lust beyond control or dominance, his primal side driving him, and the feel of her hand against his back did nothing to rein him in. No, like the rest of her luscious naked body, it offered permission.

He could take her; she would buck and moan and cry out in pleasure at his touch, at the feel of him inside her. But he would not do it while at the edge of sanity's tether. It had to be real, motivated by true emotion. Not the pounding drive of this madman, a demon touched by a wicked curse.

He became paralyzed, bracing himself on his forearms, which framed her face. Blinking, he stared into her accepting blue eyes, and felt appalled at himself. He *was* a monster, and it was no wonder that he'd never successfully bedded any female at this stage of his change. He was horrific, beastly, the sort of creature who raped and pillaged entire villages full of women. That was what a berserker did in the flush of violence and bloodlust.

"River, what's wrong?" she asked.

With a roar, he buried his face against her shoulder, rocking and thrusting his hips, mimicking the motions of sex in the hope that he'd come right away. And he knew that he would, even if he'd only harden again immediately, the tense demand spiraling even higher in his body. But if he could bring himself past the edge enough times—maybe two or three—before actually entering Emma, then their first time might still have a chance to be lovely and beautiful.

"Have to ... come." He ground his hips, and she kept meeting the motion, but he tried to still her hips beneath one hand. "Don't. Got to do this ... myself."

She tried to push against his shoulder, but he moved faster and faster, determined to gain release before plunging inside of her. "River, look at me."

He growled, his hair a tangle against his face, his hips working a fevered pace.

"River!" She shouted it, shoving him hard in the chest. He panted against her, gasping as he pressed his face into her warm, soft neck and shoulder.

"Sorry," he mumbled, his body jerking with tremors. "Don't know what else . . ."

"You don't have to do this by yourself. I'm right here. Make love to me," she told him fiercely, still trying to force him to look at her. "I'm here. I'm yours. I want you."

"I'm cursed. . . . Don't want to be in you . . . until controlled."

"That's the thing, River." She stroked his hair, her fingers winding all through the tangles, and she made a soft sound of comfort. "You don't have to be in control with me."

"Don't," he barely managed to growl, feeling power ripple down his spine. Gods of Olympus, even his wings felt on the verge of exploding through his skin. Normally it was only the needs or the silver. The wings had never been so explosively close to unfurling during the craze.

"Yes," she said. "I am giving myself willingly. Offering myself to you. Come inside of me, River. Please."

He shook his head, making a guttural sound of pained desire.

With firm hands, she took hold of both his shoulders. "You're going to do what I say, okay? You know how on the island you helped me? I listened to you?"

He nodded, digging fingers into the mattress, praying he didn't cross to a more dangerous place.

"Now it's my turn to help you. Lean up, River," she urged him. "Kneel back between my legs, like before."

Somehow his body listened; she was soothing him, with her gentle voice, her loving, tender touch. Maybe that was it, or maybe she controlled his curse in some mystical, un-fathomable way—just as it had been her blood that freed him. He didn't dare question, as he lifted onto his knees. Staring at the dark, silky thatch of hair between her legs, he calmed a little more. It was odd, but as he looked at her, appreciated her naked, gorgeous form, the sheer beauty of it had an almost liberating impact. Brought him back to his human self more fully and pushed the berserker's evil demands further out of his mind and body.

With a shaking hand, he reached down and traced the little concave indention by first one hip, then the other. Emma had the strength of a natural athlete, her feminine muscles toned and firm. Her upper body in particular was one flowing line of gorgeous definition, and it brought the humming, buzzing flow in his body under her sway. He felt lighter suddenly, still filled to the hilt with longing for her, but it all flowed through him so ... rationally. Normally, even.

"See?" she said, smiling up at him. "You're calm with me. You just have to trust me and trust yourself with me."

His eyes drifted shut as she kept touching his body. "Oh, Em, I trust you, love."

"Then let me give you this release. Let me show you this freedom you crave."

He gave a slight nod, eyes still shut. "It's myself I don't trust. Not you."

"But I trust you," she whispered, sliding her hands down his lower back, trailing fingertips along his tight buttocks. "I trust you to be gentle and loving with me."

"It's not the curse in me, Em, that's making me so wild ... it's you."

"Then make love to me."

"But this makes the curse come alive. . . . It's like throwing wood on a blazing fire."

"River," she told him in a steady voice. "I trust you. Just keep hearing that, feel it in every pulse of this gorgeous body of yours. Oh, God, you are breathtaking."

"I have never wanted any woman so much in my entire life," he told her, opening his eyes again. He had to see her, couldn't shut her out, not even from his line of sight. "I want you to know that. I crave you more than any female ever before, more than when I was in Sparta, or over all the centuries since then."

"Show me," she told him, her words a warm, seductive purring sound. "Show me how you feel. How you want me ... to make love with me."

He couldn't move. He was paralyzed by the anxiety that

he might grow violent or take her too roughly. Again, she urged him onward, took his hand and slid it to her right breast, but he pulled back.

"I'm afraid I will lose control and harm you," he told her in an anguished voice. "No matter how much we both want this . . . I might hurt you, kill you if the violence surges over me. It could come from nowhere, blindside me at any time. I couldn't live with harming you. You're precious to me and I won't, Em. I won't risk it."

She shook her head once, then a second time, much more strongly. "You're wrong. With me, you aren't like that." Her eyes widened as if she'd gotten an idea. "But if you're afraid to touch me, at least for now, then let me be in control. I'll pleasure *you*."

She reached toward him, planting both of her hands against his chest. Her touch was warm, erotic, and she began rubbing his pectorals with sweeping strokes. Then she began beading his nipples, which hardened beneath her firm motions. As she focused there, her gaze grew far more daring, sliding down his chest, to his waist and hips, and then lingering at his groin.

For a long moment she stared at his thick, heavy erection, and he wondered if she was pleased by what she saw. Or, like some of his few lovers over the centuries, if his size intimidated her. As a mortal he'd been slightly larger than average, but upon being transformed by Ares, the male portions of his anatomy had expanded to exceptional dimension and size. Not grotesquely large, yet definitely far above average.

Ares had even laughed about what he described as "an additional, extraordinary gift for our servant."

"River, your special skills as a weapon are now clear," he'd said after returning River to human form. "But your other sword, the thick, natural sword of your manhood . . . this, you surely see, has been transformed, too. It's such a perfect symbol, don't you think?" Ares had tossed his head back in amusement, golden hair shimmering in the fiery hues of Styx. River had glanced downward, feeling his cock lengthen and strain as if commanded by the god himself. "What a mighty asset I bless you with. As a sign of your warring nature, I have given you a pulsing, mighty shaft of victory. Just be sure to take some spoils along the way."

River had not known what to say or how to react, gaping down at the surging length between his legs. Only later had he seen his special *endowment* as Ares' idea of a cruel joke. That even then the god had known the wicked, lustful cravings that he'd seeded inside of River, so of course it had amused the deity to grant him such a straining and monumental cock. Oh, dark, evil humor, indeed. River burned for sex with an unstoppable need, yet could never slake his lusts with a woman without worrying about harming her.

Maybe it was remembering that moment while Emma caressed and stroked his body, or perhaps because she'd finally looked at his shocking length, but all at once he had to get off of her. Put as much distance as he could between his soiled, ruined nature and her sweet, good one. If he remained naked against her for even one more moment, he feared seizing her in a brutal sexual display . . . and in the process, he might taste the bloodlust.

In one single and graceful motion, he hurtled away from her, leaping to the other side of the room. He planted his hands against the painted surface of the far wall, his lungs seizing for air as if he'd been drowning. He heard movement on the bed, thought he detected the sound of bare feet on the rug.

"Don't come near to me."

"I have to help you through this," she told him, her voice coming closer. "If you don't take me, I think you'll wind up back in the dagger."

She was right; he'd known it the entire time she'd stroked him. He pressed his forehead against the wall, his fingers curling in agony at how much he wanted Emma, and how painfully he needed her. "I won't hurt you. I . . . I don't want to do anything to hurt you."

"I know that. That's what I keep telling you." Warm hands slid to his hips, her touch closer to heaven than anything he had known in his long immortal life. Closer to it than he'd felt that day of his death at Thermopylae.

She was sweet, perfect. The feel of her hands on his body

was soothing and pleasuring and arousing him like some divine nectar from Olympus.

And that was what finally settled the matter in his mind, and he knew what had to be done. It wasn't what he wanted, or the hope that his heart had entertained, but perhaps they would have another chance. Another day. Because even if it wasn't what he ached and longed for with every ounce of his will, calling on his brother would keep Emma safe and that was most important.

"Tell me one thing," he asked, his chest rising in quick, short pants. "Where are we right now?"

She pressed a kiss against his spine, her mouth warm and gentle in the center of his back. "We're at Shay's house, and some of your friends are here. Ari, Ajax . . . Nikos."

"Good, that's good, Em." He swallowed, trying to calm down. "Now if you care for me at all, and I know that you do, I ask only one thing."

She made a soft, plaintive sound, her cheek brushing against his muscular back. "I'd do almost anything for you."

Pressing his forehead against the wall, he moaned. And shook a little harder. "I . . . know," he barely managed to say. Oh, why was she still touching him? Being so kind?

"Just don't ask me to leave you," she murmured softly, placing a kiss against his shoulder. "I can't leave you like this, sweetheart."

His body seized up on him then, his hands curling into fists, his shoulders rolling with tension. "Back off," he snarled between clenched teeth. "Right fucking now."

Ripples of bloodlust surged through him, and all he could picture, all he craved, was the thought of taking life. Of turning on Emma, anyone else in the house; they were his enemies . . . weren't they? They sought to chain him, own him, harm him somehow.

*Not right, wrong!* he tried to tell himself, but he was blind with the compulsion now. Gone over to it, lost in its thrall.

He burned to feel weapons within his grasp, to choke away life with his bare hands. *Emma, no! Get away while you're able.*

"Leave," he begged, slamming both fists against the wall,

somehow holding himself by that last fragile cord of sanity.
"Now, Emma . . . now!"

He was dimly aware that she stroked his back with her
hands, attempting to soothe him. *She doesn't understand
the danger.*

"Leave me. Em, get Ari." He growled, turning to gaze at
her with his wicked silver stare. "Tell him to come armed."

# Chapter 18

A ri got to the closed bedroom door first and heard Emma's muffled cry from the room's interior. "Don't, River," she said. "You can't. Please *don't* do that."

*Oh, River man, not good*, he cursed inwardly, about to give a swift knock on the door—and River an even swifter knock on his ass. Or worse, depending on how badly he'd treated Emma.

Nikos was faster, however, hitting the closed door at a dead run. He didn't bother stopping to knock, barging into the room without slowing his furious pace. Nik sputtered curses, pulling to a sudden stop. Ari was moving fast and slammed into the guy's back with an awkward thud, and careened backward; Nikos had blocked his view and Ari couldn't tell what was going on inside the room.

"Is she okay?" Ari asked, regaining his balance. Nik did an about-face toward the door, looking embarrassed, and that gave Ari a full view of the scene inside the room.

Nikos headed toward the hall. "I'm going to get Shay for this one."

Ari caught the warrior by the forearm. "Not yet, man. Let's see what's going on here first."

Ari felt protective, knowing that River wouldn't want Shay seeing him like this; his friend wouldn't want anyone seeing him so far gone.

"I want to make sure he's really all right," Nik said quietly.

Ari felt an immediate gut-kick of guilt. The man really had proved himself when it came to River, staying steady and concerned when others of their cadre had moved on.

"I've done this drill plenty of times." Ari looked into

the Spartan's black eyes. "He's still with us . . . at least right now. I'll tell you if we hit Defcon Five. Why don't you wait out there?"

Nikos gave a stern nod and Ari guided him toward the hallway. Satisfied that Nik was squared away and wouldn't create even more drama, Ari turned back to face the music. He let his gaze roam the room as if he were an immortal detective, taking in even the smallest details as he pieced together events. Emma sat huddled on the floor, naked, a sheet clutched across her chest. She looked a crumpled mess, her face streaked with tears. She hadn't looked at either of them, almost as if she wasn't aware they'd barged in on her in such a vulnerable state.

"Are you okay, Emma?" Ari tracked her gaze. Her eyes were fixed on the other side of the room, focused on the wall that was flush with the door itself. It took actually stepping into the room to see what she stared at.

"He wouldn't let me help him," she said in an anguished voice. "I kept trying and he started hitting the wall, and then he . . ." Tears filled her eyes. "He . . . backed me over here."

*Oh, shit*, he thought, getting a pretty vivid image of how threatening River would have been while "backing" Emma to the floor.

"Our boy was probably just trying to keep you safe," Ari told her, but wasn't entirely convinced of that fact.

River stood off to the side, naked, gleaming with sweat and shaking all over. His face was pressed against the wall, his hands braced overhead as if held in place by invisible manacles. Ari took a slow, cautious step toward his friend, wondering if he'd truly gone violent or if he'd just been crazed for sex. Emma didn't appear hurt, he decided with another quick look at her. At least not physically; the emotional part of whatever they had going here was obviously damned messy.

"River man, how's it going, friend?"

River growled like a rabid, cornered animal, saying nothing more.

"Oh, that good, huh, tough guy?" Ari laughed low, trying to keep the humor between them. He knew from experience that River calmed when he recognized his familiar voice. That of all the corps, he alone had the power to help River come back from his berserker frenzy.

River hissed, his bare body tensing and flexing so hard that the muscles rippled and moved all down his back.

"Now *that's* not very polite," Ari said with a low chuckle. Behind him he heard Emma sniffle, and he wondered where the hell Nikos had gone to.

Ari tried again. "How about a nice hello for your best pal, huh? It's been a while. I've missed you, man."

River knocked his forehead against the wall a couple of times, rocking a little bit as if trying to still his crazed thoughts.

"And that," Ari continued, taking another cautious step closer, "looks downright painful. I mean, you don't have much rolling around in that brainscape of yours, anyway, so you should look after the little that's there."

River's hands slid along the wall, spreading farther out to each of his sides. "Is she still here?" he asked in a raw voice.

"Yes, right here," Emma answered, and to her credit her voice sounded much stronger and more assured than she looked. She definitely cared about the guy.

"Emma's doing fine," he assured River, taking two more steps closer. He was almost right up to his friend, in position to capture and subdue him if he turned violent. "Don't you worry about Emma; she's looking great. Feeling great, aren't you?"

He never looked back at her, but had confidence that she understood his operation.

"I'm feeling really great," she agreed. "Never better, really." Her voice did finally waver a little, and that fact caused River to jolt in obvious awareness, his body jackknifing against the wall as if electricity shot through him. Finally he grew still again, panting hard, and even more sweat began rolling down his back.

"Get her out of here," he growled in a low, pained tone. "Get her away from me now."

There was movement behind him, and he heard Nikos enter the room again and begin talking to Emma in low tones.

"No," she argued sharply. "He hasn't hurt me. I'm not going."

River began shaking all over. "Please take her, Ari. Please get her somewhere safe."

Ari kept River in his sights, but spoke to Emma over his shoulder. "If he's asking, Emma . . ."

Nikos's voice became stronger. "Here, Emma, you can come with me."

Well, that? That, River didn't like at all. In a blur he wheeled and pounced toward Nikos. "Not with you. Not Nikos." River grabbed Nik and hurled him against the wall where he'd been huddling, hands wrapped about the warrior's throat. "You don't fucking touch her; don't even breathe around her, or think your stinking thoughts near her. Understand?"

River's eyes were wild silver, and that power moved and shimmered all over his back and bare skin. Nikos didn't answer; damned if he could with River's gripping choke hold about his throat. He just worked at prying River's fingers loose, meeting the frenzied stare the guy was throwing him.

River made a harsh sound. "Do you understand me, warrior? Emma is mine. She's mine and you won't touch her or talk to her."

Ari cast a quick glance at Emma, expecting to find her scrambling from the room with a horrified expression on her face. Yeah, he had that guess dead wrong. She'd straightened her posture, wrapped in that sheet and looking much more composed than she had only a few moments ago. She seemed to be doing all right with the guy's volatile emotional state, which was impressive. Even ugly-ass, cold-hearted, nothing-rattles-him Straton couldn't stand to be around River when he got like this, for crap's sake.

Ari moved toward River, ready to yank him off Nikos. "Let him go, dude. Now." Nikos closed his eyes, no longer trying to work River's hands off his neck, and Ari continued, "You hate Nikos? News alert! Nobody likes Nikos. Not even *Nikos*. Look at the guy, will you? He's uglier than a yard snake, sucks at poker, and last I heard, he's a big disco fan. We can hate him together."

Nikos gave him a searing glare, one that said he'd make Ari pay later. Ari shrugged apologetically, rolling his eyes toward River in explanation. River seemed unaware of the entire interchange—his eyes glazed over and his chest rose in quick bursts. He still held Nikos in his grip, but not quite as harshly.

"So, yeah, you can hate the guy, that's cool," Ari continued. "But guess what. You don't have to kill him. Let's leave that to . . ." *Who? Who the fuck should he say they'd leave it to?*

"Me," Nikos rasped. "I'll do the job."

"Look!" Ari patted River's back. "Nik's gonna take the problem right off your hands. Gonna off himself for you. Isn't that nice of the bastard? See, he's not all bad."

River cast Ari a confused look, and Ari acted with instant precision, seizing his friend from behind in a bear hug. Stumbling backward with River in his arms, he shouted at Nikos, "Get out of here. Go! Take Emma and get her someplace safe."

Nikos barely made it to the upstairs veranda without getting physically sick. He fell against the railing, his entire body covered in cold sweat. What the fuck? He'd never seen River in such bad shape, and it had brought the horrid memories back in a heartbeat. Probably because of how River had been flat up against that wall, stripped bare with arms wide as if he expected to be . . . beaten. Punished. Abused.

Nik's stomach seized on him, but he choked down the urge to be ill. Reaching a shaking hand to his forehead he tried to take hold of his reaction.

*River does not remember*, he promised himself. *You took care of that years ago.*

Still, he shook from the inside out, wondering how he'd lived with all the bad shit inside his soul for so long. But with River gone for the past four months, it had all come alive in him again.

*He does not know, will never remember.*

But what if he did recall the truth someday? The way

he'd gone for Nikos's throat, the pure hatred in his soul moments ago had been chilling. Stone-cold deadly.

*If he remembers, you can explain. Tell him the truth.*

Nikos's belly drew tight again and he bent over the railing hoping the wave of nausea would pass.

"You all right?" the deep, familiar voice called out to him. Nikos gripped the railing harder, shaking his head.

Mason walked up behind him with slow steps. "Nik, what's wrong? You sick or something?"

He couldn't find his voice, and pressed his eyes shut tight. Finally, he shook his head again, unwilling to look at the mortal.

A firm, strong hand came down on his shoulder and there was comfort in that grasp. "Let me help you over to one of the chairs," Mason said, trying to guide him.

Nikos froze. Unable to move. Unable to talk or deal with this good friend who he'd fucked things up with lately.

Mason kept his hand fixed on his shoulder for a moment, but then eased it away. "Or," he said with a quiet laugh, "you can stand there turning ten shades of green."

"I am not," Nikos croaked, rubbing a hand over his mouth. He was feeling a little more stable, less spooked and sick.

"Oh, come on, Nik. That swarthy Greek skin does not mix well with ghastly gray. It's just not that becoming." Mason elbowed him, and then walked back toward the inside of the house.

"Don't go," Nikos called out, keeping his back to him.

"No?"

*I don't want you to; I want you here with me, quiet with me. Talking or shooting shit, anything at all with me.*

He heard the sound of Mason's returning footsteps, and kept staring out to the land below, listening to the harmony of the cicadas. "You sure have some loud insects here in Georgia."

The mortal laughed from the darkness behind him. "Yeah," he drawled in his softly beguiling Southern accent. "One of our tourist attractions. That and the palmetto bugs."

"Also known as roaches?"

"A rose by any other name, my friend."

There was another long, endlessly suspended silence between them, one in which the symphony of night noises reached a crescendo. Finally Mason said, "Okay, well, if you're feeling better, I'm off."

"Just so you know," Nikos admitted in a rush, "you're probably the only thing that could have settled me just now." *Oh, gods, why had he said that? What the fuck had happened to his brain?*

Mason stayed quiet, but Nikos sensed him still standing at his back, felt the buzz of strong, mortal energy. Damn, he should have kept his trap shut, should have held the line.

After what felt a full minute, he heard a deep, quiet sigh. "You've helped me, too, Nik. A lot. And for that, I'm grateful."

Then there was the sound of Mason's footsteps moving away, the door opening and closing behind him. He was gone, leaving Nikos with his crazy, swirling thoughts and a body that was rippling with forbidden desire.

River catapulted within his grasp, but Ari wasn't about to release his grip on the guy. It was like trying to control a herd of slippery oxen, with River sending the two of them in a staggering dance step back and forth across the room. Ari not backing down or letting go had them crashing into a tall dresser, bottles of perfume and trinkets flying everywhere, glass shattering. Then River lunged in the other direction, knocking them back into the wall with painful force.

"Gonna get a shiner off that," Ari shouted with a curse, wrestling to maintain hold on his roaring madman of a friend. Once more River gained a surge of strength and they went flying, landing in an awkward, uncomfortable heap in the middle of the rug, barely missing the broken bits of glass. Ari was definitely the bigger guy, and he took advantage of River's prone position by basically sitting atop him.

"Stop moving, Kassandros." Ari planted a knee in the center of River's chest, but River kept trying to lurch upward, his silver eyes staring blindly. Ari punched him in the jaw, hard, hoping it would get his attention. River blinked back at him, looking like he'd been woken from a bad dream that he didn't understand.

River let his head roll back against the carpet. "Nikos is a real shit."

"He's all right," Ari said, wondering where that sudden animosity had surfaced from. "He worried about you a lot while you were gone."

"I don't believe that for a minute," River said acidly. "No wonder it took so long for me to make it home. I doubt our tracker was interested in locating me."

Ari had shared those qualms before, but Nikos had won him over in the past few days, including the patient way he'd handled River's attack just now. It had been pretty brutal, but Nik had stayed calm.

"Nah, Nikos did right by you, man. He worked it hard and never gave up."

River's eyes blazed anew. "Even for a *slave*? The dirtiest and lowest of you all? I don't believe he would do that, not for me. Not for a second."

"You know we've never treated you like the lowest or dirtiest . . ." The words had stung, they really had.

His friend never talked with such bitter, cold resentment. That, plus that otherworldly, silver gaze, made him feel like he was staring into the eyes of a ghost.

"I am the lowest rung, Aristos. Maybe the ocean was the perfect place for me, after all." He laughed harshly. "The true home for a bottom-feeder of a helot slave."

"You're not talking like yourself," Ari said without self-editing. "I don't know what you're even getting at."

River jolted, the silver force traveling visibly through his entire body, shooting through his veins and lighting them up like tributaries from Styx itself.

"Hey, buddy. Calm down." Ari tried pushing him back into the floor; he shouldn't have given the guy crap, not when he was like this.

"Nikos hates my ass," he hissed, eyes rolling back in his head. River's body jackknifed with convulsions, washed out completely by silver. "Nikos always hated my ass, even . . ."

He never finished the sentence. That consuming, clawing

force folded into a whirlwind, trying to claim him. Ari knew it in an instant and pinned him down against the floor with tight fists. "You're not going anywhere," he said. "You're here to stay, River. Here. To. Stay."

"What . . . ?" His head jerked sideways and he looked out toward the hall. His swirling eyes closed briefly and he sank against the floor. "Oh, God." His voice was full of agonized regret. "Why didn't you stop me?"

Ari wasn't going to be swayed by River's momentary clarity. He didn't budge or move a muscle. "You were just doing your usual routine," he said.

Only it hadn't been usual at all, Ari thought, shocked to realize that he was shaking. He'd talked River down more times than either of them could count, but this one had been uglier, harsher . . . and much more sinister.

"No." River's eyes opened slowly, the silver brighter than before. "Why didn't you stop me from showing Emma . . . that? All that horror that lives in me? She'll never want to be near me now."

"I don't think you've got anything to worry about there, buddy, okay?" he reassured him. "All good."

River scowled up at Ari, the silver in his eyes fading just as the fight in his body had begun to diminish. "So you gonna let me get up or not?"

"Not anytime soon."

"You're crushing me beneath that monstrous weight of yours." River smiled wanly. "You obviously took my share of the rations while I was gone."

Ari lifted an eyebrow. "What'd you eat, huh? Chicken of the Sea?"

River's eyes drifted shut. "Just don't let me hurt Emma," he murmured softly. "Please, Ari, you know what's inside of me. Don't let me harm her or . . . worse."

"You know that I won't."

River nodded, his chest pulling in tight, quick pants. After struggling for a moment, he spoke in a subdued voice. "She calms me. I've never experienced anything like it before. You fight me off my ledge, Aristos, but she . . . she eased my berserker. For a little while, she backed me down and centered me."

"So what went wrong?"

River shook his head slowly. "I don't know. I do not know. So keep her out of my reach until I'm myself again. Whatever you do, even if you have to tie me down, you keep her away from me."

Ari hesitated, considering what his dearest friend had just asked. After a moment he spoke in a low voice. "Tell me. Just how serious are you about that?"

# Chapter 19

Leonidas stood in the middle of the horse pasture, watching the moon rise. On the crest of the hill, lights blazed within their shared home, although only Straton and Kalias remained tonight. The others had gone to Shay's home to talk to her cousin about River. It was almost midnight, and he hoped they'd receive more news about the warrior soon.

River had always been special to Leo, although he'd never admit it to his other men. Never bitter or complaining, the warrior carried himself with a pride and honor that belied his humble roots. But it was the way in which he approached life, with such passion and openness, that touched Leo the most. There was honesty to it, a true innocence that made him want to be less reserved himself.

He walked the property perimeter, testing the wards, making sure they held in place. The compound had been hit by demon attacks several times since they'd moved in, the wards threatened each time. They would have been stronger, but they weren't nearly as old and therefore solidified as the ones that guarded his castle in Cornwall, so he gave them extra attention as a result. He and his men couldn't afford to be caught unawares with all the uncertainties that surrounded them now.

He trailed his fingers along the wards' sparking line of protective power, feeling for any weak link in the supernatural chain. As he moved farther down the line, Leonidas kept a firm hand on the flowing band of energy, playing with it absently as it bounced and reacted to his touch. He'd always considered his wards to be living things, the way they moved and responded to him, and he felt gratitude toward their protections, too, because they were the first line of defense against demonic attacks.

With River finally back, he felt particularly grateful for the security, for knowing that their Savannah home was safeguarded. He didn't want to lose a warrior ever again. With Ares having turned on them, he felt as if unseen threats teemed all about their cadre. Whereas the wards made him feel secure, the crumbling compact between Ares and their corps had the opposite effect, making him feel on edge and unsettled.

If only their Oracle would return; if only she would whisper some insight into his ear. She was the one who'd first hinted at Ares' traitorous change, guiding them toward the One who was far more powerful, the Highest God. Yes, if the Oracle returned, she would advise him, help him decide his next steps.

*Keep convincing yourself that it's only her words of advice that you miss. Not her company. Her sweet kisses . . .*

He shook his head. The woman was their guide, not his own to love or to hold. Only it was far too late for him on both counts, and he was already lost to her.

She'd come to him one final time months ago, right after the battle in Bonaventure, and asked him to hide Ares' Looking Glass of Eternity. The fact that she no longer trusted Ares had been the most compelling argument that the war god had truly abandoned them, and that their bargain was shattered beyond repair.

And so he'd done as the Oracle had asked of him, concealing the priceless object. Its location would never be discovered on his watch, not by demons or his warriors. Nor by Ares, not as long as he had fighting breath, because that's what he'd promised the Oracle. He refused to betray her trust in him. Since that day, however, she'd vanished like the wind over a brutal summer battlefield. Not a whisper, not a hint of her ever since.

Day after day, he continued protecting the looking glass, knowing how dangerous it would be for it to fall into the wrong hands. They'd learned of its power from Ares; no wonder he sought its return. Anyone who gazed into its surface could pass from this life and into Elysium, whether mortal or immortal. Ares had already attempted to capture Ajax's soul by having him look into it, but Jax had fought him off.

So with the mirror being something of a portal to heaven itself, it was the type of object for which warlords and dictators would spill the blood of millions. Leonidas also wondered if it couldn't potentially allow a way for the powers of darkness to invade Elysium.

As he considered the object's other potential properties, he wished fervently that the Oracle were here to advise him. Without her, they were drifting rudderless, a derelict ship out at sea. She'd been their guide from the very beginning, stepping into Hades with her long black hair flowing in the breeze, her rich-colored skin gleaming golden by the fires.

Ares had just completed their transformations when she appeared, and the heat in Leonidas's restored body had reacted immediately to her exotic beauty. For one small moment on the banks of the Styx he'd imagined that, here in this afterlife of sorts, he might find a way to have that mysterious woman who fired his blood to share eternity with him.

Lightning had flashed at that moment and the Oracle vanished before his eyes, destroying his hope as Ares made her invisible to all of them except Ajax, who would convey her prophecies to their cadre. She'd remained invisible, too, until the past year when, by some unknown miracle, she'd appeared to him out on the Cornish moors. She'd been standing there, just watching him with those gloriously blue eyes—eyes that had bewitched him completely.

"She may yet return," he whispered to himself. "For she said she watched you from afar for more than a thousand years. What is four months when compared to that?"

But what if that fickle war god would not *allow* her to return? The thought made him feel old once more, as if his body had aged a full century in that single heartbeat when he'd considered that he might never see her again.

"Stop with the fear, Old Man," he told himself. The nickname had never been more apt than in recent days. The war injury in his knee ached constantly. The horrific scars on his body, earned at Thermopylae, seemed to grow more hideous every time he glanced in the mirror. His lower lip had been disfigured since that day. It didn't hurt; it simply ruined his smile.

Ares had restored each of their bodies after they accepted his bargain. But after Leonidas's death the Persians had paraded his corpse as part of their victory celebration, shifting him from shoulder to shoulder and brutalizing his form. By the time he'd reached his fellow Spartans there by the banks of Styx he'd been ruined. Never fully redeemable. At least that was how he'd thought of himself ever since.

He was still fairly young by all visible accounts. His curling, dark brown hair wasn't streaked with gray, nor was his neat beard. With the exception of the scars, his face held few lines, although it would never be handsome, not since the Persians had played their knives and swords across it. And if he'd been decently attractive, surely his Oracle would have returned by now. She would have burned for his touch as powerfully as he did for hers.

*She's not my Oracle*, he reminded himself, feeling an overwhelming amount of melancholy. And he cursed himself for the emotion.

He glanced upward at the moon and humbly apologized to the Highest God who watched over them all. "I have no right to be so selfish," he prayed aloud. "Even though Ares gave her to us, you are the one who has allowed her to speak your own words. You've let her continue as our true spiritual guide, Mighty One. It is not right that I ache for her so."

Maybe it was the sight of the full moon rising over the pasture, bathing their horses in ghostly light, maybe it was the light breeze that stirred the grass all about him, but something caused him to look to his right side.

And words failed him as they always did whenever she appeared.

Emma appreciated the sanctuary of Aunt Joanna's former bedroom. It felt like family and home, and obviously Shay had realized that she could use a little "normal" after tonight's craziness.

She wore one of her aunt's old bathrobes, thankful for such everyday comfort. After what she'd just experienced with River, her emotions were ping-ponging all over the place. One minute she was painfully worried about him, and the next frightened by what she'd seen he could become and what he was clearly capable of doing when he changed like that.

She and Shay sat on the sunporch off the bedroom, talking about superficial, safe topics. Shay's relaxed mood began to ease Emma off the emotional tightrope she'd found herself teetering on after River's freak-out. That was one way of describing what she'd experienced; another would be intense sexual frustration; yet another would be witnessing murderous rage in the eyes of your boyfriend. She'd understood why River had kept trying to get her to leave as soon as she'd witnessed him lunge at Nikos.

The cozy sitting room did wonders for her mental state, with its potted plants and plantation shutters and small sofa covered in bright floral fabric. That, along with the scent of Pacquin hand cream and Givenchy perfume, made it seem as though Aunt Joanna were still alive. Suddenly Emma's medium gift began to open in reaction to the strong sense memories. She jolted at the unexpected phenomenon, and with a quick shudder slammed her internal gift tightly shut. *Not now*, she thought. Now was so not the time for one of *those* conversations.

She forced herself to focus on Shay and her casual chit-chat. Her cousin rambled along, but she couldn't stop worrying about River, wondering if he'd been able to stay in human form this time.

"He's doing all right," Shay said after Emma blanked out on their conversation once again.

Emma affected a casual tone. "I'm sure he is."

Shay looked into her eyes intently. "But I'm not sure that *you* are, Em. Doing all right, that is."

Emma stared into her lap, working her hands together nervously. "He was in such bad shape," she admitted after a moment. "I knew what to expect, you know, but it was more intense than out on the island. A lot worse than what I'd seen before."

"Weren't you fighting demons when he emerged the first time?" Shay leaned back into the deep sofa. Sliding an arm around Emma, she pulled her close. "As in, battling for your lives?"

Emma nodded, leaning into the comfort of her cousin's warm shoulder. "He saved me from them."

Shay made a knowing sound. "Exactly. The demon fighting channeled his violent urges."

"He explained that to me. That the sex thing is how he keeps from murdering whole villages and such."

Shay snorted. "He did *not* say that."

"No, you're right, but then tonight . . . was when he seemed really on the edge."

"And the island was different how? Apart from the demon battle, which obviously helped stabilize his bloodlust."

Emma shivered at that term.

"The island was . . ." Emma wondered if she was really ready to talk about all that had happened; the thought of reliving it made her even wearier. But it also gave her something to focus on other than worrying about River's well-being.

"He kissed me," she finally offered, feeling shy for some reason. "And I mean, really kissed me. In a top-to-bottom, take-the-curlers-out-of-your-hair-'cause-you-don't-need-them-anymore sort of way. That kind of kiss."

"You don't mean it." Shay grinned hugely in response to that news, her light blue eyes flashing with excitement.

Emma leaned her head against Shay's shoulder, sighing into the physical contact. "I've missed you so much, Shay."

Shay turned and kissed her on the forehead. "I've missed you, too, sweetie. We all have." She gave her shoulder a small squeeze. "It's been a long time."

"I'm sorry."

Shay turned to her in surprise. "For what?"

"That I never came back." Tears burned her eyes suddenly, and she tried to blink them away. "I'm sorry that I didn't. Couldn't. I loved you so much, you know that. All of you, but it hurt. It was just too hard. But I'm still so sorry."

Shay kept her close, not saying anything for a while, just

nodding her head. "I can't imagine how it was for you when your ... when Leah died. I know how much Mason and Jamie mean to me, and she was your twin. You had a special connection. And deep down, I always understood that."

*Deep down.* Emma's chest grew painfully tight. She knew she'd hurt Shay, all of them, but she just wasn't sure she could handle hearing that sad truth right now. The reality of it brought almost more guilt than she could handle at the moment. "*Deep down* you knew it," Emma finally repeated, swallowing hard.

"I was little, too, you know," Shay said, "and you were my world. I didn't have a sister, and you and Sophie, and Leah, you were so much more. You were it. *The* 'it' in my world back then, and ..."

Emma's tears began to come in earnest, her shoulders heaving with sobs. "I feel horrible that I hurt you so much, just totally dumped you. All of you. And then Mason needed me this year after he came home from Iraq, and you called, and I didn't do anything."

The sobs intensified, pulling buried emotion out of her like vine-deep roots, unearthing the hard pain of it all. "I hate that I haven't been able to figure things out, but once it was gone between us, all that specialness, it seemed so broken. And every time I thought about coming around, the idea just got scarier, and harder, and more and more ... undoable."

Shay wrapped Emma in a tight, comforting hug. "You didn't let me finish," she said gently.

Emma sniffled against Shay's shoulder. "Finish what?"

"I'd been saying you were the whole world to me, but what I didn't get to add then was that as much as I loved all of you, and Leah, of course—*you* lost your 'it.' Leah was that one most special person in the whole world for you. And when she died, you just did the best you could. I know that. Mason and Jamie do, too. They always have."

Emma sat up straight. "I am such a ball of mess." She wiped at her eyes. "I'm having some kind of meltdown, maybe. Spartan Shock Overload or something."

"Oh my God, that's classic. S.S.O. It's a syndrome; we've named it."

"Let's write an article and submit it to some self-help journal," Emma suggested jokingly, then growing more serious asked, "So how'd the syndrome hit you at first? Bad case or low-grade version?"

"It's a lot to get used to. There are things that . . ." Her voice trailed off, and she seemed to be holding something back. But Emma wanted it all now that she'd gone underground with this crew.

She gave her cousin a little nudge in the arm. "No way, you started something there," she said. "Don't back down now."

Shay seemed to consider for a moment. "Let's just say River's not the only one who can change forms. They've all got something of that. He's just the only weapon-shifter in their midst."

"What do they change into?"

"That's not really important right now. Let's deal with one shape-shifter at a time. Namely the one you're already in deep with."

Emma nodded, wadding the tissue in her hand. "Could you go check on him? When I left him with Ari, he was really having a tough time of it."

"He'll be fine. He's got Aristos taking care of him."

"But if he didn't stay in human form," Emma wondered aloud, "that would be dangerous, wouldn't it?"

"I think it would be okay with the guys around, keeping him from killing anyone." Shay laughed.

"Glad *you* think it's funny."

"Hey, I'm shacking up with his fighting partner, so don't look at me."

That made Emma curious. "Do they work in pairs or something?"

"Huh. River didn't tell you about . . . uh . . . Ajax? The way they team up?" Shay's gaze grew a little guarded and Emma had the sense that maybe she was dancing around the edge of something important.

"No, he didn't mention Ajax, really."

Shay nodded. "You'll probably see it in action soon," was all she said.

Emma decided not to press the topic, once again worrying about River. "You think he'll be able to stick around eventually, though? I'm just hoping he's still human right now." Emma leaned forward a little, listening for any sound from the hallway.

"I'll go check on him, if you really want me to." Shay started to get up, but for some reason Emma wasn't ready for this moment to end. She had a pretty strong feeling there might not be much downtime around this operation and she wanted to hold on to this closeness for just a bit more.

"Let's give them all a little while longer." She patted the sofa. "Hang out with me for a few more minutes. Answer some more of my burning S.S.O. questions, cool?"

Shay sank back into the sofa, propping her bare feet on the oversized basket that served as a coffee table. The warmth, the closeness with this cousin whom she'd always missed, was one of the best gifts she'd received in years.

"You know River well, then?" Emma asked, but her cousin surprised her by shaking her head.

"I know him somewhat, but he disappeared right after I came on the scene." Her expression darkened. "Long story about that, but I kinda blamed myself. I think we all blamed ourselves, and really it was his idea and his choice. I still feel bad about the way it turned out, though."

"What did he do? I never asked how he'd wound up in the ocean." She was surprised such an obvious question hadn't come up, but there had been so much else to wonder about.

"He stayed in the form of a dagger for much longer than he'd ever been in weapon form before. We're talking a full day longer, and it was dangerous. Ajax didn't want him to do it, but River was hell-bent on going along so he could protect him."

"They're that close, huh?" Emma wondered why none of the other Spartans had felt such a strong need to be part of that mission.

"It's . . . a little different. They're a special fighting team, and River should explain how it works to you, not me."

Emma could accept that; if it was something important to River, then he should be the one to tell her. She nodded for Shay to continue.

"It happened in the middle of this big battle over in Bonaventure," Shay explained. "One of their demon enemies tossed River's blade out into the Wilmington."

Emma felt a fevered anger grow inside of her: hatred of the enemy who had mistreated her love so harshly. "That makes *me* want to fight."

"And maybe you will," Shay said cryptically.

"Oh, no. No, no, that's you, babe."

Shay searched her face, then said, "Well, don't be so sure. You might be surprised what happens when hanging with the boys." She laughed.

Emma didn't. She was too busy feeling slightly freaked by Shay's suggestion that she might wind up battling demons herself. But then Shay blew out a long sigh, changing the subject.

"River's an absolute sweetheart, of course. I realized that the first time I met him." Shay smiled at some memory. "And kind of shy, too, which is really bizarre given the way I hear he's Mr. Sex Machine after his change."

Emma snorted. "I'll believe he has a shy side when I finally see it."

"Might not." Shay shrugged. "Maybe he's just comfortable with you."

"Maybe. I don't even know him yet," she said with a hard sigh. "But I'm already halfway in love with him. Geez, I'm nuts."

Shay moved her feet off the table, straightening her clothes as if she intended to leave. "You're totally sane if I'm any basis for judgment," she said. "I fell just as hard for Jax. Keep in mind, our own special gifts help us hear or know more than the usual mortal woman making her way in the dating pool. And when you add in their supernatural powers? I think it's a situation where you're bound to fall hard because you know that you're meant for each other."

"I'm reassured." Emma burst out laughing. "Not. Not even close. I'm not in Kansas anymore, but might be in *The Twilight Zone* or somewhere even weirder." She hit the base of her palm against her forehead. "I know! Even weirder could be my imagination, dreaming all of this up."

"Nope, Em, it's real. For better or worse, you're wide

awake." Shay stood up, brushing a hand through her hair. "I'll tell you this, though, it gets easier once you learn all the rules and what makes these boys tick. You've got a guy who obviously fell hard for you in about two seconds flat, and I can tell you this. My own husband has known him for ... well, let's just say it flat out, for thousands of years. And Ajax loves that man. Loves him to the ends of the earth and up to the moon and all the way to God himself. You're not making a mistake in falling for him."

"That's not what I was thinking." Well, not thinking it *much*, at least. The exhaustion was painting shadows in the corners of her mind, the kind you couldn't help fearing might hide monsters.

"You sure?" Shay smiled.

"All right, you busted me. I was thinking this," Emma answered, standing up, too. "Why couldn't my sweet, amazing, honorable guy have the ability to turn into something equally sweet and honorable and easy?"

Shay just rolled her eyes. "Where's the sexy romance in that? Give me complex and deep any day of the week."

Emma had to admit that she was starting to agree— even with the scary and edgy side that River possessed, he was also capable of more passion than any man she'd ever known.

"You go grab a shower, if you want," Shay told her, heading toward the door. "I'll let you know how he's doing in a little bit."

# Chapter 20

The vibrant blue of his Oracle's eyes shimmered like the moonlight that limned her. Leonidas felt overwhelmingly grateful for his hawk's eyes, vision that was capable of penetrating even the darkest night.

Bright blue streaks shot through her black hair exactly as they had when he'd last seen her, only she'd grown it much longer. It spilled down her back, gleaming and shiny, begging to be touched. She was forever changing her appearance, and tonight was no exception.

"No words for me, my king?" She inclined her dark head, not taking a step. "Are you angered by my absence?"

His chest drew tight as a drum; he felt his breath catch, but he could only gape like a bumbling idiot. No words. Not a one. *Oh, you shy imbecile*, he cursed inwardly, searching for something—any damned thing in the universe—to say to this woman whose presence he'd craved so painfully.

"I—I . . . am . . ." *An asinine moron*, he finished in his own mind.

She did not lift her gaze, did not move, but simply stood before him in that bowed posture of respect. "My lord, please do not be so angry with me." She looked up at him, that lovely gaze bright with tears. "I can handle any punishment from you. Anything but the loss of your affection."

And then, his heart beating furiously inside of him, no words coming at all, he *roared*. He opened his mouth, threw back his head, and released a shout so loud, so intense, that the petite woman before him jolted visibly. But her entire expression transformed the moment he spread his arms wide to embrace her. Still running, reaching, ready—gods of Olympus, hoping . . . He stormed toward her with every bit of intensity that his ancient soul possessed. His armor felt light as air, his feet as fleet as Nike's.

The moment they reached each other she made an agile leap and he swept her upward, swinging her into his strong embrace. Despite his brass breastplate, she managed to wrap strong graceful legs about his waist, locking them tight down along his buttocks. Those muscles tightened in instant arousal the moment her heels dug into the leather that bound his lower body.

"My sweetness," he murmured. She tangled small arms about his neck with a fevered kind of desperation.

"Oh, Leo." She pressed her face against his cheek, plunged fingers into his curling hair, twisting tight. "I am sorry. So sorry." Dampness touched his beard as she nuzzled her face against his.

"Shh, love. No tears. We're together . . . now."

She didn't look up, but bobbed her head obediently, just clinging to him as if he were the one who might vanish at any moment.

What had happened to his dear Oracle? She trembled as if terrified. Or was she simply overwhelmed?

She kept her legs wrapped about him, and his hands locked tight about her lower back, securing her against his chest. Keeping that compact, graceful body of hers pressed against him, he turned in a slow circle of wonderment. She had come to him, finally. He could hardly believe she was real, not some figment of his mournful imagination.

He pressed a kiss against her ear. "Have I captured a moonbeam?"

"It's me, Leo. It really is." Her words were muted because she spoke them against his shoulder, keeping her head buried against him.

"You won't vanish?" Damn, but he needed reassurance, the promise that he could hold her for more than a fleeting second.

"Forgive me," she murmured.

He tried to take hold of her cheek so he could look into her eyes. Kiss her. Truly see her. But she only burrowed closer, her small body shaking with tremors.

"I don't understand . . ." He paused, again trying to see

her face, but he couldn't pry her head up. "Dear Oracle, why these tears?"

"Happy." That was all she said for a moment; then she hiccupped slightly and lifted her face toward him. Her vivid eyes grew even more vibrant, alight with wonder and obvious tenderness. "I am so, *so* happy to be with you, sweet king."

With that one simple comment, an idiot's grin spread across his features. "With me." He couldn't quite believe it, and even more vain, he craved to hear it again.

"You silly man, yes!" She tightened her arms about his neck and kissed him full on the mouth. Just a swift, playful brush of her lips against his that sent a shock wave through his entire body.

His grin grew much wider, and for once he didn't care how his smile must appear to her. That the rough scar on his lower lip pulled ungraciously, giving him an expression that was more leer than smile. He laughed low in his throat. "You missed me."

She kissed him in the center of his forehead, showering him with several quick kisses. "Terribly, terribly. All I wanted was to get back here, to you."

He didn't bother questioning why she'd stayed away or why she hadn't been bounding to his side every single day, many times a day. Nuzzling against his beard, she made a little purring sound, and arousal hit him like a hot wind straight out of Hades. His groin tightened beneath his loin wrap, the leather constricting him painfully.

"I have counted every single second since I left you," she told him. "The past four months felt even longer than the thousand years when you couldn't see me. I didn't think that I would survive them."

He silenced her with a kiss. The very one he had imagined giving her for all their months apart. Unlike any time he'd kissed her before, however, he didn't hold anything back now. Teasing at her lips with his tongue, he kept hold of her, slowly sinking to his knees. His armor creaked, but he ignored the sound as he lowered them to the grass.

She plunged her tongue inside his mouth, and their kiss quickly became much deeper, tongues warring and twining.

Hands caressing each other, breaths coming desperate and fast, bodies aching to join. He had to get that sexy, feminine body beneath his own even though he was in full armor.

With a gasp, she broke their kiss, and sat panting before him. For a long moment, a hushed stillness came over them, only the sound of cicadas filling the night. But the loudest sound, by far, was the rushing beat of his heart. So loud it nearly drowned out every other sound that folded about them.

Slowly she reclined against the fresh earth, unfolding that graceful body in sweet invitation. Even once she lay back, those enchanting blue eyes stayed fixed on him; her T-shirt-clad chest rose and fell quickly, her breath coming in quick panting bursts of desire that caused the heat in his groin to nearly boil.

There would be no hesitation this time, no stopping this intensifying rush of need. He had to claim her, had to mark her as his. For an insane moment, he fought the heady desire to allow his wings to form, to make love to her beneath their covering. To say to nature, the elements, to all spiritual powers: "She is mine."

With shaking hands, he fumbled with the leather bindings along the side of his breastplate, keeping his heated gaze locked tight with her own. Those blue eyes grew unfocused, filled with such lust as he'd never seen in any woman's. Especially not directed toward him.

"Damn it," he cursed as he fumbled with the armor.

She sat up, tucking her legs to the side as she scooted closer. "Let me do that." She glanced up into his eyes, a playful smile upon her lips. The last time she'd done this very thing it had ended in their first kiss. Letting his hands fall to his sides, he nodded, and her delicate fingers made quick work of releasing him. But she didn't stop there. When he moved to pull the armor off, her hand stilled his.

"Please, Leo." Her voice was husky-rich, filled with more desire than he'd ever heard. "Be still and let me undress you, love."

He growled in the back of his throat. She knew that for a simple warrior and king like him, allowing anyone to attend to him—to treat him with such tender reverence—was almost unbearably difficult. As he watched her, he was struck by a palpable sadness in her eyes, still wet with tears.

Doubt hit him full-on at that moment. Both as a warrior and as a man, he'd trusted this beautiful woman totally, but now she was being dishonest with him somehow. She was touching him as she'd done before, but the heat of it . . . was gone. He gazed down, seeing the way her hand trembled as she worked at his armor.

"Sweet Oracle, look at me." He cupped her chin, forcing her gaze to meet his. "Tell me why you've really come tonight."

She beseeched him with her eyes, making a slight shaking motion with her head as if she were a hostage, being forced to do this. "You do not want me?" he asked to cover the moment, all the while searching the pasture with his hawk's sight, sniffing at the air.

She didn't answer and he prompted her in an intentionally rough, cold tone. "So, my lady, that's it? You no longer want my battered body?" He made a scoffing sound, his gaze still roving the property. "For that, I can hardly blame you."

"You're . . . hard to look at, king. You've always said so yourself."

Although he knew it an act, he still winced at those harsh words, but she caught his hand, squeezing it. Not letting go until she finally met her gaze.

Soundlessly she mouthed the words, *I do.* She bobbed her head with emphatic force, adding, *I want you . . . so very much, my sweet king.*

His own eyes burned and he squeezed her hand in return. "Well, at least you didn't mind the feel of my lips against yours before."

She melted before him, eyes drifting shut as if he were kissing her all over again. "Poison," she lied, swaying slightly in obvious remembrance. "Terrible kisser. You might use your teeth in battle, sir, but kissing isn't the time."

"Why have you come to me, then?" he snarled at her, their fingers threading together. "Why have you bothered at all?"

"Our lord Ares sends me," she told him in an overly

loud voice. "He wants to discuss the return of the slave Kassandros." Her eyes grew wide and she made a subtle motion of warning with her head. "He'd wished to help you locate the missing warrior, but now he celebrates this man's return." She bowed slightly. "He has interest in this servant, in freeing him after so many years of service. Just as Ajax has requested of him on so many occasions. Ares believes that bestowing the gift of freedom upon Ajax's servant will bring peace between you immortals and himself."

Leonidas stared into her eyes simply aching for her guidance, to know her mind at the moment. It was obvious that Ares had threatened her, and he began examining her, looking her over for any abuse. She placed a staying hand on his forearm and reassured him with her gaze. And she loved him with her gaze; he'd have sworn it.

He touched her face and stared into her eyes for a long moment, then with an ugly growl said, "Ask Ares what he plans to give me for River. I assume he wants my warrior servant, seeks the man's actual appearance in his Olympian court?"

"Yes, king." Her tone was a chilling warning.

"Well, then, tell him that I require a gesture of goodwill," Leonidas said. "He tried to kill one of my best warriors, and responsibility for River's long absence falls on Ares' shoulders as well. So I must have a sign of his favor if I'm to trust my warrior to this summons."

"Tell me what you wish, my lord."

He lowered his voice to a bristling demand. "Tell him I want you, dear Oracle."

She gasped slightly at his words, obvious fear in that light blue gaze. "Yes," he went on, "tell him that as a boon for my years of service, as a sign that he can be trusted, I expect him to give me . . . *you*. Let him know that if he wants to build a bridge with me, then from now on—and for as long and often as I wish—you will be my war prize. That's what I require, so go tell your war god of my request."

She dropped her head, staring into her lap, but he saw her lower lip trembling, and then several tears rolled down her cheeks. "Yes, Leonidas."

"Bah, no tears over this horrible fate, little fairy." He

feigned a harsh, cruel tone, even as he reached to touch her cheek, his fingers stroking away tears. "You'll not find my touch entirely repulsive. And even if you do, perhaps I can convince you of my more ... sensual qualities."

She looked into his eyes one last time, and his heart ached for her; he felt a deep, murderous rage that he'd not known in a very long time. And he wanted to unleash that venom against Ares for hurting his sweet, gentle Oracle. He had obviously manipulated her into coming to him to force some kind of entrapment that she didn't feel free to vocalize.

As she'd done earlier, he mouthed silent words, *You are my heart*, and the dull, broken pain in her eyes subsided a little. She answered with a slight bow, folding both hands over her own heart, letting him know that she felt every bit the same as he did.

"Go to your god," he snarled. "Tell him what I demand, Oracle."

With a quick wave of her pale arms, she vanished. And Leonidas hit his feet, already at a breaking run.


"What did that king intend with his words?" Ares had worked himself into a frenzy, pacing his throne room that had filled with morose darkness the moment the Oracle returned from her meeting with Leonidas. "Daphne, I heard the entire interchange, but I want to know what you *truly* said to the man. There was more going on."

He strode toward her, grabbing her arm in a vicious grip, and Daphne began to tremble. "Nothing. I said nothing that you didn't hear."

Although a god, her brother was not omniscient; he had availed himself of spying on her meeting with Leo, as she'd known he would, but he did not comprehend the nuances of what she'd communicated through her eyes and her touch.

"Liar."

"Brother, I speak the truth," she told him, but her voice cracked, betraying her fear.

"He honestly believes that I will give you to him in—what is it to be? Payment? Retribution for my own recent misdeeds?"

His grip tightened, became bruising in its strength, and she tried not to flinch. "You're hurting me, Ares."

"Good. For you, sister, have certainly wounded me. Such disloyalty and treason you display in aligning yourself with that pitiful king."

"I—I only relay what he told me, my lord. You know that it is only your bidding I do."

"No, I do not know that," he told her in a calculating tone, his shrewd eyes growing dark as a moonless night. "I think you wish only to rebel against me these days. You've told me so, often enough in recent times. There's just too much of your mother in you, isn't there, Daphne?"

Daphne pried at his fingers, trying to loosen them from her arm; then suddenly Ares released her. He marched to the far side of the room, his cape floating behind him. She fought the urge to hurl herself at him in a frenzy, to try to murder him for all the injustices he'd done to her, to Leonidas, to Ajax and River . . . to countless thousands of other nameless innocents throughout the ages. She was no match for him in strength, but she actually took a few fast steps toward him in her rage.

She stopped cold as her brother turned back to her. His facial expression had transformed into a mask of cool calculation, and this new temperament was reflected in the palace atmosphere.

"Well, then, our laconic king chooses his words oh so carefully, doesn't he? Very few words he speaks, but always with infinite meaning."

He gazed at her in mild regard, and she wasn't sure if he expected an answer or affirmation, so she kept quiet.

Ares laughed low. "Surely you would agree, Daphne. The shy, quiet man has even fewer words for you than the rest. You know this much by his own admission."

"He is quiet."

"His words are always purposed and, as if he aspires to be a god himself, those words are full of powerful meaning." Ares stroked his goatee, a faint smile forming on his lips. "My theory is obviously correct, which means that by demanding you for himself he knows how much I treasure you." He gave her a lascivious glance. "He is in fact making a declaration of war. That simpleton has stupidly, foolishly declared open war against me, the god of *all* wars."

She reached pleading hands out to him. "You don't know that, brother, not at all," she said. "You are only making assumptions. You have no basis for—"

"Silence." He raised a hand, furious fire shooting from his glowing fingertips.

She bowed her head obediently, fear for Leonidas and the Spartans almost choking her as the merciless god spoke again.

"If Leonidas wants war," he said, "then he shall have it. Until mighty Styx flows red with their blood and the blood of all those who aid him, he and his immortals shall certainly have it."

# Chapter 21

Emma couldn't sleep, not with the restless energy that thrummed through her coupled with the unfamiliar sounds throughout the house. So, these men were immortals; did that mean they didn't need to sleep? It could have been daytime based on the raucous voices downstairs, the heavy clamor that kept echoing up to the second floor.

She rolled onto her side in the bed, fluffed the down pillow under her head, cuddled another one close, but none of the physical comforts alleviated the deep swell of loneliness she felt inside. Where was River? It was as if she couldn't even sleep without holding him or knowing if he had remained out of that damn dagger. But Shay had never come back to give her a report on his condition; that commotion downstairs had started up almost as soon as she left Emma alone.

Emma sighed, rolled the other direction, and tried to get her serious brain buzz to quiet down. But she'd experienced too much in the past twenty-four hours to achieve peaceful silence. She sighed again, turning onto her back to stare at the ceiling, and then became resolved. Reaching over to the side table, she flicked on the light and began digging in her overnight bag for something to wear.

After dressing, she opened the bedroom door a few inches, peering out into the long hallway, which was lit only by a table lamp near the stairs. Where would River be? Maybe down with the others?

The last thing she wanted was to come off as desperate or needy with him. She'd always sworn that she'd never be one of those women who flung herself at a man, and not even a gorgeous immortal was going to make her change. Plus, what if he was only into her physically?

She stood in that doorway, listening for any sound of his voice, hating how much she longed for him when, really, she hadn't any proof that he returned her feelings. He'd said all sorts of sweet things to her, been out of his mind with desire, too. But was any of it real? As tired as she was, as surreal as the entire experience had become, the doubts found fertile ground within her heart.

*Guys don't respond to me like he has*, she thought, gripping the doorframe. *Not very often.* Pretty but not truly beautiful, that had been life's ringing endorsement of her appearance. River, on the other hand, was the stuff of women's fantasies brought to life, with his long golden brown hair, his mesmerizing catlike eyes, and that lean, long, chiseled physique. She'd never seen a man with such defined ab muscles in real life. Apparently it took finding an immortal Spartan dagger to see such a thing.

She shook her head, easing the door shut. She needed to wait right now, let Shay bring her news or see if River needed her help again.

That was the strong, self-respecting position. So why did it make her feel heartsick with worry for the vulnerable warrior?

Maybe what she needed was to go downstairs and figure out what all the banging around, full-throttle noises were. Obviously nobody else was sleeping, so why should she?

Emma padded down the stairs in the direction of the numerous voices coming from the dining room. She reached the first floor, and although her heart did a fast jig in her chest at the thought of trying to explain what had happened with River earlier, she held her chin high and walked into the dining room. Pausing on the edge of the room she struggled to gather her nerve and saw what was only one more world-rocking scene in her crazy day.

Evan Foster, best friend prior to that moment, was standing in her cousins' dining room with a peanut butter sandwich in his hand. His blond hair was mussed, and he was covered in grime, including some brackish substance that streaked down both arms. But that wasn't the cursable part of the whole thing. It was the way he was chattering with the whole lot of them, her cousins and the Spartans, as if he owned the place, standing there in . . . God, was that body armor? And was that an automatic rifle he had slung over his shoulder?

"Oh. My. God," she exclaimed, and every pair of eyes in the room looked in her direction. "Evan, you little fuck ball. I'm gonna kill you!"

Evan's own gray eyes grew wide and alarmed. "Shit, Mace, I thought you said she'd gone to bed."

"What?" Emma shrieked, rushing him. She slammed a fist against his chest. "You bastard! Don't you talk to them like I'm not here! You have fucking got to be kidding me." She sputtered, waving a hand up and down at his military garb. "You are not—I mean *not*—one of the Shades."

Evan's shoulders slumped and he dropped his weaponry to the dining room floor with a clatter. "Emma, give me a chance here," he tried in a placating tone that was not going to work.

She backed away, flattening herself against the wall. "No freaking way. You've been lying to me! For months at least, I'm guessing."

His eyes shifted slightly.

"Longer than that?" she squeaked, glancing around the room until her gaze locked with Shay's. One glance at her cousin told her the truth. "Oh, geez," she said in disgust. "I guess I'm just the stupidest, most gullible friend on earth." She glared at Evan, but he just dropped his head.

"You better look contrite."

Mason was the one to step forward. "Em, doll, look . . . I know this looks bad."

"Bad?" She shot daggers toward Evan, her *former* best friend, seething with fury, but he didn't look up. "*Bad*, Mason Angel, don't come close to covering this shit."

Mason reached for her arm, but she sidestepped out of his grasp. "Don't try to soothe me, Mace." She gestured furiously at Evan. "Nope, not when that *friend* of mine left me out there on the island. Not when demons *attacked* me after he *abandoned* me there to that storm."

Evan's head jerked up at her words, anguish in his usually warm, kind eyes, but she didn't stop. "And after I almost died while he was—just guessing here—off with y'all fighting demons. When he could have been protecting me. Me!"

"Emma, I would never have left you in danger, never," Evan told her fiercely, his eyes filled with obvious pain. "I am so sorry. So incredibly sorry. By the time I realized how late it had gotten, your mother had called me."

"Mama phoned you tonight?"

"Yes, and gave me an earful, trust me," he said in a low voice. "I wanted to come over right then, but she told me you were sleeping."

She sighed, but couldn't shake her feeling of bitter betrayal. "That doesn't cover the past. All those lies, lies, lies, all the time! How many dates have you stood me up on?"

Mason laughed a little. "They aren't dates, baby doll. He's gay, remember."

"I oughta hit you for that stupid joke."

Mason gave a grudging nod, but still grinned. "Emma, listen to me for a second, okay? You and I go way back. We've been really close, yeah?"

For the first moment since she'd walked in on Evan, she felt an emotion other than betrayal and fury: she ached inside. Why was Mason bringing all that up now? To remind her that she, too, had once let down people who were close to her?

"That was different. I didn't walk away from y'all because I didn't care," she whispered, biting her lip.

Mason's eyebrows lifted. "No, no, Em, that's not what I mean." He touched her arm very gently. "You and I are square about the past and all that. I just mean that you trust me. Don't you?"

She gave one firm nod of her head. "I'd trust you with anything, Mason. That never changed."

"Good, because that guy"—Mason pointed over at Evan, who now stood, back propped against the wall and staring at the floor—"that guy worships you. He was only trying to protect you."

"From what?" she blurted. "Geez, I'm not some frail southern blossom or something. I'm a strong, kick-ass woman."

Mason smiled much bigger this time. "I've seen that. You grew up on me, Em."

"What were you trying to protect me from, Evan?" she asked loudly. "What possible reason did you have for being in league with my cousins and lying about it?"

He pushed off the wall, walking slowly toward her. Mason stepped out of his way, but kept near her, sliding an arm over her shoulder, offering her a feeling of safety and support.

Evan stood in front of her, silent, and then finally looked into her eyes. "I knew how afraid you are of your own ability, Emma. When mine started coming out, I tried to tell you. Don't you remember?"

She shook her head. "I don't know what you're talking about. I have no memory of that at all."

"We were seventeen; you'd just gone to State with the swim team, and when you got back we went riding around. Just shooting the crap, and I told you two things that night. That I was gay—and that I saw demons sometimes."

She definitely remembered the big coming-out chat, and also that it hadn't been the newsflash Evan thought it would be. "I talked to you about being gay; that's all we discussed."

Mason's arm around her shoulder relaxed a little, and he shifted on his feet. "Evan remembers it . . . uh." He cleared his throat. "He recalls the conversation a little differently."

"You must've blocked out the rest." Evan extended his hand, palm up, seeking hers. Grudgingly she gave it to him, and he squeezed it. "Emma, when I told you about the demons, you got so upset I had to take you home. Your mother had to give you a sedative. She told me then that it was something you probably couldn't handle, at least not at the time."

Emma shook her head. "I . . . how can I not remember that?"

Mason pulled her a little closer in the crook of his arm. "Emma, we all know what pain you've had with using your ability. Because of . . . Leah." He whispered her twin's name as if he were afraid she might shatter at hearing it.

"You can say her name. Leah. I say it all the time, think it all the time, Mason." She turned to look into his eyes. "And I'm stronger now than I've been in a very long time." She glanced at Evan and back at Mason. "I don't want any of you trying to protect me anymore. I want to operate in this calling of mine, really use it for good."

Mason and Evan gaped at her. "Are you serious, Emma?" Evan asked. "What changed? You weren't ever gonna go down that road again."

She sighed. "River changed me." She thought of how she'd begun seeing the demons after she'd used his blade on herself. That was probably something she should come clean about, actually. "I mean, guys, he really did change me. When I used his dagger to draw my blood, well, the last time I did, I didn't just hear the demons anymore. I started seeing them."

Shay walked into the dining room right then and all but screeched to a stop. "You what?"

Jamie began grinning wildly. "She sees demons, Sissy Cat."

Shay walked closer, her eyes as wide and filled with excitement as Jamie's were. "But you've always been a listener. You're a medium. You don't share our demon-hunting bloodline, either."

Emma shook her head, toying self-consciously with the hem of her shirt. "I was telling them that it happened after I'd used River's dagger on myself several times. I went from hearing the demons to actually seeing them."

Shay nodded very slowly, eyes sweeping back and forth as she thought about the revelation. "That means it was something about how he healed the wound, then, I bet."

"It's something about River's own power," Mason added reflectively. "That in healing her, he must have opened her up somehow. Created a new ability? Or maybe just opened up her existing gift of hearing?"

"It might only be temporary," Jamie layered in. Emma felt like she might get a case of conversational whiplash as the entire crew volleyed theories and opinions, all their voices growing louder and vying for the floor.

Shay looked over at her after several long moments with a cringingly apologetic expression. "Guys, guys, guys."

She made a karate-chopping motion with her hands. "Chill out. You're starting to freak Emma and she's had enough going on today."

The three men turned toward her as if seeing her for the first time; she'd been that forgotten in the midst of their debate. Evan opened his arms, offering a hug, and after giving him a grudging expression, she accepted his embrace. She held him tight; well, as tight as she could with the body armor. She dragged in a deep breath, wanting that comforting, familiar scent of her best friend. Instead, an acrid, burning odor wafted into her nostrils.

"Eww! Evan, what's that horrible smell all over you?"

"What smell?" he asked, releasing her, and Emma started rubbing her nose.

"It's just awful. It's making my nose burn because I inhaled it." Suddenly Emma realized that the hunters were all staring at her, that eager curiosity reignited in their eyes.

"Great. You're about to tell me that I've got some gift of supernatural smelling. . . ." She saw the answer in Shay's barely suppressed smile. "No, wait, don't tell me. Two demented abilities are enough; I don't want a third." She rubbed her nose again, hating the stink that still stung her nostrils and made her feel nauseous.

Mason slid a hand on her shoulder. "Look at it this way, Em. Really, it could be temporary. All but your natural gift; we don't know what impact River had on you."

Shay disagreed. "I've never heard the boys talk about River changing people when he heals them. Heck, he healed me, remember? Jax used his sword on me when Sable had tried turning me to stone and he brought me back to life. I didn't get any new gifts from that . . . well, none that weren't already mine anyway."

Emma became aware that Jamie was staring at her even harder than he'd been before. "Uh, Shay," he said, gaze still riveted on Emma. "Maybe it's because of the Daughters—"

Shay shut him down. "Not that. Nope. No."

"But, Shay," Jamie started again, and once again Shay cut him off.

"You know what Emma needs?" Shay said, linking elbows with her. "To get some sleep." The words sounded pointed, and Emma knew that Jamie had been about to reveal one more freaky piece of the overall picture.

She'd have demanded to know more, except a deafening, high-pitched squeal filled her ears and her mind. It was blinding, and brought an immediate blast of pain clamping atop her head.

She moaned slightly, planting a palm on the wall to keep from doubling over. Behind her she was aware of the others asking if she was all right, what had happened, but she could barely hear them over the intense, blinding noise.

The horrific sound grew louder until Emma screamed at the pain exploding through her mind. "Don't ... you ... Don't you hear it? Oh my God, that horrible sound. And there's ... cackling." She heard squeals that, while not exactly like those of the water demons, were familiar enough.

Wide-eyed she turned to Shay, grabbing her arm, but she couldn't find her voice. She could only feel the world careening from underneath her, the piercing, cruel demon calls in her mind. By force of will, she finally cried out, "Demons! There are demons outside!"

And as if in perfect choreography, the four hunters moved as one, rolling into action.

# Chapter 22

W hen Leonidas arrived at the Angels' plantation, ready to warn his Spartans and the Shades that he'd called Ares to battle, their first skirmish was already beginning, the property under siege from a demonic scouting party. Good thing, he thought, that he'd brought the other immortals with him, because Ares hadn't wasted any time setting a demonic assault upon them. Kalias and Straton had shifted into winged form along with him, the three of them moving with supernatural speed through air and shifting dimensions.

It had been less than fifteen minutes before they had landed at the edge of the Angels' drive, but enough time, obviously, for Ares to mount his first wave of attack. They'd trounced those minions, tearing them to pieces in moments, and now awaited the next wave.

Leonidas used his forearm to wipe a smear of black demon blood away from his eyes. The thick substance covered his face and chest, residue from the three leather-winged minions he'd decimated. His forces had spent the past ten minutes battling back a small surge of similar creatures, a band of middling demons whom Shay's brother identified as "low-country boil."

Leonidas had been confused until Shay explained that it was the name of a local culinary specialty, one with spicy shrimp, corn, potatoes, sausage, and onions, cooked in boiling water for many hours. He smiled, understanding the joke, the comparison to local demons being roasted in a fiery hell quite obvious.

Jamie colored in more details. "Yeah, we take their kind and peel 'em, boil 'em, and shuck 'em. Then we fry the rest of 'em up for Sunday lunch. That's how we roll down here, King Leonidas," the human told him proudly.

And from what the king had observed recently, Jamie Angel had a right to that pride. His Shades were a deadly force when it came to battling demonic entities, utilizing a full arsenal of weapons that, although very different from what the Spartans employed, were quite effective.

Jamie's team relied on a mixture of slick weaponry and spiritual warfare, their protection and power coming from the same source the Spartans had turned to recently, the Highest God. All other gods bowed before that One—*including Ares*, Leonidas thought, praying that the Highest would defend all of them in the coming dark days. He'd thrown down a gauntlet earlier with the message he gave the Oracle to take back to the war god.

Jamie Angel sputtered a few curses and then turned to face Leonidas. "Sir," he said, "what I'm sensing is that the spiritual walls are coming down all over this place. I'm talking really old wards that my ancestors erected. Incredibly powerful barriers that have stood against attacks without breaking for a very long time." Jamie looked into the darkness. "But I'm seeing gaping holes in the things now."

Leonidas nodded, reaching with his spiritual sight. He didn't like the confirmation he received. "Fissures are forming, yes. Almost like a dam that's slowly shattering, and it's allowing evil to seep through."

Jamie and the king were crouched on the slope of land behind the house, the one that led to the river. It was a tactical choice because the shadows were thick here. Not that the demons' vision wouldn't pierce the night, but they were protected more adequately by the darkness down here. The front side of the house was bathed in moonlight that didn't reach the back hill.

More important, they could take to the shallow creek water that grew high with marsh grass and that would allow for stealthy maneuvering during battle. The group of them huddled low, weapons ready. The humans with their twenty-first century automatics, the Spartans with their old-school, supernaturally upgraded shields, swords, and spears.

Mason and Nikos held the front perimeter, watching

over Emma and River—if that warrior even needed protection. Leonidas hoped that although his current condition was unstable, he could still act on Emma's behalf if
necessary.

Jamie shifted on his haunches, moving closer toward
Leonidas. He kept his voice low. "But why would our
protections suddenly fail like this?" He cast a worried
glance toward Shay. "My family has been safe here for
generations."

Leonidas nodded, studying the landscape, listening with
his supernatural hearing. In the distance the keening howl
of a demon rent the night. Tightening his grip on his spear,
he answered without looking at the mortal. "It's not an attack on your clan, James. It's aimed directly at me, at all of us
Spartans. You're just caught in the cross fire, I'm afraid."

A solid hand came down on Leonidas's shoulder. "Sir,
with all respect," Jamie told him, "this isn't cross fire. This is
looking after our own. My sister is married to one of your
men. We're in this deal together."

Leonidas smiled, feeling the scar on his lip tighten. "I'll
remember you said that. I have a feeling I'm going to need
all the warriors I can get in the coming days."

He wondered if the human would feel so eager to volun-
teer if he understood that it wasn't just the powers of dark
aggression they would be battling, but the long, merciless
arm of Olympus itself.

She was terrified. The entire gang had rushed to arm
themselves, Ari, Nikos, and Ajax way ahead of them on
the way out the front door. Shay had at least turned back,
promising Emma that they'd protect her. Saying that the
property was almost always safe, but they had experienced
a few demon assaults recently.

Great, like that was supposed to make her feel better?
Especially with that horrible cacophony of demon noise
turning on and off in her head like a static-filled radio dial.
She sank onto the bottom stairstep right where they'd all
left her and, planting elbows on both knees, pressed fingertips into her ears. At the moment, she was managing to tune
out the piped-in hell music.

*Just work it like you did the spirit voices all these years, those persistent and naggy types who were harder to quiet. These demons are the same.*

The only problem with her effort at self-reassurance was she didn't believe a word of it. Not only that, although the exterior noises and shrieks were frightening, she was much more worried about something else. Someone else. River Kassandros.

She'd asked Ari about him as he pounded through the front door and he'd made an offhand comment about bondage. Just tossed that remark out while moving on to battle the forces of evil.

"He's a little tied up at the moment." He'd actually joked about it, then much more kindly added, "That was bad. Sorry. The guy's doing okay—a little embarrassed. You should go see him. Just don't loosen those bindings for now."

She sighed, dropping her hands away from her ears, and was pleasantly surprised that it seemed she'd won a battle of her own: subduing the aural assault, at least for now.

So if the demons had been silenced—perhaps even on the property's exterior—and if River was still in human form . . . why was she shaking all over?

She glanced up the stairs, yearning to go see River, but feeling that same knee-knocking fear every time she thought about it. There was no good reason for her to fear him. He'd been gentle with her earlier, or mostly so. And the moment he'd thought he was losing control he'd backed away, confined himself to Ari's care. Her heart beat heavily at the image of River up in that bedroom, bound in some manner, all because he . . .

*All because he what?* she wondered, trying to fill in the missing piece. But she knew. *All because he doesn't want to harm me.* After Nikos had helped her from that room, he'd obviously asked Ari to safeguard Emma from his berserker ways. She felt tears burn her eyes and had to blink several times in order to see clearly.

With the shame he already felt about his curse, it killed her to imagine how much more humiliating it had been to ask his best friend to manacle him. How much it must have cost him, too, and he wouldn't have been willing to do that if he didn't truly care about her.

She bounced to her feet and tore up the stairs to that bedroom door.

After two knocks she heard his husky, rough voice, and it sent a thrill of desire right through her. He was still real, still human. And, quite probably, still in a state of sexual heat.

She didn't hesitate and opened the door, easing inside. The lights were off in the room, so it took a moment for her vision to adjust, allowing her to see his prone form in that pie slice of light spilling in from the hallway.

"Emma, no, sweetheart. You've got to leave me for a while," he explained with what struck her as an amazing amount of kindness and patience. "I'm not safe for you."

She stepped farther inside the room and approached the bed, finally getting a view of how he was splayed atop the four-poster bed.

Her hand flew to her mouth. "You shouldn't have done this. River, no, this isn't right."

He growled in a long, extended rumble. "You must leave me!"

"So my friend is back, huh?"

Another long, roaring growl. "Which friend?"

"My berserker."

Now this apparently gave her fevered warrior pause. So, she'd discovered a tactic for dealing with his crazed mind and body: Make a stupid joke that barely makes sense and he'd back down a few seconds. Sort of like those FBI shows where they screamed things like, "Doughnuts! Doughnuts! Hair spray!" while arresting criminals in order to confuse them.

River jerked against the mattress, his back arching as if he could barely keep his body controlled. "Emma. Em." Her name was barely more than a pained plea, a heart-wrenching groan.

Her gaze snapped to the bindings on his hands and feet, which looked pretty tight and secure. Yeah, Ari had done his assigned job thoroughly. It didn't change the fact that seeing this brave, alluring man spread-eagled and mostly naked tore her to pieces.

"I want to free you."

"You're not listening, Emma. You're worse than me, not in your right mind. I am lethal as hell to you. Do you know what berserkers do? They rape, they kill, they lust for blood. To taste the tang of it on their tongue, swirling within their mouth, pouring down their gullets. They crave the feel of their bare hands on flesh and bone, ripping and destroying." He jackknifed, straining his hands and arms with a cry. "Set me free! Emma, I have to feel you, taste you."

Oh ... God. He'd unleashed his own berserker just by talking about it. She took a protective step backward as the bed frame made creaking, bending noises. He was going to rip the frame apart at any second.

"I'm going to mount you, Em, my body sliding atop yours. I'm going to thrust inside of you, take you. Hard. Maybe even rougher than that ... from behind, against a wall. ..." He sounded almost incoherent as he described a half dozen scenarios of increasing sexual intensity.

She could help him. Deep in her heart, that place that still vibrated with their blood-tie, she knew that she was the one. With a deep breath she took several steps closer until she stood by the bedside.

"River," she announced calmly, "I want you to look up at me." He mumbled to himself and she barked at him. "Now! Look at me, River! Into my face. Look."

He grew more subdued, blinking up at her in the half-light. He said nothing, his big chest just heaving at the air, sucking in gradually steadying breaths. She touched his right hand where it was bound against the headboard. "Shh, sweetheart," she soothed. "That's right. I'm here. I'm right here, and you're okay. See? You're back to yourself."

He nodded after a moment, swallowing visibly, and his eyes drifted shut. "You're the one, Em. I've never been calmed so easily before. Never."

She settled very gingerly along the edge of the mattress, slowly stroking a hand across his chest. Although it could have been an arousing gesture, she made it the sweetest and gentlest of caresses. "I told you that you'd never hurt me."

He nodded again, eyes shutting slowly. And she took another step of faith, reaching to untie his hands.

Ari scowled, wiping the oily waste of demon's blood from his eyes, but no matter how long he squinted, he couldn't square the current scene with any version of normal that he knew. In the past ten minutes, every manner of imaginable shit had erupted all over them.

The battle had started with pip-squeak-sized demons who'd squeezed through the wards, oozing venom and foulness. As soon as they'd decimated those fleas, a troop of leather-winged creeps had come marching down the front drive. Then a little crackpot minion had swiped in next, actually having the gall to land on Leonidas's shoulder. As if any shithead should try *that* with the king of all Spartans and immortals.

Yet all of that had been a fucking dress rehearsal compared to the unholy and heinous Djinn who'd just galloped into their midst. Ari cursed under his breath. *Sable.* On the Angels' property somehow, rearing up with those famous jeweled swords of his and thrashing his forelegs at the air that separated him from the group of them.

"I've come with a message." Sable dropped his forelegs back to the ground while still brandishing his swords.

Jamie fired on him right then, but of course ammunition didn't do jack against the demon. With his extremely fast reflexes, Sable raised his shield and deflected the incoming rounds. As good as Jamie was, his demon-fighting powers were pretty much useless in the face of a demon as strong as Sable.

"You want a piece of me, then?" Ari stepped forward with a growl, ready to take on the Djinn, demon to immortal.

Leonidas caught his arm. "Wait," the king said coolly. "See what he says."

Sable laughed dully, his scarred, ruined face twisting into a cruel mask. "Smart, king. No wonder they made a

few movies about you ... even if you did lose at the Hot
Gates."

Ari growled louder, straining to hold himself back from
the bastard who had once destroyed his brother Ajax's life.
And who had nearly ended River's life for good.

Sable noticed, his eyes flaring a blazing shade of red.
"But I'd keep your boy there on a leash, Leonidas. He seems
to have spent too much time with his friend ... that"—his
mouth twisted in distaste—"butter knife. Or is it a fork?"

"You know exactly how powerful River is, freak show,"
Ari shot back, taking a step forward, but this time Kalias
grabbed him by the back of the neck like he was a kitten,
for crap's sake.

"Pipe down, Ari," his ever-cool big brother cautioned,
hand still clamped along his nape.

"We wish to hear your message," Leonidas called to
Sable, shield firmly in place, their whole line intact.

The demon turned in a circle, apparently thinking he cut
a majestic and threatening figure. He was tall; Ari would
give the ugly centaur that.

"Ares makes a demand," he announced. "Of that
weapon-shifting slave. You're to surrender him two nights
hence, at sunset."

"For what purpose?" Leonidas replied.

"Ares needs no purpose!" Sable roared. "You swore an
oath to him, and this is a duty he requires of you. But as it
happens, have you forgotten that it's August? Do you no
longer recall the significance of the date?"

Ari knew instantly that Ares did, in fact, have the lot
of them pinned by their balls. Every August for the past
eternal years, they'd affirmed their vows to the deity. This
year was the very first, the only one, that they'd not already
been preparing to make offerings and show respect as a
matter of standard course. Because none of them believed
in the god's bargain anymore, or his word, for that matter.
By demanding this display of honor, and by requiring them
to give over River, he was calling their hand.

"Surrender the slave or face Ares' wrath," Sable said.
"Your choice. In two nights my legions and I will return to
this riverbank, and you will surrender River Kassandros.

You will do this out of fealty and loyalty to your god. And River will meet his fate, once again—and oh-so-poetically—by a river."

"We do not surrender any man," Leonidas announced, raising his shield ever so slightly. "Ever. We fight as one among the Spartans and Ares knows that fact."

"Is this the message you wish to return?" Sable trotted backward several steps, a leering expression on his wicked face. "That you dishonor your god?"

Aristos grew tense, and felt the same tension roll like a wave through their gathered corps. Through human and immortal alike. How Leonidas chose to answer would determine their fates. But he'd told them upon arrival that he'd already given an ultimatum of his own to the god, so this decision would only up those stakes. Make the path of their future more clear.

Their commander took several slow steps forward, leaving the protection of his warriors. "You may tell Ares that King Leonidas of Sparta does not ever make deals with the lives of his men. We stand as one in all things, whether our god has turned upon us or not."

# Chapter 23

Emma held the thick leather bands that had bound River's hands until moments before. She felt the rough texture between her fingertips while watching him take long, slow breaths. "That's it," she encouraged, scooting a little closer to him on the bed. The room was dark except for the hallway light that spilled across his features. So far, he appeared downright tranquil. She tossed the restraints onto the bedside table, feeling assured that he was out of the berserker danger zone.

*Bad idea,* she realized almost instantly as his eyes flipped open and his electric gaze hit her like a pair of high beams at midnight. Silver blazed from his eyes and at once his face was transformed into something sinister and threatening. She didn't dare move; not because she feared him or believed she might awaken his berserker any further, but because she didn't want him to sense any fear from her. The thought of how that impulse might set back their progress was almost more than she could take.

He stiffened against the mattress, his entire body suddenly rigid, and his back arching in reaction to whatever urges were awakening inside his body again. A rabid, plaintive growl rumbled forth from his chest and his left hand shot out, seizing her forearm without warning.

"I'm not afraid of you," she told him slowly, doing her level best not to wince at the tight manacle he'd formed around her arm. He ratcheted his hold tighter, a much deeper-sounding growl vibrating through his entire body. It wasn't a human sound at all, and for the first time since his violent streak had reemerged, she did feel a flicker of fear. But she wouldn't bow to it.

"Do you hear me, River Kassandros?" She kept her body perfectly still even as his wrenching grip on her tightened. "I am not afraid of this . . . part of you. So stop trying to scare me."

"You should . . . fear . . . me." He barely managed to force the words past his lips. With an anguished groan, he closed his eyes, wrestling the darkest part of the berserker's thrall. That conflict manifested physically as she felt his hand flex and tighten around her forearm, the pressure alternately easing up and clutching harder. Then he truly surprised her by sitting up and climbing off the bed with a calm, cautious demeanor. His eyes remained wild, but his body? Well, his body seemed focused intently on one very rational goal as he reached out and drew her flush against him. Was he under control? She couldn't be sure, but he no longer seemed ready to seize her against her will. He slid both arms around her, keeping her tight against him, and began to move his hips in a slight thrusting motion, moaning in pleasure as he did so.

One large palm clasped her lower back, urging her into the same rhythmic movement he'd established. God help her, but she felt her whole body react. Felt her panties grow damp as she fell under River's dark spell, joining her hips willingly in the rough, primitive gyrations he was establishing.

A soft moan escaped her lips and she pressed her face against his bare, smooth chest. "Oh, River," she told him softly. "You are so intense . . . and beautiful."

His teasing motion grew gentler right then, the way he touched her less desperate. His chest, which had been dragging at air, suddenly fell into a more normal rise and fall, even as those longer, slower strokes of his hands along her buttocks, her back, her hips, grew more focused. The motions and his behavior shifted then, and he seemed much more aware of her actual presence in his arms. With a low groan, he buried his face against the top of her head.

"My Emma, my sweetness," he murmured. "I went a little wild, didn't I?" He actually laughed. She wanted to punch him—and she wanted to fall beneath his body and let him ravage her.

"Are you back for good?" she asked, not able to hide the uncertainty in her voice. "You're my River now, right?"

He nodded, pressing her close against his chest. She could feel his heart's fast beating, but sensed that it grew less frantic with every passing moment. "You calmed me. Again. It just took a few moments."

"I shouldn't have untied you, huh?"

"Well, that depends." He released her, backing up a few feet until he leaned against the dresser.

"On?" She watched him, unable to keep from smiling in her pure joy at seeing the return of the man she cared about.

"Whether or not you like the feel of my hips grinding into yours," he said, watching her languidly. "Or the sensation of my hands all over your body."

Heat hit her face hard. "You jerk of a berserker. No, new name for you. As of right now. You're my jerkserker."

He began shaking with laughter and nuzzled her closer against his chest. "Come here, Emma. Let me hold you. I will drink in so much of your calming effect this time, the beast won't come back again."

River had asked her to wait for him in Aunt Joanna's bedroom. He wanted time to be absolutely certain that the berserker was at bay. Once he was, he told her without so much as blinking, he planned to come to her and woo her. To make love to her for a very long time.

He'd now fulfilled that promise, a soft knock sounding from the other side of the bedroom door. She drew in a deep breath and told him to enter, but kept her eyes closed, almost afraid to see what state of mind he was in. She heard his footsteps on the carpet, then felt the mattress bow beneath his heavy body.

"You going to look at me, Emma? Or did I scare you off last time?"

The bed rolled a little beneath her, and she finally opened one eye for a hesitant peek. He lay on his back, arms folded beneath his head, looking wonderfully calm and collected. And he was clothed, wearing a soft black T-shirt and faded jeans. Oh-kay. This was different.

She'd been helpless when he was in his ancient garb, had swooned and begged when he was naked. But blue jeans and bare feet and more than six feet and several inches of him right next to her and so relaxed?

She opened both eyes, and turned toward him. "You look . . . different."

"Clothed, you mean?" He rolled to his side with a lazy, relaxed yawn. "Or perhaps the less crazed version of me is a new one for you?"

She swallowed. "Jeans. Nice." It came out like some grunted tribal greeting, and a slow, satisfied smile spread across his features.

"Emma. Beautiful," he returned, sliding one large tanned palm around her waist. "Sweetest thing in my world."

"I keep thinking that if I breathe you're gonna vanish on me again. Or . . ."

He shook his head. "I'm under control." His smile grew a little wicked. "Well, mostly. I'll stay if you're okay with that."

She swallowed again, bobbing her head vigorously. He released a quiet laugh at the eagerness of her reaction. "And here I was thinking you might run screaming the minute I came to you."

"Uh, yeah, more like screaming to get you to finish what you started," she blurted. "You can be quite the tease, you know. Get a girl ready, willing, able and then poof! No delivery. I'm thinking I should spank you for that."

"Spanking." He rubbed his jaw as if considering the idea. "Perhaps, although not yet. I'm a much bigger fan of the rubbing and stroking and nibbling side of payback."

"More a carrot than the stick kind of fellow, are you?"

"Sweet love, what I have for you is neither carrot nor stick," he drawled, tightening his arm around her waist, tugging her closer. "But then again, you're already aware of that fact. Extremely well aware."

A sexual thrill shot to her core, causing a sweep of pure heat to rush through her entire body.

He gazed up at her for a long moment, his green-gold eyes more clear and focused than she'd ever seen them. The swirling threat of silver from earlier was gone from his gaze, replaced by this vibrant, natural color. His eyes were so exotic and beautiful; they were downright breathtaking.

*Yeah, that's why I can't breathe. It's all about the man's eyes. Not the cowboy-gorgeous way he's lazing beside me or the way he's looking at me.*

And how had she missed his golden eyelashes before? The way he was looking up at her through them at the moment—not to mention how thick and long those lashes were—should have been flat-out illegal. He lowered them slightly then, giving her an even better look at their rare golden shade. Surprisingly, his eyelashes were a lighter shade than his golden brown hair.

She reached down and ran her fingers through that long and tangled hair. It was still disheveled, but not nearly as much as it had been every other time she'd been with him. He'd cleaned up somehow, just as he'd grabbed hold of clothing before coming to her now.

She brushed fingertips over his cheek, feeling the light beard stubble. "You're dressed and, damn, but you almost look like you had a shower."

"Almost?" He raised both eyebrows in question. "Well then, I guess I didn't completely achieve my desired impact."

"Which was?"

"Clean, combed, and gentlemanly." He gave her an almost shy grin. "I tried hard to arrive with everything neat and intact."

"Naked was okay," she admitted quietly, loving how his eyes flared at her remark. "And definitely neat and intact."

He propped an elbow under his head, adjusting to look at her. "You like the jeans, though. I see it in your eyes."

"It's the bare feet, actually," she confessed. "They've totally done me in. Well, that's part of it."

"And the other?" He blinked up at her, innocent curiosity in those striking eyes.

"You're beautiful," she confessed on a breath. "It's almost sinful how beautiful you are."

He beamed beneath that praise, edging her closer. She still sat facing him, knees pressing into his left thigh, but his gaze traveled between them and she could practically hear him trying to figure a way to get her down on her back.

"You're not exactly where I want you," he said softly. "But with the way I stormed at you earlier, perhaps it's for the best just now. You can see that I have a more mannerly side."

He rolled a little closer to her, a long section of hair falling across his eyes, and she reached to brush it away. She needed to see him, to have that connection between them that only really came with looking into his eyes. So much between them had been about their souls, their mental communication, and, yes, their bodies.

"Talking is really nice," she agreed, still stroking his hair. "We haven't exactly had much time for that."

A frown played across his face, his eyebrows drawing together. "I'm sorry about the berserker. Sorry for scaring you." He sounded grieved, ashamed, and her chest tightened.

"I told you it was okay. You're safe here with me," she assured him, pausing in the middle of stroking his hair. "I'm just curious why this last time was different."

He stared up at the ceiling for a moment. "I didn't want to lose you," he admitted hoarsely. "I couldn't show you that side of me again; I have so little control over it, but as I focused on you, thought about you, I was calmed. You centered me, Emma. You do . . . crazy things to me. You make me out of my mind with need, but you have the power to bring me back to myself, too."

She threaded her hands gently through one long section of his hair, shocked by how silky soft it felt, how lush. She was about to say as much when her fingers caught on a tangle and he winced.

"I'm sorry," she said, eyes widening. "Did that hurt?"

He smiled again. "Surprised me, that's all," he said as she cautiously extricated her fingers from his hair. "Then again, everything about you surprises me."

She rolled her eyes. "This from my dagger-boy sex fiend? I'm about as shocking as a Sunday afternoon compared to you, bub."

"When you live on the borders of eternity, Emma . . . when you spend your life fighting demons and protecting mortals, normal is the shocking thing. Don't you see that?

Your gentle steadiness, your rational calm in the face of my storm—it's the most arousing and erotic thing about you. And trust me; your hot, firm, downright gorgeous body has me enthralled. But it's you—you—that seized hold of my heart from the first moment."

He sat up slightly then, opening his arms to her. She swallowed hard, intensely aware of his muscular arm pulling her closer, urging her to lie right beside him. This collected and calm River actually terrified her far more than the frenzied, half-deranged one. It gave her less power, and him much greater command over her, body and soul.

He wrapped his arms around her, drawing her into his warm embrace. "Em, come lie with me. It doesn't have to be about sex, but I need you closer. Need to feel you up against me, to smell you . . ." He laughed a low, sexy rumble. "And, yes, making love would be the best way to accomplish all of that. But only if you want me as much as I want you."

River held his breath awaiting Emma's response. What if she didn't want him, not in the way that he did her? He'd blustered ahead, confessing so much in the past few minutes, and although she appeared to be aroused, her pupils large and dark, her nipples beading beneath that thin T-shirt . . . he was terrified. Why had he asked her so bluntly? The fact that she stared at him, slightly wide-eyed as if she were afraid of him again, it was like the worst demon assault that he'd ever experienced.

He closed his eyes, unable to face her possible rejection. As he braced for it, tried to think up some clever way to laugh it off, he felt the gentlest, most tender kiss brush his forehead.

"River," she murmured, "it's probably good that you have such a dense side."

He opened his eyes, and she was leaning down, her mouth so close and welcoming, her pale blue gaze filled with obvious desire. "Why's that good?" he asked.

She lowered closer, kissing him again, the quickest tease of her lips. "Because I hate to think how much more vulnerable I'd feel if you realized how gorgeous and sexy you are."

He couldn't help it; he actually purred upon hearing those words. He slid a hand behind her nape, pulling her closer.

"Yes," she added as he drew her down atop him, "I want you . . . I want you enough to beg you to make love to me."

"No need to beg." He opened his mouth to her. "I just need you."

# Chapter 24

Emma was straddling his hips, that full mouth already swollen from the few kisses he'd given her. His hands were moving under her shirt, and his mind had moved much further along than that, filled with vivid ideas of what he planned to do with her. And for her.

"Uh, River, there's something you should know."

A dim part of his mind understood that she had something to tell him, but the most blazing, intense portion of his anatomy was raging onward. This moment was all about her, the two of them, and he wasn't about to be deterred, not this time.

At that thought, he slid a palm along the silken skin of her lower back, outlining her spine, feeling the indentations above each of her buttocks. Oh, by all the gods, yes! He lifted his hips, shifting them so that his groin pressed upward and his erection nestled between her legs, and all the while he kissed her deeply. Using his body and mouth to pour out every emotion hidden in his heart. Love. Need. Freedom. Want. And a thousand more that spun through his head.

"You're not paying attention." She arched her back in a way that made her breasts jut out even more, and caused his erection to punch upward within his pants.

"Surely you feel how attentive I am to all aspects of you, Em," he argued. "I am very, very rapt."

"You're making me crazy right now." She flushed just then, running a hand through her hair. The small gesture made her look shaky, on the verge of losing control with him.

"My intention precisely." He lifted her shirt, peeking under, then raised it higher and craned his neck so he could get a better view. A pair of luscious, creamy breasts was his reward, and they weren't even bound by a bra or other lingerie. He reached out his hand and tested the weight of the right one, loving the way it filled his palm, forming so gently into his grasp. Gods, but he loved the way her nipples puckered with desire for him, and their budding texture was the best he'd ever felt or seen.

"River, listen to me."

He sighed and closed his eyes as his fingertips grazed over that nipple. "Your nipple loves me," he said. "I'm listening to *it* right now."

She slid her own hand up over his and forced his thumb's motion to stop. "No more," she told him in a stern voice. "You're on suspension for a moment."

"Sounds like you're back on that spanking idea." He nudged her hand off of his for a second, resuming his careful exploration of that tight little nipple. "Threats like that only motivate me to be a very bad boy."

She arched backward, ducking out of his reach. "You're still totally high."

"High?" He lifted off the pillow, tracking her motion, not willing to be thwarted. "I'm right here."

"High! Stoned. Flying out of your mind," she said, eyes growing wide.

He gave his head a slight shake, dimly thinking that he'd not even shown her his wings. "Not flying. Right here, right now."

While he did have a roaring little buzz floating all through his system, he knew that she was the cause of it all. He'd never been so happy before, felt so desired, or so damned ready to just be with a woman.

He made a purring, sexual sound and then in one graceful movement, he pounced. Rolling her before she'd realized he was in motion.

She lay pinned beneath him, breathless, her pupils dilated with heated arousal. As he lowered to kiss her once again, undaunted and aching, she stopped him. She clamped one hand over his mouth. "Stop."

He frowned, trying to reply, but she kept that hand in place, not letting him speak.

"Look, I should've mentioned this earlier, but just so you know, Shay told me that there was some sort of demonic problem outside the house. All of them went out to deal with it, but just in case—in case we get invaded or whatever—I wanted you to know. Okay? Done."

Immediately his amorous haze was shattered, his entire body drawing tighter than any bow he ever used. He stiffened atop her, arching his back and listening. Whipping his head toward the window, he heightened his sight, needing to know the threat.

"I guess I should've told you right away," she was saying, but he held his hand up, and shook his head to silence her. The burn began in his belly right then, that alert, violent burn in him that he always got when he sensed Ajax needing him. It had been months since he'd felt his master's summoning pull, but the familiar need was undeniable. He couldn't help answering, as if it had only been days, moments.

He lifted into a push-up, then, with a last glance at his sweet love, bent down and brushed a fast kiss across her lips. "I have to make sure I'm not required," he said, searching her face to be sure that she understood. In her pale eyes he felt the same throbbing frustration that hammered his own body. "I'm sorry. I don't want to go. You're what I want."

She forced a smile, stroking his cheek. "You're a warrior. I understand, baby."

*Baby.* She hadn't called him that yet. "For that, you're getting kissed again, and then much more soundly when I return."

"For what?"

"Baby." He rolled off of her and practically sighed the word. "Yeah, I like that one a lot."

"Baby," she repeated, trailing fingertips down his forearm as he moved away, "please be safe, and please, please, hurry back to me."

He didn't want to leave her; it made his chest feel hollow and dull. Not to mention the way his erection still strained inside his jeans. All his male parts were as unhappy with this turn of events as he was, but he still had his duty. Though he'd been unable to serve Ajax for these past months, if his master needed him now, he had no choice but to heed the call. Much as he hated leaving her, much as it brought out those ugly and resentful feelings about being owned by another, this was the pledge he was bound to honor. The one that he'd sworn on that long-ago day down in Hades.

*You're not thinking of duty, man*, he realized. *You're thinking of Emma. You're desperate to keep her safe.*

Then he knew that it wasn't really Ajax he worried about now, nor his fellow warriors, but Emma who had become his first priority. She was his protected, and soon—incredibly soon if he had any control over it—she would be his lover. And as soon after that as he could manage it, she would become even more. They were already blood-tied as it was, and for a man like him, that bond was as close as you came to having a true mate.

He crept to the adjoining sitting room, which had the only windows in the bedroom suite. Moving cautiously he edged up against the wall, standing between two windows where he wouldn't be spotted from below. Listening keenly to the outside, and lifting his nose into the air, he worked to perceive the atmosphere beyond the closed windows. His senses far exceeded a normal mortal's, and just getting close enough to the window enabled him to learn more about the demon activity.

There were some cackles out there, a few light roars, but they were distant. His own team and some of the human demon fighters were deployed in full force. He stood, silent and waiting, back flat to the wall, and reached inside himself, trying to sense if Ajax was about to reach for him or summon him.

He let his gaze move to Emma where she lay on the bed, and watched her as he listened. She stretched and stared at the ceiling as she waited. She reached one hand toward her breast, touching it quickly, then pulled down her T-shirt.

*She's remembering what my hand felt like there*, he thought hungrily. Just like me, she can't stand that I've left. . . .

He forced his attention back to the reality of the moment, to the sounds of possible battle outside and in the distance. After a long, quiet moment he realized that things seemed quiet enough. Besides, it was okay to let the others handle things for once. He'd served Ajax and the others for so long; it was only fair that tonight should be one occasion when he put his own needs first. Talk about a radical, outrageous change inside his slave's heart: that he could place himself, and now Emma, first of all.

Maybe not often, but at least for this one night. There would be many more eternal days to serve his master over the course of his life. But there would only be one first time to make love to this woman.

Emma was going to be his, in every way now. A few steps to where she waited on the bed, and they would fall into each other's arms. They would lie together, joining, moving. River watched her through narrowed eyes from his position by the window. The rough material of his jeans stretched tighter with his arousal. He reached down, adjusting himself slightly, and the feel of his erection beneath his hand called out endless memories of releasing himself so he wouldn't harm anyone he loved. His fingers closed over his cock through the denim, and for one moment, he gave a harsh stroke.

It was meant as a warning to the berserker that was still singing in his veins. A reminder of his dominance, and that he expected his rampaging side to behave in Emma's arms. With squeezing fingers he gave his cock another punishing touch, his eyes sliding shut in anticipation of Emma's hands roaming his body.

Although there remained a chance he might become unstable while they made love, he didn't think so. The violent, raging surges had quieted to the barest hum inside of him, and this was the longest he'd been able to reemerge from the dagger since Emma had found him. Still, he wasn't going to let down his guard against his own darker nature even for a moment. Emma was far too precious to him, and although he was calmer than he'd been with her yet, he wasn't going to leave room for his berserker to sneak an attack.

Yeah, not raping or attacking the woman you'd fallen in love with was probably a really good strategy.

He listened at the window for one last moment, reassured that the warriors outside were doing okay, and then moved back into the bedroom. It was time for him to claim Emma, to slide into her body, to feel her wet heat that would be swollen and eager for him. Beyond ready as he finally pushed inside, stretching her with his hard length.

A quiet roar built inside him at the thought, and he moved across the room.

"Is everything okay out there?"

He nodded, then leaped onto the bed, rolling her into his arms. "The battle's under control." His tone was husky and filled with seduction. "But we don't have to be. Not any longer."

With a growl he rolled her beneath his body. Emma moved her hands along his back, sweeping her hands in a circular motion, moving lower and lower. He tensed when she clasped his buttocks and squeezed.

"The jeans are totally hot, but not when I want you naked." She slid a hand into his back pocket. "Out of the pants, River. And the shirt, too, for that matter."

River's body jolted atop hers, a tidal wave of heat flowing through him at the words. No woman had ever commanded him physically. Not that he'd had many lovers over the years.

"You . . . you're telling me what you want."

She brushed his hair away from his eyes. "That's what women do these days, River."

"It's different. New. I like it."

"It's what modern women do," she explained, but then her hands tightened about his shoulders.

"I'm not exactly a modern man, though."

She seemed to catch his tone. Softly she asked, "Exactly how long has it been, River? I mean . . . physically. How long since you were with a woman?"

Gods, he didn't want her to know how pitiful his track record had been. He heard Ari's joking voice in his head. *Loser!*

He swallowed. "A while, Em," he told her vaguely. But he wanted her to know him, not be cagey just to protect his ego. "It's been a long time," he confessed. "I don't even know, Em . . . a hundred years? Probably longer."

She forced him up onto his elbows by shoving at his chest. He lifted, bracing his forearms so he could look into her eyes. Dreading the pity he might see there.

Instead, Emma's expression was radiant, beaming wide with joy. She laughed huskily. "Now that is one seriously long wait . . . which means we're going to have a great time tonight. You've had one heck of a dry season."

He tugged on her T-shirt, pulling the neckline low enough that he could trail a long, sweet kiss along her breastbone. "You smell like rain." His tongue lapped at her skin, tasting the particular sweetness of it. "Warm, summer rain in the afternoon, that's you."

He swallowed and slid a palm under her shirt. Feeling the scratch of his calluses against the creamy softness of her skin, he caressed his way from her right hip, scooping his hand up over her waist and then moving that flat palm under her shoulder.

She clasped his hips and urged him to lift. He obeyed, rising upward, and she slid deft hands between their abdomens, working at the button and fly on his jeans. As the pants fell slightly open, she peeled them back and began tugging on them with shaking hands.

He rose up onto his knees, stripping out of his shirt; she pushed his pants all the way down his thighs. Their respective items of clothing went flying into the air, tossed in every possible direction until he snuggled down between her open thighs with a happy groan of anticipation.

Emma opened wider, wanting to feel all that golden-hard skin of his body up against hers, no separation at all. As he pushed his lower body down against hers, resting between her open legs, she felt an electric sensation the moment the blunt head of his erection pressed and rubbed its way into her damp folds. For a moment, he pushed slightly against her opening, but then seemed to decide it was too soon, and repositioned himself.

She shook her head, reaching between them. "No, now. I'm so ready. Never more ready," she whimpered softly. "Don't make me wait any longer."

She didn't stop to deal with protection although ordinarily she would have. The guy had been celibate for a century so he wasn't carting around anything unpleasant. In terms of making babies, it wasn't that time of her cycle anyway. Besides, that thought made her a little giddy, and she wasn't sure if immortals could even procreate.

No, this was a right now, right time kind of moment, and she wasn't about to ruin the mood or put on the brakes. They'd already been derailed enough times as it was.

As she angled him in just the right way, he propped on his forearms, his head bent down so all that long wavy hair brushed against her face. The moment of penetration was seamless and breath-stealing. The pressure he started gave way to the sensation of being filled totally; she'd been so slicked and eager, he slid home with one strong push of his hips, driving into her deeply. He spread her wide, and she had to gasp at his size, at the sensation of accepting so much of him in one long thrust.

Her eyes watered slightly and she tightened her hands against his upper back, just trying to breathe. It was like being a virgin all over again. Not just because of how he sank into her, thick size and all, but because of all the strange, tender feelings that he'd caused in her heart.

"Are you okay? Was I too rough?" He stilled inside her for a moment and then lifted himself to look into her face. His eyes flared with protective concern, and she smiled at him reassuringly.

"Nothing about that was rough. You're so, so gentle."

"Okay. Okay," he said, but then turned his head to the side. "If I get to be too much . . . you know, if that harsh part of me shows up—"

She took hold of his face, forcing him to look at her. "River, I can handle you. Any part of what you bring, I'm in, okay?"

She could see he wasn't entirely convinced, and that wouldn't do. Not now; never again. So she decided that strong persuasive measures were in order, and angled her hips upward, taking him as deep as she could, and then wrapped both thighs about his lower back.

"Emma . . . oh, yeah, yeah. That's sweet as you are."

He started moving inside of her then, at first a restrained motion that built some friction. Back and forth they moved as one, no words spoken, no sound between them except the primal noise of desire. His hands were in her hair, tangling, seizing, and she reciprocated. Their bodies were turning and writhing in amazed appreciation, every touch a flurry of need, a fevered grasp.

River loved how it felt to be deep inside of her. Every time he lifted and sank back in again, that warm tightness surprised him anew, and it seemed he worked his way in just a little bit deeper.

Then he'd test the connection and drive her into even more of a frenzy by withdrawing to the edge of her opening and rubbing his cock against that sensitive flesh before sheathing himself fast and deep all over again. He loved the little cries of pleasure she made each time as if he were pushing her higher and higher on some great swing, stealing her breath and her fear, then sending her zooming back down to the earth.

It had been well more than a century since he'd come inside a woman. And how long had it been since he'd lain with a woman he actually loved? He wasn't sure that had ever been his portion. And given that fact, he felt his sacs grow tight and his body tense; he wouldn't be able to hold out long. Not this first time.

But he was determined to bring Emma to the edge and did everything in his power to restrain his burning, impending release. He was shaking with the need to fill her with his pulsing seed, to claim her by leaving that part of himself in her core.

*Take her now*, a demanding voice commanded inside his mind. He shivered, not wanting the presence of that bestial voice. *She is yours and you must take her.*

For a moment he stilled inside of her, terrified that he was losing himself in the wrong way. Not just in her tender, caring arms.

"Don't stop," she begged him, arching her head back into the pillow. "Not now, baby. Keep on . . ."

The darkness inside of him had no part here; it had no right to her at all. He pressed his eyes shut and buried himself deep within her again, still hearing the crescendo of need he'd lived with on his own for such a long time. It urged him harder, begged him just like she had.

He rocked his hips harder, letting loose of his tight control. Listened to her voice, her needs ... and was shocked like hell to discover that his inner voice wasn't taking control. He wasn't ravaging her, or hurting her. The voice lived inside him still, but it was being ... respectful. A gentleman. Loving her as much as he did.

In that moment he realized that he'd finally beaten the curse. Emma had soothed the monster inside of him. He'd not hurt her, or harmed her at all, and she was the perfect answer to all the restlessness in his soul, guiding him closer toward the release his full nature craved.

Suddenly Emma lifted up off the mattress slightly, clutching at his back, digging her fingers into his skin. She shouted and cried out, murmuring his name, her entire body clasping and releasing in waves. With that, the last of his tight restraints severed and he began thrusting into her with forceful, driving motions. Taking her totally, filling her with warm spasms of sublime release.

*I love you, Emma,* he murmured inside his head. *I love you more than I can even show you. But I'll find a way. I will find a way, sweetheart.*

# Chapter 25

Thank God it was morning because it sure had been one hell of a long night, Nikos thought, rubbing his weary eyes, and glancing out the window at the early daylight. They'd finally wrapped up that demon battle at around two a.m., and then he'd volunteered for patrol duty, not catching even five minutes of sleep. As an immortal he didn't require much, but even a few minutes helped a lot. During his youth, back in Sparta, he'd been able to sustain himself without sleep for days if need be, but sometimes he swore that at roughly twenty-five hundred years old, even his supernatural power didn't quite replace a few minutes in his own bed.

Now, meeting with Leonidas and Kalias about the recent breaks in the wards, he wished he were more on his game, less weary. They were in the upstairs library of Shay's house, the three of them analyzing the recent breaches at the compound and the plantation. Nikos made note of the data, listening and scribbling the details on a pad.

"So if we can create a schemata of the vulnerabilities," Kalias explained, looking toward their king, "then we might be able to detect a pattern. If there is one, that is."

Nikos listened, noting that this plan had Kalias's name all over it. It was emblematic of how the guy thought and always had, with order and precision, as if he lived life by neat design. Though he was Ajax and Ari's eldest brother, his personality was very different from theirs and he was definitely the most intense and logical of the three.

What was it these modern people called that way of thinking? Right brain? Left? Nikos was too tired to recall which one it was at the moment, but his own brain was wired similarly. He agreed that identifying and tracking the break-in points could, indeed, reveal their potential next points of vulnerability.

"Nikos, is your mapping ability geared to handling this sort of projection?" their commander asked, rising to his feet. "Can you process this information and then upload it for display on one of your grids?"

"Yes, my lord." Nikos was already reaching in his mind, delving for preexisting maps and considering the best way to attack the problem. "I'll need a computer first, though, so I can access the server back at the compound."

Kalias stood, too. "Let me go ask Shay about that," he said with a serious nod. "She already gave me use of her laptop this morning, and it's one of the latest, very fastest models. My sister-in-law does love her technology," he added with a half smile. "And I love that about her."

Leonidas clapped the warrior on the shoulder. "I wouldn't share that sentiment with your brother," he said, making his expression grave and stern. "You know how possessive he can be about her."

Kalias rolled his eyes. "I have no need for a female, least of all his," he said as the two men strode out of the room. "Isn't that right, Nikos? What would either one of us do with that sort of duty?"

Nikos forced a laugh, waving them on, but couldn't find his voice. He watched them leave the room, sitting perfectly still in the chair. Panicked, unsettled. Feeling as if he must be transparent to every one of the men whom he fought and lived with. They wouldn't judge him, not with how commonplace it had been for Spartan men to take male lovers back in their ancient days. The practice had even been encouraged as a source of bonding and unity within the ranks. Still, out of the seven immortals who served side by side, he was the only one who had carried such needs in his heart throughout eternity.

He stared toward the doorway where Kalias had been, his words still ringing hollowly in the air.

*No need for a female.* Nikos could agree fully with that statement, but for all the wrong reasons.

\* \* \*

River's eyes felt too heavy to open, his body relaxed and pleased, and even though he could hear the voices of his comrades out in the hall and throughout the house, he didn't want to rouse himself. Not with Emma's cheek resting against his chest and that warm hand of hers lying square upon his belly . . . extremely low down there. Just a few tempting inches from his morning salute, also known as his post-sleep erection.

Immortal or not, some bodily functions simply never changed, and waking up at full mast was one of them. The only difference was that he'd never once awakened with a lover in his arms, or even imagined what it would be like to be able to roll over and make love to someone he cared so deeply about as he did Emma.

He slipped fingers down to his cock, lightly rubbing the swollen head of it, then let it fall back against his right thigh. For a moment he'd considered waking Emma, guiding her hand just those few inches lower so he could reintroduce the two of them. As he glanced down at her, his cock twitched slightly in her direction, almost as if it were trying to reach her itself.

A tight ache filled his groin and he shifted his hips gently, trying not to wake Emma. But as soon as he moved, she stirred, and damn if her sweet palm didn't slide much lower, her fingers tangling lightly at the edge of his wiry pubic hair. All at once her hand tensed and she lifted her head to meet his eyes.

"Forget where you were?" he teased, keenly aware that she had not moved that palm of hers yet. "Or perhaps who you were with?"

She laughed and nuzzled her cheek against his chest again with a happy-sounding yawn. "I needed that."

He stroked a hand through her waving dark hair. "I assume you don't mean the past six hours of sleep," he said flirtatiously, "but waking to find me in your bed."

"Actually," she said with another yawn, "I meant waking to find my hand practically brushing your balls. So there."

Oh, gods, he'd been busted. He coughed, feeling his face flush.

"I—I didn't place it there, if that's what you were thinking."

She pressed herself up to a half-sitting position, staring down into his eyes for a long, sensual moment. With a lick of her lips, never breaking that stare, she moved her other hand all the way down, stroking his curling hairs, locating his sacs.

"Gentlemen first, right?" she asked, beginning to roll the heavy weight of his balls in her palm, squeezing and massaging until he pushed back into the pillow. Until he had to bite down and suppress the loud groans of pleasure that erotic touch elicited.

She didn't stop there, however, moving her small hand up the base of his cock, rubbing the long vein that pulsed on the underside of it. "But I can't ignore the senior gentleman, of course," she said throatily, "or he might become jealous."

"Whole package," he barely managed to say, his hips riding up off the mattress with her motions. "Oh . . . Em . . ."

She halted her slow, lengthy strokes for a moment, gazing down at him. "Should I stop?" He would have leaned over and nibbled her in punishment if only he could have moved at all.

In a tight voice, he begged, "Never!" His hips moved in rhythm with her gripping pressure, and he gloried in every touch.

With Emma establishing their motion, he rocked up and down, reveling in her pleasuring. She had control of him, and it felt . . . good. To be commanded by someone so gentle, and loving, who cared for him this deeply, oh, it was Elysium itself.

"You better . . ." He strained to speak, to talk at all. "Em, I'm going to . . . you better . . . oh fuck!" He screamed and felt a rolling, powerful intensity rip loose from his core. "*Fuck!* Emma . . ."

In warm, coating spasms his body released, his hips thrashing and thrusting until the tide rolled all the way out. Until he lay there with his chest rising heavily, feeling the sticky warmth of his seed on his abdomen and thigh.

"I wanted to get inside of you," he explained, struggling for breath. "Tried to stop . . . you."

Emma rubbed her hand low, spreading his thick seed between his legs. "But you deserved for me to pleasure you."

He had his eyes squeezed shut, but opened them slightly to look at her. She stared down at his body, focused on attending to him. Her eyes were narrowed, a rich flush in her cheeks, and as he felt her fingertips graze over his pubic bone, he realized that she was enthralled with him. Studying him like some work of art, inspecting the way every intimate part of him reacted to her touch.

He blinked, more moved by that worshipful notice than perhaps anything else she had ever done for him. She slid fingertips along the small trail of hair that led upward toward his belly button, and whispered, "You've had to take care of your own need so many times, just to keep from hurting those you love." She looked up at him then, her light blue eyes shining with unshed tears. "Haven't you? Always with your own hand."

He swallowed, humbled by the love he saw in her eyes, heard in her voice. "Yes, Emma."

She nodded as if resolved. "You're not alone anymore, River. You'll have me for as long as you want. And as long as you do? I'm the one who will always—always—pleasure you in any way that you want or need."

He was speechless, moved; his chest downright ached. He had wanted for her to take him in hand and stroke him, just as she'd done. But how had she possibly realized his yearning? Was this what it was, being in love, that you simply knew the heart and mind of your mate?

"I ... didn't dare ask," he told her softly. "But I woke with that thought in mind."

She looked up, meeting his gaze and smiled hugely at him. Absolutely radiantly. "I know."

"How?"

She slid up his body, curling against his side once again, and settled in with a sigh. Placing that warm, sweet palm atop his abdomen again, she leaned closer and kissed his right nipple, suckling it for a moment.

"Seriously," he asked again, "how did you know?"

She laughed. "I wasn't entirely asleep earlier, you know. I felt it when you touched yourself."

"Oh, damn" His face flushed even hotter. "I'm not used to waking with a woman in my arms. Better grow more polite."

"Actually, I liked knowing what you wanted." The words were slightly muffled as she worked her mouth against his nipple again. With a final, lingering suckle, she kissed his chest and laid her cheek there. "It's good to know what my guy desires because that helps me deliver it."

"I want to give you what you want, too, though." He rolled with her in his arms, pulling her near until they were facing and flush against each other.

She wrapped an arm about his neck, drawing him toward her for a kiss. "I never said we were finished this morning, Kassandros. We're just getting started."

It was well into midmorning by the time Emma felt any sort of motivation to leave River's arms. The man had done things between her legs and to her body that she'd actually never heard of before. She decided that creative lovemaking was greatly enhanced when your man had a very muscular, very strong physique. He could hold you at angles that allowed for deeper penetration, suspend you up against walls. The possibilities were obviously endless with River Kassandros, she thought with a dreamy stretch of her bare, sweaty body.

He'd fallen quiet in the past few moments, like her lying flat on his back. His arm was folded behind his head, and he seemed to have grown more serious and thoughtful now that they'd worn themselves out in sweet pleasure.

She didn't know what troubled him, but wondered if it could be the same thing on her mind. The truth was, she had been awake for a while this morning, and had wanted to stay there, snuggled close, so afraid that if she startled him or moved the wrong muscle, that his prison would consume him again.

Even in the night, whenever she woke, she'd wanted to weep in relief at the feel of his solid, warm body up against hers. At the earthy smell of him, at the light snoring sounds he made periodically just before he stirred.

Maybe he was thinking the same thing about her. Not

that she might vanish into a silver genie bottle, but that he might be forced to leave her.

She rubbed his chest in big sweeping circles, loving the smooth feeling of his warm velvet skin over the much harder muscle beneath. His eyes drifted shut in pleasure at her caresses, a slight smile on his lips—still real. Still here and physical with a steadily beating heart.

The question had to be asked; otherwise she was going to live in too much fear. Even if it upset him for a moment or made him worry about her, it still had to be asked.

"You think you're here to stay?" She wanted to fling herself atop him and hold him tight enough that he'd never leave. Wanted to know he wouldn't be sucked back into his prison. But she controlled the urge to do so.

His eyes fluttered open again, the thick lashes looking lazily beautiful. "I've passed out of the danger zone," he told her. "I'll become a weapon again, but only by choice and as needed by Ajax in battle."

Emma's relief was immense, and there was so much she wanted to tell him, but all she could seem to do was bob her head and smile down at him. "I'm so glad. So happy," she finally said, but something he'd said already had her slightly fearful again.

"You don't look quite as happy as I'd hoped," he said softly, studying her face.

"It's just . . . why does Ajax need you to be a weapon? I don't understand. And if you do change again, what if you become trapped? It could happen, and then . . ."

He lifted a hand to her cheek, rubbing his knuckles there tenderly. "Em, I'm a warrior. That's what I do. And a big part of that is what I'm able to become, the weapons I can transform into. Jax relies on me for that, and needs me. I'm his . . ." His hand stilled against her cheek, a frown forming on his face.

"His what?"

He opened his mouth, seeming ready to answer, but then hesitated.

"You're Ajax's *what*?" she pressed, needing to understand. Shay had intimated a special connection between them earlier.

"His weapon of choice," he said softly.

"Oh, what? Ajax isn't a big boy? He can't take up a normal, soulless sword or dagger? He has to use you?" She knew she sounded angry, but she didn't care because something that they were touching on here did make her livid on River's behalf.

"It's not Ajax's fault, Emma," he told her with an intense look into her eyes. "You cannot blame Ajax."

"You're a gorgeous weapon, trust me, I've seen that. But seems to me that he has plenty of others he can use so you can fight as a *man*. Not endanger your soul again like what you just went through."

"I don't have . . . There's not a choice," he said in a voice that was rough and thick.

"No choice? That's bullshit!"

"It's the truth." He seemed ready to tell her more, to explain what he truly meant.

"You're not telling me something here; there's got to be more."

"I have a duty as a warrior to protect mankind." He stared past her at something unseen, at some place in his mind. "I took a vow years ago, thousands ago, and Jax wields my weapon in his hand as a result. It's the way that it has always been."

"I'm sorry, I can't accept that." She shook her head, resenting Ajax and this requirement for River's service. "It doesn't seem fair to me, that he's going to ask that of you again, not when it almost killed you this last time."

"I have powers you don't understand yet . . . within my blade and the way I fight. When Jax wields me, he summons those skills."

"I know," she said softly. "I realize there's so much about you that I don't know. But I'm scared, River," she finally admitted, pressing her forehead up against his. "Scared that if Ajax calls on you to fight as a weapon, that next time, there won't be any way for you to come back."

"Sweet Em, I will always come back to you," he promised. "For as long as you want me, I will always return to you."

She wrapped both arms around him, clinging tight, and

told herself that he knew what he was doing. That he understood what he was.

The thing was, she'd have to learn to trust that promise of his.

River dozed, a strange dream state working at his mind. During the night his sleep had been so peaceful, his body fully sated and relaxed. Now as he danced along the edge of slumber, something darker tried to claim him.

He groaned slightly, rolling closer to Emma, but holding her against his side; the troubling half-dreams kept pulling him under. It was an unsettling sensation, one that reminded him too much of the dagger's ability to claim him against his will. His thoughts began drifting in disconnected fashion, a kaleidoscope of subconscious images dragging him under sleep's heavy cloak.

Suddenly he pictured Nikos's muscular, dark neck within his clawing hands as it had been the night before, saw how close he'd been to strangling his fellow warrior's life away. He'd lusted to smell death and blood, especially from that man.

All these long years and his so-called brother had treated him cruelly, had reminded River of his place on the outside of their circle. River had taken it without comment, but now enough suddenly felt like far more than enough.

*Nikos tried to take my life.*

Where had that thought come from?

It persisted. An image came to him. *Lit torches flooding the barn where River slept.* He'd been young, only fourteen. Her father was a Spartan officer. She'd only given him small tokens, smiled at him. But he'd been naïve, foolish . . . so very foolish to accept her innocent trinkets.

*Torches blazed, masked faces surrounded him. Swords were drawn, ringing in the fire and light.*

Then from the throng a voice emerged, one that he'd lived with for more than two thousand years. Nikos. That killing mob followed him, wanted his blood to flow like a river of Spartan crimson, to soak the hay and stones and manure of the barn that was his home. *They were dragging him, stripping him bare, hauling his kicking legs up between their bodies. The sound of sharpening blades rang through the night.*

Violence strangled River from the inside of his mind, silver painting over the dream imagery until he became terrified that he'd actually been reclaimed by the dagger while he slept.

He thought of Emma, ached for her. There had to be a way that he could break free of this nightmare, and go to her, stronger, saner.

*Focus on Emma. She is the key to your freedom.*

Seizing hold of her scent and image, River slammed awake with a terrified shout.

# Chapter 26

He should have been in a divine mood as he walked downstairs to the main floor of the Angel plantation. After all, he'd made love to Emma three times in a row; he'd loved and held her all night long. By all rights River should have been soaring to the heavens, but instead he felt . . . foul-tempered.

It had to be the result of that disturbed, odd dream he'd had about Nikos. It had left him in a piss-poor mood, had plagued him ever since he'd woken up. All because it raised one horrific possibility: that the berserker still simmered in his veins. That it was ready to roar to life again in some new and deceptive manner.

He reached the bottom of the stairs, raking a jittery hand through his damp hair, realizing that any moment he would be confronted with the Spartan brotherhood. Now would be the moment for all those welcome-home shouts and cheers that he'd yet to experience. Yet all he wanted was to turn around and sprint back up the stairs.

"And there he is." That voice. The one that had summoned him countless times, and that he'd long loved and followed. But now the sound of it felt like cold, deathly winter, made his bones grow brittle.

"River?" Ajax called to him again, his voice uncertain. "Are you going to look at me, friend?"

The warrior was behind him in the hallway, and he didn't even want to turn around or see him. Not that he had a choice; this was his master after all, the man who commanded him.

River pivoted slowly. "Jax," he said coolly, "good to see you."

Ajax's large dark eyes searched his face, and his black eyebrows knit into a sharp furrow. His master appeared more vulnerable than River had ever seen him in all their years together, so many questions in his expression. "Are you well?" Jax asked him, taking a small step closer. "You're feeling okay now?"

River shrugged indifferently. "I'm back. I guess that's what counts."

"What's that mean, old friend?"

"What do you think it means?" His tone was seething, his anger from all the months of drifting and imprisonment swamping him. Boiling over so that he couldn't hold it back. "Ajax, master of mine, you tell me what you think I mean."

Jax straightened his shoulders as if River had just slapped him. He said nothing. So River decided to do that work for both of them.

"I did everything in my power to protect you, and what did I get?" He stalked closer, the whisper of violence and fury buzzing through his body. "You didn't do jack to bring me back." He shook his head in disgust. "And you did nothing, absolutely nothing, to keep me out of that demon's hands when *I* couldn't help myself."

Ajax dropped his gaze to the floor, a genuinely pained expression on his long-familiar face. "I guess I deserve this."

River lunged toward his master, shoving him hard in his chest. "Damn right. Damn fucking right you do." He kept cursing, a long stream of ancient and more modern profanity streaming past his lips as his whole body became wracked with tremors.

Ajax's black eyes narrowed like closing shutters. "River, you're not yourself." He whipped his head around as if seeking backup.

"Don't look for Ari to help you here. You can answer yourself. Do I still have the bloodlust?" He shoved Ajax harder this time, fueled by the rush of violence in his soul. "Am I berserk?"

"You are not . . . yourself." In a quick maneuver, Ajax spun River back against his chest, but River countered and outmatched him.

He placed a wrestling choke hold on Jax, employing deathly force. "Nothing wrong with me at all, *master.*"

From the doorway, the voice of his nemesis spoke with chilling calm. "Let Ajax go."

"Fuck off, Nikos," River snarled, never looking at the approaching warrior. "You're next, so unless you want to move to the front of the line you better back the fuck off. Now."

Nikos moved in toward them, suddenly flashing a long blade. River felt Jax attempt to shake his head, but he had the Spartan held too tight.

"Oh, you want to take me on, Nikos?" River shouted at Nikos, staring at his weapon. "You ready to go another round with me?"

"Find Ari," Jax said hoarsely, the words an urgent, gasping sound. "He'll get through to him. It's not River, it's the curse."

Nikos didn't move, seemingly transfixed by River's berserk state. Everything played out as if in slow motion, fevered by the wickedness burgeoning inside of him.

"Go get Aristos. Now!" Jax shouted, and that command incensed River's berserker, hit the beast like boiling acid.

River growled low and long in the back of his throat, Jax still hooked close in his forearm. "Good gods, I'm not an animal in need of a keeper."

"Then don't act like one!" Nikos sprang on them both in a graceful, unexpected move.

River's dream about Nikos flooded his mind right then, that weird half-memory. River shoved Jax out of his grasp and lunged after Nikos. This time Jax held onto his arms, keeping him at bay . . . but just barely.

River strained to reach the Spartan who had insulted and belittled him for thousands of years. "You got some problem with me, Nikos?" River shouted, feeling the veins along his forehead pop out from his intense fury. "Why should I shock you right now? I'm what I've always been, you bastard. A cold-blooded, murdering fiend. Owned by a cold-blooded fiend of a master."

"Ajax is right." Nikos shook his head, eyes narrowing. "You're not yourself at all. Listen to what you're saying.

What you're doing. We're Spartans," he said. "We treat each other with respect."

Ajax loosened his hold on River slightly, just enough that River leaped free. "Oh, and that's a riot coming from you." River shoved his chest against Nikos's. "I'm not your equal. I learned that by your hand long ago. That I'm not like you, not a glorious, proud *Spartan*."

"Watch yourself, *Kassandra*." Nikos's cold eyes grew even colder.

River was just reaching to slam him against the wall, when he heard clamoring footsteps. Ari was catapulting down the stairs, heading right for them.

"Stay out of this, Ari," River cautioned preemptively, keeping his eyes trained on Nikos.

Ari forced his way between them. "Guys, cool it. Time-out for both of you." He eyed River hard, in that way he did whenever River came down from his berserker rush. "You and I are gonna talk, River man."

Then he flipped a glance toward Nikos. "And you, brother, are getting the hell out of here for a while. Head over to the compound, go to Starbucks, whatever." Ari shook his head and gazed at Nikos with a pained expression. "What did you do to get him going like this, Nik?"

"I didn't do shit. He just went off on Jax, then me." Nikos lifted both hands, stepping sideways and out of River's reach while Ari kept River held back.

"You've still got it coming from me, Spartan," River threatened viciously. "You've had it coming for centuries."

Nikos's dark eyes narrowed. "You can't take me on and win. You're a slave," he barked in a bitter tone. "It's all you'll ever be. A slave chained to his master . . . throughout eternity."

Nikos strode past him with a defiant air, leaving River and Ari alone in the great room. River let out a tensely held breath, watching him go. "Yeah, fucker," he muttered as the front door slammed. "I'm a slave, but not your slave."

A muffled cry caused River's head to snap toward the stairwell. His heart plummeted to his stomach at what he saw. Emma stood, bracing herself against the railing, blue eyes wide and filled with pain. Damn it, she'd undoubtedly heard at least some of that interchange; certainly the most important part. The one he'd been dishonest about when she'd asked him how he served Ajax. The deepest truth about what he truly was: a slave. At the sight of her, he no longer understood why he'd ever become so angry, felt calmer and soothed as if by magic.

Why had he lost control of his inner curse, his dark side, and with such venomous fury? He couldn't even remember. His head suddenly hurt with a throbbing pain, and he buried his face in both hands.

"Ari," he said with a low moan. "Make sure Jax is okay . . . gods, even Nikos."

He felt Ari's reassuring hand clasp his shoulder. "They're fine, but yeah, I'll go check."

He kept rubbing his eyes, his head pounding with that slicing pain. Emma was there and he knew she was waiting; that the moment he dropped his hands away from his face, he'd see shock in her expression. Doubt. Disgust.

"Emma, I'm sorry you heard all that." Slowly he lowered his hands.

"You . . . you told me that you were a slave to the dagger," she said, tears welling in her eyes. "To your weapon form."

A roiling wave of nausea shot through River. Could she truly be so repelled by what he was?

"Emma, let's go outside and talk," he tried, but she wrapped her arms about herself in protection.

It seemed that he was making a bloody mess of every relationship in his life. And now the only woman he'd ever loved was staring at him with pure revulsion in her eyes.

River had never felt more ashamed of what he was, of the invisible manacles that bound him, than he did right now. He dropped his head forward, staring at his bare feet, and for a moment saw them as they'd once been. Grimy, covered in dust and dirt from the fields. A slave's feet.

"I didn't want you to know," he admitted softly, too afraid to even lift his head and meet Emma's horrified gaze. "But it's true, Em. I was born a slave. I am a slave even now."

He waited, hoping to hear some sound or movement,

but there was only silence. At last he lifted his gaze, keeping his head lowered.

"Don't do that," she told him in a quavering voice. "Don't you dare do that. Not with me, River."

He kept his head bowed, wishing like Hades that he could take that pained, appalled sound out of her voice. "Do what?" he asked in a wavering voice of his own.

She was in front of him in a heartbeat. "Don't look at me like that . . . or not look at me at all. That body language, or whatever I should call it, just don't," she sputtered. "Bowing your head to me like you really are a slave!" She grabbed hold of his jaw, forcing him to straighten from the subservient posture that he'd adopted without even intending to do so.

"But it's the truth. I am a slave, Emma," he told her as she maintained an iron grip around his jaw. "I am Ajax's servant. That's why I'm his weapon."

Slowly she let her hand drop, and River turned away, too ashamed for her to see how her reaction devastated him.

"Do you think I care?" The words were shockingly quiet; in fact, he almost missed them.

"What?" He slowly turned toward her, daring to meet her gaze.

"I asked if you honestly, truly think I give a shit if you're Ajax's . . ."

"Slave," he finished for her. "I'm a helot slave. I was born one in Sparta and I have never, not once, lived as a free man," he said in a boiling, low tone. "Ares made sure of that fact."

"Again, how can you think that would matter to me? That it would change my feelings for you after everything we've shared?" she demanded, grabbing hold of his arm and squeezing it.

"Because it should." River dropped his head subserviently again, treating Emma as he would any female of Spartan lineage. She was highborn; he was her inferior. "It should matter in every way, Emma. I am not of your class."

Emma couldn't even find words. But standing in that foyer and watching River's inclined head, seeing the way his body shook and trembled from the reawakened berserker in his blood, she began to cry. Gushing, soul-breaking tears, not the suppressed few she'd shed since she'd met him.

"Emma, look at my hands." He lifted his head, extending his palms. "You see how calloused and weathered they are, and how sun-darkened my body is. Because I have been a servant from the day I was born. You? You are . . . amazing."

She let go of his arm, feeling torn and broken in the deepest part of her heart. "So I guess you did think it would matter. And that doesn't say much about your opinion of me."

He tried to reach for her, but Emma didn't want to feel his touch, and sidestepped him. "Don't," she told him icily.

The gaze he turned on her was heartbroken, devastated. "Emma, it wasn't you," he said in a ragged voice. "It was me. Me. I didn't want you to know; don't you *understand*?"

"Look, I'm going over to my house for a while. My mom's worried sick, I'm sure, and I've got her car," she said, trying to sound calm even though it was the last thing she felt. "And, no, River. No, I don't understand why you couldn't realize that I'd accept anything about you. Why you don't realize how much I love you already." She stared at the keys in her hand for a moment.

"Love me?" she heard him murmur. "You love me?"

"You could have told me anything," she said, "and I'd have accepted it. Anything, River."

"Then don't you know my heart now? Why I couldn't tell you this *one* thing?" he cried out, and when she looked up he had both hands over his heart, and his eyes were wild with emotion.

"Tell me now," she whispered, taking a step closer.

"Because I'm ashamed!" He gave a pained, broken cry. "I am so ashamed of what I am. That you"—he gestured toward her with a shaking hand—"you're from money and sophisticated and full of all the best things. Me? I'm nothing more than what I have always been and will ever be . . . a slave. The lowest of all castes."

"River, look, please . . ."

She tried to move toward him, but he took several more

steps backward, moving toward the stairs. Then, very slowly, very powerfully, he gave words to his pain. "I ... am ... *not worthy* of a woman like you." He turned on his heel, sprinted up the stairs.

And was gone from her sight.

For a moment she stood, stunned, unable to believe all that she'd just learned—and equally stunned that he'd kept something so important from her. Not that this whole servant concept mattered to her one bit. This was America, after all, and the twenty-first century, and although his world was obviously defined by such antiquated ideas, he wasn't a slave. Not a servant. Not really. Except in the way that he served as a protector—the duty she'd glimpsed in him out on the island as he'd given everything inside himself to fight off the demons that wanted her.

No, she didn't care if he was a servant or was tied in some ancient way to Ajax. But what did matter—what did hurt—was that he'd had a chance to tell her about it, the full truth, and he hadn't.

Good lord, she needed a break from the insanity, at least for an hour. She needed to get her mama's car back, and, basically, figure out that she hadn't lost her mind. She glanced around, thinking she should let Shay or someone else know that she was leaving, but she didn't have the emotional energy to deal with it right now. She started moving toward the door, fumbling with her purse and keys as she walked.

A strong hand caught hold of her arm. "Whoa, Emma, where you off to?" Ari asked, his voice kind and sympathetic. Way too sympathetic, which told her that he'd obviously heard at least part of her conversation with River.

She sighed, not wanting to get into the whole thing with River's best friend.

"I see." He made a low, clucking sound. "Running away then, are we?"

She shook her head. "Home. I'm going home."

"Sorry, doll, but I don't think so," he disagreed. "Not safe for you to take off right now."

"Oh, no, no, no. I am *so* going home now." She wrestled her arm out of his grasp, but as he released her, it sent her pocketbook crashing to the floor. She squatted low, wiping a hand over her eyes, scrambling to gather the spilled coins and lipstick and keys. "I have things I need to do today."

"You think that's what he needs?" Ari sank to his haunches beside her, scooping up her belongings and dropping them in her purse. "For you to take off, run away?"

"I didn't say I wasn't coming back," she snapped, closing her purse.

He lifted a skeptical eyebrow. "Really? Well, that's what he's gonna figure."

"He has no reason to reach that kind of conclusion, not after . . ." *After I told him I was in love with him, and basically swooned at his every touch.*

Ari wasn't on that page, however; how could he be? "After that particular fireworks display, Emma? If you do a runner, he's going to take it as proof of all that shit he just told you."

She stared at her purse, mind racing. "I love him, Ari. He knows it. If he reaches some absurd conclusion, then maybe we don't have the shot I thought we did."

"And if you don't get it, you might not be the girl I thought *you* were," he said, managing to look truly disappointed in her. That only frustrated, hurt, and pissed her off loads more.

"Aristos. Mafia man. Don't give me shit right now." She stood slowly to her feet. "He lied to me. I asked him and he did not trust me. And I really do need to run home; it won't take long, but I've got to come up with some kind of story for my mama before she reports me as missing to the police—figure out where my car is, and clear my head a while."

Ari rose to his feet, too, towering over her. "Come on, then." He started walking toward the hallway.

"What are you doing?"

"Going with you to your mother's," he explained, extending a hand. "I drive, though. You go shotgun."

"Not in my mama's Volvo."

"Yes. *Because* it's your mama's Volvo. I don't get a chance to be sporty very often." He flashed a big grin. "We'll talk about the rest on the way."

# Chapter 27

River hung his head guiltily, feeling sick. He'd railed at Ajax, torn into Nikos, who, although he clearly did have something to hide about that night in the past, had seemed rock solid in his assurances that he'd never meant River harm. Still, the questions hammered at his mind.

And none of that came close to how he'd hurt Emma. She was right, he'd been dishonest with her. He'd been given plenty of moments in their conversation to answer her questions about Ajax, but he'd taken none of them. How genuine and real could love be if you didn't even trust your partner with the most basic facts of your life and your soul?

He buried his face in both hands, waiting for Leonidas. The king had asked for a private meeting with him in the upstairs library, and River waited there now, a heavy feeling of dread eating away at him.

"Are you feeling all right?" Leonidas asked, entering the room. River looked up and watched as the commander closed the door, giving them privacy.

"Yes, my lord." He bowed his head. "Thank you, sir."

The king gave him a sturdy pat on the back. "It's good to see you again, young River. We have missed you a great deal."

River inclined his head farther, feeling even more like an ass. "Thank you, my lord."

"River, at ease."

That was Leonidas's way of telling them to stop bowing, especially River, who spent much more time genuflecting to their leader than the rest. It was an impossible habit to break; not only did he adore their king, but even all these years later he remained in utter awe of the man.

River lifted his head and Leonidas drew a chair up closer to River's so that they sat face-to-face. He settled back into it, folding his hands on his thigh. "I need to talk to you, River. And it's not an easy conversation to have, so forgive me if I move straight to my point."

River's heart sped fast. He was going to be reprimanded for speaking to Ajax with such disrespect, and perhaps for attacking Nikos. Both men were full Spartans, after all. He swallowed and gave a half nod.

"When we were attacked last night, Sable appeared on the property. He made a demand." The king regarded him for a moment, letting the revelation sink in.

"The place is warded, isn't it?" River asked. "I assumed that only minor minions attacked."

"We're trying to determine why the security perimeter is weakened, although I have a theory in mind about that." Leonidas paused for a moment. "That's not my chief concern at the moment, however. You are."

"Me?" Yes, he'd suspected that this conversation would involve his recent misdeeds. "My lord, I did not mean disrespect to Ajax, and not to make excuses, but the time in the weapon . . . it did things to my mind," he rambled, but stopped when he noticed a flicker of confusion in the commander's eyes. "Or with Nikos," he tried. "I wasn't truly intending to harm him. Well, I was at the time, but I wasn't in my right frame of mind, so forgive me—"

"River." Leonidas cut him off and raised a hand slightly.

"Yes, my lord?"

"I must admit, I have no idea what you are talking about."

River's shoulders dropped heavily. "I apologize for rambling."

"Please, let's slow down, and you tell me what's on your mind and what's happened. I think we have much to discuss right now."

"What about Sable? And what you asked me here to discuss?"

Leonidas planted hands on both knees. "I think," he said gently, "we'll work our way up to that."

\*       \*       \*

"Mama, I'm sorry, I wasn't trying to scare you," Emma told her mother yet again. "I was at Shay's; it's not a big deal."

"Since when isn't *that* a big deal?" Cecilia closed the front door to their house, and then walked toward the parlor, Emma and Ari following in her path. "Last I recall you haven't gone over to your cousins' house in nearly twenty years, so you'll need to work a lot harder than that, Emma Lowery."

"Mama, what is this, the Southern Inquisition?" Emma thought on her feet. "Shay wanted me to meet her new husband, and the time just got away from us."

Her mother eyed her oddly and then regarded Ari with even more suspicion, pushing her glasses down the bridge of her nose so she could study him. "Where did *you* fit into this plan?"

Emma forced some laughter. "It's crazy! Would you believe that he's friends with Shay's husband?" Brothers, friends, Spartans, she'd keep some details for later. "Who knew? Don't you just love small-town life?"

"Next thing you know it will turn out he's related to her new husband, won't it?" She glanced between the two of them pointedly before making a big production out of clearing her throat. "Aristos, you still seem familiar to me. And while Emma was missing—"

"Mama!" Emma disagreed vociferously. "I was not."

"While my daughter had vanished, and I didn't know where she was, leaving me to worry horribly ... I kept thinking about you, young man."

Ari shifted on his feet, a sheepish and slightly guilty expression on his face. "Yes, ma'am. I'm sorry you didn't know where she was." He cut his eyes at Emma. "I would have told her to *call* you if I'd *known* that."

Cecilia ushered both of them into the living room. "Please sit down; I have something to show you." She directed her words toward Ari. "My point was, while I worried and fussed over my daughter all morning long, I kept trying to understand why you seemed so familiar, Aristos."

"Mama, how long have you been awake?" Emma asked,

flopping onto the sofa. Her blanket and pillow were still there. "Be honest."

"It's almost ten thirty, Emma."

"You never wake up until at least eight."

"That doesn't mean I didn't worry about you," Cecilia told her, moving toward the large bureau of drawers that stood near the fireplace. "Once I made it downstairs I noticed that you weren't here on the sofa, of course," she said, opening one of the drawers. "So I called over to the carriage house, and I tried your cell. Then Sophie, my *good daughter*"—she narrowed her eyes at Emma—"told me you were over at Shay's. At that point I realized you'd absconded with my vehicle, and decided you must be in some kind of trouble."

"Why didn't you just call Shay?" Emma cried in exasperation as her mother riffled through that drawer as if searching for something.

"Well, darling, I did do that not long ago."

"So, in short," Emma said, "you were worried for, what? Twenty minutes?"

Her mother pivoted, clutching a large album in her arms. "Twenty very long minutes, Emma dear."

She padded on her bare feet toward Ari, and Emma got a better look at what she held in her arms. It was their oldest family photo album. "What are you doing, Mama?"

"I have something that Aristos is meant to see," she said mysteriously. "Doesn't concern you right now."

"You're mad at me." Emma sank back on the sofa, heaving a sigh.

"I am. A little bit," Cecilia answered in a light, musical voice. "Next time you head out in the middle of the night and take my car, please do me the courtesy of leaving a note. I raised you better than that." Then she sat down on the arm of the sofa beside Ari, flipping through the album. Emma wondered what on earth her mama was doing or trying to embroil the Spartan with.

"It's here, I'm sure of it," she said offhandedly.

"Ma'am?" Ari asked, and Emma couldn't help grinning at his ridiculously polite tone. This from a man who cursed routinely and was totally irreverent with nearly everyone in his life, at least from what she had seen so far.

"Yes, yes." Her mother's voice grew more animated as she stared down at one particular page. "She was right, it is here."

"*Who* was right?" Emma asked. "Mama, Ari doesn't even know you, so please don't make him think that we're weird."

Ari lifted an eyebrow toward Emma, making sure her mother didn't see.

"Take a look, Aristos," Cecilia said, sounding proud of herself. "On this page—it's right here."

Emma studied Ari's face as he hunched his large shoulders to lean down and stare at the album, figuring that he was going to be forced to indulge some whimsy of her mother's. Nothing could have prepared her for the way he visibly paled, bolting upright with wide, almost frightened eyes.

"I was right, wasn't I?" Cecilia asked, placing a gentle, reassuring hand on his arm.

Ari didn't answer at all; he sat there in shock, his big chest rising and falling as if he couldn't breathe well, and then after a very long moment, he bent back over the book and stared at whatever her mother had shown him.

"I knew that she hadn't misled me."

"I . . . I don't know . . ."

Her mother patted him again on the arm. "Don't be upset by this," she said softly. "It's not meant to frighten you."

He turned to Cecilia. "And you're not?"

"Afraid of *you*?" She laughed. "Lord, no, Aristos. I spend my whole life communing with the dead."

He stared at her for a long moment, but Emma couldn't see his face. Finally he said, "But I'm not dead. I'm not . . . like her."

"That's what I heard, and I don't need any more explanation."

Very slowly Ari nodded his head, and then her mother reached into the album and removed something. Handing it to him, she whispered soft words that Emma couldn't hear.

* * *

"Why does Nikos hate me, sir? I have heard you hint before, something about our fathers, or the past?" River asked, his throat tightening in long-standing pain. "He does not like me, and he never has."

Leonidas's expression became guarded. "Why are you bringing this up again now? It's been a long while since you asked me that question."

River's eyes drifted shut. "I need to know."

"He does not hate or despise you, River, and he never has. While you were missing, only Ari worked as tirelessly as he did in trying to find you. Nikos has never hated you."

"Then what was the history with our fathers that you once indicated?" he asked. "You know something, sir, but I don't know what it is."

"And you are frustrated that I won't betray the confidence?"

"Did Nikos tell you? Is that what you mean?"

The king leaned back in his chair, staring into his lap thoughtfully. When he looked up he gave River a sympathetic smile. "It is Nikos's story to tell, and when the time is right, he will do so."

River shook his head. "He'll never tell me anything. It's a losing proposition."

"I wouldn't be so sure. He's been a little more . . . open lately. With those around him, I've seen it. Give it time, and perhaps a relationship will grow."

A *relationship*? He didn't want a damned relationship with the cold-ass warrior. He wanted to know if Nikos hated him enough to have led a death squad against him back in Sparta. But he could never admit that to their king.

"Anything else on your mind?" the man asked him, closing that discussion, obviously.

They'd already talked about Ajax, and Leonidas had reassured him that Jax was well aware of his loyalty, and of his issues because of his shape-shifting.

River shook his head. "Nothing else, sir."

"Then you need to know what concerns me today, and it's not your place in our ranks. I wish it were as simple as our occasional struggles for unity." Leonidas heaved a very tired-sounding sigh. "Ares has demanded that we turn you over to him. Tomorrow night."

River could only stare in shock. "Wh-what?"

"Our relationship with the god is now severed, and this is his first play for power." The king's eyes grew hooded. "Our Oracle has been . . . stripped from us, as well. But now, we are told to give you over to the god tomorrow evening as a sign of our renewed pledge of fealty. That Sable will come to claim you and take you to the god."

River blinked, trying to imagine what fate the god had planned. And what possible worse fate was in store than what he'd already endured when he'd been lost in the water. Then he thought of Emma, and his heart clutched in his chest; he'd just found her, fallen in love with her, but now he'd be taken away and she would be lost to him.

"When?" he asked in a thick voice. "When will you hand me over, then? Tomorrow night at this deadline?"

For the first and only time since River had served his king, the man actually became angry with him, raising his voice. "River Kassandros," he said sternly, "do you believe I would ever turn on you, ever treat you cruelly like that? Do you think, possibly, that I wouldn't summon every force at my disposal to protect you? Defend you?"

River's eyes stung at the words, and he bowed his head. Humbled, affirmed, accepted. He had no words for his king. Nothing came to him at all.

"You are my own, young River. You are one of us, and we will defend you to the death," Leonidas vowed. He stood and faced River, and planted strong, firm hands on both of his shoulders. "You are my own," he repeated solemnly. "You are a Spartan as I am."

River kept his head lowered for a long time, unable to meet his king's gaze. Those words quietly singing in his mind, entering his soul, healing him.

At last he found his voice and gave a quiet reply. "And I am yours, my king," he said. "I am yours."

Ari's heart had actually stopped beating in his chest. At least he'd have laid big money on that fact, and he was very much a betting man. He held the small black-and-white image in the palm of his hand, squinting in order to get a better look.

It was Juliana, no mistaking that fact. And not only that, he stood beside her wearing that damned Victorian suit, the one with the vest and the buttons he'd been sure would pop off. But how would Emma's mother have known to give this to him, and how did she have this picture?

Not that he even cared at the moment. He was too enthralled by the faded image of the one woman he had ever, truly, and with all his heart, loved.

"How . . . why do you have this?" he finally managed to blurt. "I don't understand."

"That's Emma's great-great-aunt."

"Juliana."

"Yes!" Cecilia clapped her hands together. "And of course it is you, as well."

Beside him he heard Emma murmur something, but he couldn't even focus on the words. "I can't believe it," he muttered. "You've lived here? All this time? I mean, the family has?"

"Ari," Emma asked, her voice filled with amazement, "did you *know* her?"

"It was a very long time ago."

"I was told not to ask why you're here now," Cecilia said. "I am not to ask any questions, except there is one that I can't hold back . . . if you'll permit me, Aristos."

After a moment he nodded, gaze still locked on the photo.

"Did you love her?"

He rubbed a palm over his chest, wondering if his heart was beating still. He felt a heavy pounding and let his hand drop. "Yes," he admitted. His voice was barely recognizable, even to himself. Filled with unshed tears, a hundred years of regret and heartbreak. "Yes, I definitely loved her."

Cecilia bent closer to him, slid an arm about his neck. "That question," she said, "I *was* supposed to ask."

"Is it her?" He snapped his head up, looking hard into the woman's eyes. "Did she tell you this? Is it Juliana?"

Cecilia's expression grew guarded, maybe a little somber. "I don't know, Aristos. I'm not sure. It could be someone else from her life, another spirit who sensed you when you came to the house the other day. I'm never completely sure, and in this case, I wasn't told the spirit's name. But you were meant to have that photograph, and I was supposed to ask the question."

He nodded slowly, enthralled once again by the faded image in his hand. But for some reason, he felt compelled to say the words one more time.

"I loved Juliana with all that was in me. I never loved any other woman like that."

# Chapter 28

A ri paced back and forth in front of Emma's brownstone. Why the hell did this town believe so deeply in preserving history? In allowing their lovely buildings to stand for so many years? Here he was again, with fate landing him on this same doorstep; he, the only one of their brotherhood who'd ever done a tour of duty in this town before.

He turned and read the plaque mounted on the front of the place: BUILT FOR JULIANA TIADES, 1889. He knew from personal experience that her father, an iron magnate, had commissioned the four-story dwelling for his favorite daughter, a young spinster woman who'd planned to maintain her independence and fortune by never marrying. Not even when confronted with a mysterious—and charming, if he did say so himself—Greek man who did his level best to woo and claim her as his own. She'd not resisted his affections, but she had let herself die.

He stared up at the steps that led to the main entrance, that old familiar ache twisting in his gut. Time dissolved and once again the house was ablaze with golden candlelight, Chopin floating out from the parlor. The night air was heavy with the perfume of gardenias and expensive champagne. The front door stood open, two well-heeled gentlemen smoking cigars on the balcony overlooking the cobblestone street. Ari joined them, happy to breathe a bit. He'd felt cornered and overheated inside the crowded gathering. He'd come to the society party on a mission, but the two scoundrels he'd been pursuing weren't in attendance. He trotted down the marble steps, glad to inhale fresh air.

Suddenly, in the darkness, he heard lighter steps behind him. Spinning to see who followed, he discovered an auburn-haired beauty, dressed all in white, with a high collar that only served to accentuate her long, sculpted neck. The oak trees kept her in shadow despite the gaslights that blazed overhead.

"You followed me," Ari said, blunt as ever. He'd been struggling during those years with the flowing poetic language of the Victorian era. A tough task for a plainspoken Spartan like himself.

"I just want to know," she said softly, dipping her head low, "how it is that someone like you, sir, moves so easily in the physical realm?"

Then she glanced up at him, her pretensions of shyness melting away. A mischievous gleam shone in her eyes, the streetlight catching it as she moved out of the shadows.

He was nearly speechless. "What the blazes?" he finally sputtered, wiping his mouth with the back of his hand.

"Nor do you possess the fine manners of this age, sir." She stepped closer to him.

She was shorter than his six feet, five inches, yet quite tall for the era. Perhaps even five-foot-eight. She tilted her head upward, narrowing her catlike, eerie blue eyes. "I would say that you are far, indeed, from your own time."

She tapped a delicate finger against her chin, studying him as if he were a puzzle to be solved. "But not a ghost or spirit. Obviously quite solid." She swept her gaze up and down his form with a suggestiveness that no woman of society would ordinarily have dared. Her lovely, perceptive eyes gleamed with mischief. "Yes, *quite* solid, it seems."

"You, ma'am, are clearly a bedeviled spiritualist," he countered, stepping much closer. A slender waif of a society lady wasn't going to get anything over on him.

Then a slow, delicate smile curled the edges of her rosy-colored lips, and something about that look made him burst out laughing at the absurdity of battling such an elegant and beautiful woman.

"Well, milady, since you seem to take great pleasure in assessing my qualities"—he paused, giving a gallant half bow of respect—"I will accuse you of possessing a keen and challenging intellect. Further, I suspect you conceal a surplus of clever humor behind that sweet smile of yours."

In reaction, that smile became less coy and more genuine, and her eyes lit with amusement. "Well, sir, now you've displayed your most intriguing aspect . . . splendid taste and judgment."

He was lost to her then, already, and he hardly cared at all. Sliding a hand through his hooked arm, she guided him back inside the town house, taking floating, graceful steps that made it seem as if she weren't part of the physical world herself. She led the way up the marble steps to her front door.

The very one that had, oddly enough, been part of his finding River again. No wonder he was shaking down on the inside of his body even if his large hand, the one holding Juliana's faded photograph, wasn't trembling at all.

Emma walked down the front steps of her house, looking for Ari. He'd said he needed air after receiving that photograph of Juliana Tiades. *Talk about lost loves*, she thought, searching the sidewalk for her new friend. This situation was like the mother of all lost loves . . . and apparent heartbreak.

Once her mama had finished scolding her privately—and after Sophie had come in the room all but drooling over Ari—she'd told them that she better go check on the poor stunned man.

"He lives outside of time," Cecilia had whispered in her ear. "But you know that already, don't you?"

"Yes, Mama," she'd said in the most appeasing tone she could summon.

"He's tied in with Shay and her brothers somehow, isn't he? With the demon hunting?" her mother had persisted, walking her toward the front door.

Emma had only sighed and drawn her mother into a reassuring embrace. "I don't have time to talk about it right now, but I'm fine, Mama. Please don't worry so much."

Cecilia had held her an extra-long moment and then kissed her cheek. "You're grown now. I do know that. And you're beyond my control anymore, too. But just be careful, Emma, especially right now."

Emma wasn't sure what that meant, and almost asked

her mama for more, but her mother was already heading back into the parlor. "Go now," she called over her shoulder. "Go on and be safe."

She shivered, pretty sure that her exceptionally gifted mother somehow had already gotten wind of River and the true nature of her current situation. Still, with as famously overprotective as Cecilia Lowery was, then surely this new hands-off approach meant that things were going to work out okay. Didn't it?

"Hey, Mama!" she called out. "Can I keep your car for a few more days?"

"Of course." Cecilia sighed as if the heavy weight of motherhood bore down on her shoulders. "And Sophie and I will retrieve your VW from the beach."

Emma stood in the hallway watching her mother vanish from sight. "Hey, Mama!" she shouted. "In case I haven't said it lately, you're the bomb! Bomb and a half! Best mama ever!"

Cecilia's head had reappeared around the doorway, and instead of laughing as Emma expected, her expression was serious. Not fearful or frantic, just highly sober. "It's your time, Emma, darling. Much as I worried earlier, I've heard that truth now. You're strong; God made you that way, and never forget it. You can handle the harsh hurricane winds when they come, the fires when they burn," she stated seriously. "Your calling is now, so walk in it with power and grace."

Emma gaped, dumbfounded and not sure what the bizarre prognostications meant. She thought about following after her mother and asking for an explanation, yet some force or instinct told her to let those eerie words stand as they were. And to give her mother space that she needed, necessary room for letting go.

"I'm over here," Ari's accented voice called, jolting Emma back to the present moment. She'd been standing on the sidewalk at the base of the steps, staring at the salon across the street, lost in her thoughts.

She looked in the direction of his voice and discovered Ari on a bench beside Mrs. Wilkes' Boardinghouse. The usual long line of prospective diners was missing from the sidewalk, the tourists who normally started gathering by ten thirty every day, drinking lemonade and jonesing over the aroma of fried chicken that wafted from the old Savannah restaurant.

None of those milling folks was around right now because it was Saturday, Emma realized. That one small anchor to real life and schedules and mortality gave her pause. Had River ever even eaten fried chicken? Or collard greens? Those thoughts gave her pause, too. She'd fallen in love with him so fast, absurdly so, and given her body to him totally. She barely knew the man ... but then again, she knew him better than most in his life, of that she was certain.

She strolled to the cement bench where Ari sat hunched forward, still studying the photograph. Maybe she should give him more time and a little bit of space, she thought, but he glanced up and motioned his head, indicating the open spot beside him.

They sat in silence together for a while, and Emma kept watching the salon across the way. She had friends there, and her pal Casey had come home from New York for the summer and was working there part-time as well. If Casey caught her sitting here with a hunk like Ari? Well, there'd be no end to the grief she'd receive. Joni and Brenda would latch on to that gossip for sure even if it wasn't true.

She slid down slightly and hoped that the small-town gossip wheels weren't already cranking into overdrive.

"I should've figured that you might be related." Ari gestured with the picture, fanning it lightly toward her. "I mean, maybe not. It was such a crazy long shot, that the place had been in your family ever since." He shook his head. "Just like the woman, let me tell you, to freak me out like this."

"How did you know her? Meet her, I mean."

He released a low, sad-sounding laugh. "What were the chances, huh? A man like me, here in your town. But long before you were even a thought."

"You believe someone actually put any thought into me?" she teased, wanting to lighten his mood. His normally warm eyes were haunted, such melancholy pain in them.

"Oh, yeah, Emma, you're great," he agreed absently, staring at the picture again. "You've made my best friend a very happy man and that makes you my number-one gal. Since I don't have anyone of my own, guess I have to cheer on the happiness you two have found ... plus Ajax and Shay. Shit, all my peeps are finding love."

"Oh," she blurted, "I don't know if it's ... love."

But it was love, wasn't it? She'd told River that very thing earlier at the house. But hearing Ari say it aloud made her a little jittery, scared of how fast things were moving.

"I heard you tell River that you love him," he said plainly. "I didn't need to hear it, though, because from the moment I met you at the beach, every one of your actions said as much. You do love him, and he's crazy gone for you, too."

"It's all happening so fast." She shook her head, wishing that she didn't feel so off the grid. "It's real, I know it, but it's all so totally weird."

"It's weird to love someone like that?" Ari cocked his head back, studying her. "I'd say it's a goddamned miracle, Emma, and don't you forget it. You're blessed. River's needed you ..." He shook his head, frowning. "He's had a hard life, Em. Don't hold that shit against him from earlier, about not telling you he's a helot, all that."

"You love him, too."

He nodded, eyes growing distant. "Yeah. Yeah, we were always close. Grew up together."

"But he's Ajax's servant, not yours."

Ari brushed a long wisp of hair from his eyes. "He served my father; his whole family did. He's actually five years younger than me. Ajax is closer to him in age, but for some reason that kid just took to me. Followed me around everywhere when we were growing up. I went off to the Agoge—the military training school—when I was seven, but whenever I was home, he was my shadow. So I started teaching him stuff ... wrestling, drills, you name it. My father had a big soft spot for him, and tried his best to help, and eventually as we got older he joined us as a battle squire, serving my brothers and me."

Emma fought a mix of curiosity and the same indignant emotion she'd felt earlier when talking about Ajax's dependence on River's fighting skills. But she had to know more because it was like being offered a window into this huge part of her lover's life.

"Why didn't your father free him, if he cared about him so much? Why didn't Ajax?"

"My father died ten years before Thermopylae," he said simply. "At the battle of Marathon."

Emma's heart skipped at least two beats. "Okay, no. No, no, no. Your father died at *Marathon*?"

Ari gave her an odd look. "What's so strange about that?"

She snorted. "Don't go there, Ari. Just don't."

He got her meaning and laughed, too. "Yeah . . . yeah, so I was twenty-two then, Jax twenty-one . . . and River was seventeen, getting much stronger all the time. He had a ton of promise with the military side of things." He stopped talking, closing his eyes briefly. "I'd always figured my father would give River to me when he died. I hoped to find a way to free him, you know? But no matter how much my father tried to tell me it would leave him unprotected and in danger, I just couldn't hear it. So he'd arranged that River would go to Ajax's care."

"Oh, God," she breathed. "That . . . hurt. Didn't it?"

"You think?" He gave her an anguished look.

"Ajax wouldn't do it?"

He shook his head. "Ajax loved him like I did, and he's always had both feet on the ground . . . far more than me, I'm the first to admit. If River had been freed, he would have been a target for angry classists. Would have gone hungry, and life in Sparta was inextricably linked with the military, so where would his place have been? I was naïve and River didn't even want freedom then, not really."

He fell quiet, looking back at the faded photograph in his hands. She wasn't sure whether to speak or stay silent just like he was, and was about to suggest they hit the road, when he turned to her one last time.

"Emma, the sweetest kind of love sometimes happens very fast." He offered her the photograph, and Emma took it gingerly into her hands, chill bumps forming over her arms. Her great-great-aunt had been stunning, and even in the blurred image she could see that Juliana had very light blue eyes like Sophie's and her own. Also like Shay's and Aunt Joanna's and Cecilia's. How could something so rare, such a recessive gene trait, be *that* dominant?

Emma kept studying the image. "Wow, she was beautiful, Ari. She had such an ethereal, magical quality to her. And, man! Would you get a load of you, all trussed up and pretty in that suit."

He growled. "Hated that damned thing." But he looked far from unhappy as he complained. "She liked it, though," he added much more quietly. "Loved my sharp-looking duds."

"You made quite a striking couple."

He nodded, chewing on his lower lip. "The thing is, Emma? About you and River and how fast it all feels . . . when it's right, when the gods or the Highest God of all ordains a union, you know it. You know it fast as a heartbeat."

He took the photograph back into his big hands. "Don't question what you've got. Like I said, it's a damned miracle in my book."

Emma knew to trust what she already felt for River, the reality of it, and the way he'd already changed her. Her heart had opened since meeting him, and it was like coming awake for the first time in years.

"There you are!" Sophie came peeling down the steps with her corkscrew black curls wildly askew. They flew up from the sides of her head as she scrambled down the last of the steps. She all but screeched to a halt in front of Emma and Ari, clutching a book against her chest.

She stared big as life at Ari, extending the book toward Emma. "Mama said to give you this."

"Stop ogling," Emma muttered under her breath, low enough that Ari wouldn't hear her.

"All the fun is never mine." Sophie plopped down gracelessly on the edge of the bench beside Emma, squeezing and forcing her way onto the postage stamp–sized space.

"Like this. Big mystery journal to give *to you.*" Sophie drummed the book she'd been holding. "Big mystery message from Mama *to you.* Meanwhile nobody's telling me anything about what's going on."

Emma stared at the leather-bound volume curiously. "What is it and what did Mama say?"

Sophie tilted her chin up and stared straight ahead. "That you need this right now. Or you will soon."

"Says who?" Ari leaned around Emma so he could see Sophie.

"Not your girlfriend, Aristos, don't worry," Sophie said lightly, nudging Emma with the journal. "*Mama's* spirit guide. Apparently Shay already has a similar book."

"I've seen another one like it," he said just as cryptically. "Emma, your mother's right. I think you're going to need this right now."

# Chapter 29

River left the meeting with Leonidas feeling lighter, humbled—and desperate to talk to Emma. She'd gone off with Ari earlier, he knew that, and until he could see her and apologize for being dishonest, he wouldn't feel peace.

He headed toward the bedroom that they'd shared last night, hoping that maybe she'd returned and he'd find her there. When he opened the door and saw the empty bed with its rumpled sheets and blankets, and realized that she wasn't back, he felt a crushing sense of disappointment. It was possible that she wouldn't come back at all. He hadn't shown faith in her, and that fact had obviously hurt her deeply. So she might have decided never to return. He didn't think so, not based on what she'd said, but it wouldn't surprise him. The thought brought a crushing, heavy feeling over him; it seemed to fall over his shoulders as a physical weight.

He sank down on the edge of the bed, trying to gather his thoughts. Leonidas's meeting had left him wondering about Sable. How did the king plan to fight the Djinn tomorrow night? And what about Ares? Was there any way to actually combat a god? It seemed the world that they'd lived in for all these years was starting to crumble at its foundations. Right now, when he'd never wanted to remain a vital part of the world as much as he did now.

He raked a hand through his hair, thinking about all the revelations from Leonidas. He was lost in thought, staring into space, and that was probably why he didn't hear Emma come into the room. Suddenly, she was just there, in front of him, staring into his eyes.

"Have you been sitting here since I left?" She smiled slightly, but approached him as if he might bolt.

He stared up at her, feeling lost, and then did the only thing that made sense. He opened his arms wide to her, begging her forgiveness with his mournful gaze.

She flung herself into his embrace, burrowing her face against the top of his head. "I'm sorry," she said. "I'm sorry I hurt you and didn't try to understand."

*She* was sorry? He was the one who'd been dishonest, who hadn't trusted her. He should be apologizing to her. He pried her out of his arms, needing to look into her eyes.

He patted the spot beside him on the bed. "Em, sit down, okay?"

"I don't care, just so you know."

"Let's talk about this. I have a lot to say, and—"

She cut him off. "River, listen to me." Her eyes were bright with unshed tears. "I said, do you think I care? What or who you are? I've accepted that you're immortal, that you can become a shield or a dagger. I mean, next you'll probably tell me that you can become a sports car, any particular kind that I choose—or failing that, that you can heal my body, or step into my dreams."

"Yeah," he said, "there is that," breaking into a sheepish smile. For all the gods' sakes, why had he ever figured this one piece of his story would be such a big deal in light of the full picture?

Emma wiped her eyes, laughing. "Oh, I'm just getting started, baby." She opened her arms, wrapping them about him and nuzzling her face against his cheek. "There's your rowdy troop of fellow warriors," she continued, the words somewhat muffled, "the no-holds-barred testosterone levels around here . . . there's you talking in my head. On the whole, I'm thinking that you being at Ajax's service isn't really a deal-breaker for me. Nope, not at all, in fact."

"Thank you." He pressed his nose against her face, loving the fresh lavender scent of her silky, thick hair.

"What is an issue, though," she continued softly, "is you not telling me the truth. Not trusting me to handle anything you could toss at me."

"I should have told you. I'm sorry." River sighed, rubbing his thumbs up and down the elegant cords along her nape, wanting to soothe any upset that he'd caused her. "It's defined me for so long, though, what I am. And deep down, all I've ever wanted is to be a full Spartan."

Emma pulled back, staring up into his eyes. She had a ridiculously big smile on her face. "You know, sweetie, sometimes words are just empty vessels. It's the truth and the heart of things that really counts."

He frowned. "I'm not sure I follow."

"You are a full Spartan!" She pounded a light fist against his chest as if it were a gavel. "It's so obvious to me that you are totally part of this group of warriors, no distinctions. I'm sure it's even clearer to all of them."

He sighed, recalling the fight with Nik. "Well, obviously one of them would argue with you about that point."

"Nikos? Yeah, well, I heard most of what got said." She gave a shrug as if the thought wasn't even worthy of a moment's attention. "And as far as I'm concerned, Nikos's opinion doesn't count because he seems like a jerk, maybe an asshole. Am I right?"

"Those words definitely have application to this situation." River burst out laughing, and for the first time in the past day, that brutal edginess that had been chasing him eased up completely.

She leaned in to kiss him. "One thing I love about you . . . I can curse like a sailor and you won't ever mind. And that's only one of the many things I love."

"That's still such a shock to me."

"I told you before that I love you, and I meant it." She clasped his face within her palms, forcing him to look at her. "River, hear me say it. I love you. I really love you."

He'd wanted to believe her words earlier, but somehow his heart hadn't been able to fully accept that she could. It had been easier to pretend that he'd not heard what his heart hoped for. But now, looking into her pale eyes, he thought about how real and honest every moment between them had been. Every kiss, every touch, truly genuine.

"River?" Emma still searched his face, her eyes filled with vulnerable questions.

He bent forward and kissed her forehead. "I love you, too, Emma. I love you with my whole soul, my full heart."

She bobbed her head up and down eagerly. "I know."

He laughed at that. "I'm sure that you do. You know everything inside of me now. . . ."

"Actually," she confessed, "I heard you say it when we made love last night. I heard your voice in my head."

"That's kind of cheating," he teased, tilting his head so he could kiss her. "But I'll take it."

"I'll take you right back," she said as he covered her mouth with that kiss.

He wished they could linger in that simple moment, hating that he had to tell Emma what he'd learned from Leonidas. It would have been so easy to dream in her arms, lost in the fantasy that nothing sinister hunted them or would want to destroy them. He slid his hand along the back of her neck, kissing her harder, wanting to enter the center of her soul and being. And wishing he never had to give her anything to fear. Only there wasn't a choice.

He broke the kiss, wiping the back of his hand over his mouth; she looked back at him in surprise. Her dark eyebrows knit together slightly, a small furrow of confusion forming. "What is it?"

If he'd had the power, he would have rearranged the universe in order to choke back the words he was about to say, but they'd already talked about being truthful and open. *No choice*, he thought. *She's got to know.*

"I met with Leonidas while you were at your mother's," he said. "You need to know what he told me."

"I don't understand," Emma told him softly after he'd finished speaking. "Why would Ares demand *you*?" She gestured toward River, her brow crinkled in confusion. "I mean you as a person. You like you are now."

"I'm not worth it?" He laughed at her question, which could have so easily sounded insulting, but which he knew was spoken only out of concern.

"I'm not answering that question," she said. "I do believe that we made love no less than four times in the past day, and that should prove how valuable I think you are."

"Come here." He growled and pulled her back down beside him. He brushed a thick lock of hair away from her eyes, and looking into them, thought how very much like Shay's they were. "You have your cousin's eyes. Same shade. They're like jewels." He felt his groin tighten as he stared into them. "Absolutely breathtaking."

"My mama always said they were wise eyes." Emma looked up at the ceiling. "I never really knew what that meant, but I love that *you* love them."

He drew in a breath, knowing that they needed to discuss Sable's ultimatum. "Em, I need you to understand something. I'm not going to sit on the sidelines tomorrow night. When the attack comes from Sable and his crew, I have to be part of the battle."

She stiffened beside him. "Are you joking?"

"No. No, I'm not," he told her. "I'm very serious. My comrades are going to be under great threat, and Ajax will need me. . . ." He winced, knowing that the mention of his master could touch off more pain because of their earlier discussion. "I . . . I told you before that he relies on me, and now you know why."

"What does he need from your weapon self while fighting?" She looked into his eyes. "I'm not arguing or debating. I'm just genuinely curious."

River laughed softly, brushing a hand through his hair. "Long story, that. And we'll have time to talk about all of it, but the main thing is that there's special power in my blade." He glanced over at her and she was listening in rapt fascination. "Remember how I cut you on the island and it healed? Ares placed the power of life and death in my weapon form. It's more than being a sword. My capabilities are much greater than that."

She chewed on her lip, her dark eyebrows drawing together. "You really believe you should be in that fight, then. Even though this Sable Djinn is coming for you and has already shown that he'd love to kill you."

"The brotherhood is on the line for me, protecting me," he said, cupping her cheek. Hoping that she could understand why he would do something that, in her mind, must seem so frightening. "I have to do the same in exchange."

"Where will I be? Do I fight, uh, too?"

He wanted to burst out laughing at that sweet, charming, and totally adorable question. "No, sweet Em."

"Shay is my cousin and she's a demon hunter, so I'm not being totally moronic with that suggestion. And my mama gave me a book, something about me being a Daughter of Delphi."

"I'd sort of suspected that was the case. But no, you won't fight, at least not yet," he told her. "Maybe you *will* train with Shay, I'm not sure. But tomorrow night, you stay inside this place where you're safe."

She nodded, and then, seeming to think of something, rolled to kiss him. "Actually, that's any place where you're likely to be. But in this one instance, I'll stay out of the way."

Emma found Shay in the kitchen making a huge tray of sandwiches. She wasn't sure how to approach her about the very old, leather-bound journal she held against her chest, but Ari had said Shay would have explanations.

"Uh, Shay?"

Her cousin glanced over her shoulder, mayonnaise jar in her hand. "Hey, you. I'm making some lunch for the boys. What is it with us Southern women, huh? No matter how modern we are, no matter how empowered, we always wind up back in the kitchen."

"Food is a Southern woman's love language," Emma agreed.

Shay held out the tray of sandwiches toward her. "You want one?"

Emma didn't answer, but held up the book. "I wanted to talk about this."

Shay's pale eyes flared with recognition. "Oh, wow. You went to see your mama," she said. "And your mama wanted you to see something, too."

"You know what this is all about?" Emma waved the book again. She'd read over some of the pages on the drive back to the house, but there was so much to absorb and try to decipher. "Daughters of Delphi? That's what it looks like this thing says we are. But is it true?"

Shay placed the knife and jar on the counter, washed off her hands in a slow and methodical manner, then turned to face Emma. Dish towel in hand, she walked Emma toward a drop-leaf table that had been folded down to seat just two people.

"I knew this would come up sooner or later."

"Just didn't think it would be this soon?" Emma laughed wryly, taking the seat across from Shay.

"The minute you got involved with River and the rest of our Scooby gang, it became important. But I'd thought maybe we could give you a while to get used to things first. Did you tell your mother about all of this? Is that why she went ahead and gave you the book?"

Emma shook her head. "No way, but you know Cecilia. She's as perceptive and attuned to the supernatural world as she ever was. She spoke some pretty mysterious words about me having a destiny and this being my time."

Shay watched her intently as she spoke, taking in the words. "Did she explain what you are? What all of the women in our family line are?"

"Nope. Just had Sophie hand me this book."

"I see." Shay hesitated, seeming to search for the right words. "Well, it's like this. All of us are descended from the original oracles of Delphi. That's why we're prophetic."

"Prophetic? Huh?" She frowned. "I hear voices and spirits, Shay. I'm a medium, that's what we do, but I am not a prophetess."

"Uh, yeah. You are. Sorry." Shay laughed slightly. "I see the demons because of my father's line, that's where that comes from, but I also get prophetic visions that manifest in my drawings. I saw Ajax and sketched him for a long while before he showed up. And you . . . well, you don't have my father's bloodline, so this 'hearing' that you do, that's exactly what it is. You may not see the future, but you hear things supernaturally and that's precisely what a prophetess does. And your gift is going to change now, probably, because it's finally opening up fully and because you know what it is and you aren't resisting it anymore."

Emma's mind reeled. "So I might start hearing the future, too? Like you see it in your sketches?"

"Maybe. Maybe not," she said. "The simple fact that you hear and then translate supernatural messages is a prophetic gift; it doesn't have to be events from the future that you hear. It might even be events from the past."

Emma tapped the book that sat on the table between them. "And where does this book fit in? It doesn't seem to have much in the way of helpful information."

"It traces our bloodline back to Delphi," Shay told her. "Oh, and by the way? One of the original oracles is the Spartans' special guide. So if a fairy-looking woman comes to you and has blue streaks in her hair that make her look like a punk rocker?"

"Yeah?"

"Don't be fooled. She's actually a real-deal oracle. She might seem quirky and adorable, but she's tough as nails and a really powerful woman. You'll like her, just don't let her sneak up on you."

"Great, one more crazy thing to dread."

"Oh, don't dread her . . . she'll save your butt when you need her." Shay reached for her hand, squeezing it. "She'll probably come to you at some point, maybe tell you about your calling as a Daughter. Don't be afraid, seriously. She looks like some Goth chick, not a mythic one."

Emma opened the book and began flipping through the pages again. She had a long, anxious wait until tomorrow night's confrontation with the demon Sable, one when she'd be worrying about River's future fate. Reading over the book and learning anything that might help her fight, too, seemed the smartest way to pass that time.

"Thanks, Shay," she told her cousin, standing to leave. "I'm glad you're in this insanity with me."

Shay smiled up at her. "And I'm glad I'm no longer the only human woman."

"Two mortals to their seven, right? Well, of course there's Jamie and Mason. They help balance the odds a little more in our favor."

Shay's facial expression grew a little harder to read, sending up warning flares in Emma's mind. She sank back into her chair. "What else?"

"Hmm?" Shay asked oh-so-innocently.

"You forgot to mention something else." She folded both arms over her chest and waited.

Shay smiled. "It's not a big deal, really. I mean, don't let it freak you out or anything, but, yeah . . . I'm not exactly mortal anymore."

Emma jerked back so hard, she almost knocked her chair over. "You're not what?"

"I chose to join Ajax in immortality," she said with a sheepish glance. "To be with him forever."

Emma placed a hand to her temple, which suddenly throbbed like it might explode. "You chose that. You could choose that, as in someone *gave* you a choice."

"The Oracle."

Emma sucked in a breath. "And that probably means I'll have a choice like that, too."

"Not necessarily, not at all," Shay rushed to assure her, but the words had the exact opposite impact.

If she wasn't given that opportunity, she would grow old and brittle and die while River remained as vital and gorgeous as he was now. Without meaning to, she released a choking sound, working her lungs for any kind of air.

"Don't panic, Em." Shay moved out of her chair and knelt by her side. "You and River have something very special, and one thing I've learned while hanging with these boys is that all sorts of miracles take place. You and River are meant to be together, and however the whole mortality issue's meant to work out—it will."

Emma closed her eyes. Shay seemed so confident and assured; she had to take comfort in that fact. Even if yet one more fear had been thrown over her shoulders like a suffocating weight.

"I love him," Emma whispered. "I'm going to keep faith in that fact."

Leo walked out to the end of the dock. It was early evening, just after eight p.m., and he'd spent the afternoon drilling the men. The Shades had joined in, too, and everyone had finally gone off to hit the showers.

But not him. He needed this quiet moment when so much was on the line tomorrow night. He scuffed his boots along the worn wood planks, listening to the bubbling of the flowing water and the symphony of summer insect sounds. If the Oracle were here, she would help still his embattled thoughts.

But she would not come, perhaps never again. It seemed that Ares had stripped her from his life just as he had stripped away his own sponsorship. They were alone. In the twenty-first century, he and his fellow ancient warriors were now drifting in the wrong time without a clear mission.

A small noise behind him jarred his thoughts. Whipping around to inspect its source, he found the one thing his heart hadn't even dared to hope for: the Oracle. She wore a slinky halter top and denim shorts. A very short pair that was cut to her upper thigh. And she was barefoot, a tiny toe ring glinting beneath the moonlight.

His eyes were riveted on her. "Did Ares decide to grant you to me?" He had to keep up their pretense. "And did he force you to come in such an appealing manner, Oracle? Surely you know that my desire for you is already plain fact. You needn't appeal to this old man's vanity."

"Old Man." She narrowed her mysterious, thick-lashed eyes at him. "I never want to hear that again." She sounded a bit ticked off with him, and that fact caused his body to run hot in reaction.

"You didn't answer my question," he said, working to keep the emotion from his voice. "Has your war god sent you as my boon? Fulfilled my request?"

She stepped closer, her small bare feet weaving around a few broken boards as she moved near. Pressing fingertips to her lips, she urged silence until she was right up against him, pressing against his chest. She lifted onto tiptoes and wrapped her thin arms about his neck. Her warm breath fanned against his cheek and his ear.

"My love, he wants your life. He seeks to destroy you ... all of you ... and plans to use River to accomplish the task."

He folded his thick, muscular arms around her back, pinning her close, and whispered against her ear, "I will not let him win. River will be safe."

She trembled against him, pressing even closer until he

felt her warm, soft breasts tight against his rib cage. "But what of you, Leo? You have to be cautious. He's cruel, you know that now. He will do everything he can to ruin you and hurt you. Not just kill you, Leo, but punish you and make you suffer."

A haughty, calculating voice interrupted them. "Yes, well stated, Oracle of mine," Ares called out from the river that ran behind them.

Still clinging to each other, they jerked their gazes toward the water only to find Ares gliding past in an ancient funeral barge. As if he were the Ferryman there to usher them into the afterlife. Torches blazed at both ends of the craft. He reclined with the laziness of a well-fed czar or emperor, and fanned himself absently.

"I knew you'd try warning the noble king," he observed with a yawn. "But it's pointless, *Leo*. You and yours are already finished. I simply take my time with this sort of thing as it's much, much more satisfying."

"Ares, betrayer, you underestimate me and my warriors," Leonidas challenged, shuttling the Oracle behind his back in a protective gesture. "You chose us as your immortals for a reason. Our skill, our mettle, our strength."

"I chose you because you could be controlled, frail king. Old Man. She may disagree, but I do not. How you creak these days, those old war injuries pained and aching. How your immortality seems to be fading from your veins. Are you really sure that you've not started the mortal aging process? Perhaps those fears in your head and the brittleness in your bones are true."

The Oracle lunged from behind him, pointing an accusing finger. "You have no right to taunt this brave soul. No right to be so vicious. I can go to—"

"You will not!" Ares leaped to a standing position as the barge slid past the dock's end. "You will not intercede. You are the one who has no rights!"

"If you bring it to that ..."

"I've indulged this fantastical whimsy of yours for too long," he announced, and lifted both hands. "It's time for you to realize who's truly in control here."

The Oracle began trembling, backing toward Leonidas,

and he took hold of her, wrapping her from behind with his arms. "You . . . won't. Please."

"What's he doing?" Leo whispered, but she shook her head, clinging to him as if afraid he might vanish.

The god swept his arms through the air and gold light passed like a cloud from his boat to the dock. Leonidas squinted, trying to understand what sort of cruel magic the god had just done. He couldn't tell, but had to blink against the gold dust in the air.

"No!" the Oracle cried in a wounded voice and he squeezed her even tighter, murmuring words of reassurance.

Only he realized a heartbeat too late that he murmured to no one. She'd been stripped from his arms.

"Ares, what did you do to her?" Leonidas demanded, rushing toward the water. But the god's craft was already moving much faster down the river.

"Invisible again, that's all," he called with a laugh. "Just as she always was. She can see you, of course, as that's fitting punishment. But you, old king, you will never kiss her again. Never hold her or even see her. She's dead to you now."

Leonidas dragged at the air, hands bunched against his sides. He spun around, searching, aching to find his love, but it was exactly as the god had threatened. She was gone.

*Oracle!* he screamed out in silence, not willing for Ares to hear his torment. *Oracle, my love!*

The last sound he heard was that of a god's pleasure: the floating, musical sound of Ares laughing in delight.

# Chapter 30

The time to face his maker had arrived. Well, *re-maker* was more like it, since Ares had taken the man that River once had been and re-formed him in his own war-ring image. And now? Well, it seemed that the deity was done with him, exactly as River had suspected during those months of aimless, trapped drifting. So getting a chance to offer a little payback to the Djinn who'd put him in that condition? And thumb his proverbial nose at Ares while he was at it? It felt damned good. Better than good, actually, to be heading out to confront the very forces that had turned on him four months ago.

He stood at the door of the Angels' home along with the others, fully clad in armor, ready to fight. And knowing full well, of course, that he'd likely shape-shift, perhaps many times, in the course of the night's battle. They'd spent the past day preparing, drilling, running scenarios. That, too, had been the best kind of rush, and it had been like coming home to be back with his fellow warriors.

What didn't feel good, however, was the way Emma stood at the door's threshold, staring at him as if wanting to memorize every last detail of his features. As if she were terrified that she'd never see him again. And that fact tore at River's heart. The others filed out in a strong, purposed line, moving into formation at the front of the house. Shay was the last besides himself to leave, and she paused, hugging Emma very close.

"Sweetie, it's going to be all right," she assured Emma with a laugh. "We've done this before, and these guys are, well . . . old hands at this. Really old hands, right?"

He watched as Emma clung to her cousin, forcing a hollow laugh. "Win one for the Spartans, huh?" She gave her cousin a playful slug on the shoulder, the two of them stepping out of the embrace.

Shay walked out slowly, eyes fixed on her cousin. "Emma, it really will be all right. Believe me."

"If she won't believe me," River said with a halfhearted smile, "she's probably not going to listen to you."

Emma nodded silently, her gaze fixed on River's face again, eyes roaming his features. Memorizing again, he thought.

Shay left the house, calling over her shoulder one last time. "We're strong, Em—and they're the strongest God ever made. You're strong, too, so pray hard tonight."

As soon as Shay had moved on, Emma hurtled herself into his arms. "I hate this."

With his heavy breastplate and greaves, it was hard to feel her much softer body, but he sure as hell tried, wrapping his arms about her lithe form. Holding and clutching and needing her so damned much it robbed his very breath from him.

"No man has ever had greater reason to come home from battle," he murmured against the top of her head, bending lower and showering her with soft kisses. Her cheek, her neck, down toward her breastbone.

"You take care of yourself, baby," she told him in a husky voice, her strong arms wrapping about his neck. "You made me a promise, you know. That you would always come home to me. If you don't keep it . . ."

"I will, sweet Em. You'll hold me in your arms again."

"If you don't, I'm gonna find you again." She released a quick exhalation of breath. "And next time? I'm kicking your little silver dagger *ass*."

He moved into the night still laughing. His heart swelled with how much he loved her. Thank the Highest, he thought, that of all the potential soul mates who might have been his destiny—of all the women he'd encountered throughout the centuries—this one woman who finally belonged to him had just done the unthinkable. She'd sent him off to perhaps the most intimidating, harshest battle he'd faced in years . . . making him laugh.

*     *     *

Mason held position in front of Nikos, crouching beside the veranda steps. It was a relatively secure, fortified position, the house behind them guarding their backs, the steps protecting them from the side. Nikos had to hand it to the former Marine. He'd been trained well. Assault rifle gripped in his hand, Mason kept the weapon's barrel ready, his body taut and prepared for any possible attack.

Nik kept two fingers against Mason's lower spine so that his fellow warrior would know where he was at all times. Last thing they needed was for Mason to mistake him for the enemy. He held his beloved eight-foot spear in his left hand, ready to conjure fire straight from Styx at the slightest demonic provocation. As he crouched close to Mason he had to smile at the incongruity of their weaponry, and yet they'd already proved what an effective and powerful fighting pair they could be.

Together their two bodies, their mutual training, all of it made them one complete fighting weapon. His fingers tensed against Mason's back, a wash of heat filling his hand. Gods, if he wasn't careful the hunter would feel that swell of supernatural power.

But it was too late: Mason had already sensed that spiral of heat. His spine stiffened and he lifted his chin, glancing backward at Nikos out of the corner of his eye. *Have you seen the enemy?* That's what the alert green eyes transmitted.

Nikos gave a slight shake of his head, raising his gaze beyond the human, far into the night. The heavy darkness was ripe with sounds: the cicadas, the breeze, the gurgling creek as it flowed nearby. Far off, somewhere down the long driveway, a demon howled, a raucous, soulless sound that cooled the fire in Nikos's blood.

With his supernatural eyesight, he scanned the trees, peering through every inch of the thick Spanish moss that the demons might use to obscure their presence. His nose twitched, that rancid scent of demon's sulfur burning his nostrils. In front of him, Mason lifted slightly on his haunches. His weapon clicked, the safety disengaging; he'd spotted a threat. Nikos mirrored the human's physical stance, keeping his own body right up close. All at once, he felt a rush of protectiveness for the man; Mason was only mortal after all, and any one of their demonic enemies could snuff out his life with one prime strike.

*Why did I let him take front position? That should be me, ahead of him, shielding him with my much less vulnerable body.*

He was about to whisper as much in Mason's ear when the attack came over them in less than a millisecond. Like a swarm of hell-fevered bees, a full pack of smallish demons was upon them. Gods, not six, or seven, but more than a dozen that had seemingly sprung from nowhere, without scent or sound.

Mason fired on them, a rapid tat-tat sound that sent several falling earthward, but Nikos was instantly on his feet. He bounded into the melee, hurling molten fire that had already filled his spear. Over and over he ran at the attackers, shield up, spear riving the beasts even as Mason's weapon scattered hellfire of its own.

He'd be damned if the human hunter got hurt, not while fighting with him. Suddenly, that mortality within the man meant everything, was something precious that Nikos would have laid down his own life to defend.

But the fucking beasts just kept coming. Behind him he heard Mason curse, reload, and cock his weapon once more. Then the human came forward, taking the lead again.

That was the moment when true hell rained down on them.

Ari and his brothers were the first to see it. From down the length of the driveway a blinding explosion of light appeared in the darkness. They'd been on patrol, the group of them spread out over the property, working off of Nikos's projections as to where the next likely weakness would occur in the wards.

"It's like being a goddamned sitting duck," Ajax cursed low.

Ari hissed under his breath in agreement. "Sable's the master showman. He's got us here, waiting for his big fucking deadline. . . ."

Kalias took a step forward. "It's Ares' deadline, boys, don't forget."

"I want to kick some ass," Ari added. "On River's behalf."

Ari was actually a bit ticked at his best friend. It was ridiculous that the guy wanted in the middle of the fight, being, as he was, the chief prize booty. But it wasn't like they could make him stay out of the battle, and when push came to shove they definitely needed him. The other Spartans hadn't balked at River's participation, but maybe Ari's own feelings were just a little too complicated. After getting the guy back after so many months, he was admittedly reluctant to see him in the line of fire all over again.

The three of them moved down the long line of live oak trees, bodies tensed, supernatural abilities at maximum intensity. Waiting, ready.

From the night they heard a harsh set of cackling calls. All in the trees, it seemed, echoing through the Spanish moss.

"Holy fucking hell," Ajax muttered, as all three brothers dropped to their haunches.

"Okay, what was that?" Ari added.

They'd heard it at the same time: a sound layered atop the shrill cries and demon barking. A beating, drumming drone.

Louder it grew. One beat, a second, and then another. All the while the reverberations began to shake the very earth.

"Not good, boys," Kalias whispered, crouching low against the earth. "Not good at all." He looked up, his harsh face searching the night.

Ari had his palm splayed on the sandy ground, and like his two brothers tried to determine the source of the chilling drumbeats. The sound wasn't musical at all, but more like what they had heard during their three days of facing the Persians. A chill chased down Ari's spine at the memory, at the connection. . . .

Right then the earth beneath his hand began to tremble and quake, thundering with every new pounding on what had to be some unearthly drum.

"Oh, my gods," Ari murmured, understanding at last.

Chilled to his marrow, he sought his brothers' eyes in the dark. Surely they understood—surely they knew.

They said nothing, poised deathly still and ready.

"It's Ares," Ari whispered to them. "That is his battle call . . . his drum."

"I need River," Jax told them fiercely. "I'm going to summon him to my side. Then we'll split up and begin a stealthy advance."

The earth pounded much harder at that precise moment, and Ari flinched. It became real to him right then. Ares, the god they'd long served—the deity of all bloodshed and violence and battle—was calling them to war.

River was knee-deep in the marshy water of the creek bed, slamming his shield in the face of a demon with red beady eyes. He lifted his spear and summoned fire, wondering if he'd still be able to call it forth; it came from Hades, after all, but he was pleased when his weapon erupted in a burst of flame.

*We were born there, made there . . . but Ares can't take our power back. Not yet.*

He slashed and moved, hurling the fiery balls from his spear, but all at once it seemed that there were more of the demons coming at him. Behind him Ajax made a harsh cry, but he didn't dare look back even though his mind raced with fear for his master. Had he been injured, falling in battle?

And it was a horrible, gruesome fight, no doubt about it. The more they slugged it out, wielding every weapon in their arsenal, the bloodier and harder the situation seemed to get. *Emma*, he thought, *why didn't I tell you to leave this place?*

He should have sent her back to her home, or the compound, but he'd worried too much for her safety, whereas here he'd felt they had a chance of protecting her. Now that the fire was raining down on them, he was no longer sure.

There was a stumbling, sloshing noise behind him; he glanced out of the corner of his eye and saw that Ajax moved close behind him.

"River," he said, his voice weakened, "I'm hit . . . fall back."

"Where are you injured?" River hurled more fire as two low-flying brittle creatures launched at them both. "Tell me where you were struck."

His mind was already moving, thinking of how he could help his friend and master.

"No," Ajax told him weakly, grabbing hold of his shoulder. "Fall back . . . the others already have."

"This shit's still coming! I have to keep going or they'll get closer to the house."

*To Emma . . .*

Ajax's grip tightened on his shoulder, but he felt the man waver on his feet. River backed up several steps, eyes trained on their attackers. "Come on, Jax," he said, "I'll get you back to the high ground. Get you to safety . . . and heal you. But then I've got to get right back into the fray."

Jax nodded, held to him, dragging his right leg. River could see the vicious wound in his upper thigh, saw a shattered bone protruding. It was an ugly one, possibly lethal had they still been human.

"Hold on to me," River told him, Ajax's heavier weight sagging and pulling at River's own strength. "Keep going, Jax. Keep going."

They stumbled in the darkness, River already summoning his otherworldly power, already visualizing what he needed to do. By the time they were out of the water, back on the side of the hill, the silver was already engulfing his full form. He felt the humming power. It filled him to the hilt; the silver washed in his veins and colored his eyesight.

As it seized hold of his soul and his body, he cried out to Ajax, "It'll only hurt for a moment. Be ready!"

He morphed into a flaming, healing sword at that exact moment, and hurling himself through the distance that separated the two of them, River spun through the air. He turned end over end, full of bright, glorious power, until his sword ran deep into Ajax's injured leg.

For a moment he was blinded; the rushing life force in him burst forth, and in a spasm of horrific pain, he absorbed Jax's injury, released healing and life. In a rush he layered in prayer. *Highest God, bring your healing. Heal this man . . . my friend. Heal him, please, Great One.*

A bright circle of light exploded through his senses, and he instantly knew that Ajax was well. Therefore he could change back to human form and launch himself back into the fight. He allowed the hard, silver substance of his sword form to melt away, to flow back out of him, all that healing energy rolling like a wave toward the universe. From his deepest, most primal core, he reached—several times—and was relieved when his human form began to take shape once again.

Gasping, coughing, he fell to the grass, landing unsteadily on his knees. Ajax lay on the ground beside him, looking woozy and halfway out of it. "Jax," he said, looking around for the others, but saw no one. "Ajax, get up. We've gotta move, man. Come on."

Ajax looked at him through glazed, distant eyes, but nodded. River stood quickly and extended a hand, pulling the other man upward, helping him onto unsteady feet.

"You all right, Jax?"

The other man gave his head a shake, reaching for his sheathed sword. "Thank you, dear friend," he said. "You are far too good to me."

River winced as he recalled how coldly he'd treated Ajax the day before when his master had been so genuinely happy to see him. Now he regretted that he'd never found a private moment to apologize. With the way the current battle was going, this might be his last chance.

"You are a true friend, Jax. I love serving you," he said. "You know that."

Ajax smiled faintly, said nothing more. But River wasn't quite done.

"I'm sorry . . . for the way I was yesterday."

"I always told you, Kassandros," he said, starting to move forward. "You're not right in the head."

They both laughed, and River's heart sang in gratitude, thankful for that familiar, long-standing camaraderie they'd always shared.

*Truly thankful*, he thought, *that I'm back.*

Nikos watched in horror as a demon lord, the one who had apparently set these devouring minions upon them, emerged. At least eight feet tall, the towering creature was one of the fiercest and most hideous that Nikos had seen in years. He wondered if the creature terrified Mason the way it did him at the moment. The being possessed more appendages than Nik could easily count and was whipping them about viciously, sweeping its own little underlings aside like yesterday's trash.

Its glowing red eyes became brighter with every advancing step, the blaze filling the darkness. In reaction, Nikos's own supernatural power flushed through his body. He *felt* the silver wash into his veins more than saw it, his instinctive reaction to such a devilish threat. The silver that filled him was no less than pure fire from Styx itself and it instantly infused every single part of his anatomy.

He glanced back at Mason, whose eyes widened at what had to be a shocking sight: the wild, out-of-control blaze in Nik's own countenance. "Get behind me," Nikos roared, his vocal cords drawn tight as a bow. "I'm transforming . . . shifting. Can't stop."

Mason ignored him, raising his weapon once again. "Fuck that. I'm in this fight, Spartan."

Nikos grunted, feeling the overpowering pulse of Hades itself roar into his muscles and sinews. Felt his bones lengthen and morph. His body was on full alert, his silver-filled eyes trained hard on the monster that was stalking toward them.

*And toward Mason*, he thought, all his protector's instincts crackling like wildfire in his mind.

"I am immortal; I will shield you, Angel. Stay back! Behind me, human!" This time, Nikos wouldn't hesitate. He couldn't; the urges in his blood were too damned strong. "On my mark, I take lead. Three, two, one . . . go!"

He leaped over Mason, the bounding as easy as breathing because of his change. His physical transformation was pure impulse: Guard humanity at all costs. Serve them as their own dark angel. This was everything he'd sworn to do, every bit of his soul's calling. But because it was Mason's life and safety . . . oh, gods, the instinct was hitting full throttle and faster than he could keep it leashed.

Mason kept behind him, getting off several rounds against the approaching demon lord. He growled, "I am right with you, Nikos. I'm a fucking Marine. Don't treat me like a pansy!"

Nikos growled back at him, feeling his T-shirt rip to shreds as his wings grew wild upon his back. It wasn't the time for a macho pissing contest. The thing coming at them packed more force and more death than Mason ever could have encountered, no matter how many demons he'd slain before now or how many enemy soldiers he'd faced.

"Fight with me," he barely managed to shout over his shoulder. His voice was that changed, the hawk assuming control of his body. Of all their cadre, Nikos's raptor was the most sinister, the most volatile and angry, and . . . rude. Or so he'd been told. Like that mattered.

With a shrill warning cry, Nikos lifted off the ground and flew at the demon. His human body remained, but his hands curled, long talons forming. His face morphed into a hawklike one, growing harsh and brutal; soft feathers covered his human chest.

The demon attacking him stared, beady red eyes widening in shock.

"Never seen anything like me before, have you?" Nikos roared. They were hawk words, not human. He knew from experience that his harsh raptor calls threw the demons off, at least the ones that hadn't encountered him before. His talons ripped into demon flesh, and in response the creature's long tentacles whipped Nikos hard and flat across his right wing.

"Now you're pissing me off!" he shrieked in his raptor's language and swooped at him again, driving his blazing silver sword right into the beast's chest.

With that, the repulsive thing exploded. Literally. The power of Nikos's supernatural sword, the strength in his wings, all of it literally caused the idiotic demon to spew blood and guts and acid fire in every direction.

Nikos did a reverse turn midair, got right out of the way before that fiery shit touched his skin or wings, and watched the demon crumple to the ground.

He whooped and was about to fly earthward when he caught sight of Mason. Oh, dear God above all. Oh, Highest God . . .

Mason lay on the ground, his leg boiling with what looked like a heavy showering of that demon's acid-blood. He didn't scream, didn't cry out, but he lay on his back curling onto his side, gripping his leg. His eyes were shut tight in obvious pain, his face twisted into a mask of—

Oh, gods, it was a horrible wound. That was all Nikos could think as he dropped to the human's side. He absorbed his wings for the moment, but kept his talons, and used them to rip into the khaki fabric of Mason's cargo pants. He sheered the pant leg off, exposing the boiling flesh. The hot stench of burning skin hit his nostrils hard and made his eyes water. Mason gave a muted cry of relief, pawing at his leg, but Nikos caught his hand, absorbing his talons so he wouldn't cut him. "Don't," he warned. "You'll burn yourself, but any wound of mine will heal easily."

He planted Mason's hand atop his chest and the human nodded weakly. "Just get it off me, man," Mason told him, his voice tight with pain, but remarkably calm given the circumstances. The wound was horrific in magnitude, the acid continuing to boil and rend the vulnerable human flesh of his left leg.

Nikos reached for the shredded fabric of his own shirt, wiping as hard and fast as he could to get the searing substance off. But it was literally eating Mason alive. Nikos's eyes watered as he worked; all around them there were shouts and roars and hawk cries. Demon laughter filled the night.

After several moments, Mason waved a hand at him. "Go," he said. "Go back to the fight. Go . . . okay. I'm . . . gonna . . ." Mason's head lolled back against the ground and his eyes drifted shut. He'd passed out before he could finish his sentence.

Nikos glanced over his shoulder once again at the unfolding battle, then back at Mason. "Fight's under control," Nik said softly. "I've got to save you."

Mason shook his head. "Firefight . . . back to it, Kell. Get in the game."

"*Kell?*" Nikos repeated. In his delirium, Mason clearly thought he was someone else. Another demon hunter, someone Nikos hadn't met yet?

"Kelly . . . he's here. I saw him. Tell him not to save me, to get to safety. Kelly . . ." Mason's eyes fixed on Nikos, clarity filling their dazed green depths once more. Then sadness. He shook his head, soul-wounding despair in his eyes. "Forget Kelly." Another shake of his head and his jaw ticked with visible pain. "Kelly's gone."

Nikos pressed his thumb against Mason's mouth, silencing him. "I'm getting you to higher ground. To help."

Mason's eyes closed heavily again, unconsciousness overtaking him once more. Nikos reached down and took hold of both his hands. "Good thing you're out cold," he grunted as he lifted Mason's heavy body upward. "You don't want to be awake for what I'm about to do."

He heaved Mason over his left shoulder like dead weight and in a rush of transformation became a hawk protector once again. Then, with Mason secure across his shoulder and back, Nikos flew into the night.

River glanced around. "Where is everyone else? I don't understand where they are."

Ajax shook his head. "The demons are everywhere. They're trying to divide us, pick us off one by one." Then Jax reached a hand out, stopping River from walking. "What's that?"

River didn't hear anything, and waited in silence, trying to pinpoint whatever dark force Jax had just heard. They'd been hunkered low in the tall marsh grass for several moments. With the next wave of attackers they'd be in prime position to nail them stealthily. River hated the murky feel of the water, though; it brought back bad memories of his recent trauma.

*Different river, different time*, he told himself, glancing about the darkness.

That awful drumming noise that they'd heard earlier started up again, and Jax cut a glance at him. River had no idea what the rhythmic sound meant, but it definitely chilled his soul. Still, he sank down lower in the tall grass, some instinct warning him that the heavy, beating cadence was a dark sign.

Yet the thundering rhythm only intensified. It was right

atop them. Ajax whipped his head around, looking at River from his position in front. At once his eyes widened, filled with some horror that River couldn't yet see ... as if an attacker was bearing down upon his back.

River craned around to look, and understood why Jax's eyes had filled with that fear. It wasn't drumbeats anymore ... it was hoofbeats. At that exact moment, Sable galloped past him, reaching down with both hands. River felt himself hurtling through the air. The Djinn lifted and tossed him across his back as if he weighed nothing, were still just a dagger.

River tried screaming, but couldn't find his voice or think clearly. A blinding, explosive pain stabbed hard in his chest; it speared into him completely the moment Sable flung River across his back. Then another ripping pain tore his thigh. And the intensity of both wounds was so powerful that his world started to grow dim.

*Some kind of weapon*, he thought vaguely. *Sable has spears along his back.*

With a weak hand, River tried to struggle. It was pointless, he discovered. He'd never be able to move at all.

The demon had impaled him on sharp stakes that ran the length of his horse's back. River was literally and violently bound to his greatest enemy's body.

Feeling the warm surge of his own blood, smelling the heavy metallic odor of it, he fought to stay conscious, except the long rolling gait of the damned centaur lulled him even more.

Sable finally spoke then. "How do you like riding side-saddle?" He laughed. "Of course, you're facedown, so it's not really the same. But I thought for a true girl like you, it would be the perfect thing. The ideal way to deliver you to Ares ... to undo my own curse," he said threateningly. "And solidify yours."

The blackness rushed over River in that moment. His last thought was that he was lost beneath the waves again, even though he knew he was still human. But the despair, the bottomless, aching feel of it, was precisely the same.

*Chapter 31*

River squinted as very bright light flooded his eyes. He blinked, confused to find himself resting in a soft, plush bed. A very spacious and luxurious bed, he realized, and sitting up quickly he knew it was a mistake. He immediately grew light-headed, and flashing spots shot through his vision. Where in Hades was he?

Every direction he glanced he saw gold: the light, the drapes over the windows, even the sky just beyond. Something sticky clung to his chest, and glancing down he saw his clothes were covered in dark, dried blood. He felt underneath the T-shirt, where his skin was warm and unscathed, which reassured him only briefly. Every battle memory came rushing back to him: being captured by Sable, those horrific protruding horns that had impaled him.

Was this Elysium? Had he died after his latest injuries? *So much for immortals not being able to die*, he thought grimly, easing off the bed. He'd been laid out atop the gold-engraved covering. Apparently with great care and ceremony, he decided upon seeing the opulent pillows that had been spread under his head, and as he spotted the heavy jug of wine and another of ice water displayed on the side table.

*Emma*, he thought in panic. Where was Emma and how would she know where he was if even he wasn't sure?

"That bumbling moron was not to have harmed you, brave one," a silky, familiar voice announced.

Ares stood in the room's doorway draped in a flowing, diaphanous cape of golden silk, open to his belly but flaunting the masculine physique that he'd always been so proud of.

The god drawled on, "Sable can never seem to get his assignments quite right, and I apologize for his ineptitude, fine warrior."

"He dumped me in a river last time," he said bluntly, not believing the war god's simpering words, not for one second.

"That was not my intention, Kassandros. You know how valuable you've always been to me. Precious." The god extended a muscular forearm, flexing the muscle. "Made by my own hand, forged with my power."

The god's eyes assumed a wicked gleam. "You've always been mine, young hero, and that's why our time has come."

*Our time?* River's throat tightened up on him; these words from Ares were more sinister than any he'd ever spoken to their corps, all the more so because of their seductive hint at power.

River thought fast and knew that he didn't have a chance if he argued or balked. Playing as fast and loose as the god did was his only hope.

River took one bold step toward the deity, inclining his head. "My lord, tell me what you envision. Talk to me of this, our time."

Ares closed the distance between them, draping that powerful, golden-haired arm over River's shoulder in a show of camaraderie. Guiding River out the door, he bared white teeth in a smile. "Come with me, strong one, and I will offer you what every mortal craves." The vicious smile grew brighter. "I'll give you the world."

Emma sank to the floor of the shower, her whole body wracked with sobs. She crouched there, raking shaking hands all over her body. River was gone. She'd felt the attack on him at the moment it happened. She'd heard him crying out over the distance that gathered between them. With every passing hour, their blood-tie gained more strength, and she'd begun to feel his most intense emotions within her own soul. Like now, when she sensed the battle's outcome without hearing from any of its observers.

River was injured and in pain. She didn't need Shay or Mason or any of the others to come tell her because she *knew*. She felt it deep in her spirit because of their connection.

Why hadn't she argued harder to stop him from fighting? Why hadn't any of the others? she wondered, still sobbing. It was a warrior mentality that was totally foreign to her, but what else could she expect? She'd taken a lover who was a weapon . . . fallen in love with a man so mystical and totally other, of course his world and values were foreign to her. And she'd never stand in the way of his being all that God had called him to be. He did have a powerful destiny; it just didn't come from that murderous Ares.

River had been anointed by God himself to protect humanity. Maybe Ares was the one who'd empowered him initially, but he was a hero to all mankind. He'd sacrificed everything out of duty for those he loved, and even those he didn't know at all.

God would honor that. He had to; she knew it. That kind of devotion and honor would not go unrewarded. The kindness in River's soul was too strong and powerful to be extinguished. God had sent her to him, too, hadn't He? So that he wouldn't die in those drowning waves.

River would be protected now. He would, she assured herself, stopping her tears. She sat on the floor of the shower, the warm spray rolling down her back. Somehow, even though her heart was breaking, even though it made no logical sense, she became certain that River would be okay.

He would fulfill that promise he made her. It had been a promise, one he had repeated several times. This from a man who'd taken that long-ago oath to serve throughout time, and had never wavered in that duty—not even now.

"Come home to me, baby," she murmured aloud, closing her eyes. "You have to come home."

Then she focused her words toward River himself, reaching hard and shouting across their blood-tie connection, that spiritual thread that bound them to each other, allowing supernatural communication.

*You promised me, sweetheart,* she called to him. *You have to stay true to that. You told me you would come back. . . .*

*I know that you will.*

*          *          *

"Take a look, warrior. Tell me what you see." Ares led River out onto a long stone portico, revealing a stunning, breath-stealing view. "The summit of Olympus. Power."

River's gaze swept over the rolling clouds, the bright refractions of light and energy, the distant view farther along the edge of the high mountain that revealed another palace. And another.

*They must belong to the other gods*, he realized, trembling at the thought.

Ares waved his hand magnanimously at the awe-inspiring view. "All may be your portion, young one. All may be your own." Then, turning toward River, the deity gave him a measuring stare. "If you but seize it. Not from me, but with me. By my divine ordination, it shall be yours and you will rule in the greatness I always intended."

River blanched beneath the god's intense inspection. His mind raced and felt as if it might fracture into useless shards simply from the sheer insanity of the offer. Of being on Olympus in Ares' palace, finding himself talking to a god. A slave conversing with the forces of the universe, it was more than he could comprehend.

Ares laughed. "Overwhelmed, are you?"

"I don't have words," he barely managed to reply. "My lord, my war god . . . why me?"

"You hold great power inside of you. I placed it there," Ares answered smoothly. But there was something very important he wasn't revealing; River sensed it. "And your so-called friends? The ones you're so loyal to? They've all turned on you."

River frowned, not sure what the war god meant. "How . . . ? Who?" He returned to that flashing mental image of Nikos, that long-ago day that he'd seen in his vision. The *krypteia* gathered in a shrouded circle, Nikos at the center.

"Nikos?" he asked in a choked voice.

Ares smiled smoothly. "Yes. He sought your death even then. And these past months, well, you already suspected his sabotage in their efforts to locate you."

With an illustrative extension of his hand, Ares unfurled

a series of images before River's eyes. They played for him in his mind as a filmstrip would, the god offering perfect narration.

"This meeting? See who is gathered?" He watched Nikos with a map, Ari sitting sulkily on the sofa. "Just them, and listen, they don't even sound happy about searching for you." Bits of their dialogue played through River's mind, a discussion that nobody else had bothered to come, an argument about it being pointless to search.

His heart seized painfully. *Aristos! His dearest friend ... even he had given up?*

"Of course your king was otherwise employed. He, the one who claims to protect you? Ha, quite the laugh."

The whirlwind of impressions rolled through River's spirit, brutally realistic. Straton's unwillingness to attempt to hear him when his dagger form was finally returned; Ajax's nonresistance when Sable had him thrown into the Wilmington; Shay's conniving agreement to take him to America as a dagger. Older images, too, Kalias and Ajax insisting to Ari that he be kept as a slave. The last image, though, chilled him most of all. It was a grim picture of his own body, bound and tied to pegs along the side of that old barn as the cloaked Spartan death squad gathered with whips and swords. Nikos stood in front of them all. He was the one shouting orders and leading the charge.

River stood, gasping, dragging at breath. The pain the revelations brought had him doubled over in agony. These men ... he'd loved every one of them. Damn it all, he'd even loved Nikos in some stupidly loyal way. But they'd turned on him. To the very last man, they had abandoned him.

"You see now, don't you?" Ares asked him smoothly.

River just blinked, clutching his stomach, eyes fixed on the white stones beneath his feet. The god dropped a warm hand to the small of his back and patted him as he might a child with a tiny scratch.

"There now, warrior," he said. "Rise to your feet and let me talk of our plan. Of a world where you'll have more power than any of those immortals combined. Where I'll give you more wealth and influence and acclaim than you ever dreamed when you slept in that barn in old Sparta."

River coughed, struggling to stand tall. This god had ripped out everything inside his heart, his soul. He'd stripped him raw as surely as if he'd flayed him with iron. But there was one precious hope that he prayed might be real. One vision of betrayal that he'd not been shown.

Forcing strength into himself, he looked up into the god's eyes. "Tell me about Emma. Tell me she's true."

The god glowed brighter as he heard the question. Power infused him from the top of his head, and it filled him with beautiful majesty. "Your Emma . . . oh yes," he said. "I forgot about her."

River repeated his earlier words in a pained, growling tone. "*Tell me she's true.* That her love is real."

Ares stroked his beard mildly. "If you truly want to know, yes. I can show you her heart."

# Chapter 32

Nikos couldn't stand the constraints of the hospital waiting room. The faces in the small area kept changing over the hours, the Day-Glo green plastic chairs filling with a rotating parade of humanity. So he was more than a little grateful when he spotted Shay walking toward him. He met her in the hallway.

She gave him a weary smile. "Mason's sleeping, but stable and feeling good," she said. "Thanks to you."

He turned from her and began walking toward the parking lot; satisfied that Mason would live, he couldn't flee the place fast enough.

Shay trotted up beside him. "Aren't you going to go see him? He asked for you, several times."

He gestured toward the exit door. "I . . . I have work . . . things I . . ." He babbled like a moron.

She gave his resistant forearm a tug, trying to pull him back inside. "I need to get back to the house right now, and he shouldn't be alone."

Nikos swallowed, willing his heart to calm down. He could handle this; he could go, do the duty, keep his guard up and get out soon enough. It wasn't as bad as facing down a demon pack, after all.

"You know, he's been totally shut down since Iraq," Shay continued, seeming to sense that he wavered. "Came back eight months ago and has been locked inside himself ever since. I miss him. . . . I've tried over and over, and I can't make a connection. But he relates to you. I've seen it. He talks to Jamie some, but . . . I don't know. There's something about you, Nikos. Something he needs."

Nikos felt as if all his armor had been stripped away. His

heart slammed with the speed of a Gatling gun, hard and fast, and he had to swallow the bitter taste of panic. Shay knew. She suspected what kind of man he was, the way her brother awakened him.

And all the while Shay kept staring up at him, waiting for some sort of response, that smile on her lips fading slightly. "I'm not saying you've got to take him on permanently or anything. I just . . . you know, I thought you two were kind of friends now."

"Yes."

"You *are* friends?" Why did the question—and the way her eyebrows lifted to underscore it—seem to be far more significant than the words she used?

"Perhaps fighting partners is more accurate. There is a bond there."

"He needs that kind of friend right now," she said. "That's all I'm saying."

But then a question hit him, seemingly from nowhere at all. "Who is Kelly?"

"Kelly?" she repeated at first; then her eyes widened with understanding. "Oh, he was dating some girl over in Iraq for a while, but they broke up. Her name was Kelly. Why? Did he mention her?"

He'd been dating a female; of course he had, because the handsome, sad-eyed mortal wasn't like Nikos was. That hidden desire didn't course in Mason's veins from the most ancient of times like it did in his own.

Nikos tried to remember the exact words that Mason had used during the demon battle; everything had happened so fast. *Where is Kell? Kelly is here. I saw him. . . . Tell him not to save me. To get to safety. Tell him. . . .*

Tell *him.* "Nothing. Mason just mentioned that name last night. Must've been delirious."

It seemed that Nikos wasn't the only one with dark, forbidden secrets in his heart. And for the first time since meeting Mason Angel, that slamming, skittish sensation in Nikos's chest didn't make him feel like he was drowning. It did something far more startling as it filled his rib cage this time. It gave him hope.

*          *          *

Mason's heavy snoring greeted Nikos before he'd even pushed open the door to his hospital room. Stepping quietly across the tile floor, Nikos had to squint to make out the slumbering form that was laid out atop the sheets of the hospital bed. But he saw enough that his breath caught for a moment. Mason's leg was swathed in thick white bandages, his right arm, too. Nikos sank slowly into the vinyl visitor's chair that was positioned beside the bed, keeping his focus on the sleeping face before him.

*Don't let your gaze slide any lower. It's not polite.*

The fact was, the hospital covering was thin at best and had ridden up to expose what Nikos couldn't help but notice was a pair of boxer shorts. They had devilish little cupids on them as if they'd been some Valentine's gift, perhaps from a lover. Nikos frowned at that thought, but something far more important than jealousy was pulling at his attention for the moment.

*One little glance to check out his bandages. That should be expected.*

Amazing how many excuses he could generate when it came to this sleeping man. A man who had no idea about all the secrets Nikos harbored inside or how painfully similar their own paths had been, despite being separated by millennia. At least, that was the case if Nikos's new theory about Mason's "girlfriend" Kelly was correct. Every instinct pulsing through his blood told him that he was on the mark here.

*You know what it is to hide, to keep your loss buried deep inside like this.*

For whatever reason, Mason Angel made Nikos forget every vow of celibacy and privacy and heterosexuality that he'd ever sworn in his heart. He made him want to risk things that should never—not now, not in any century—be risked again.

With a stealthy hand Nikos reached to touch Mason's arm. It was long and lean, resting only a few inches from Nikos's own hand. Inch by inch Nikos moved his fingertips closer, wanting something he refused to define or give name to in his heart. Dusky brown hairs curled along Mason's strong forearm, some lighter brown than others, just like the hair on his head.

*Much lighter than me*, he thought, staring at the slightly curling wisps that ran all the way to Mason's wrist. Holding his breath tight, Nikos reached out and let his fingers play up the length of that sinewy, muscular arm. The hairs were soft—far softer than he'd have imagined.

He studied the sun-darkened skin, such a contrast to Nikos's own swarthy coloring. Mason's skin was golden brown, tanned from living by the ocean and river, perhaps. Or simply from his time of long-term desert soldiering, the kind of tan that never totally faded. With hesitant fingers, he reached to touch just one more time. He stole one more feel of those silken hairs. And by Olympus, Mason's arm jerked.

Nikos bolted backward in his seat, ramrod straight in his posture, and found Mason gazing up at him through heavily lidded eyes.

"You're awake." It came out as a bark, and then he scowled to add further disdain to his meaning. As if Mason had violated a basic code of conduct by simply opening his eyes. Anything to deflect attention from what he'd probably been busted doing.

"You saved my ass." Mason blinked back at him, his gaze firm and fixed.

Nikos did not blink. "Actually, it was your leg."

He could have seen demons fly into the room and been less surprised by what happened next. Mason laughed, a deep-down from-the-belly snort. The long-eyed stare and sadness were gone for once.

"God, you're funny." Mason rubbed his eyes. "It's the quiet ones you've got to beware of; that's what my mama always told me."

He knew that Mason's mother had died only four months ago, and yet the human still smiled. *Happy to be alive, perhaps? High off the pain medication?*

"Let me correct myself. You saved my leg *and* my ass, you freak."

The corner of Nikos's mouth turned up. Just one little bit. Maybe Mason had no clue that he'd been trying to give him a rubdown on the sly. He decided he was in the clear, and was about to release his tightly held breath when the human turned his gaze upward at him.

That gaze was more than alert.

"So since you saved my ass and my leg"—Mason rubbed the beard stubble along his chin contemplatively—"I figure you were just making sure the arm's still intact?"

Nikos bolted to his feet and walked toward the door. No way, nohow would he stand up to this sort of court-martial.

"Oh, Jesus, come back." Mason laughed again, a warmer, more relaxed laugh than even the first time. "Had to give you shit for it, didn't I?"

Nikos held perfectly still, halfway between the bed and the door. His mind swarmed with responses, all of them too dangerous. He wasn't good at jokes or snappy one-liners like Ari or Ajax. But he came up with something, somehow; maybe he pulled it straight out of his ass. "It's an old Spartan technique. It revives the dead."

"Then it worked." That voice . . . was full of meaning and intensity. A little bit of flirtation. Nikos's smile returned, both sides of his mouth turning upward, and slowly he dared to face his interrogator. Mason's eyes were bright and filled with the same coy mischief that had just been in his words.

And he gaped like a dumbstruck idiot because nobody, male or female, had flirted with him in at least a hundred years.

"Careful, I might just have won this sparring match, Spartan." Mason laughed low in his throat, still rubbing his jaw, fingers lingering along the beard stubble. "You Spartans have a reputation to uphold. All that terse 'we'll fight in the shade' wit. Don't let me down here."

Nikos bowed with mock gallantry. "When you are recovered, I will meet you for a wrestling match. I'll see how well you do then."

Mason didn't miss a beat. "I'm game. I was on the Citadel wrestling team."

Oh, shit. The innuendo was only escalating and now he'd walked right into it.

Nikos stared toward the window. "I doubt you've ever wrestled as we Spartans do," he said roughly. "Naked."

Mason's eyes widened; then he glanced quickly away, his expression growing serious. Softly he spoke. "I've been naked with men before." Mason turned his stare back on Nikos. "But I think you know that. Still, nobody else here knows about me, so this conversation goes no further. Understood?"

"I didn't . . . not . . ." He struggled to find his voice. "We have more in common than I knew," he said at last. "Before now."

The green eyes narrowed, but were lit from inside again. "You may be funny, Nik, but I'm thinking you're not as swift as I had you pegged for."

Nikos returned to the other side of the bed, but faced the window. He busied himself by cracking open the blinds and staring at the parking lot below. "You've known about me? All along?"

"In this era, we call it gaydar. You don't live in the macho-or-die Marines with hundreds of other men without having a damned good one."

He peered over his shoulder. "Ah, so that's it."

Mason raked a hand across his short cropped hair. "Part of it," he said, and then sighed. Fiddling with his sheet, his gaze went long and far away. Thousand-yard stare, all over again.

"And the other part?" Nikos pressed, dropping into the seat beside the bed.

"Too complicated to explain." He shook his head slowly. "I can't go there, man. Not even if we do have something in common."

His voice had lost its levity, gone all heavy again, and Nikos couldn't stand that fact. Suddenly he wanted to be the funniest damned man who'd ever roamed the earth.

"I lost someone," Nikos confessed in a rush. "At Thermopylae. Someone who . . ." His throat tightened hard and he cleared his throat several times before continuing. "Doros. That was his name. I had a wife, a son, but Doros . . ."

He could not say anything more; the human would have to intuit what he himself could never give words to. That

Doros had practically flowed through his bloodstream. Lived in his own rib cage, he'd been that deep and crucial a part of Nikos's soul. "He fell the first day of fighting. He was much farther back in the phalanx. I didn't know until long after night came. I fought the next two days to avenge him. I fight now, in eternity, to make . . . sense. Of it all. To make it matter."

With a half glance, he dared to see if Mason was even looking at him. What he found was a man who had lived every emotion and thought that he'd carried inside his own skull for far too many years.

Mason sat upright, struggling for a moment as he adjusted his bed and cautiously moved his leg. "Last night, I thought you were Kelly." The words were spoken so softly, Nikos nearly missed them. "Thought I saw him."

Nikos nodded slowly. "Forgive me, but I asked your sister if she recognized the name."

Mason cursed and threw him a vicious look. "Christ, she thinks Kelly was my girlfriend over there. Not my . . ." He pointed toward the window, toward the east.

"I didn't tell her otherwise," Nikos promised fiercely.

Mason folded both arms over his chest. "You don't get it. You Spartans didn't live in a 'don't ask, don't tell' world."

"It's not like your commander is going to come busting down that door. You're out of the service."

"Honorable discharge, Nikos. Honorable. Hell, I'm so far in the closet that I could hang myself in there and still have room for an entire wardrobe. Even now. My sister? She has no clue."

"Your brother?"

"Shit, no. He knows about the demon, that's all."

*Demon? What did a demon have to do with . . . ?*

This time it was Mason who cleared his throat. Several times, and coughed, rubbing a palm over his chest. "Kelly . . . I met him over here, stateside. We were in the same battalion, later the same unit. Over there, there wasn't any sneaking around, no leaving anywhere. It was just sand in your crotch twenty-four seven, and sleeping when you had three seconds. Death and explosives and seeing innocent children get hurt. Not exactly time for visiting a gay bar, you know?"

He laughed bitterly, staring off into space, then continued. "We never had five seconds alone . . . not safe ones. But one night, our unit had taken over an abandoned palace—this crazy-ass place full of shadows and turrets, and I knew it was stupid. The slightest indication of what we were and we'd be outed and kicked out. The Marines . . . this was my life, you get it? I know you do. It was what I lived for . . . apart from him."

"Tell me what happened that night." Nikos pulled his chair closer.

"It was stupid, so stupid, but it was miserable over there and staying apart was eating us alive. So we made plans to meet . . . alone. We'd been there only a few minutes, in this darkened doorway that was out of patrol range and everyone's sights. And then that's when the shrieking came . . . the howling. It was a demon like I'd never seen. A female Djinn."

Nikos went still. There were no female Djinn, not that he or his fellow Spartans had ever seen, not from the very beginning of their time as immortals. He was about to point that out to Mason when he continued, "Wonder why you never see 'em, don't you? The females? I know why." He smiled bitterly, his stare growing much darker. "Because the males keep them bound in the desert. Corralled together, controlled. And Kelly and I . . . had come across one who happened to think I was exactly what she wanted, after all those years alone. Years without any sort of man, demon or not."

Mason's eyes closed for a moment. "She was gorgeous, of course, with long hip-length black hair and full of curves. If that sort of thing did anything for me." He laughed darkly. "She wanted me. That's what she said. When I refused, she revealed her true self, all her claws and scales and fire. Made sure Kelly could see her, even though he wasn't a hunter like me. Kelly stepped between us, ready to fight. And she tore my lover apart from the inside out. Right before my eyes she ripped him to shreds without drawing so much as a breath."

There was no comfort to offer, no touch that could alleviate this kind of guilt and pain. Nikos struggled internally,

reached into every part of his Spartan mind for ancient wis-
dom to ease the mortal's burden. He found nothing.

"He died in my arms," Mason added, sinking heavily
into the mattress. "I lost my lover, the only person I *ever*
loved like that ... and had to pretend he'd only been my
buddy. Had to lie to everyone about what went down, including about what happened with the demon. So that's my
story. Not glorious or brave like how you lost Doros, not
even admirable. Kelly died because I wanted to hold him in
my arms, and I got my wish in the end, damn it. And I died
that day, too, because I'm a coward who couldn't keep him
from protecting me."

They remained quiet for several long moments, but then
a nurse entered the room. "Time for more medication," she
announced brightly with a glance at Nikos. "Is this your
brother?"

Mason shook his head, eyes still closed. "A friend." Then
those gorgeous green eyes flipped open again, locking with
Nik's own as if he were waiting for something more.

"Yes, friends," Nikos agreed, swallowing several times.
"Good ... friends."

Mason sank back into the pillows then, smiling.

# Chapter 33

"Do you believe him?"

River started at the light feminine voice and, turning, discovered that a gorgeous woman stood off to his side. He'd been sitting on the stone steps that led down the mountain's long drop-off, a part of him considering the idea of throwing himself off the great mountaintop. Wasn't that what you did after discovering everything and everyone you'd ever believed in had turned out to be a vapor, a deception of the highest, most soul-wounding type?

She moved closer. "He's the liar, you know. Not the ones you love. And I don't care if he hears me say it, either."

"Who are you?" River looked back toward the palace, figuring this was more of Ares' confusing assault on his mind.

She smiled, running a hand through short black spiking hair. Wait! Were those blue streaks he saw glimmering there? *Blue Streaks.* That had been the nickname Shay gave their Oracle back in Cornwall.

Blinking up at her, he finally recognized the fey woman, drawing on his memory of the ancient day of their bargain. "Oracle," he murmured in awe and relief. Oh, thank the Highest. This one, this one he could trust; he knew it. "Our dearest, beloved Oracle." He hadn't been cast aside after all, not by the Highest. And perhaps, if she spoke the truth as he knew that she must, not by those he cherished.

She cast a semi-nervous glance over her shoulder, sitting down beside him on the stone step. She spread her gown out carefully and with one last look toward the palace, lowered her voice. "He's being *entertained*." She waggled an eyebrow. "He can't help himself from indulging his bodily desires . . . many times a day. No discipline." She clucked her tongue. "None whatsoever, the creep."

River wasn't sure if he should laugh, agree, or demur. So he did the smart thing—the tactic that every slave memorized early on—and kept his trap shut.

"We won't have long, so I'll tell you what I know," she said in a quiet voice. "He wants what's inside of you, River." She reached one small, elegant hand out and planted it over his heart. He almost laughed when he saw that her fingernails were painted in sparkly blue polish as if she were some punk-rock goddess.

"Ares wants the power *inside* of you, do you understand?" She patted his chest emphatically.

"No, my lady." He shook his head, feeling more confused than ever. "I don't know what you mean."

"I was there, the day of the bargain, remember that. I know what he did, what he gave you."

"The power of life and death?"

She smiled. "Yes, but there's more. What he gave you was far more than just that, as great as it must have always seemed. But I dare not speak it now." Her expression grew grim once again, and she cast a nervous glance toward the palace interior. "He already controls and owns me, and he can't hurt me anymore than he already has these past days. So I have a plan, River. But you must not trust any of those images he showed you. I know what he did to you; I heard him gloating over it after. None of what he showed you was true, River."

He stared down at his hands, holding his tongue. Those scenes had felt so real, so vivid and genuine, even as his heart had decried them.

She tilted her head sideways, and gave him a playful shove in the chest. "River! You know your brothers and friends. Your Spartans love you, value you with their lives."

He rubbed a hand over his eyes. "I know." And he did; although the god had done a powerful, impressive job of filling his mind with false images, they had still felt wrong. "I do believe you, my lady. Not him."

"Good. That's important."

"He has never brought me anything more than pain. He's not my god. Not anymore."

She slid a hand over his arm. "Even better." With a quick smile, she confided, "I'm sending you back to them now. And this act of defiance is going to bring the current battle to its climax."

"How? Will you create a portal?" He knew that the Oracle often created supernatural doorways that he and Jax traversed as a fighting pair.

"Yes, my dear portal jumper," she said with a light laugh. "P.J., right? Isn't that what Ari always calls you?" That was the nickname Ari used whenever a portal jump left River woozy.

"I'm not sure what to make of our Oracle calling me by that nickname."

She leaned forward and pressed a chaste kiss to his cheek. "You go, good warrior, and prepare your comrades. Tell them to gather and summon the Highest God. This will bring Ares to the table, and he'll be ready to fight."

"Where will he battle us?" River asked, his mind moving quickly over the revelations.

"I'm not sure, but I imagine the place of your making."

"Hades," he whispered in fearful wonder. "We can't fight him there and win. He's a god."

The Oracle tilted her chin upward, challenging him with her look. "River Kassandros, Ares has attempted to destroy you here on Olympus. He tried to kill Ajax, allowed your blade to be misused and lost. . . . He is cruel and must be stopped. He hasn't won yet, and he won't do so if you all join together."

"But we've always gained our power from him."

"You have more strength and force inside each of you—and yourself in particular—than you realize right now. Not to mention your secret weapon."

He shook his head in confusion and she continued. "Emma. You have Emma, a second Daughter of Delphi, and she can combine her power with Shay's. Ares does not know that Emma is a Daughter because Sable never told him. I heard the interchange when he returned with his report. Two Daughters focused in will and strength to protect their mates is a powerful force to reckon with. The only thing stronger would be three or perhaps four." She smiled as if considering something, then dismissed the thought with a little shake of her head. "But two aligned, unified Daughters of the same bloodline will be able to bolster all of you and your fighting strength."

"I don't want Emma in danger," River argued, trying to visualize his beloved in a descent to Hades. "He won't transport them anyway, will he?"

"If you are together when you call upon the Highest, all will be conveyed to wherever Ares determines to battle you. And you can't keep Emma out of the charge, River, because she's a warrior like you. Just a different sort of one." The Oracle gave him an impish, charming grin. "She's like *me*. A seer and a listener ... and, hmm, seems there's something about being able to smell spirits. That's a rare one."

"She's rare," he said, feeling his chest tighten as he thought of Emma, and of how much he loved her. Yes, he would fight any demon or any god who wanted to harm her in any way. "I will defend her to the death."

The Oracle rose, touching a warm hand to his shoulder as she stood. "Go and tell the Spartans," she said firmly. "I can free you for now, but it must be right now."

His mind rushed with questions. He opened his mouth, starting to ask them very quickly, but it was too late by then. He'd already begun moving through the eerie, rushing fabric of time and space.

River found himself flat on his back, woozy, half unconscious. Voices were all around him, warm, kind, familiar ones. There was a cool cloth pressed against his forehead. And that touch, the one he recognized, just as he did the soft, feminine voice.

"He's coming around, I think," Emma said.

River groaned, rolling onto his side. It was worse than any portal jump he'd ever made while serving Ajax.

He felt Ari's big hands groping at his arms and shoulders. "He's solid at least."

River tried speaking but his tongue felt as if it were glued to the roof of his mouth; he groaned again.

"Aw, come on, P.J.," Ari urged. "We want to know how you got back to us, man."

"Oracle," he finally managed to say, cracking open one eye long enough to see Emma's knees. And her upper thighs. Shorts. Nice. *Welcome home, bub*, he thought and started to laugh.

"What about our Oracle?" That was Leonidas's voice, and hearing his authority and concern finally brought River back to himself.

He sat up slowly, Emma wrapping her arms about him and helping. She kept him held tight, never letting go even once he'd reached a stable sitting position. He didn't care if the others were watching: he turned his head and gave her a slow, warm kiss on the mouth.

She smiled. "You kept your promise."

"I will always come back, Em. Always."

She flung her arms about his neck, holding him close. "Welcome home, baby."

"Bub," he corrected with a glance down at her very small shorts. "Welcome home, bub."

Emma couldn't stop touching River; she needed to feel that he was solid and whole and alive. During the time of his capture, waiting and wondering if he was all right had been almost more than she could stand. Now they sat on the floor of the library facing each other, she all but climbing into his lap.

"I really am all right," he promised, petting her hair in a tender manner. She closed her eyes, burrowing against his chest. Wanting to drink him in, still afraid that somehow, someway, he would be ripped away from her all over again.

"For now." She inhaled his woodsy scent, pressing her face right over his heart. "But what about this much bigger fight that's coming?"

For a long moment he said nothing, until Emma pulled back to read his expression. "What aren't you telling me?" she asked.

He smiled, reaching a thumb to her mouth and trailing it back and forth thoughtfully. "I'm not worried about myself," he told her after a moment.

"Well, gee, there's a relief." She didn't even care if she sounded snappish. It felt as if she'd come incredibly close to losing him for all time and so maybe that did bring out her hidden inner bitch. That inner lioness who wanted to be sure her mate was free of all predators.

"I'm worried about you, Emma," he said, letting his hand fall back to his side. "Because I need you in this fight that's coming. What's brewing is unlike anything we've ever faced, and"—he sighed, bowing his head—"I have to ask you and Shay to join us in this Armageddon of sorts. And I hate that I must. But the Oracle has spoken and she has never misled us."

Emma wasn't sure she'd just heard him correctly. She had the ridiculous urge to stare at him and say something utterly inane. Like, "Huh?" Which she did, and was surprised when the word actually popped out of her mouth.

"You're a Daughter of Delphi and so is Shay. You have power that can bring down the walls of protection Ares has erected around himself. You, both of you, will be our secret weapons in this imminent and epic battle."

Emma felt a thrill rush through her whole body, but she would have sworn it was more than a physical reaction to his words. It was downright spiritual, like an answer to a mighty call had just gone forth. A call that her lover, her other half, had issued; their very nature as a couple and a team instantly had her ready to fight.

*You were made to battle together*, she thought, almost as if the words had been whispered in her ear from another dimension. *You were made for this moment, for him, for this particular war.*

Emma gave a resolved, emboldened nod. "Let's go find Shay, then. And gather the others so you can tell us what we need to do."

Daphne peered out of her room, watching Sable trot back and forth in the expansive hallway. Ares had clearly summoned him for a debriefing, yet couldn't be bothered to meet the Djinn in a timely manner.

*Too busy satisfying his sensual side, as always*, she thought with a scowl. Her brother was greedy, insatiable and—to top it all off—cruel. The evidence of that trait exhibited itself in the poor demon's slow movements. She'd had enough opportunities to study his elegant strength, even if it had been misappropriated for Ares' purposes. But now with the harsh spikes covering the centaur's body, his physical torture and suffering were more than apparent to her.

And it also gave her a better avenue for defeating her brother. Perhaps the Highest himself was offering this moment.

With a furtive glance she ducked out of her room and moved straight toward Sable, holding her head high. "You," she said firmly. "I have prophetic words for you."

Sable jolted visibly, rearing around to face her with his usual sneer. But she glimpsed vulnerability in his red, beady gaze that she'd never seen before. "What could you have for me, Oracle?"

She stood even taller, sweeping her long robe behind her regally. "You might be surprised at my words, brave Djinn."

He rolled his red-filled eyes sarcastically. "Me? Since when would you call me brave? You despise me for my long-standing opposition to your Spartans."

She shook her head, bunching the folds of her gown within her right hand in an effort to remain calm. "No. No, Sable, you have worth. I saw it in your eyes that day four months ago at Bonaventure. When you refused to harm Shayanna Angel any more than you already had."

The demon snarled, clomping backward several steps. "You and I, fair Oracle, have nothing to say today."

She wasn't going to back down from this opportunity. Such a moment might never present itself again, and gaining Sable's support could literally turn the tide of battle. "I have words for you, Djinn. You would dare disdain what the Highest has for you?"

He blinked back at her, silent, and for the briefest instant his bloodred eyes turned in hue. They shifted to what she'd glimpsed so briefly that day in the cemetery and became light, ethereal blue.

\* \* \*

Sable had listened to her quick words, his eyes remaining that lightest shade of blue that identified him as a descendant of the oracles of Delphi. Half Djinn and half oracle—she'd recognized his bloodline that day four months earlier. Now that she'd finished speaking, the red haze filled his vision once more and he spat out his reply.

"I'm not a *Daughter*," he said with a hissing sound. "Not chosen, not *special*."

She shook her head. "No. You're wrong, Sable. You have a destiny the same as any other descendant; it doesn't matter that you're a Son and not a Daughter."

He laughed mockingly. "There aren't provisions for bastard demon spawn like me. My demon father raped my mother. You do realize that, right? And I am of his loins, of his seed. I am what he is and has always been. Evil. Twisted. Wrong."

She threw a cautious glance toward Ares' chambers. Any moment and he would interrupt them; these few moments were it. They would define everything, determine whether Sable could be brought to their cause of righteousness.

"I'm the half-breed spawn of my own father," she answered simply. "But I am the woman I was called to be. Just as you have within you the seeds of goodness. Not to be like your father. To be something epic. Something glorious and much more than he has ever been."

Sable tossed back his head, laughing, but the sound hit a hollow note. "Do you know my father? A dark demon lord, that's what he is. He bred me for darkness, too. It was his only purpose with me, ever. Darkness and fire and smoke."

"Your mother loved you."

"You do not know that!" he thundered. "You never knew her."

"Are you sure?" she countered.

There was a long, heavy pause and he took several slow steps closer to her. "Did . . . you?" There was quiet, almost desperate hope to the question, and she wished with painful intensity that she had known his mother. But at least she had the truth, words being offered to her from a much higher source.

"No, good Sable, I did not know her. I'm sorry." She bowed her head with honest regret. "But I hear the words the Highest is offering you, and I know that she did love you. She kept you as a babe, did she not?"

She lifted her eyes and saw the truth in his flinching gaze. She dared to continue, feeling her whole body tremble with the intensity of what God was revealing to her—and this time, unlike so many others, she was lucid and aware of what the Highest showed. "She held you there at Delphi until you were no less than three years old. She prayed and hoped to keep you safe from your father's cruel wrath, but . . ." She pressed her eyes shut, feeling tears threaten. "She did not succeed and he murdered her, taking you with him into the desert. But not before she showed you the good, kind portion of life. She did show you that, Sable. I know that she did because the Highest himself has revealed that fact to me."

He shook his head, his expression guarded and unreadable—but less cruel than she'd ever seen it. "It was too soon. And it's too late for me now."

She moved toward him, her hands extended in supplication. "It's not! Ares will never be anything but a cruel taskmaster for you. You can fight him; you can rebel and join the Spartans in their battle to thwart his plans. You can end his constant and ongoing torture of your soul. You are worthy, Sable. You are still worthy of freedom."

He dropped his head to his shoulders with a weary, soul-deep sigh. "I will never be free of his hand. My own god shackled me to him."

"Sable," she said slowly, "there is a Higher God. You know it and you can still listen to him. It will never be too late for hearing him."

He didn't answer—just stared at the floor. In those endless moments she prayed and begged with all her spiritual strength that the Highest would take hold of Sable's lost half-breed soul . . . and finally set it free.

# Chapter 34

They were assembled in the upstairs library. There had been some debate as to the best place for such a warlike moment, but in the end it was the ordinary world that seemed most important to Leonidas's warriors. He hardly blamed them.

Night had fallen and they'd filed into the dark-paneled room, the Spartans in full armor, Shay and the Shades in their military kit. Emma had joined them, too, and knelt beside River, their hands locking them together as one.

Candles flickered about the quiet room, the play of light and dark an eerie shroud over the somber moment.

"We're here, gathered as one, warriors, that we might summon our Oracle. That we might hear her advice." These were the words that River had brought back from Olympus: the ones their guide had said they should use.

He'd seen enough of Ares' temper and jealousy regarding the woman to know she was undoubtedly right. By declaring allegiance to her—and to the Highest God—they would bring forth the battle. Would it be their end? Perhaps. But Leonidas saw no good reason to delay this inevitable showdown, and every motivation to act now. That the Oracle guided them to do so only reinforced that fact.

Leonidas bowed his head, beginning the prayers. "Our Highest God, we humbly bow before you. We ask for your assistance this night. We call for your Oracle, who gives us your words. We serve you and ask to hear your divine will."

The candles around the room flickered, a surge of wind billowed from nowhere, extinguishing all the light. Leonidas pressed forward, offering prayers of love and gratitude to the one true God, the one whom Ares despised.

"Oracle, we hope that our prayers have been heard and that the Highest will offer his hand to us, and send you as our guide."

The wind around them increased, a whispering sound entering on it. It was deep and rich, filled with a peace that Leonidas had never once known. Not his Oracle . . . it was the voice of the Highest himself.

*I have heard, my children. I have heard. . . . Prepare now to fight.*

All at once that forceful, driving wind blew every door to the upper porch wide open, shattered every window with a high-pitched noise.

Emma watched, stunned, as a giant mist that had enveloped them all suddenly parted. She still clung to River's hand; whatever space or force they'd just experienced had been gentle enough that they'd kept hold of each other.

She blinked as one by one all the Spartans appeared around them. And she saw Shay, too.

"Where are we?" she asked River under her breath.

He hesitated, eyes wide, then looked down at her. "Hades. This is Hades and that"—he gestured with his head toward the distance—"that's Styx."

"Oh, holy crap."

He nodded at that comment, but said nothing more.

"And so it begins," a thundering, frightening voice declared. All the Spartans searched, obviously working to stay calm, but she could feel the ripple of tension that moved through their midst.

From the last remaining fog, a tall figure emerged. A man with long golden hair, bearing a spear and a shield. He arrived in what looked like a chariot, drawn by powerful horses; he pulled them to a halt, and Emma would have sworn on her life that those horses reacted by breathing fire.

*Crap, crap, crap,* she thought. *Not Oz, not Kansas. Not even a Terry Gilliam movie.*

The heat was stifling, humid, far worse than Savannah in a record heat wave; it was as if someone had taken that same sweltering dampness and turned the dial up by about twenty more degrees. Within moments Emma felt her shorts plastering against the backs of her legs by rivulets of sweat. Her T-shirt clung to her bra; her hair stuck against the sides of her cheeks; her panties glued to her bottom. And still that hot, damp, acrid wind blew.

As she continued to hold River's hand, a slick sheen blossomed between their two palms. But it was the burning, smoky smell wafting from every direction that bothered her most. Mostly she associated fire with happy memories, but this toxic, foul smell rose from every crevice in the realm, oozing in the humid air, flowing through the River Styx that she saw some hundred yards across from where they stood.

Ares rose from inside his chariot, fondling a barbed golden whip, rolling it in the palm of his hand absently. "My beloved immortals, come to see me at last. How many months, warriors? Four since you last worshipped me or made offerings. Obviously we must work on our communication issues." He laughed dully. "Of course, the time for talking and worshipping is long past."

Leonidas stepped to the forefront of their gathered crew. "We no longer serve you, Ares. You're well aware of that fact from our previous . . . messages."

Ares sneered at the king. "You should never have tried to use the Oracle to manipulate me."

Emma watched a troubled expression travel over Leonidas's face, but it quickly morphed into fighting fury. "You should never have begun that game, but I will ensure that you never harm or threaten her again." There was a protective tone to the words, one Emma wouldn't have quite expected from the king.

"You reach beyond even your hubris, Leonidas, believing that you can step into Hades and threaten a *god*?" Ares laughed in a low purr. "But perhaps I should consider this a social call. It is, after all, the anniversary of our bargain, the very date that you've come to me every year since." Ares moved closer to the king, still fingering the thorny whip within his palm. "You've come and pledged your fealty. Your willingness to uphold our bargain. Perhaps I've merely miscalculated the purpose you displayed by bowing before *the Highest God* on this, *our day*!" Dozens of thunderclaps resounded through his loud words, seeming to echo within his voice somehow. Emma began trembling at the sound of the god's voice as it became so much less human-seeming. So terrifying.

"I made all of you!" The god's lightning gaze shot among the Spartans, actual strikes that leaped out of his eyes and licked at the warriors. Emma saw Ari's whole body grow electrified, jolting from the force; she watched in horror as Straton's bulky form seemed to shake like a rag doll beneath the assault. He thrashed about, his arms whipping disjointedly, his head jerking.

For some reason, Ares kept at the silent, dour warrior, ripping that electricity into him until Straton convulsed beneath the assault. Then for one horrifically distended moment the Spartan's shield went flying out of his hand, tumbling toward the ground. There was a collective gasp among the Spartans because the warriors treated their shields with reverence, but Straton lunged, taking hold of his bowl again as he collapsed to the ground.

However, it was the match to the impending battle's kindling. One millisecond of silence, then a clamoring, crazed roar of warfare arose. River thrust Emma toward a boulder, already moving in unity with the other Spartans. "Stay over there, Em," he told her roughly. "You and Shay . . . you do your thing. We need you in this fight. Go!"

Shay sprinted forward, the two of them bounding toward the rock that River had pointed out. "Over here!" Emma urged her cousin. "We can use the biggest boulder for cover."

There were several smaller ones, and then a misty outcropping beyond them that led to a roaring, black vacuum. Emma stared at it for a moment, shaking and transfixed, until Shay's strong hand came down on her shoulder, shoving her to the ground. "We'll think about that later," Shay told her in a chilled voice.

"Just don't go any farther than here," Emma said, looking back at the swirling cauldron of nothingness. It was what she'd always thought hell would be: the absence of life, negative matter. A soul-draining, spirit-destroying spiral of anti-life.

And no matter how hard Emma tried, she simply couldn't stop staring at it in horror. The spiraling funnel had her in a kind of thrall, she realized when Shay began pulling at her arm, tugging, then yanking.

"Em, look away! You have to force yourself to break the spell." Was it a spell? Like a magical force? She couldn't make her mouth work to find the words to ask.

"Emma, now. It's an attack on you, your gift ... our unity."

"It is death," she murmured, chilled at the thought of going anywhere but heaven at the end of her days. "It's all that it is. No life, no joy, nothingness ..."

Starting to her feet, Emma wanted to go gaze down into the black thing. Perhaps, she thought dazedly, if she could simply see that it wasn't nearly so void.

With a painful crack to her head, Emma went sprawling on her back, a jagged rock hitting her spine. She cried out at the pain, staring up into Shay's worried face.

"Good, you're back with me," Shay told her, rubbing a palm over Emma's cheek in obvious relief. "Now don't go look at that horrible thing again. Stay here and focus. The boys' fates depend on it; our lives do, too."

Emma bobbed her head. "I don't know why that happened."

Shay huddled close to her. "It's called spiritual warfare, sweetie. You'll learn more about it when we get out of this mess. *When.* Now take my hand and let's unite our power. We have to pray out loud and fast ... both of us must invoke the name of the Highest God as well as the blood of Jesus Christ."

They'd talked about these tools for battling darkness before they'd called upon the Highest God, but they hadn't had nearly enough time. So Emma was appreciative that Shay was recentering her now after that first onslaught she'd experienced.

"One thing, Shay. Ares isn't a demon, so why will spiritual warfare work against him? I thought that was just for battling spirits of darkness."

Shay drew their hands together, to join them in physical unity. "He is a force of darkness ... we just don't un-

derstand what that means precisely. But the Shades have
lore and scriptures; that's how we learn the tools to practice
spiritual warfare. One thing we know is what the scriptures
say, 'that all other gods must bow before him.' The Highest
God of all."

Against her back Emma felt a fierce, suctioning wind
begin—and it seemed to be coming from that unholy cauldron that had mesmerized her earlier. Was it rising up now?
Coming to claim her? Emma shook off the fearful thought
like she'd kick away a snake.

Focusing on Shay's hands against her, she thought only
of the Highest. He would save River and defend him. He
could defeat all other gods.

This uneven, impossible battle wouldn't last long. And
the realization filled River's heart with an immense sadness
that he had no time to acknowledge. The storm of bronze
against bronze, of clashing weapons, filled the smoky haze
of the underworld. From every invisible crevice demons
emerged, descending upon their cadre of seven like locusts.

The minions were armed in ancient battle gear, perhaps
Ares' idea of an ironic joke. River was too busy slashing
and hacking his way within their unified phalanx to care.
One more step forward, hold the line; two more steps, keep
shield in place.

Over the melee he shouted to Ajax on his left. "I should
transform! If I can, then you'll have a more impacting
weapon."

"Too risky to you. You stay as you are."

He understood the risk factor, but the argument still
pissed him off. This was a battle for their lives, and he
should serve in his highest capacity; they could sort out any
transition problems if they survived. Of course, that wasn't
the true reason Ajax didn't want him weapon-shifting. Because if he were in weapon form and Ares seized him, it
would be far too easy for the god to cast him back into
the fiery current that had formed his blade in the beginning. Then, Styx would consume his weapon-body, melting
it back down, swallowing him into the same force that had
birthed his immortal form.

The phalanx staggered forward several rushing steps. Every advance they made, they moved closer toward Styx. He understood the king's fighting approach: to drive the attacking demon hordes forward until they reached the river, which would lock them in from behind. They'd used the same strategy at Thermopylae, sending thousands of Persians tumbling over the cliffs of the pass, and into the crashing waves far below. But in this case, their surging advance toward the water threatened to destroy them in the process because Styx might hold death for all of them this day.

Emma kept her eyes sealed shut as a tomb, following Shay's prayerful lead. Some of her words were in ancient Greek, special incantations her cousin had learned from the same journal about the Daughters that Emma now owned. Why hadn't there been more time? Why hadn't she pored over that book during the car ride home instead of feeling skeptical? Now River's life hung in the balance, all of theirs did, and her fecklessness during that fifteen-minute drive might mean their deaths.

"You can't doubt, not right now, Em. Stay focused." Shay gave her hands a reassuring squeeze.

"How did you know I was . . ."

"I don't know thoughts. I just know how scared I am, but we have to keep our minds on the Highest and his power to defeat Ares. To uphold the righteous."

Emma kept praying, and then a flowing musical sound instantly made her feel less afraid. Shay began singing, her beautiful voice firm and defiant against the evil that threatened to engulf them. For one small instant, Emma felt soothed . . . until a roar from Styx's direction cracked across the open space, causing both of them to open their eyes and stare.

What she saw was worse than any nightmare she might have conjured, and more chilling than the worst of what they'd seen and experienced so far. Her heart seemed to hesitate and spasm within her chest. Her throat tightened with unspent sobs.

*Oh, God, no*, she prayed, wanting the image to be a nightmare, untrue. "Anything but that . . ."

Emma watched as Ares lifted her beloved high into the air, suspending him far above even his own head by the sheer force of his god's power. Dark, tinkling laughter drifted across the field that separated her and Shay from the warriors. It seemed to practically seep across the space, filling her terrified imagination with dark images of what he planned to do to River.

"You should have accepted my offer." The war god laughed in that falsely light, musical tone. "You could have had Olympus and power beyond that. I laid it at your feet. You only had to serve me."

River lunged and struggled where he was suspended midair, and although his deep voice didn't project like the deity's did, Emma heard him plainly. The words were strained, slow in coming because of the physical torture he was enduring. But she did hear them. They all did.

"I . . . am . . . not a servant. I am . . . a free . . . man. I am free. . . ."

Ares roared and with a blistering flash of power River was gone, no longer suspended at all. Emma bolted to her feet. What had Ares done to him? She felt sobs building inside of her chest. Could the god have made him vanish into nothing?

She moved beyond the boulders, desperate for any sign of River at all, her whole body quaking with emotion. That was the moment when she understood. When she knew in her heart and soul the cost that had been exacted from the man she loved so deeply.

Ares smiled in admiration, turning a gleaming, exquisite broadsword in his grasp. Against her lover's will, against every instinct he'd just expressed about freedom and equality . . . the god had just turned him into a weapon once again.

Emma was already at a dead run before she realized that she'd begun moving at all. She was graceless in her panic, sprinting and stumbling wildly as she crossed the distance that had separated her from the warriors. Ares glanced up, obviously detecting her movement, and by then she was near enough that she saw his lips curl back in a sneer.

He greeted her by raising River's sword form high in the air as if it were the booty of a conquered nation.

"Ah, my handiwork is gorgeous, indeed," he said, his white teeth gleaming in the wafting heat of Styx. "What a shame that I must—how shall I put this? Dismantle you now, River."

The Spartans surged against the encircling demons that held them corralled, and Emma heard Ari curse and threaten Ares, but he didn't look toward the warriors. He kept his calculating, golden stare trained on her, watching her approach in a predatory manner. She knew he wanted her, that it was a part of his diabolical attack against River. But how could she hold back with his life hovering on the brink? She knew from their earlier conversation that if Ares returned his blade to Styx, he would be destroyed.

Emma reached the place where Ares stood, and steeling every fiber of braveness in her body, she faced the god and did the unthinkable. She thrust her shoulders back, stood tall and proud. "Ares, that sword you're holding belongs to me. I'm here to claim him."

Then, praying silently the entire time, she did something even braver. She extended her right hand and waited for Ares to place River within her expectant grasp. For a sliver of a second he seemed a bit amused. He clucked his tongue next, staring at her trembling hand. Then the mild humor dissipated, a cruel expression moving over his features.

The shift in mood apparently signaled the release of a foul odor, one that blossomed across the god's skin. The moment Ares' face twisted into that mask of hatred, a scent so rank and putrid emanated from him that she could barely keep from heaving in reaction. She swallowed and tried not to breathe much at all, but the vile odor kept pouring off the god's body. It was the evil scent of his true nature, she thought. She alone could smell it because of her gift, but it reflected the truth nonetheless. It was the smell of decay and death, of endless, ageless rotting.

Ares kept his gaze locked on her and strolled casually to the edge of the river. "I'm sorry, mortal, but I won't be giving River into your hand today. I regret to inform you that he is going to be otherwise *dis*engaged." He laughed, dragging the tip of River's blade along the surface of the rushing river. "Disengaged, disemboweled, dismantled, dismembered. However we put it, it seems I've been forced to 'dis' your lover in the same manner he has chosen to disrespect and dishonor *me*."

With those threatening words, Ares allowed River to slide out of his hand like dead weight and plunge into the ravenous river that waited below. Emma screamed, surging forward with extended hands, slashing them at the god until he captured her wrists, manacling them in his iron grip. "Now, that's not very grateful."

She struggled in his painful hold. "You're hateful . . . cruel."

"Why, thank you!" he said in genuinely pleased surprise. "How lovely of you to say. For that compliment, my dear, I will grant a boon; I'll allow you to join River in his watery fate."

As if she were no more than a feather, Ares flung her toward the water with brute force. And she felt thick, warm water wrap about her entering body like glue.

# Chapter 35

Emma couldn't see anything at all except the rushing fire and currents that swallowed her and dragged her down. The force was almost impossible to swim against, pulling at her legs, making the water thicker and movement harder with every thrash of her limbs.

She would not drown in these depths. No one in her life would ever drown again, not River, not any person she loved. It was just what she'd vowed that first day on Tybee, she realized. That she would never allow another person she cared about to die in waves or water, not if she could do anything to stop it. Remembering that day at the beach and how they'd beat back the demons—how she'd managed to find River in the water against all odds—empowered her.

She didn't care how suffocating this eternal river was, or if she had to fight the hounds of Hades to do it, but she would find her love. She would save River even if she lost her own life in the process. He deserved to be safe and free after an eternity of serving mankind and of living in bondage; finding him now was the truest gesture of love she could ever give him.

*I will not drown*, she resolved. *I'm going to find River and save him.*

At that moment she stopped struggling against the current, and began to swim. She actually dove deeper, and feeling with her hands she reached blindly for River's sword form. She refused to panic or listen to the words Ares had spoken, but it was hard not to feel desperate. She had to find River, and fast—before his sword melted in the torrent the way Ares had threatened it would. A flashing image of his beautiful, very human green eyes filled her mind, urging her to swim faster and to find him. Another image filled her thoughts, one of his shining sword form melting and dripping down to nothing like some overspent candle.

*No!* she screamed inside her soul. River wasn't going to dissolve in this eternal river. She prayed as hard as she could, choking on her own desperation, wanting to breathe and cry and sob. From nowhere, a thought came to her—or perhaps it was her answered prayer. The idea hit her as a question. If Styx was intended to destroy them both, then why was *she* surviving right now? And not just surviving, but becoming stronger. Once she stopped fighting against it, the flow filled her with energy. It didn't bring pain or fear; in fact, it seemed to diminish those emotions.

Here on the brink of life and death, everything became crystal clear, as bright as the gleam she'd seen on River's sword moments ago. The truth burned brighter than the fiery waves that engulfed her body. Waves that were as mystical as the warrior she'd fallen in love with; engulfing her with intimacy and life, yet not burning her at all. These waters had given her love, her River, life and rebirth. They could never rob her of that same animating pulse.

*Ares had been lying!*

The god was a master of lies, and his claim about returning River to Styx was yet one more deception in an endless train of them. He'd had one motivation: to make them believe River was destroyed so they would leave him behind in Styx, languishing and abandoned yet safeguarded for Ares' own cruel purposes. Once he'd destroyed the rest of them, he could take ownership of River, using him, and the power inside of him, for his vile plans.

Ares had only been lying, she repeated to herself, focusing on the words in order to remain calm. She swam harder, deeper still, sweeping her hands all about her, aware that her air supply was nearly exhausted, but she ignored the urge to surface. She thought of that very first time he'd cried out to her, and she'd dove in to help him.

*River!* she cried out in her spirit, hoping to hear him. *Where are you, River? I've got to find you!*

*Deep*, she heard him reply, *too deep, Em. Go back. You can't reach me.*

*Don't say that!* she told him. *I will find you.*

*He won't ever let you.*

*I have to find you.* She screamed the words through their connection, making him hear how determined she was. *He can't win now; I won't let him take you from me.*

*He already has.*

*Stop it! Fight, damn it. He can't take your freedom.*

She would have screamed then if she could have, because from the surging, fiery current she was gripped by a pair of strong, human-feeling hands. Seizing her arms and holding on in a clamping grip, those hands tugged Emma down. Down, far down into those eternal depths. With strength she couldn't possibly fight back against.

The very last oxygen left her lungs, and she felt a sad, exhausting acceptance about her fate. This was it; she would die here, trapped below the surface and unable to breathe. What an ironic situation. Here she'd been determined nobody else would drown if she could help it, and she was the one about to die. Another female in her family line pulled down to the merciless depths.

She thought of River and how he needed her, of Sophie and her mother, of Shay and Mason and Jamie. Her heart ached with that harsh, sad sense of loss, of the times they'd never share now. Her thoughts turned toward Leah last of all, sadness filling her, that emotion the most suffocating as her life began to ebb away. This was how Leah had felt; this was how alone and lost she'd been at the very end.

*Forgive me,* she offered on a whisper. To River, to Leah, to everyone she loved. *I tried. . . . I tried so hard.*

Nikos watched the churning tide in horror, searching for a sign of River, for any hint of where Emma might be struggling to surface. He'd never felt so furious or so helpless as he did knowing that his brother had once again been tossed into a surging river without the ability to transform or change back to his human self. Too many years he'd wasted when it came to River Kassandros, and that thought slammed him with the worst sort of remorse. They could have been close, might have been brothers in the truest sense of the word.

"Yes, the fire of Styx will swallow that slave whole. Take back what never belonged to him in the first place," Ares announced, rising taller and larger on the riverbank. Looming over each of them by at least six feet, a terrible tyrant; a grotesque horror, not the mighty figure he clearly hoped he could be.

"I am returning River Kassandros to the place of his creation by my own hand," Ares announced regally. "I am emptying him. Draining away that excess greatness that he never deserved, was never worthy of. A god's power! In a slave?" Ares began laughing. "It should have been a marvelous plan, but it was doomed to failure by my choice of recipient. Such a weak, incapable receptacle."

The god stomped toward the edge of the river, staring into the depths, the huge cloak across his shoulders rippling like a cruel battle flag.

"Perhaps I should have selected more wisely, not chosen one as primitive and unschooled as the slave." Ares glanced toward the Spartans as if measuring each of them and finding them wanting. "Leonidas, too moral and good. Aristos . . . too irreverent, of course." His harsh glance moved among them. "Straton, you're cold enough, perhaps there would have been hope. Kalias, too uptight." Ares turned, and Nikos knew he was being sought for evaluation, but he slunk down behind a boulder beside the river to conceal himself. The god would sense him, but hopefully would be distracted and lose interest very soon.

There were murmurs among the cadre, the warriors forming into battle lines, but Nikos didn't move. He stared at the river as it leaped and surged against the banks, knowing that if River was going to survive—if Emma was—he had to take action, and fast.

From the mist a thundering form appeared, seizing Nikos's attention, and he cursed upon recognizing Sable. The centaur rode at them, swords gripped in both hands, the jeweled hilts glowing with otherworldly power. Not what they needed at this moment, Nikos thought, palming his own sword.

"My favorite Djinn," Ares called out in a voice that echoed like several thunderclaps. "About time you arrived."

Sable cantered toward the god to join his side. Ares gave him a smile that revealed white, devouring teeth. Sable neared the god, but then all at once cut back, and began galloping with a charging cry, both swords extended overhead. He stormed toward Leonidas as if he meant to take those swords and run him through.

The moment seemed absurdly long as the Djinn rode furiously, his swords aimed toward their beloved king. Nikos was too far away to take action, and he was almost out of time if he hoped to save River and Emma. He gave a quick glance toward the flaming river and then watched as Leonidas's massive ebony wings unfurled across his back. Their commander shot upward, out of Sable's hurtling path, but Nikos wasn't prepared for what that twisted Djinn did next. None of them could have imagined such a radical, unexpected move.

Nikos's jaw fell slack as he watched, unable to believe Sable's actions.

Emma couldn't fight the strong hands that dragged her down. She felt herself growing faint and light-headed from lack of oxygen, but also overtaken by a strange kind of surrender. As if these stranger's hands brought safety, comfort. Maybe they belonged to an angel of some kind.

*River*, she tried calling, but she'd grown too weak. The powerful hands that gripped her shifted, and she found her right hand being clasped tightly. She tried to see who tugged her, but her vision filled with a bright blur that forced her to press her eyes shut again.

And then the pulling motion stopped, and the stranger clasped her right shoulder, keeping her steady. With the other hand, she felt a hand stroke her cheek.

*Look at me, Em.* It was a woman's voice, strong and kind and sure. *Open your eyes now.*

Emma blinked against the water, and forced her eyes open as instructed. The woman hovered in place right in front of her, dark hair floating out in all directions, face glowing in the unearthly brightness. The woman smiled then, moving her face right up to Emma's, and pressed a slow-motion kiss to Emma's mouth. At once Emma's lungs surged with oxygen and strength, and the woman smiled even more brightly.

Emma immediately became convinced that she'd already died and was having an out-of-body experience. The woman smiling at her had her own pale blue eyes, her same full mouth, her straight nose. The savior angel floating in front of her was her mirror image, identical to her in every way.

*Leah.* Leah had come to help her!

Like a magical mermaid, her mirror image bobbed her head up and down, that beautiful, eternal smile spreading even wider. *Yes, Em, you will be safe now. . . .* Her voice was lilting and peaceful.

Leah wasn't a little girl as she'd been when she died; she'd grown and developed just like Emma. She was complete, not lost or broken beneath the ocean's waves. Emma felt a sob build in her chest.

*You prayed and I was sent to you,* Leah said. *God let me come save you.*

Emma's pain welled like a torrent. *But I never saved you.*

Leah cupped her cheek, pressing her face against Emma's. *That was too big a job for you. You were only a little girl. You can't blame yourself anymore. I never did.*

*I should have known what was going to happen to you, Leah.*

*You weren't supposed to know, Emma. I love you. I'm living all the time, just not in the way you are.*

She clutched at Leah's shoulders, needing more than just this fleeting moment with her, wanting to hold her a moment longer. *Don't leave me now, sweet sister. Stay.*

Leah held her close, wrapping a strong arm about her shoulder. *You can see me again. You will see me again, I promise.*

With those words, Leah released her, pressing something solid and heavy and warm into Emma's right hand. River. Leah had brought him back to her!

His sword felt powerful and reassuring in her grasp and she tightened her hold on his hilt. She looked upward, seeing bright light at the water's surface; it moved and danced with shadows, the rhythmic pattern of Hades' fire. She blinked, and one last time searched the waves for her twin, but Leah had vanished the moment she placed River in her grasp.

*I love you, sister.* She sent the words into eternity, and for the first time since all those years ago, she no longer feared an answer. In fact, she longed for one, she realized, as she swam toward the surface, empowered enough to fight the Styx's mighty pull.

# Chapter 36

S able stared back at Ares, undaunted by the wrath in his cold god's eyes. The Spartans who stood behind him didn't seem sure what to do; well, obviously it was a bitch when your second-worst enemy decided to align with you right in the midst of battle.

Ajax grabbed hold of his arm. "What do you mean by this, Sable?" he demanded, raising his sword toward Sable. "You came charging over like you intended to murder my king, and now we're supposed to trust you? Believe that you're joining our side today?"

Sable snorted, stomping at the ground. "I was duping your perfect war god."

"Not my god," Ajax told him, watching Ares move closer with a menacing, furnacelike heat in his eyes. "Not anymore. You're the one who stays under his thumb."

"Not anymore," Sable echoed. "Or ever again."

Aristos lifted a shield, stepping forward. "Sorry if we don't quite buy this maneuver," the mouthy Spartan said. "Kick his horse's ass back to Ares' side, Jax."

"Too late for that." Sable looked upward, watching Ares' approach—and not unaware that his furious intent seemed aimed especially toward him. "Just look at my body."

"I'd rather not, thanks," Ari fired back.

"See these horrible horns and stakes that he's cursed me with? Don't you understand why I have to fight him?" Sable shouted in a shockingly genuine tone. Beside him Ajax stiffened slightly. Ari blew out a sigh, glancing toward Leonidas, who swooped down and landed in their midst.

"Commander, he's seeking asylum in our ranks," Jax told him simply. "At first I was inclined to kick his horse's ass all the way back to Ares just as Ari suggested, but it seems that he now hates the god as much as we do."

"I've been ruined by his hand." Sable seethed, daring to touch one of the spikes that jutted out from his chest. Nothing eased the pain or made it subside; Sable had lived with it nonstop since Ares had formed the protrusions, the unrelenting agony driving him perilously close to madness.

Ajax turned to him, dark eyes narrowing. "I thought it was me you blamed for all that happened to you."

"That was before." Sable returned the warrior's steely gaze, thinking of the long-standing, swelling hatred he'd felt toward this Spartan. Somehow, perhaps only today, that old vendetta felt pointless, as dried up as an old husk blowing on the hot wind.

"Before?" Ajax clearly wasn't going to let this one go, even with Ares practically on them.

"You going to fight now or not?" Sable spat, raising his swords.

"You won't get in this fight until we hear you say it," Ajax told him from the side of his mouth, hunkering low with his shield as he prepared for Ares' arrival.

"Say what?"

"That you know I didn't cause your blasted ruination. It was because of your own mistakes, your own evil. That it was also the fault of war."

Sable stomped his hooves, blowing out furious breaths as Ares stalked closer. "The vendetta is ended," he told Ajax swiftly. "From here on, we fight this god together."

Leonidas stepped forward. "At every turn you have opposed and thwarted our purposes. Now you align with us? Why should I accept your fealty?"

Sable glanced between the warriors, then fixed his gaze on the king. "I surrender, King Leonidas of Sparta. I surrender and offer my warrior's strength to your cause. Even in the oldest of times, you accepted the arm of defeated forces, did you not? Conquered nations were brought to heel and made to serve." He extended both of his scarred and withered hands. "I am yours to wield, good king."

Ajax raised his shield. "Not quite good enough, but it works for now." Leonidas himself counted off the charge, and Sable felt a rush of battle lust. And for some reason, the thought of impressing that famous, brilliant commander gave him a thrill that he'd not known in centuries. He responded to that feeling by surging ahead, leaping out in front of them all.

In that moment he became the Spartan's truest cavalry, a dark Djinn who'd chosen to side with his erstwhile enemies. A Djinn whose only mission was destroying the god who'd done his level best to destroy him. But no more. *And never again*, Sable vowed, galloping without that god's bridle or restraint.

Hooves flying, swords flashing, Sable ran like the very wind. A blazing hot wind of destruction, he fervently hoped, hearing the loud war cries of the Spartans in his wake.

Ares had grown even larger, truly becoming a giant, and Leonidas wasn't certain that their swords would have much impact against his titan-sized legs and thighs. Still, he led the warriors in a surging attack, following behind Sable, who slashed both swords into the god's right thigh. The centaur never broke his galloping stride, those swords slamming into Ares' leg with speeding force. Ares looked down—his upper thigh at Sable's eye level—tossed back his head, and roared furiously, yanking out the two weapons, barely bleeding at all. He wasn't even in pain, Leonidas realized as he and his Spartans charged forward, slashing at the injured spot. Ares was angry at Sable, incensed that the Djinn was fighting on the side of the Spartans, but not badly wounded.

Ares reached down and, ignoring their efforts to wound him further, scooped Sable into his glowing golden hand, grabbing him as a little girl would a plaything that had caught her fancy. With a bitter snarl he said, "You have been useless to me for far too long. Let's see how that coat of yours does when consumed by hot fire."

Without another word Ares tossed Sable toward the river, and the Djinn struggled with his forelegs, trying to climb out of the supernatural waters. He tossed a spear against the earth, gaining purchase on the bank.

Ares didn't even give his former minion a parting

glance. Never realizing that the Djinn remained in the battle, he spun on the Spartan corps bracing into a fighting stance. "You've enjoyed my gift of immortality for far, far too long," he told them in that thunderous voice. "And now, like Sable . . . you will die for your disobedience and rebellion." Then that calculating, pitiless gaze swung right on Leonidas. "Starting with you, 'good king.' Isn't that *her* affectionate name for you?"

"You are clearly jealous, war god," Leonidas said, feinting to the right as Ares swatted toward him. Threatening the woman he loved was a mistake the god would pay for.

"Jealous? Of *her*?"

Leonidas tightened his hold on his sword. "That I'm the one she wants, who has her heart."

Ares stopped midstrike, amused. "Jealous of my own sister? Why would I ever feel that way?"

Leonidas felt as if all the blood rushed out of his body. Sister? That couldn't be. Although his sweet Oracle was immortal, she wasn't a goddess or divine creature. If she were, then why would she want him, and why would she be controlled by this dark deity?

Ares laughed, a cunning, satisfied smile forming on his mouth. "She never told you, did she? And here I'd assumed that she had confessed our familial secret. She's my half sister. Our father, Zeus, bedded a gorgeous young woman, you see, only . . ." Ares rubbed his beard casually. "She just didn't return his affections, and that made Daphne . . ." He glanced at Leonidas meaningfully. "Our bargain's over, so you may know her name. In fact, I'm sure she would have loved to be the one to first whisper it in your ear, to offer it up to you like the pearl of her virginity. So allow me to rob her of that tender moment. Daphne. Daphne. Daphne is her name," he chanted in a singsong melody. "And when Daphne's mother spurned my father, well, dear *Daphne* became something of a liability, you see. Daphne had to be controlled. Confined."

Leonidas's hands clenched about his weapon, and it was all he could do to keep from rushing the brutal creature talking about his love that way. *His Daphne.* He finally knew her name, here at what was likely the end.

"You're not worthy to speak her name," Leonidas challenged, glancing back at his remaining men.

"She belongs to me, you pitiful king. She's always belonged to me because our father gave me control over her."

Leonidas knew that most of what Ares said couldn't be believed, although the part about the Oracle being his half sister had a bizarre ring of truth. She possessed so many gifts and such beauty, was truly beyond this world. But it hardly mattered to him in that moment; the only thing he cared about was doing his best to defeat the god before them.

Leonidas and his men prepared for the charge. Kalias, Ari, Straton, and Ajax moved closer together. Where was Nikos? He'd not seen him fall in battle, but he wasn't anywhere nearby.

More than two thousand years ago, they'd made a hollow bargain with this deity; they'd danced and bowed before him for too long. Been devoted to and honored by their calling as protectors of mankind, and in exchange they had been hunted and betrayed by the very god they'd sworn to follow. Every moment of Leonidas's immortal life had led to this confrontation. To freeing their brotherhood from the cursed bargain and to freeing Daphne so she could be his own. Free to love, and free to be loved.

Leonidas threw back his head and released a long, piercing war cry. The earth thundered beneath the pounding steps of their feet. With that forceful charge, he and his warriors confronted much more than a betraying, murderous god; they reached much farther than simply fighting for comrades. They moved past an epic destiny and assumed an Olympic one.

They cried out, weapons drawn, bodies moving, and as they ran, their individual voices came together as one voice. Melded into the sound of one warrior, one force in defense of goodness and justice, they did what they'd been born to do: they faced down that god and became even more glorious.

# Chapter 37

Nikos knew what had to be done, and although he might not survive it, there was no other choice. Stripping off his breastplate, he moved toward the fast-flowing river. He would dive in and find River and Emma; if he expired in the effort, so be it. With all that he'd held back from Kassandros for all these immortal years, he would not deny this man the one gift he could now give—saving his life and that of the mortal whom he loved.

As he prepared to launch forward, holding his breath, however, one of the strangest, oddest sights appeared out of the watery deep. In fact, in that moment he knew if he lived another twenty-five hundred years, it might remain the oddest thing he would ever see.

Sable's forelegs came up from along the water's edge. Nik had watched the centaur flailing against the embankment moments before, but had turned away, focused on helping River and Emma. Now that feisty demon launched upward onto solid ground with a roar, swords extended in a downright gallant gesture. But it wasn't just Sable who bounded onto solid ground. There astride his back ,with one arm about his human torso, seated carefully to avoid all his protruding horns, rode Emma. Mounted like some goddess born of Olympus, River's sword gleaming, glowing bright in her outstretched hand. With a thundering shout, she and Sable galloped forward.

Damn, had he died somehow without noticing? Was he having a vision because of where they were? Otherwise, what he was witnessing made no logical sense.

There was no time to decide, he realized, bolting up and onto his feet. Taking off at a dead run, he chased in their wake. They, and all the other Spartans, would need him if they were to have a prayer of winning this battle.

"Go, Sable! Faster!" Emma yelled in his ear. "Over there to Ajax, okay?"

"Mortal, you are pushing your luck." He growled low. But she had to hand it to this mutinous demon—he did gallop just a little bit harder.

Ahead she saw Ajax and the other Spartans battling Ares, the god hurling thunderbolts and fire and epic weapons at their much smaller forms. The warriors dropped low, holding up their shields, but she could see their situation looked dire.

But if she could just manage to get River into Ajax's hand, there was hope—they knew now that River had greater power than any of them had ever imagined. His blade might prove brutal against the god's massive body.

"To Ajax," she repeated to the demon whose body she clung to. "Please, just get us to Ajax so that I can give him River."

"You're so sure you can trust me," he said, and looked over his shoulder at her with a bitter glare.

Oh, God, what if she couldn't? What if she had mistakenly placed her faith in him—what if he was going to veer and take them to Ares? Take River right back to the god who wanted him dead?

"Please . . . please don't let me down," she said softly, but the demon just laughed.

A few moments later they came abreast of the Spartans and Sable reared—a perversely glorious image, she thought, barely managing to hold to him. But it caused enough of a distraction to make Ajax look up from the fighting; their gazes locked, and Emma saw his eyes becoming wide in shock . . . hope.

She extended River, beaming at the man who could and would wield him. Ajax rose to his full height, opened both hands, smiling back at her. "River Kassandros!" he shouted. "My friend, my brother . . . come fight!"

She tossed River's glowing blade toward the Spartan, and she would have sworn—she was absolutely certain—

that she watched wings form along the hilt. His sword, more glorious than ever, flew through the air and toward Ajax's extended, grasping hand.

As the Spartan seized hold of her lover, the air began to make a loud, shattering hum. All of Hades began to quake in reaction to the master and servant joining together to fight.

River felt a surge of power roll through his sword form the moment that Ajax used him to pierce Ares' body. It crashed through his core like an unholy tidal wave, one that sent many more vibrations in its wake. The god had been weakened. He sensed it, just as he knew the moment that Ajax used him to strike the god again . . . and again.

*Ajax, don't relent!* he transmitted, hoping his master could hear him urging the man onward in the fight. *He's weakening!*

Motion jostled River; he was aware of Ajax's grip tightening about his hilt in determination. So many years of fighting as one—it was natural to read the Spartan's battle intentions. And he knew one thing as he felt the man's human grasp grow determined: that the next blow would be the most powerful they would deliver the god in this tandem assault.

River braced himself for the impact, knowing that he would taste the vile deity's blood for days to come, long after he returned to human form. There was a rushing motion, one that told him Jax was charging toward the god.

*Yes!* he urged. *Take him now, Jax. Now!*

A shuddering crash rocked through River at the moment of impact. He sensed the god falter, stumble.

And then, most glorious of all, River knew the instant when Ajax urged his return to human form.

"Well done, River Kassandros!" he heard his dear friend shout. "Very well done!"

River transformed in one flowing motion of silver and focused visualization, relieved to feel his own flesh and bones re-forming to the body he preferred to inhabit. He'd not wanted to admit it until this moment, but some part of him had feared that he might become trapped in weapon form again. All the more because Ares had cast him into the sword against his will. But now, kneeling and gasping, he ran hands along his thighs and chest, exultant to feel so undeniably human once again.

He scanned the scene before him, shocked to see that Ares had actually fallen. Still monstrously huge, the god struggled and bled. River couldn't help grinning like a fiend at the knowledge that his own blade had done that damage. That the sword he'd been forced to become had, even if only temporarily, felled their nemesis. What he didn't understand, however, was why none of the gathered Spartans was charging forward to finish his handiwork. The lot of them was clustered together, surging yet withheld as if straining against invisible bonds.

"Jax! We have to finish this job," he said as the Spartan pulled River to his feet. "Why aren't they doing anything more to fight Ares?"

Right then a piercing sound rang all around the gathered warriors, and it was obvious why they weren't advancing any closer to the wounded war god. A bright band of power held them all at bay. Ares seemed to be slowly healing himself, his body doubled over and trembling.

"How can we get through that?" River called out to the others, searching for Emma as they joined the corps. He breathed easier when he spied her. Kalias had her protected in the lee of a grouping of rocks.

Leonidas answered. "I don't believe that we can. We wait and when he emerges, surge forward again."

Suddenly a beautiful song pierced the raging fire and darkness. Pure, divine music reached down and engulfed them all. River tensed, searching the scene—and a gorgeous woman materialized in their midst. She had long flowing hair, midnight black, down to her waist; he recognized her instantly, although she had changed her appearance since he'd last seen her on Olympus. Their Oracle had come as promised.

"My brother has finally overstepped his bounds," she told them all with a sweeping gaze. One that lingered longest on their king, River noted. "You met me once . . . all of you did on the day of your bargain. Since then only Ajax and Leonidas have seen me. And I spoke with River the other day on Olympus." She smiled at him briefly. "Well"— she paused, looking toward Shay and then Emma—"the Daughters of Delphi can see me, too. Emma and I will meet after this battle."

She turned back toward them, and marching past her fallen brother, gave him a spiteful glance. Leonidas stepped forward and they clasped hands.

"My king." She bowed her head. "Do you have the object I gave you months ago? Or is it back at your compound?"

"I've never let it go."

She held out her hands, expectant. "I require the looking glass now, my lord."

Behind them Ares growled, struggling to move. It was the Oracle who'd restrained him, River realized excitedly. The god wasn't holding *them* at a safe distance. He was the one held in that encircling prison.

Their king made a motion with his hands, producing what had to be the Looking Glass of Eternity. "I've kept it warded and with me at all times—even in battle, my lady."

He placed it within her hands very gently, and the Oracle said, "My father, Zeus, charged me with protecting this item—in any way that I saw fit—and in return for doing so, I've been promised my freedom." Her eyes lifted, meeting Leonidas's. If River wasn't imagining it, he would have sworn . . . no, they couldn't have feelings for each other, not like that.

"Yes, hear *that*, my wicked brother?" she shouted, holding the glass overhead. "I am free from your domination as of today! Our father decreed it."

Then, with a supernatural force unlike any River had seen, even from Ares himself, she hurled the mirror into Styx. He braced, half expecting thunder and bolts of harsh lightning, but there wasn't any sound at all as the looking glass slid beneath the water's surface.

She moved toward her fallen brother, ablaze with fury. "You're not done, I'm sure, Ares of Olympus," she said. "But this day . . . this day belongs to me and my Spartans. The ones whom I will serve until I draw my last breath."

Without any warning Ares vanished from before their

eyes, and the small, miraculous Oracle began to laugh. She doubled over, big gasps of laughter rolling out of her, until she finally stood upright. Wiping a hand across her tear-filled eyes, she said, "He's ashamed. Humiliated! Isn't that perfect, my warriors?"

She swept her gaze about them all, then turned to face Leonidas with a graceful, deep bow. "The world will be safer now," she pronounced quietly. "And you will be, too, dear king."

She rose tall again, and lifting her face toward the sky, murmured words that none of them could hear. The last bit, though, River caught, or at least he thought that he did.

". . . take them home."

# Chapter 38

As Emma came roaring through the air of Hades, back to what she immediately recognized as her cousins' property, she wondered if this was what it was like being catapulted out of some giant cannon. She was the circus act to end them all as the brightly lit house came into view. Her cousins' home had never looked more reassuring, even if she did land in the middle of their driveway, and very hard, on her ass.

"Great, it's not just Oz. Now I've become Dorothy's house," she muttered to herself, a sandy cloud of dust rising in the air. "If I'm really lucky, maybe I'll land on the witch. Or Ares." She glanced beneath her bottom hoping to see a swatch of his glowing cloak. No dice.

But she was very happy about someone else's appearance. About ten feet away from her, there was a clanging sound. River's sword landed with the same ass-slamming force that had hurtled her home. She tried to get up and go get him, but as she rose, she immediately sank back down to the ground.

When a silver hum began in the air around River, Emma started to smile. So she didn't have to go get him, after all, she thought, watching the long-limbed, lean figure of her lover emerge from the penumbra that had formed around his sword. It only took a moment and then he stood, gloriously naked this time. Once he spotted her, he began running toward her, clothing himself midsprint.

Damn, khaki cargo pants and military tee just didn't have the same allure as his gleaming, nude body did. Still, any version of her man was a welcome sight. Especially right now.

"Are you all right?" He knelt breathlessly in front of her. "Good gods of Olympus, sweet Em, please do tell me you're all right."

She answered by flinging herself into his arms, holding and squeezing him as tightly as she could. "I was so afraid I'd never get you home again. So worried that I would fail you."

"I promised you before, Emma." He ran warm hands down her back, nuzzling against her cheek. "I will always come back to you. Always. I'll move the universe itself if I have to, but I will return."

She nodded, burrowing her face against his chest. "I believe you now."

"And with you always saving my life, I don't think I have a choice," he whispered against her ear. And although he joked, she heard the heartfelt emotion in his voice. "You saved me, Em, there in the river. I don't even know how you did it."

"Long story, baby, and it's a good one. But I'll have to share that with you a little later."

"I . . . thought I sensed some other person there, though." He stroked her hair. "I swear, I thought I did."

"Sable helped us out; you know that, right?"

"No, I mean *another person*," he insisted, and her smile spread even wider. If she'd doubted Leah's appearance before, or wanted to write it off as a hallucination, River's words dispelled any of those doubts. "Em, it was so strange, but she felt . . . a little like you."

"Imagine that." She laughed, and pulled him closer, if that was even possible.

Right then Emma heard a noise from the main house and was shocked to find Sophie, of all people, barreling down the driveway.

"Oh, my God, Emma! I was sure that the rapture had happened or something. All of you just whisked away."

"What do you mean?" Emma rose unsteadily to her feet. River was immediately at her side, sliding an arm about her waist to keep her legs from buckling. Yeah, the whole OK Corral Hades-style had definitely left her weak.

"I was here when you guys did the Houdini vanishing

act, that's what." Sophie held out both hands in wild exaggeration. "You didn't hear me come in, I guess, since a glowing cloud of silver and gold was all over the room."

"You were here?" Emma didn't understand what her sister was saying. Maybe it was because she was too addled by what they'd experienced, she thought, and looked to River, who seemed even more confused than she was.

"Who's *this*?" Sophie asked, those flirtatious, big blue eyes widening just as they had when she'd met Ari.

"Oh, no, no, you don't." Emma laughed, sliding her arm around River's hips. "This one's mine."

"Whoa, ho. Very nice, Emster." She raked her gaze down River's full form.

"River Kassandros, meet my wonderful, amazing little sister, Sophie Lowery. Light of my life, craziness of my universe. All of it in a nutshell, standing right in front of you."

Sophie smiled as if moonbeams suddenly infused her, she was that pleased by Emma's introduction.

River extended a hand, but then stopped, rubbing it on his pants, which were already covered in grime and soot. He stared down, laughing. "Let's shake another time, how about it, Sophie? But it's nice to meet you."

They started walking toward the house. "Soph, you know what all Shay and Mason and Jamie are into. Right? You know the whole 'battling the forces of darkness' thing they do with the Shades."

"Yeah. So? Yeah? Yeah?" She made a little impatient sound, following beside them.

"It seems," Emma answered slowly, "that I'm neck-deep in all that now, too. Details to follow once I'm not falling-down tired."

Sophie didn't answer; her eyes were focused ahead at the sandy turnaround in front of the house. Cars were there, as always, but she frowned as if something disturbing had caught her attention.

"What is *that*?" Her voice had a strange catch to it.

Emma looked, but saw nothing unusual. It was River's reaction, however, that set her heart pounding like it had back in Hades.

"Oh . . . shit. Sable's here."

"What's a sable?" Sophie asked, eyes even wider. "Does it have horns and withers and a tail and a human head ... and torso?"

"No way can you see that, Soph!" she cried. "You don't see demons!"

"Oh, shit is right," Sophie blurted, stopping cold. "That's a demon? That's what that is?"

River put a restraining hand across Emma's shoulder. "You stay here for now. Both of you."

It killed Emma that for whatever reason she couldn't see any of what was transpiring between River and Sable. And although she might have heard it, since that was her other ability, she wasn't close enough to do so. Sophie stood beside her watching in avid interest, craning up onto her tiptoes for a better view.

"What's happening? What are they doing?" Emma whispered as if they were watching some elicit scene never intended for their eyes. "River looks like he's just talking."

"That's what the big creepy horse guy's doing, too. Man, he's awful, isn't he? Oh, sorry, Em. That's right, you can't see him."

"But I did. Down in ... well, I was in a special place where I could see him, and yeah, he's pretty hideous and mangy, poor guy."

Sophie turned wide, luminous eyes on her, looking up at Emma. "I thought he was a demon?"

"Yeah, he is, but he's been on the wrong end of some bad treatment. I guess you could say he's turning out to be ... complex. He helped us out when we vanished."

Sophie continued her narration, never missing a beat. "Still talking, not smiling, not angry, though."

Emma decided that it was time to head inside and find the soft pillows and sheets that were practically screaming her name. "It's fine; let's just go inside. Maybe there's a Diet Coke around somewhere if I'm really lucky." She started walking toward the house with weary, heavy steps.

They approached River, and Emma caught a strain of Sable's low, rumbling demon's voice. He was muttering something about Spartans being crazy if they thought Ares would ever leave them alone.

"Then where are you going?" River asked the demon, his head tilted upward as he talked. It took a lot to dwarf the Spartans, although River wasn't quite as large as the rest of the group.

"Oh, wow." Sophie made a pained sound. "Oh ... that hurts too much." Sophie moved closer toward River without stopping. Almost gliding. As if she were being drawn by a force outside herself.

"Sophie, wait!" Emma called out, but her baby sister was already moving right to the spot where Sable seemed to be standing.

The mortal approached him with eerie light blue eyes that were disgustingly familiar, and made his fiery demon's blood run cold. *Delphi. Daughter of Delphi.* He wanted to heave, the image was so unsettling. What was it with these women and the way they kept popping up lately, hounding him like beasts from Hades?

"What does she want?" Sable directed the question toward River, but never took his eyes off the small human who came up to him with idiotic boldness. "She doesn't realize what I *am*?"

"Sophie, don't go near him." River caught her by the crook of her arm, but she wasn't going to be stopped.

"That's right, tiny human. Pathetic mortal. Daughter of Delphi." He released a low-pitched growl of hatred. "I may have relented with these ... people." He spat the word, unwilling to give them the respectful title of warriors. "But you, *you* I have no compunction about trifling with. Ah, soul-sucking you to a paper husk might be nice. Then again ..." He stomped a hoof against the sandy earth. "Your kind is untouchable. Pity, that. Still, I'm feeling rebellious tonight—your friends will tell you that much—so perhaps I might handle you inappropriately. Or suck inordinately. Or rape insubordinately. At any rate, you shouldn't count yourself safe while standing this close to *me*."

His own soul ached inside of him right then, as if it an-

ticipated the quick rush that action would bring. But he had
to give his horned head a light shake at a horrific realization. It wasn't the thought of emptying this frail mortal's
soul that brought on the burst of longing. It was that pair
of light blue eyes that had revolted him at first glance. Had
electrified him quite against his will.

That human gaze was fixed on him, filled with tears,
heartbreak, grief. He attempted a smile because those
emotions were his own life and trade: He fed off them and
gained energy.

Yet the forced smile died right on his lips. This one odd
human's pain did *not* strengthen him or thrill him with possible pleasure. Instead, for reasons he could never name,
not in an ageless age, he ached deep in his dead soul as he
saw that pained expression she gave him. It made his coat
prickle, his protruding horns throb, and his fire-mottled
skin tighten.

Sable lowered his head until his eyes were locked with
her human ones. "What are you doing?" he roared, vaguely
aware that River Kassandros attempted to pull her away.
She shook off his grasp with an odd hiss. A sound he instinctively knew didn't naturally pass her lips.

She kept coming toward him, reaching with both of her
soft, unscathed hands, he realized in horror. The idiot was
going to touch him!

He reared back. "Don't you dare," he cautioned in a
seething tone. "I will crush you beneath my hooves if you
even try it."

She stood only a foot or two in front of him, so perversely
small that she had to crane her neck at a sharp angle to
even meet his gaze. He glowered at her, unsettled, hating
her. Despising those gentle, nurturing, sad eyes of hers.

"I . . . I am so sorry." She kept looking at him, and then,
damn the small freak, but she burst into gut-wrenching,
shoulder-heaving tears.

That outpouring of humanity paralyzed him. He could
only stare down and wonder why this pathetic mortal
would bring such fruitless emotion to his feet. But that was
before. Before the moment that changed every thought in
his head. Before she did what no blasted human had ever

dared . . . she reached out a trembling hand and touched his chest. "Oh, Sable, I am so sorry."

"For what?" he growled, snapping his jaws.

She dropped her head heavily, and kept that warm palm flush against his scarred chest. "Your pain. Oh, your terrible pain."

He wanted to rear back, wanted to stomp her to bits under his hooves. He wanted—oh, Ahriman—he wanted a thousand things, not one of them right.

She cried even harder, and with extreme gentleness moved that warm hand to the first of his new protruding, excruciatingly painful horns that Ares had given him.

"I can help you. . . . I'm going to, I promise." She placed fingertips against the raw place on his chest, and he actually thought to warn her that she would bleed. But the sudden rush of relief he felt blinded him to anything else but the peace. She touched him again. And again. All along his chest, each time absorbing his horrific mutations into her hand until they vanished.

"You . . . stop. Have to stop," he finally managed to warn her. This selfless act of hers would come with a price, he was certain. He knew enough about Ares and the balance he exacted from things that she'd never get away with touching him and healing him like this.

"Am I hurting you?" Sophie lifted her bowed head, blinking back tears. "I don't want to cause you more pain. Oh, it's too much for any living creature."

He came back to his senses. "I am no creature, pitiful one!" He raged and trotted backward. "I am a Djinn born of fire and blood. You dare to show me mercy? You deign to heal my curse?"

She gazed up at him weakly then, wobbling on her feet. "Yes. Yes, I do because you have suffered too much."

What he saw in her countenance was more horrific than any punishment from Ares. Her eyes were filled with . . . compassion.

With his thorns only half healed by her touch, he reared in a circle and galloped far, far away. To the ends of the earth he would go to escape the look in the one called Sophie's kind blue eyes.

*     *     *

River watched as Emma caught Sophie, collapsing with her as she slid toward the ground. Emma held her younger sister close within her arms, looking up toward him for an explanation of the strange moment they'd both just witnessed.

"Oh, my God, what's going on with her?" she asked River. "Why would she go up to Sable and ... how could she have done that with him?"

He examined Sophie's body for any sign of injuries. "You're gifted as a medium, and Shay is a hunter," he said, thinking through the possibilities. "What's Sophie's ability?"

"She doesn't have one!" Emma nearly shouted, stroking her sister's hair away from her closed eyes. "Mama always said that Sophie hadn't received a spiritual gift."

He nodded, silent for a moment, then smiled at his soul mate. "Sweet Em, I hate to tell you this ..." He laughed, hoping she'd find some humor in what he was about to say. "But Sophie just showed you and me—and Sable especially—the exact nature of her calling."

Emma gave him an adorably confused look, still holding her sister in her arms. "I don't get it. Talk to me like I'm really, really new at this. Which I am, so there you go."

"Sophie's a healer. And she has the gift of compassion." He stared down at his mate's sister, at her crumpled, small form. Amazed that anyone could ever—in any century or lifetime—feel the true mercy that she'd just displayed toward that demon. But she had, and Sable had been terrified by it. That much had been obvious. And he'd also found relief from his intense physical pain.

"That's amazing." Emma stared down at her unconscious sister with a look of genuine wonder. "But Sable didn't hurt her or anything? I mean, that's not why she passed out?"

"No. I think it was probably very powerful for her. Has she ever done anything like this before?"

"Never. Not that I know of." Emma brushed a wild curl away from Sophie's closed eyes. "This is brand-new."

River couldn't help giving her an exuberant smile. "It's *all* brand-new, Emma. For both of us ... all of us. This is the adventure of my immortal life, but I don't want it to end, not ever."

Emma leaned forward and kissed him on the mouth, lingering and savoring what he gave her. After a moment, she pulled back, staring into his eyes. "I love you, River. I never would have survived if I'd lost you during that battle. You've redefined every one of my expectations or hopes out of life." She glanced down at her sister. "So I think Sophie's got her own journey to make. Like me."

"I love you, too, Emma. More than I can tell you."

Her eyes took on a mischievous, downright wicked gleam. "I can think of a few ways that you might express that sentiment."

He could, too, he thought. But only after a very satisfying sleep with Emma curled up in his arms.

# Chapter 39

Nikos was dead weary after the battle, and he planned to wing it back to the compound as soon as he tracked down River. After watching the servant nearly die in the depths of Styx, he'd reached a conclusion: It was time to tell River the truth about their shared past. Moving as if he felt every one of his more than twenty-five hundred years, he followed the man's scent trail to the second story of the Angels' home and toward the library. He heard Emma's laughter first; then as he hit the landing and rounded the corner, he saw Kassandros sitting on the leather sofa inside the library. He held Emma tight within his arms, the two of them nuzzled together as an inseparable whole.

Nikos pulled to a stop just outside the doorway, knowing that he couldn't intrude on the sweet moment of reunion. And feeling a hollow, throbbing ache in his chest at the image before him. To come home from such an epic battle, greeted by the one you most wanted to hold . . . well, it was more than Nikos could seemingly hope for. He rubbed a palm over his chest, hating the way his heart ached, despising the bottomless emptiness that filled his soul. Year after year, he warred against demons and darkness, but he always came home to loneliness. To solitude and silence and an empty bed—and his own empty arms.

But for the first time in far too many years, that homecoming wasn't enough. *Not close to enough*, he thought, watching Emma and River kiss as if he were a voyeur. Yes, there was much he had to explain to the young servant whom he now watched in secret: truth that would have to be told. But not tonight. Tonight it was obvious that his fellow warrior and brother was occupied with a much more rewarding return to the human realm. There would be plenty of days to come when he could confess his sins.

"Mama's never on time," Emma said, squeezing River's hand.

Good lord, did he clean up pretty. He wore a nicely pressed pair of khakis with a deep green linen shirt—open collared just enough to reveal his burnished skin. He'd pulled his hair back into a neat ponytail, and although she would never have thought she wanted to see that wavy, golden brown hair away from his face, it only enhanced the rare color of his eyes. Just like that shirt did. Bringing out every facet in them, a lovely play of gold against green.

He started to smile, and she blushed, realizing that he'd busted her ogling him.

"Better than the faded jeans and bare feet?"

She shook her head, releasing an extremely appreciative sigh. "You keep raising the bar, baby. Eventually you'll run out of ways to outdo yourself."

"Don't count on it." He bent down and, tilting his head slightly, caught her in a slow burn of a kiss. "Who needs dressing up when I can *undress* for you?"

"You have a serious wicked streak, Kassandros." She looked away from him, making a big show of watching for her mother. "Maybe I'd rather undress you myself."

"And maybe your mother forgot about lunch," he offered, glancing around hopefully. "This is a hotel, after all. We could get a room here and put it to good use."

Although he was keeping up their exchange of innuendo, she saw his eyes grow troubled. Reaching for his hand, she held it tight, giving it a quick squeeze. "You're gonna love Mama. She's the least intimidating woman in the world."

He nodded, but his expression remained serious as he stared out at the street and beyond it into Forsyth Park. Maybe changing the subject was the best idea, she decided, and she pointed to the park, explaining some of its history and telling about the huge fountain that she'd always thought made it a downright magical place. "People get married by that fountain all the time. Every weekend there's some wedding over there."

"We could do that." He studied his finely polished loafers for a moment and then gave her a tentative glance. "If you wanted, I mean. Get married . . . there."

She didn't know what to say; she just could not make her thoughts stop spinning fast enough to form a reply. Had he really just asked her to marry him? She felt her eyes burn, and her vision turned blurry.

"Or we could get married anywhere," he added even more softly. "A barn or a field or a church, it wouldn't matter to me. If you were just willing to marry me." He turned, cupping her face in both hands, and bent his head lower until his mouth grazed her cheek. "Emma, I'm even willing to beg," he whispered into her ear, his tone husky and urgent. "Please, marry me. Please."

She flung both arms around him and repeated the words he'd told her the first time they'd made love. "You don't need to beg," she said. "I only want you."

He wrapped her within his arms, holding her so close that neither of them remembered the traffic or that they were standing outside a hotel lobby, or that her mother might arrive any minute. The only thing—the absolutely only thing that mattered at that moment—was the solid, quick beating of her lover's heart. She felt tears burn anew, thinking how close they'd come to never having this moment. If she'd not heard his voice that day out at Tybee, this steady, very human heart would probably never have beaten again.

His life would have been smothered within the silver of his weapon form, and he would have remained lost forever beneath the waves. And if not that, she could have lost him in Styx—would have—if God hadn't sent Leah to save them both.

"Your heart is beating so loud." She laughed, turning so her ear was right over that spot in his chest. She tried to imitate the staccato rhythm aloud a few times, and enjoying the feel of his hands stroking her hair, she kept mimicking that pounding sound of his heart.

River rubbed the nape of her neck. "Is that noise supposed to tell me you like what I'm doing?"

"No, it's that *you* like what you're doing," she told

him, rubbing a palm over his chest. "I'm listening to your heart."

"Sounds like you're saying *bum, bum*," he observed.

"I *am* saying that," she said, closing her eyes, still listening. "It's the sound a heart makes."

"No, that's the sound of being turned down, that's what it is." He nodded as if fully convinced of whatever nonsense he was talking about. "It's your mother saying you can't marry *this* guy." He thudded his chest a couple of times, nodding some more.

She pulled back, not sure what he meant. "River, what are you even talking about?"

His expression was serious, but she could see him fighting hard to suppress a smile. "Bum. Bum." He lifted an eyebrow. "That boy's a *bum*. Not going to marry that *bum, bum*."

She swatted him hard, and he was already working to steal another kiss when she heard her mother's lilting voice. "Who's marrying a bum?" Cecilia asked. "Emma, darling, sorry I'm late."

River made a low sound of embarrassed panic, trying to release Emma, but she anchored him close. She looked up into his face, giving a quick smile of reassurance, then turned to meet her mother's extremely curious gaze.

"Hey, Mama. Meet River. I love him. I really, truly love this man."

Cecilia blinked, clearly caught off guard by Emma's announcement. She glanced between them, inspecting and curious. All the while River squirmed, wanting to let Emma go, but she forced him to be still.

"This is interesting indeed," Cecilia said, sliding her dark sunglasses atop her head to examine both of them more closely.

"No, Mama, it's more than that. It's the best thing that's ever happened to me," Emma continued. "I love this man, and I'm going to marry him." She looked up into River's eyes and swore that they shone a little bright. "You're going to love him, too, Mama."

Cecilia's eyes twinkled. "Darling, you have my approval. This man, no matter what he might occasionally think," she said, eyes narrowing because she was obviously using her gift, "is certainly no bum. He's more like a king. That's what I'm hearing." Cecilia began bobbing her head, her smile widening. "He has the highest, best blood flowing in his veins."

Cecilia reached out a hand just then, and River, who had yet to utter so much as a peep, gave her his elbow. Emma's mother slid her hand through that crook, gave his arm a small squeeze. "So what's this, though, about changing form so much of the time? You become a weapon . . . a sword? Or is it a dagger?" her mother babbled. "Fascinating. I'll want to know more over lunch. Emma will always be safe with you—that I can tell."

Wide-eyed, River looked at Emma and she shrugged. "I didn't tell her a thing. Not a thing, so don't look at me. Don't forget she's where I get my own gift."

Cecilia was unfazed, chattering as they approached the lobby door, clearly fascinated by everything she'd begun perceiving about her future son-in-law. She made a slight gasping sound, eyes wide. "Thermopylae, too? Oh, Emma's great-great-grandfather would be so proud. And, no, River—he wouldn't care that you're a servant."

Emma stopped right in her tracks; River's eyes grew wide as saucers, and her mother never stopped prophetically chattering.

". . . he came here without a pair of shoes to his name, you know, so he would have nothing but respect for a man who'd lived so long as a servant. It's the humble things that God uses in this universe, River."

Emma opened the door to the lobby, wiping her eyes. She'd never loved her mother—or her crazy family gift— more than at this moment. That was when Cecilia dropped the true bombshell.

"Not that it matters," she said offhandedly, "because you're not going to be a servant for very much longer."

River halted, turning to Cecilia. "What did you just . . . what are you saying?"

Cecilia leaned onto her tiptoes and patted River's cheek with all the love a mother might show: as if he had been in their family for years, and she'd known all his heartbreak.

"River, darling, I'm saying this," she told him softly. "You'll marry my daughter as a free man."

And with that pronouncement Emma thought that River Kassandros, fighter of demons, hero of epic wars, shifter of weapons, just might faint dead on the spot.

"Yo, Nik!" Aristos came barreling down the front steps of the Angels' house, chasing him. "Glad I saw you. The Old Man's called a special gathering tonight. Big mysterious gig, not saying much about it, except to come in the old garb."

It had been two days since their battle against Ares, and life had already started to seem spookily normal. But they all knew that the war god was far from done with his vengeance; it would only be a matter of time until he made another strike. For now, or even just today, Nikos preferred to believe the happy illusion of peace.

"No indication at all about the reason?" Nikos asked, but he was already looking out toward the dock. He'd been on a mission when Ari interrupted him, totally on target.

"It's going down here, eight p.m.," Ari told him, turning back toward the house. "Commander says it's important. That's all I know."

Nikos thanked him for the update, and went back on point. Target in his sights, Nik was already on the move. He'd caught Mason's scent trail at the front of the house, and knew it led down to the river. At the very end of the dock, which was really more a long pier that ended in the shallow marsh grass, he could see Mason balancing a couple of fishing poles. Without a word, Nikos approached and then dropped to his haunches beside him. Mason held a journal on his lap, but he closed it abruptly.

Mason lifted an eyebrow. "I suppose it's the Spartan way to walk quiet as a fox, then." He wore a sleek pair of black sunglasses that, while blocking out the sun, made his green eyes unreadable. Nik instantly hated those fashionable shades.

"Ha. You're masterful, Angel. You find a way to cut through all the bullshit and just like that." Nikos snapped his fingers.

"Right now you're squatting like you plan to bound

away, so I'll use my ready weapon.... You gonna fish, or not? I assume an ancient man like you can still find his way around a river like this one."

Nikos hesitated, unsure if Mason truly wanted him to stay or was simply displaying that famed Southern hospitality. After deliberating, he settled quietly into a sitting position, making sure there was plenty of room forming a buffer zone between them.

"You didn't answer me before." Mason released the line and stretched his legs out. The bandage moved a little and he rubbed the thigh muscle above the injury. "Why the cautious approach?"

Nikos shrugged. "I figured I'd overstepped my bounds at the hospital."

Behind the shades Mason's brown eyebrows lifted in what looked to be surprise. Then he glanced down at the journal that he cradled in his lap. "Actually, I was just reading about you."

Nikos propped his elbows on both knees, trying to see if the journal had a title. Nothing, just plain leather. "Reading what?"

"Some pages I transcribed from an ancient text, *The Final Crossing*. Doesn't say much about you seven individually, but it describes the bargain that you made."

Nikos grunted fiercely. "It seems that bargain wasn't worth the blood it was written in."

"No, it's changing, that's all," Mason disagreed. "You've won a first battle with Ares, and the stakes are going to get higher, but I'm not concerned. I have a lot of faith in you Spartans."

Nik gestured toward the closed journal. "Is that why you're reading that book? Hoping to find some clue about us all?"

"I told you, I'm reading about *you*." Mason glanced at him, a true smile playing at the corners of his mouth. He tapped the journal with his fingertips. "Lately I find I'm a bit fascinated by you. That I want to know exactly what makes you tick. I thought this book might help me."

Gods, why did Mason have to have those sunglasses on? It annoyed the bloody hell out of Nik that he couldn't read the man's emotions, always so vibrant in his wide green eyes. And so he did something impulsive and daring: Nik reached forward and slid the sunglasses down Mason's nose. The green gaze staring back at him was open and a little shocked, full of unvoiced questions.

"Needed to read you," Nikos said, gesturing toward the journal. "Never been much of a book guy, but your eyes don't need a lot of translation."

Mason exhaled softly after a moment and looked away, out at the water again. "I should get cagier, then." His smile opened even wider. Gods, it was a beautiful expression to glimpse on the guy's face after the months of melancholy pain.

After a long, powerful moment, Mason drew in a long breath. "If you were married back in Sparta, like you said . . ." He looked into Nikos's eyes for a long, still moment, then quickly dropped his gaze. "Then how was it with your wife? I mean, if you . . . you had someone else. I don't get it. It's not how I'm built, to be with a woman. I've never been wired that way."

Nikos answered with carefully chosen words. "Marriage was compulsory. It was loveless, a duty. Danae and I respected each other, but we were strangers. I lived my whole life in the corps, stayed in the barracks. She owned our land, managed it; I fought the wars. We both knew that our duty was to Sparta, to create future soldiers who would defend our land. We expected nothing else."

"Did you ever see Danae again? Or your son? After the bargain?"

"They thought me dead and I let it stay that way. She married another; my son grew to manhood and was slain by the worst and most unbeatable type of demon . . . plague. I watched from afar when I could, from the shadows where their human eyes couldn't see."

"And then?" Mason asked bluntly, his eyes alight with undisguised curiosity.

"I . . . what do you mean?"

"You took other lovers over the years? Other men?"

Nikos slid backward, his face burning. "That's not in your book?"

Mason rubbed first one eye, then the other. "I want to know if I'll ever fall out of love with a dead man. If I can . . ." He shook his head. "I want to know if you ever loved anyone else."

Nikos stood slowly, walked to the edge of the water. "Do you even have bait on these two poles?" He peered down at the still lines.

He heard Mason give a smug laugh. "I got you out here, didn't I?"

Nikos's heart beat like a fiend inside his chest. He could hardly let himself hope; but the man's prying questions instantly gained more life. After careful moments he finally turned and stared into the expectant green eyes.

"I never allowed myself to touch or love another after Doros fell at the Hot Gates. I have never loved again since then. For a long time, I wondered if I ever would."

Mason nodded and slowly slid his sunglasses back over his eyes. His own book was closing yet again. Because Nikos could never find words, the right ones, to unlock his own heart.

"I think I'll learn from your experience," was all the human said, frowning intently.

"No!" Nikos barked. "No, don't copy my choices," he said much more quietly. "They've not been very smart ones."

"Give me some good advice, then. Tell me what I should do, how to feel like I'm still alive in here." He thumped his chest. "Not a ghost that's wandering alone."

Nikos dropped to his haunches beside Mason once more and knew that this was it. His one big chance, the sort you might never get again. Anything he said next would forge the course of whatever treacherous, tentative bridge they'd been building. It might determine how every future moment between them would go.

Planting a firm hand on Mason's shoulder, Nikos took the biggest risk he had in eons. Did something far scarier than slaying a hundred rabid demons or facing down a fully armed battalion of Persians without backup. He opened his mouth and quietly said, "One thing. Just one piece of advice, my friend."

Nikos clasped the warm shoulder, felt the firm muscles

beneath. "Simple, Angel. When you've mourned long enough, when the grief's not so raw, and you'll know when that is . . ."

Mason nodded. "I'm listening."

Nikos drew in a deep breath. "Then give me a chance."

# Chapter 40

They'd gathered in the old manner, a large bonfire lit near the river that edged behind the Angels' home. It was nearly dark, the last pink and gold light of the day fading from the sky. River hadn't been sure what to expect as he and Emma had walked down the pathway toward the water, Ajax and Shay chattering beside them.

Now they stood as one in a circle about the fire, listening to Leonidas. "We've come for a very important purpose tonight," he announced in a booming, unusually chipper tone. "To welcome home River, our friend and comrade who we feared was lost forever."

River's eyes burned as a tremendous uproar exploded among his friends. There were clapping, chanting, and shouts of approval. Just like he'd thought he would hear when he first came home, he realized, remembering that night when he'd still been trapped in the dagger. He'd been so shocked by the silence all around, driven to doubt the very friends who now applauded his return.

*I belong here*, he thought. *This is my home. . . . These people are my home.*

And he glanced at Emma, knowing that with her as his future wife, soul mate, and friend, he'd found a sense of completion he'd never really expected would belong to him.

Leonidas turned to River. "Warrior, we have something special planned to honor your return. Tonight is truly for you."

River sucked in a breath. When had their king ever convened one of their sacred nights, declaring it in honor of just one man? He blinked, stunned, unsure how to answer.

He was a servant, not a full Spartan, and didn't understand what Leonidas had in mind.

"My lord, I . . . I am honored," he answered uncertainly, keeping his gaze on the ground. "But I am curious, too."

"Yes, I'm sure you are." The commander chuckled low. "I'm sure everyone gathered by this fire is full of questions. And so we shall begin."

Next Leonidas did the most unusual thing. He asked that each of them assume their winged warrior form. River stalled because he rarely made that winged transformation; it just didn't suit his warfare style. Sure, he'd do it now and then if he needed to cross vast distances in flight or if it proved useful in battle. But for the most part, it had been Ares' gift to the Spartans, and not being their equal, he felt an impostor if he called upon the ability very often.

Leonidas stepped in front of him. "Yes, River, you most of all should summon your true form." Then the king offered a reassuring smile to Emma. "I'm sure you've not seen him that way yet, but he's a mighty, fearsome warrior, as you'll see. It's what we all are, how we were formed by Ares when made protectors of mankind."

River hesitated a moment, but he wasn't about to defy his king. Sucking in a deep breath, he threw back his head and released a mighty, hawklike cry. As he reached upward toward the full moon, he closed his eyes and began to transform. Hot tension spread across his shoulders, seizing him in a painful, gut-rending spasm. He opened his mouth, releasing another piercing cry—and heard the answering shrieks of six other hawk shifters. Rolling power shot out from his spine, and in one glorious, rustling explosion, his huge wings emerged across his back.

Emma watched in amazement, shaking slightly as she studied the primal warrior beside her. She thought of Shay's words several nights ago, how she'd said that River possessed many gifts, not just one, and that over time Emma would eventually see all of what her lover could be.

Staring up at him now, listening to the soft rustling of those wings, she became convinced of one absolute fact. That as gorgeous as River always was to her, whether in blue jeans or naked or gleaming with silver, he'd never appeared more beautiful than at that precise moment. The moonlight glowed off those shimmering silver and black wings; his face lifted to the night sky and his eyes pressed shut in ecstasy, and she was awed.

He was allowing her to see something even more intimate and rare than he'd done as a weapon-shifter. This avian change, this extraordinary, miraculous form of his, was the purest part of him, and it didn't come with a berserker's curse like the dagger or sword or other weapons. It was something he craved; she could tell. A freedom that he ached for yet mostly denied. She sensed it. Something he treasured, but rarely gave in to or allowed to happen.

*He doesn't feel worthy of this noble form.*

She heard the words in her mind, and knew that it was her ability as a Daughter that had whispered the truth. Her prophetic gift would begin emerging faster and faster; that's what the Oracle had promised, and this was one of those moments.

She watched as his chest rose and fell, pulling at the night air, and sweat rolled across his bare chest. She needed to touch him, to let him know that she was still here, but didn't dare interrupt the sacred hush of the moment. A quick glance around the circle surprised her. She'd been focused only on River, not even realizing that the rest of the warriors had transformed as well.

Their black wings glimmered beneath the light from the bonfire and torches, and as she slowly gazed from man to man, she saw that each of their forms was slightly unique. Straton's wings, spread wide behind him, had streaks of rich red mixed in with the black. His face, normally harshest of all, had become starkly elegant: his nose longer and his eyes wide and almond-shaped.

Ari's wings were a pure shade of midnight, fluttering and shifting along his back with the same high-test energy the guy always seemed to barely hold back. Nikos wouldn't meet her eyes when she glanced toward him, but she smiled, thinking that he'd used his own wings to fly her cousin Mason to safety a few nights ago. All around the fire she looked, seeing that each warrior's wings and hawk form was slightly unique, possessing some unique touch, whether a hint of crimson or cobalt blue to his long wings.

But her beloved was the only one whose feathers were touched by silver, she realized with unexpected pride. She turned toward him then and found him staring at her, the usual warm color of his eyes replaced by that same luminous, beautiful silver.

"All that I am," he told her in a hushed voice. "All that I will ever be. You have all of it, Emma. I am yours. Every change in me, every part . . . all of it belongs in your hands."

She swallowed, and stepped closer, daring to touch a few feathers along his left wing. "Magical. And to think that you're mine. All of this beauty. Mine. I can't express how much that means to me."

"Yes, it is yours," he pledged softly, his voice filled with emotion. It almost sounded as if he were sad.

Had she said something to hurt him without meaning to? She panicked, realizing that her words touched dangerously close to his feelings about being a slave. "I mean, you're free, not owned, or . . ."

His eyes opened and he touched a hand to her cheek. "Love freely given is the most powerful love of all, sweet Em," he told her. "You're right, I am yours. I truly belong to you, and just as equally, you belong to me."

He bent low, pressing a searing, long kiss against her lips. She felt supernatural power in that connection, as his mouth opened to hers, his tongue exploring deeply. Little sparks of electricity moved between them, and she felt almost faint, like all the blood had rushed to her extremities, fled her heart. She reached out, clutching both of his forearms in order to steady herself.

He pulled back. "You all right, sweetheart?"

"Swoon moment, that's all."

She heard murmuring among the other men, and then Ari called out from the other side of the circle. "All right, all right, lovebirds"—he let loose a rolling laugh—"and *that* is an apt description for River right now."

Leonidas stepped up to them, bearing something in his arms that Emma couldn't quite see. He walked up to River, facing him, the hint of a smile on his brutally scarred face, and gave Emma a slight bow of acknowledgement.

"There is another reason that I've brought us together this night," he said, warm gaze fixed on River. The king was taller by a few inches; River's physique was different than that of all the other men, she'd noticed. Leaner, not quite as tall, more the long, defined body of a swimmer than the bulk of a football player.

Leonidas reached a hand out, clasping her lover's shoulder for a long tender moment. Finally with a last gentle squeeze, he withdrew his grasp, taking his place beside River within the circle.

The king cleared his throat and addressed the group. "River Kassandros, we welcome you back to the corps. You were missed by each one of us."

Thunderous cheers resounded, followed by the pounding clank of fists against shields. Emma's gaze was riveted on River's reaction, and even in the firelight she saw him flush with pride and acceptance. He lowered his head slightly, wordlessly acknowledging his friends.

"But I have called us together for an even more powerful reason," the commander told them quietly, gaze turned back to River. "We have entered a new time, a new era. What our future holds, none of us can say, for all that moors us to the past has been severed. We serve the Highest God now, not Ares."

More shouts and cries of approval rang out, and Emma found that she held her breath, impatient to hear what this heroic king would say next.

"All the old vows are shattered, and from here on, we make our own rules and laws," Leonidas continued, waving a hand without turning away from River. "Ajax, come near, please. Kalias, bring us a torch."

The two warriors moved near. Kalias's face, so like that of his brothers, danced in golden light and shadow. Both brothers moved in front of River, still winged, standing so close their feathered appendages brushed together with a rustling sound.

"River Kassandros," Leonidas said firmly, "I ask something of you this night. It will require sacrifice, duty, the greatest part of your immortal soul." He hesitated, searching River's face. "Are you willing, young servant?"

Emma's heart began to race insanely, and she saw a flash of doubt in River's eyes. What were they about to do to him? And why did he look frightened, here on a night of celebration, and with men whom he trusted so much?

He didn't blink or waver, didn't back down, but stared up into his king's eyes. After a silent moment transpired between the two, he whispered, "I am ready, my king. As always, I am your servant . . . servant to all of you, and to my master Ajax. Tell me what you wish, and it shall be done." River bowed his head low, assuming a servant's posture, humble and deferential.

Emma held her breath, deathly afraid of what would be asked of him. River would give everything for these men, but surely they wouldn't require even more than they already had. Surely her good, noble love had given enough.

Leonidas reached a strong hand out, cupping River's chin, and very gently forced his head up. "Faithful warrior, brother, friend," he said softly. "Here is the question I ask. If you will accept a gift from me . . . from Ajax. From every Spartan and human gathered with us here." The king paused, clearing his throat. "Young River, will you accept your freedom? Will you let us sever your bonds of slavery this night?"

The shaking started somewhere in his hands, or maybe his arms. For a very long moment, River actually feared he'd break. His vision did blur, the dancing firelight making the beloved faces in front of him swim like a kaleidoscope. He felt strong, familiar hands reach out and take hold of his arms, then other hands along his back.

They would never let him fall, never let him break; he knew it.

Ajax stood tall and proud just in front of him, his own face awash in powerful emotion. "You are my friend, not my bound servant," Ajax affirmed. "I wish you to be free of bondage, now, this very night."

"Jax . . ." He didn't know how to answer, and this incredible gift scared him somewhat. "I love fighting with you . . . it's all I know."

Jax reached out and held firmly to River's forearm. "That, my friend, will never change. I rely on you and need you too much. But we will work as a team, a pair of equals."

Kalias spoke next, his rough, deep voice like gravel. "My brother is right, River. You were birthed into slavery, but you don't have to live that way ever again."

"But it's your choice, River," Leonidas added, clasping both of his shoulders. "It takes your own words to break the unequal chaining that Ares placed between you and Ajax. You must say the words, you must make the choice to renounce the way he bound you in eternal servitude."

River's heart sang, soaring to a place of hope that he'd never fully known, at least until he'd met Emma. But to have her as his wife, and in freedom, it was almost more than the overworked muscle in his chest could contain. And he thought of Ares, that vile, hateful god, of all the pleasure he'd taken in shackling him, and of how he'd intended to turn River against all of the Spartan brotherhood. And Emma. Oh, sweet fate, what if that hateful god had turned him against his love?

With a single, purposed nod he spoke. "I renounce the slave chains that Ares placed on me. I will walk among all of you as a free man and an equal."

Ajax took hold of both his shoulders and moved very close, his eyes bright and shining. "You accept my gift of freedom? You take it right now?"

River whispered, "I accept."

Ajax broke into a broad, beaming smile and, leaning close, pressed a chaste kiss to River's forehead. "Then, my brother and friend, you are free."

Leonidas rubbed a quick hand over his eyes, making sure none of his men saw how emotional he felt. The corps was shouting and drumming, cheering River's release. It was the night any king dreamed of, that rare, sweet moment when all were well, and only good deeds and hopes abounded.

He looked down at the folded crimson cloth that he held within his hands, and turned to River once again. "One more thing you must do, warrior."

River's eyes widened in curiosity. "Anything, my lord."

Leo pressed the sacred fabric into his expectant hands. "Bear this Spartan cloak, and accept your place as an equal among our circle. Full Spartan citizen of our homeland long since passed away; full Spartan warrior in our immortal campaign."

River clutched the cloth, his eyes filling with true tears as he pressed the sacred Spartan crimson against his chest at last. He worked his mouth, but no words came out, and Leonidas couldn't help smiling. River possessed such honesty and nakedness in everything he approached, but this cloak, this gift . . . Leonidas knew it was the deepest desire of his heart. Ares had robbed him of it on that long-ago day in Hades. It had been obvious how much the young man ached to wear the item. And that being given the crimson was all he truly wanted out of the entire bargain.

So more than a thousand years ago Leonidas had brought his immortals together on a night much like this one, with torches and bonfires blazing, and he'd led each of them to burn their old cloaks. They'd laid the crimson folds on a funeral pyre out of mourning for their fallen ones, and as a tangible way to express their grief for all those they'd left behind. But Leo had encouraged the offering for another reason, one he never shared with a soul. Because of how many times he'd seen the pained envy in River's eyes as he secretly watched the rest of them in their billowing Spartan cloaks.

River turned the thick wool folds within his hands now, stroking the material with infinite care. "I . . . I'm not sure I should accept this," he stammered, blinking his eyes quickly. "None of the others have theirs. I'm not sure that it's right."

Leonidas smiled at him, signaling with his right hand. "Aristos, you'll do the honors?" With a wave, he directed Ari toward a large oak tree where he'd concealed a neat stack of six additional crimsons.

The corps exploded in jubilation, handling the garments

like sacred objects given from high above. Leonidas slipped
into the shadows, into solitude, not wanting to intrude on
their moment. These were the bravest, finest men he'd ever
commanded. As he watched them unfurling those glorious
garments in the firelight, heard them snapping the crisp
fabric as sharply as battle flags, he knew that a new era had
truly begun.

# Chapter 41

Daphne concealed herself in the very darkest shadows, hiding more skillfully than Leo did at the moment. He'd never looked more handsome, more kingly, or more beautiful than at this moment when he stood silently loving his own men. She'd never known anyone like him, so capable of kindness, yet not afraid to show brutal strength.

At that exact moment he spotted her in the darkness, eyes flaring. He stood transfixed, his scarred face dancing in the fire's shadows, and her heart soared. Taking a step toward him, she remembered how he loved her Goth Girl outfit and changed her clothes in midstride. And that plan, well, it made her king's eyes grow even more filled with obvious desire.

There were murmurs among those gathered, all of whom recognized her from the battle in Hades. She gave a wave. "Not trying to interrupt. Just stepping. Right. Over. Here." She took big exaggerated steps, her thigh-high leather boots making crackling sounds as she moved to Leonidas.

"My lady." He bowed low, extending both hands. "You honor us."

She wanted to throw her arms around his neck and cling to him, to hold him tighter than she ever had. But she also knew that even though Ares no longer dominated her, he would always remain a dangerous threat to Leo, as would her love for him.

She leaned up on her toes, looping her arms tightly about his waist. "It's Daphne, sweet king," she whispered. "I'm called Daphne. I've wanted to tell you for so very, very long." She gathered a handful of his linen shirt within her grasp. Needing to hold him.

Leonidas reached a weathered hand and cupped her cheek, his lips turning upward in that quirky, rugged smile that always made her quiver a little.

*Oh, I want to stay with you. Need to be with you,* she thought, feeling tears sting her eyes. "If only I could."

She hadn't meant to say the last part aloud, but she knew he saw the pain in her eyes. He glanced past her toward the others, obviously making sure they didn't watch, and then bent low. He pressed his mouth against her ear, his breath arousing and warm. "Ah, but we *can* be together, my darling. My *Daphne*. You're free."

His words, their unlivable promise, brought tears to her eyes. Reaching a hand to his cheek, she caressed it in one long stroke, like a paintbrush outlining a form upon a rare canvas. She was all too aware that she might never trace this beloved, bristling face again.

"I have work to do here, my lord," she told him, her throat tight from the barely restrained tears. "And you know, too . . . that I cannot stay." Her tears spilled then. "I'm sorry." She blinked, sniffling in several short bursts. "I would . . . I would be with you, if there were a hope of it. If my brother wouldn't still hunt you."

She squeezed her eyes together, almost willing the facts of her bloodline to vanish, pretending that she was human. Just some cool girl with a good budget for thrift shops and vintage clothes and lots of blue or crimson hair dye.

In a loud voice, his blazing eyes locked on her, Leonidas shouted, "One moment, comrades. I need to speak with our Oracle."

Murmurs of understanding arose from behind them as Leo walked her into the shadows. He had her against that hidden tree in a heartbeat. He wasn't gentle, didn't make any pretense of it, bending low and ravaging her mouth. His beard prickled and scratched her skin, as just this once, she gave in to her king's kiss completely. She tangled her hands through his short curls, twining them, needing to somehow capture him, too.

"You must stay now, Daphne. Your brother's no longer controlling or hurting you." He growled, and that possessive sound sent chills rushing across her skin. "He's taken so much from me over these centuries, but *not you*."

"Then how about this?" She stroked his cheek. "Because *I* love you. If I came to you, he'd make sure to steal you from me. The only way I can protect you now is to make sure he doesn't believe we're together. He has to believe that, or you'll never be safe."

Leonidas pressed her flat against the tree, a low rumble in his throat as he gave her one last, probing kiss. Then he moved back several steps, abruptly done. Resolved. She could see the painful decision in his eyes, the look of the stalwart commander who always sacrificed when duty required it of him.

"I love you, too, Daphne," she heard in that rough and gentle voice that filled all her dreams. "And ..." He looked at her as they reached the ring of firelight. "I will not give up. I will make you see the truth."

Without looking at her again, he stepped back into his role as king, and she dutifully filed into the circle as his Oracle. "I've come to speak to Kassandros, my king," she projected loudly enough for all the gathered warriors to hear.

"That is your purpose?" There was the subtlest challenge in his question. His sad, weary eyes focused on hers. It would be like this from now on, she thought. The two of them in a public, sacrificial role, hiding what they felt, denying the right to it.

She addressed the corps boldly. "I have come with an offer," she said, unable to suppress a slight smile. "Familiar words, indeed, no? Of course, I come as your friend, as well. . . . I am still your guide, dear ones."

Stepping away from Leonidas, she strode toward River. She had always held this one in such a tender spot, and even though he'd not been able to see her, she'd watched and studied him for years. His heart was huge, open and kind. Such sweetness in him, but also so much doubt and pain because of his life's course—*and because of Ares*, she thought, frowning slightly.

This moment was the purest gift she could offer this good-hearted weapon-shifter. "Congratulations, River," she said softly, and leaning up on her booted toes, pressed a kiss to his cheek. "You are a fine, worthy warrior to bear this gorgeous cloak, to be called Spartan."

He flushed, glancing slightly to the side. *Shy like Leo*, she thought, and her tenderness for the warrior expanded even more. "You heard me mention an offer, yes?" He lifted his gaze and started smiling.

"Yes, my lady."

"That offer is for *you*, River Kassandros."

His eyebrows shot up toward his hairline. "Me?"

"You're our key," she told him. "The only one who holds enough power to defeat Ares. You see, when he made those threats by Styx, talked about reclaiming his power, he truly meant that. When he formed you in Styx long ago, my brother seeded some of his own authority into you. He hoped that by placing it in a lowly servant—his words, not mine—that it would remain concealed. He told no one, least of all you, but I knew the moment he transferred that power. I saw it with my own eyes, perceived it by my own ability."

River stared at her, eyebrows knit together. "Oracle, I am sorry, but I don't understand."

"He made you a demigod, River. He gave you, literally, a portion of his own supernatural strength, straight from Olympus."

Leonidas studied her, a wealth of questions in his dark eyes. "To what purpose? He wouldn't want to lose even an ounce of his own power . . . would he?"

She turned and smiled at her king, wishing so badly that things could have been different. "King Leonidas, my brother is a masterful schemer. He always has some devious plan in mind, but in this instance, I don't know why he formed River in that way, or why he hid some of his power inside him."

She turned back toward River. "But I do know this . . . it's why shape-shifting has always brought you such torment. It's the source of your berserker's curse. And if you think about it, it's no wonder. The god of bloodlust poured some of his all-consuming thirst and power into you."

She saw the warrior's hands form into reflexive fists as

he pressed them into his thighs. Yes, her wicked brother had that kind of effect on all of them, but River had deserved so much more compassion because of his gentle nature, his huge heart. That was why she'd arranged the offer that she brought to him now.

"River," she told him softly, "you are free now, but this unstable power is still inside of you. Do you understand? It remains a part of you, joined to your marrow and blood."

He dropped his gaze and gave a quick nod of acceptance.

"You remain immortal as before, but you won't ever fully master that berserker, not with the darkness my brother seeded into you."

She reached for Emma with one hand, and then clasped River's palm with her other, drawing the pair even closer together. "Emma, I come with an offer tonight. My father Zeus took mercy on River's plight and on all that he suffered because of Ares. He won't intervene, and doesn't give over rewards or help very often, but he's allowed me to present a special opportunity to you both."

The couple stared at her with wide, curious eyes, their expressions almost mirror images, and Daphne couldn't help smiling. Yes, they deserved what she'd managed to broker for them.

She gave Emma's hand a little squeeze. "Emma, you have a choice. You can become immortal like River, so that you'll always be with him and live throughout eternity at his side." Then she swung her gaze toward River. "Or, River, you may relinquish your immortality and live a normal, human lifespan with your chosen love. But you must choose, and you must do so right now."

"What about the power inside of me?" River asked. "I thought you said it made me the key to defeating Ares. I really don't understand, Oracle. What happens to this demigod's power, to my ability to fight in weapon form, if I choose to become mortal?"

Beside him he sensed Emma's own unspoken confusion, and met her gaze by the firelight. Even though he saw no answers in her eyes, only more questions, he felt strengthened by just looking at her.

The Oracle pressed her mouth against his ear. "Kind River," she whispered, "you will fight as a weapon whenever needed, working with Ajax and sometimes the others. You'll still have that mighty power to transform as you do now. As a hawk warrior, as any weapon you choose. But you will no longer have the power to bring life. This," she continued softly, her breath warm against his cheek, "this you will lose. If you become mortal again, this power of yours must be bestowed on another warrior. All the demigod's power that my brother gave will be transferred." Still clasping his face in her hands, she peered into his eyes.

"Why won't I lose all of the power?" It was odd, but the thought of no longer weapon-shifting caused a great chasm of emptiness inside his chest.

"Because Ares formed each of you within Styx, melded that power with your body and soul. That will not be changed. My father Zeus has decreed it. You will only relinquish the unholy share of power."

She leaned in close again, whispering confidentially in his ear. "River, should you choose this course, the one who receives your overflow also receives your curse, your berserker. But perhaps, if we are fortunate, some blessings, too, for this warrior will also gain your power to bring life and healing." She stayed close, pressed against him as he weighed his decision. At last he nodded and she pulled away.

"The future of that ability and the one who would take it from you will be unknown. So choose wisely, dear Spartan. Choose well."

River blew out a sigh. So much power, but so much inability to control it, and accompanied by those berserker's rages that had hounded him throughout the centuries. The thought of heaving the load off of his shoulders was the greatest freedom, the most awesome offer that he'd received tonight. It meant that he could walk in wholeness, could take Emma in marriage as a truly free man.

He looked toward her. "Emma, I'll do as you wish," he told her. "If you want to live an immortal's life with me, I will keep the power."

She shook her head. "It's your decision to make, sweetheart," she told him. "But I think you deserve to be free of Ares' curse, just as you deserved your freedom."

All at once, her hand was reaching for his, and he clasped it as if she were about to dredge him out of the ocean all over again. He squeezed and held it, feeling her strength and natural human warmth. She moved even closer, and he searched her face. *What should I do, my love?*

She was a prophetess herself, capable of hearing voices and demons and spirits. Surely she might offer something more in this moment of weighty decision.

"What should I do?" he asked her in a very quiet voice. "It's our choice, not just mine."

She reached her free arm about his waist, tugging him flush against her. "It's not. Not really, sweetheart. You're the one who has so much to give up. And to embrace."

"Forever together, Em. That's quite the opportunity. To spend every year from now on with each other, to love each other like that."

She pressed her cheek against his chest and he had the idea she was listening to his heartbeat during the long quiet that pounded between them. She ran both hands along his back until they brushed against the long seam where his wings emerged from his human flesh. She shivered slightly at the contact.

"That's lovely." She was so gentle, barely brushing a few fingertips against his right wing, then his left. "Yet another surprise from my amazing warrior. Anything else you can do?"

He shook his head mutely, wondering what she was getting at in this moment of facing eternity eye to eye.

"Well, here's what I'm thinking." She locked her arms around his hips, leaning back so she could stare up into his eyes, yet never releasing that warm, reassuring contact of hers. "That we've got a good sixty years, maybe? Seventy? But as intense as your life is and how full of surprises you are, there's not going to be one boring second."

He swallowed, suddenly realizing that he could barely breathe. Whatever she would say, it would determine their paths from now on. "All I care about, Em, is spending my days with you. However few or many."

"I know." She smiled, then leaned into him again. "And after our sixty, seventy, fifty years—whatever God gives us—then we step into eternity together. So, either way, we're together, and either way, we still have immortal life, just not here. Not on earth, right here."

Elysium, heaven, it was the same realm: they simply used different words to describe the place that the Highest God had created for their eternal passage. "Yes, true. We have forever."

"Yeah, and I'd rather you not spend eternity with the berserker hounding you, not battling all the pain it's brought you. I mean, call me selfish, but I'd give up immortality so you can be whole and truly happy."

Murmurs of assent rumbled across the circle, encouraging him to take this final liberating gift. A melancholy thought overwhelmed him then, the image of leaving each of the other warriors behind as he aged and then died. After so long spent with each of them, the thought brought a stab of harsh pain. Just then in the firelight he saw Nikos, his face as stern and unreadable as it often was. For a second, their gazes locked, however, and the warrior gave him a small smile, nodding his own encouragement.

*Do it*, the warrior mouthed silently, and nodded again. He returned the gesture, resolved, knowing that if he asked Nikos to shoulder this burden, he would do it. But the fierce warrior was not the one; he could never tolerate or bridle the berserker's rage because he was already stymied by too much of the hard emotion. He turned and faced the circle.

*You must choose wisely*, he reminded himself, thinking of the Oracle's caution.

To offload this kind of power, and to know it would mean pain for one of his brothers, was a torturous choice. It had to be a man who could bear up beneath the dark side of it all, but whose heart was good enough, pure enough not to be bowed by Ares' wealth of temptations.

He searched the ring of long-familiar faces, considered each man's character: his skills and weaknesses. But even as he went through the motions, his choice was already made; it had been made in his heart the moment the Oracle whispered in his ear.

With deliberate steps he moved to the one man who of all those gathered was the truest brother of his heart. Ari's eyes were fixed on him, open, willing. As always, his generous warmth conveyed that he'd take any hit or shoulder any burden that River ever needed him to.

He stopped in front of Ari, working at a smile that never reached his lips. There were no words, not for this moment.

"What's up, River man?" Ari's tone was as jovial as if he were challenging him to just another wrestling match, but they were resolute, tinged with a hidden heaviness that only River would recognize.

"Brother, dearest friend," River murmured, bowing his head out of love and respect. Then he looked up and into those warm, ancient eyes. "Will you help me accept the truest of all freedoms? Will you take my demigod's power, with all that it means, both curse and ability? Will you take it from me and make it your own?"

"It depends, young stud." Ari cracked a sideways smile. "Does this mean I'm gonna get laid all the time after I use my power? Or will I be stuck like you always were, doing the business myself?"

"I think," River said, returning his friend's smile, "that's entirely on you, *old* stud."

"I'd prefer a less, ahem, *handy* route than you chose until recently." Ari made a crude motion with his hand, then seemed to catch himself. He flushed as his gaze traveled toward Emma. "I mean, you know . . . not go it alone. If I don't have to . . . you know."

Ari was stalling, of course. River knew how craftily his friend could wield humor at moments of pain or difficulty, but this particular juncture was too important to keep things light.

"I realize what I'm asking is more than I should ask of any friend. It's too much for anyone I love like I do you."

Ari's expression grew somber, his large dark eyes suddenly bright. "I've watched you suffer for too long, dear brother, and there were times when I thought I'd do anything to take the berserker from you."

"It was my path to walk."

Ari gave him a brave smile. "For a time, River man. For a time. But tonight our king rectified one ancient wrong." Ari reached out, squeezing his shoulder. "Let me set you truly free now."

All at once River had second thoughts. How could he ask any man, especially this kindhearted, good one, to assume the terrible plague that he'd known for so long? It *was* too much.

River shook his head, stepping backward. "No, Aristos. I shouldn't have asked this of you."

"I am willing." Ari's voice was sharper and more determined than he'd ever heard it before. "Kassandros, I am the one!"

River buried his face in both hands, hating the chasm of decision that stood before him. To ask his best friend, his truest brother to take on such a soul-rending struggle . . . it was too cruel a thing to do.

But then, a series of images flooded his mind; he thought of the exhilaration he'd felt four months earlier when he'd freed Shay from the deathly statue that Sable had frozen her within. Remembered that time at Verdun when he'd turned into a life-giving needle, allowing Ajax to use him, bringing life back to hundreds of soldiers in one day. Countless other memories traipsed through his mind, showing him the good that his cursed ability had accomplished—and that goodness, well, seemed most fitting in the soul of Aristos Petrakos. Slowly he lowered his hands.

"I am ready, friend. I am willing," Ari repeated, reaching out those same hands that River had just pictured him utilizing to bring healing and life. He would simply have to deny the urge to picture the darker side of that demigod's ability.

Reconciled to his choice, River turned to face the warrior.

Ari's eyes shimmered then, growing bright, and he drew River into a bearlike embrace. "Consider it done, my brother," Ari told him in a thick voice. "You know I'll always have your back."

# *Epilogue*

Some things changed, but others remained reassuringly the same. River loved caring for Ajax's horse Fresia, and now that they were living on the Savannah farm, it proved an especially relaxed pleasure. He let his thoughts wander, ran the grooming brush along Fresia's withers, whistling an old battle tune as he briskly gave the mare his finest treatment.

The first hint of fall was in the air; not in the temperature, but in the hint of crispness, a slight lessening in the usual thick blanket of humidity that covered Savannah. If they were lucky, in a few more weeks, the days would grow milder and the nights a bit chilly. Or so Emma told him. He smiled. Yes, this first fall in Savannah would be glorious. He was a free man at last, heart, body and soul.

Fresia nickered lightly and he murmured to her in ancient Greek. "Yes, my lady, I know you love the feel of my touch. . . ."

A rumbling laugh filled the doorway of the stall and he turned in surprise.

"Sweet-talking my mare again?" Ajax gave him a grin from where he leaned against the jamb. "Isn't one woman enough? Must you try to woo my own horse away from me?"

"I only pick up the slack when you fall down on the job, my friend."

They laughed together, traded more wisecracks, but very quickly fell silent.

It had been this way between them on the few occasions they'd been alone together since the ceremony. The event had marked River gaining his freedom and full status as a

Spartan . . . but it had changed every facet of their relationship. For so long he had felt as if he'd been formed out of Ajax somehow on that long-ago day by the River Styx, as if Ares had reached into his fellow warrior and re-created River, forged him into the mighty weapon that he became. Learning that the true reason was actually the demigod's power inside his soul, well, it had changed his innate feelings of how he and Ajax were tied together. Had equalized it, but also uprooted what had kept him steady and sane for so many centuries.

What could be said now, between the two of them, to bridge the strained silences? River had not one word or syllable to do the job. For so long they'd been friends, but the word *master* had always bounded that relationship, even though neither man had wanted it to be that way.

Maybe this new frontier meant friendship would simply be difficult now. It wasn't what River wanted, but he'd always been an outsider and he wondered whether Ajax would choose to embrace true friendship with him. Becoming part of the whole felt hardest with this particular man who, despite being his dear friend, was also his longtime master.

River was about to resume the brushing again when Ajax's expression grew much more intense. His thick eyebrows cranked down into an almost angry V shape; instinctively River's heart began to pound hard in response. Had he displeased Ajax? His master . . .

"What's wrong?" he asked, the words coming out in a bark.

Ajax's eyes widened slightly, then narrowed again. He gave his head a shake, staring out into the stable. "It's . . . it's nothing."

"If I've done something wrong," River blurted, "tell me."

Ajax turned back to him, black eyes blazing with fury. "Damn it, you are not my slave, River, and you're not my servant."

River focused on Fresia, working the brush down along her flanks once more, but said nothing. His heart was in his throat all at once, and he felt like a blasted idiot for his instinctive reaction. It wasn't even fair to Jax, who had never treated him like a servant since the days they'd walked the earth as mortals. Even then he had been good and fair, taking great care that River was treated better than any other helot River knew.

"I realize I'm a free man," he said softly at last, refusing to look at his friend. "I have much to learn still."

Ajax walked to him and held out his hand. "River." His voice was commanding yet gentle. River could not look him in the eye; this new world of his was more painful and alien than he'd ever imagined.

"Look at me, brother."

Slowly River turned to face the Spartan who still extended his right hand. For clasping? River didn't understand, but moved the brush to his left hand and reached to take Ajax's hand in his own.

Ajax groaned. "No, give me the brush, you bastard," he said, snatching it out of River's hand. "You're not to groom my horse anymore. Never again. I never wanted you to groom my godsforsaken horses to begin with, not at any time in the past thousand years."

"You're angry because I'm brushing Fresia?" River asked, not understanding.

"I'm angry because you keep acting like I'm a stranger and not your friend, not your brother by heart. Why can't you look me in the eye? Why do you still polish my armor and groom my horse? Again, duties I have not asked of you, not once."

"I groom Fresia because she's a gentle, fair creature and I love her," he murmured in ancient Greek. "And I do it because I care for you, friend. It's the only reason I've ever done it." River stared at his feet for a moment and smiled, then slowly lifted his gaze and met Ajax's hard stare. As soon as he did, Jax's own eyes filled with relief. River continued. "For a long time, Jax, you wouldn't take care of yourself, or be kind to yourself . . . you hadn't found Shay yet and you were so lost. We fought as one, but when I was in your hand, I felt the pulse of your pain. The loneliness in you." River looked down for a moment. "Someone had to watch over you, and I figured that would be me."

"You figured it would be you," Jax repeated, placing a strong hand on River's shoulder.

"Otherwise, your sorry ass would have been consumed in demon fire long ago; don't you agree?"

"Far worse than that, no doubt."

"And now you've gone soft from love, so I better stay on the job or this poor horse will go wild before you're astride her again."

"You're thinking of your Emma, I believe. *Astride* and *wild*, from the noises I hear in the house sometimes, would describe your activity with her."

"Ah, but if you talk trash about my woman, I'll have to take you out and thrash you. Or even better, I'll transform into a silver whip and beat you."

"Why bother? Shift into a silver-handled brush, and I'll take care of my own damned horse." Ajax began to groom Fresia himself, giving River a shove with his shoulder. "Get out of my way, you boor. Let me show you the proper way to groom a man's horse."

And just like that, the tension was broken. They traded insults and wisecracks, each trying to best the other. River hoisted himself up onto the wooden beam that separated the stall from the next, watching Ajax as he worked.

Suddenly, the scent of fresh-brewed coffee filled the air and both men lifted their heads. "Ah, the twenty-first century has much to recommend it," Ajax said as River peered down the aisle of the stable. Emma appeared, a Starbucks travel mug in one hand, a buttery bagel in the other.

Damn, his sweetness had made him breakfast. Not only that, she looked and smelled far more delicious, with her dark hair pulled up into a ponytail and the scent of perfume and shampoo all over her skin. He glanced quickly at Ajax, who gave him a wicked grin and said, "Have fun, you bastard. Just try not to be so loud about it for once."

"I can't right now; I've got to get to the school." Emma resisted as River tugged her by the hand, leading her up the stairs and to their bedroom.

"Call in sick," he said as they reached the landing. He wasted no time and slid his arms about her waist, drawing her flush against him, walking backward into their room's open doorway.

"River . . . I had a month off this summer," she argued, but all the fight had gone out of her. In fact, she was struggling physically, but not to stop him—in fact, she was working his T-shirt over his head. He kicked the door shut, never breaking their kiss.

Soon their bare bodies were joined as one, their skin sweat-slicked and causing them to slide easily together. With an eager roll, she straddled him, planting both palms against his bare chest.

"Riding me like a stud, are you?" He smiled up at her as she shifted position, causing him to sink much deeper inside of her. With a coy toss of her hair she arched her back, the position causing her nipples to jut outward, hardened and pert from her arousal.

"You do smell like you've been in the barn," she said as he clasped both of her hips in his hands.

"Now you have to call in sick. Your boss will imagine the worst possible ideas about what you've been up to in your husband's bed."

"I could just tell him I married a hawk."

"Hawks don't roam the barnyard, Em." He arched his back, raising his hips with a grinding thrust as he pinned her hard against him. "Hawks mate midair, flying and crashing and thrashing. Not unlike this."

He rolled with her then, taking her from the side, but never losing his deep hold on her. In fact, more freedom of movement enabled him to hitch one of her legs high about him and to reach even more deeply into that sweet place hidden far inside. As he felt the tip of his erection push against that spot, she moaned in response, digging her fingernails into his shoulders.

"We roll and tumble," he murmured, nipping at her neck. "And bite and mate, free-falling. Crying out . . . loudly." To demonstrate, he released a rumbling groan of pleasure as she hooked her right heel about his back, driving her own thrusting motion that sent him spiraling into bright waves of pleasure.

She murmured a cry of her own, her cascade of dark

waves falling over his chest as she rode each of his demanding surges. "If only . . ." Her words were lost amid panting and gasps.

He didn't relent, rolled her totally onto her back. With his other hand, he guided her right leg up over his shoulder and she hooked both legs about his neck, her heels digging into his upper back. "If only?" he prompted between his own greedy gasps.

"If only I could be a hawk"—she moaned again— "like . . . you. Could fly with you . . . wing . . . to . . . wing."

"Maybe," was all he said in reply. Then he grinned with a wicked amount of pleasure, speeding his rhythm inside of her to triple time. Taking her beyond any realm of pleasure that he'd ever given her before—he knew it. Knew it as he knew the heart that beat within her chest, the babe that grew within her belly. In time, he would let her know all the things that his newly changed powers allowed him to perceive about her, his beautiful, transforming mortal. And tell her about their child she now carried inside of her.

As one they reached a crescendo peak, flew together emotionally, soaring higher and higher until with final cries, they descended together. Holding each other, clinging, even though their hungry, thrusting motions grew still.

They were silent at first; then, as she let her legs drift down about him, she looked him directly in the eye, serious. "What did you mean . . . maybe? About me being a hawk someday, too?"

He brushed the sweaty hair back from her face, tucking it beneath each ear, then leaned up on his elbows and returned her intense gaze. "Oh, just that I happen to know someone—someone who would do just about anything for me, by the way . . . who now holds a demigod's power in his grasp. Perhaps we should take up the request with him and see what can be done."

Emma's mouth fell open, and when no words came forth, he gently clasped her jaw, closing it. "Anything is possible now, sweet Em. Now that I'm a free man, I feel it in here." He reached between them and touched his breastbone, then gently placed that same hand over her heart. "And here. The future is ours."

From downstairs a loud, crashing explosion sounded, followed by the blaring sounds of an old Rolling Stones song. They gazed at each other, grinning, and in unison said, "Ari."

River shook his head with a dubious grin. "He keeps experimenting with his new abilities. Says it's a gas to see what all he's capable of."

"Maybe," she ventured with a very impish grin. "Maybe—I'm just saying here—it wasn't the best idea to give your demigod's power to the biggest wisecracking smart-ass—"

He cut her off. "The most irreverent—"

"The most outrageous," she added.

"Guy we know," they said at the exact same moment and then collapsed into a fit of giddy laughter, rolling together in the bed.

"Then again," River added, popping his head up to stare Emma in the eye, "might just have been the most wickedly fun plan I ever arrived at."

Emma ran her hands through his disheveled hair. "No, I have much more wicked and fun plans in mind for you. We'll leave Ari to his own devices."

Ari knelt in front of Kalias's state-of-the-art stereo system, half of which was now fried, and knew there would be hell to pay when his stern and techno-loving big brother discovered his latest mischief.

"It's not my fault I can't control myself," he declared under his breath, even though he knew that he'd intentionally zapped the stereo system in an effort to operate it from across the room. "Why would you give power like this to someone like me, anyway? Not my fault, not my fault . . ." he kept muttering.

Then he got a fabulous idea: perhaps his power could repair the damage it had just wrought on the electronics. He was lifting his hands, forming a visualization of a fully restored bank of equipment, when the house phone rang. A zinger of electricity jackknifed out of his hand and hit him straight in the thigh.

"Damn it! Damn, damn, double damn," he cursed,

practically hopping toward the ringing house phone. If he wasn't the only one around to answer it, he'd have let it go.

He yanked the thing out of the cradle with a brusque grunt, rubbing his right thigh the entire time. Hell, he was just lucky he hadn't zapped his manhood right off. As it was, his favorite khakis were now sporting a scorch mark from the power blast. He was staring down, so busy calculating how close he'd come to scorching his jewels that he barely heard what the person on the other end of the line was saying.

"Aristos, are you there?" the woman asked in an elegant southern accent, and he realized it was Emma's mother.

"Just a moment, please," he told her. "I'll go get Emma, ma'am."

*Of course*, he thought, *gauging by the noises I just heard upstairs, she may not be available.* But he didn't say that.

"It'll just be a moment," he added, but then Cecilia cut him off.

"No, no, Ari." She seemed flustered, and he halted midstride, phone still pressed against his ear. "It's you I want to speak with."

"Me?" What would Cecilia want to talk to him about?

"I have a message for you, Aristos. An important one." She sounded very upset or emotional, he wasn't sure which, but then she cleared her throat. "It's a message for you from Juliana. Juliana Tiades." When he said nothing, Cecilia persisted. "Ari, Juliana. *Your* Juliana . . . she wants to talk to you."

And the phone fell right out of his powerful hand.

Don't miss the first
Gods of Midnight novel by Deidre Knight,

# RED FIRE

Available now from Signet Eclipse

*Coffee. Nectar of the gods.* Or at least it should be, if Ajax had any say in the matter. Which he clearly didn't.

*Strike me down for that, why don't you?* he challenged with a glance at the granite sky overhead. *Come on and fight me.*

No arrows or lightning bolts scorched the sidewalk café, and slowly Jax lowered his gaze.

*Too bad,* he thought with a dark laugh, sipping his coffee. Quite the cure when you are nursing a pounding hangover. Sure, it was a taste that he'd acquired in modern times, this era of coffee shops and triple-mocha everything, but he didn't mind being modern on occasion. In fact, he relished it, much to his brothers' chagrin.

He'd lumbered in heavy armor, worn a cravat when fashion had required it, had even donned a kilt for about a century. So drinking a bit of women's coffee hardly qualified him as an impostor, he rationalized, and took another sip.

*You have to live in the era where you find yourself.* It was his number-one rule, and so far it hadn't misled him on his winding passage through the corridors of time.

The King's Road bustled, shoppers from nearby Sloane Square hurrying home, with countless others making their way back toward the tube. He registered the foot traffic, the creeping chill of twilight that was so common for London in mid-April, the throngs pulsing and pushing their way past his table. And he noted every detail without once glancing up from his copy of the *Evening Standard*. No *Independent* for him. He remained a simple man to the core; it didn't matter if his well-heeled feet now walked hard pavement and not the fields of ancient Greece.

Scanning the paper's headlines, he could hardly focus. There was too much noise coming at him, an overload of sensory detail in every direction. And it wasn't the usual human clamor, like car horns or rap music. No, it was the mental din that hounded Jax year after year, century after century, growing louder every day. Lately he'd been choking on it, nearly drowning beneath the mental voices of London's entire population.

"Stop feeling sorry for yourself."

Kalias. Jax rolled his eyes as his big brother slid into the seat beside him. No invitation was ever necessary for the hulking warrior; he just took what he wanted and possessed every inch of land he walked or occupied.

"You don't know jack about what troubles me," Ajax answered coolly, his clipped British accent sounding particularly nasty. One good reason for having affected it during this recent London venture.

"I know that you've got a job to do, Brother." Kalias's own accent remained unchanged despite almost a century in the British Isles, as ancient and authentic as the Greek blood that pulsed through their veins.

"I know my place, and I do my work." Ajax gazed up at his eldest brother with a cutting glare. It was like staring into a mirror: the olive skin, the long, aquiline nose, the black hair. Except Kalias wore his own hair buzzed short, military-style, while Jax kept his long and loose, free, as he had in the olden days.

Kalias gestured toward the half-consumed cappuccino. "It's five o'clock. Surprised to see that's not Scotch you're drinking."

"I only woke an hour ago," Ajax replied, taking another lazy sip. "Even I have my standards."

His brother leaned closer. "So the only code you're still clinging to pertains to the satisfaction of your basest desires. Very commendable, Jax."

Ajax rolled his eyes. "Oh, bloody hell. When you put it that way"—he waved to the server, a leggy Polish blonde—"who can resist?" Then, turning to the waitress, he said,

"Irish coffee, darling." She smiled back eagerly and he added, "A double, and heavy on the Irish."

Kalias leaned in toward him. "You ignored our king's summoning. Twice."

*Leonidas. Their once and future general. Their commander for eternity.*

"The Old Man told you that?" Ajax ran a hand through his shoulder-length black hair. Silky as midnight, that was how his most recent lover had described it. They'd spent hours in that well-appointed Mayfair hotel room having sweaty, wall-bumping sex. Once done, she'd called him a god—and he'd answered by swiping a hand across her face, clearing every memory of the dark event from her mind.

He kept his gaze down, avoiding his brother's blazing, angry one. If Kalias knew that he'd taken to sleeping with mortal women in his warrior form, oh, there'd be hell to pay—and straight to Hades he'd go, no doubt about that.

And then there was the matter of Ares. Always out there, hovering on his eternal horizon like a sky full of enemy arrows.

Kalias clasped his shoulder. "So, baby brother, don't you want to know what Leonidas asks of you?"

"An assignment, no doubt."

"Not just any assignment." Kalias settled back in his chair, sipping from Jax's own glass of water without permission. "The Oracle calls you."

"Bollocks to that woman and her scheming." Ajax muttered a few choice vulgarities, thinking of the hidden prophetess and her affection for him. Too bad he liked her so damned much—and called her a friend.

He had known her, literally, for thousands of years. Back when the Spartans were originally transformed at the River Styx, the young, black-haired beauty had been assigned to the warriors as their guide. She was the Oracle of Delphi, the youngest and purest prophetess of Apollo's Oracles. Her prophecies assisted them in all their missions, but only Ajax was able to hear or see her.

"Something dire is afoot, or she wouldn't be asking for you." Kalias scrubbed a palm over his spiking hair.

"Did you tell her I'd retired from the game?"

Kalias flashed him an impatient glance. "Since you're the only one who can hear the Oracle, no, I did not tell her that you're on unofficial—and unauthorized, I might add—leave."

"Well, if I stay gone a bit longer, perhaps she'll cozy right up to you, Brother. She's quite the looker; trust me on that."

She had often determined how they drew their strength, their very life source, with her vague predictions. The supernatural law that she would be their guide in all things had never made sense, not from the beginning of their pledge more than twenty centuries ago. Still, immortal vows were lasting vows, and that had been one of Ares' rules at the outset of their agreement.

Kalias eyed him hard for a long moment, then continued in ancient Greek: "Her words maintain our warrior unity, give us needed direction. Perhaps I should mention Thermopylae ... Gettysburg ... Berlin ... Omaha Beach. Do you want me to go on?"

"Names, nothing more."

"Oh, keep telling yourself that. But we share the same memories of battles waged. Of comrades lost." Kalias sighed, his eyes filling with dark recollections. "If you won't answer our Oracle, and you refuse our king's summons, then try this on for size, little brother," he said, dropping back into English. "You do remember the name Shayanna Angel?"

"Shay," Ajax corrected hoarsely, his entire body jolting in reaction to the familiar name. Along his back, a compulsive sensation began, a ripple of power. That itchy-fingered probing of his true nature. "She goes by Shay." The burning in his shoulders spread, began to tear across his spine, threatening to burst forth from beneath his skin.

"Calm down," his brother cautioned, apparently seeing his darker temperament expose itself.

Ajax nodded, swallowing, and surreptitiously slid his palm over the center of his tailored slacks, where a swelling hard-on had quickly formed. It was impossible to think of Shay Angel and not feel that kind of achy, thick need—and he'd never met her or even glimpsed her. In fact, her name was just one out of many. But what the Oracle had said of the woman was far more than a simple name, and whenever he recalled the prophecy about what the promised human would mean to him, he couldn't help but react—physically and otherwise.

"You shouldn't talk to me about Shay out here on the street—you know better."

"I'd have figured that more than two thousand years would be plenty of time for you to master your other nature."

"Not when it comes to that little minx of a mortal." Ajax groaned, shifting in his chair.

"You have no idea who she even is." Eyebrows like winged midnight furrowed, Kalias's fury barely contained. "So I shall repeat—calm down."

Ajax blew out a breath, drew another. He crossed one expensive Italian loafer over his knee, watched a black taxi drive by. At last he observed, "You're right. This isn't about some murky future that was once foretold to me; it's about my duties."

"Well, I'm glad you concur with me, little brother." Kalias leaned back in his chair, toying with a Zippo lighter that he'd retrieved from his hip pocket.

"Why must you do that? Honestly?"

"Do what?" His brother extended the lighter questioningly, his face a mask of pure innocence.

"Not the lighter, you bastard. Why must you remind me—constantly, I might add—of our birth order?"

"Perhaps because it is my only means of containing you." Kalias's mouth turned up at the corners in a subtle grin of triumph.

"You won't *ever* contain me," Ajax shot back, staring at the darkening sky overhead. A perfect evening for flight, for soaring above the clouds, banking like the bird of prey that he was. If this conversation didn't right itself, then he would take matters into his own hands—or wings, as the case would be. He would shape-shift and leave his obnoxious and condescending eldest brother here on the street and rise to the very heavens.

"When our king requires your presence, Ajax, you comply. Immortality doesn't grant you the privilege of impudence, not with Leonidas."

"And with you?"

His brother fixed his attention on the Zippo, flicking it open and closed. "I'm not sure you ever respected me."

"Oh, please," Jax snarled. "Save the sorry guilt trips for Aristos. At least he still buys them occasionally."

Ari kept himself positioned between the two of them like the rocky pass that had once determined their battle at the Hot Gates. Their middle brother's way was always peaceful, like a trench drawn between two enemy sides.

Kalias glanced at the busy street, seeming to gather his thoughts. When he turned back to face Ajax, his expression was naked, open. "I don't understand what happened to you over these many centuries. What went wrong? You were our strongest. Our bravest. The very best of us."

Something savage broke loose inside of Ajax, the millennia peeling away as if time had never existed. He lunged forward, grabbing his brother's shirt sleeve. " 'May eternity's arms hold you,' " he pronounced coldly, repeating Ares' words from that August day so long ago. "It was a curse, not a blessing, dear brother. We're no better off than the slaves we once kept."

Kalias made a grunting sound of disapproval, but Ajax blustered on. "Haven't you ever looked at yourself in the mirror while transformed? At the blackness of your wings? At your raptor's hands, the twisting talons? We are Ares' own vile playthings, Kalias, and I am done—done dancing to his battle calls."

That was why he focused on the sex, the lusty, driven need to bed human women in his transformed body. It made him feel less dirty, less abominable. That they could worship his wings, caress his curling claws—well, it was the only redemption he knew anymore. Unless he nurtured the name of his supposed and future beloved—Shay Angel. He'd never sought her out, never tried to discern which century she might live in. That it might be this current epoch, well, it wasn't something he was ready to entertain. And yet . . .

"At Thermopylae, no one wanted to win more than you did; no man possessed a greater thirst for victory," his brother pressed. "What happened to the warrior who helped beat back four hundred thousand Persians in just three days?" Kalias shook his head. "You have the greatest calling—the most important one. You can drink yourself into oblivion, *little brother*, but your destiny won't be denied."

"It's not a destiny," Ajax answered grimly. "It was a vow."

For the first time during the conversation, Kalias beamed, his voice becoming softer. "And shall I remind you that you have always been a man of your word?"

And to that, well, there wasn't a damned thing that Ajax could possibly say in rebuttal.

"As I thought," Kalias finally murmured. "So, you will answer Leonidas's summoning. You will visit our Oracle and learn what words she has for us, the Spartan cadre."

"So why mention Shay Angel now?" Ajax persisted. "And why would the Oracle and the gods themselves have deemed her my mate? Whatever time she exists in, that's what this entire conversation is really about. We both know it."

Kalias's expression transformed, morphing into a satisfied, if not devious grin. "That much is simple. Because"—he leaned much closer—"she's the only one who might guide you back from this eternal abyss that threatens to destroy you. If only you should finally meet her."

# DEIDRE KNIGHT

## *Red Fire*

### A Gods of Midnight Novel

Eternity has become a prison for Ajax Petrakos.
Centuries after he and his Spartan brothers made
their bargain for immortality, Ajax struggles to
maintain his warrior's discipline. His only source of
strength is his hope that he will soon meet the
woman once foretold to him—the other half of his
soul, Shay Angel.

Ajax searches for his destined mate on the haunted
streets of modern-day Savannah, but he isn't the
first to find her. Shay, the youngest of a powerful
demon-hunting clan, can see the monsters that
stalk the steamy Southern nights—an ability that
draws the deadly attention of Ajax's worst enemy.
As Shay and Ajax race to solve a chilling
prophecy—one that could spell Ajax's death if they
don't succeed—a fated passion arises, threatening
to sweep away everything in its path.